ABOUT THIS BOOK

Three paranormal fantasy novellas (books 25-27) in this multi-author shared world of Havenwood Falls, home to sexy men, strong women, and neighbors who bite.

Redefined by Morgan Wylie

Hollis Blackstone is a lead assassin for her father's rogue band of witch hunters. For longer than she can remember, her father, Dante, has had two missions: rid the world of witches and locate his estranged family kept from him by his sister's rebellion. Working off a lead, Hollis finds her way through the mysterious borders of Havenwood Falls. Her father's orders were to gather intel on the whereabouts of all the Blackstones, all the witches, and the seat of their power. But then she meets the irresistible Ryne Calloway. She's finally found someone who loves her for her, but she's about to lose him before ever having the chance to love him back.

Betrayal Among the Frost by Amy Hale

Sequel to *Flames Among the* Frost—As her big day approaches, Jetta Mills is feeling pre-wedding jitters, stemming from a lot of self-doubt. When her ex-boyfriend suddenly returns to town, her concerns kick into high gear. Her fiancé Conrad is willing and ready to do whatever necessary to get Turner away from the woman he loves. But Turner's determined to claim what was once his. A unique wedding, a persistent ex-boyfriend, an untrustworthy father, a jealous groom, and Jetta's penchant for disaster may just create the spectacle of the year—if the wedding happens at all. Betrayals and lies may just be the end of Jetta and Conrad.

Forever Loyal by E.J. Fechenda

Sequel to *Fate, Love & Loyalty*—After a shifter cat fight in the middle of town two years ago, Aster McCabe and her sister, Reeve, were banished from Havenwood Falls. All memories of their hometown removed by a protective spell, the sisters have lived a settled life in Denver with their mates. But when Reeve's infant daughter is kidnapped, their parents show up on Aster's doorstep. Parents they don't remember. With her niece in danger, Aster doesn't have time to process her restored memories of a life she had forgotten. And according to her parents and an entourage of friends, she only has 28 days before she loses those memories again. But finding her niece comes first.

HAVENWOOD FALLS BOOKS

Forever Loyal by E.J. Fechenda

Fate's Demand by Emily Cyr

The Wu & the Wand by T.V. Hahn

A Demon's Redemption by JD Nelson

Also try the YA line, Havenwood Falls High; the historical paranormal line, Legends of Havenwood Falls; the darker, sexier side of town, Havenwood Falls Sin & Silk; and the local supernatural college, Sun & Moon Academy.

Stay up to date at www.HavenwoodFalls.com

HAVENWOOD FALLS VOLUME EIGHT

A HAVENWOOD FALLS COLLECTION

MORGAN WYLIE   AMY HALE   E.J. FECHENDA

REDEFINED

MORGAN WYLIE

~ A Havenwood Falls New Adult Novella ~

HAVENWOOD FALLS

REDEFINED

USA Today Bestselling Author

MORGAN WYLIE

BOOKS BY MORGAN WYLIE

YA FANTASY

Silent Orchids (Book 1)

Veiled Shadows (Book 2)

Daegan (Novella 2.5)

Fractured Darkness (Book 3)

Fading Light (Book 4)

The Sol-lumieth (Book 5) (Winter 2019)

The Rise of the Paladin (An Alandria Short Story Prequel) (Free with Newsletter subscription)

YA PARANORMAL/SUPERNATURAL

HAILEY: The Necromancer (A Shadow Realm Novella 1)

(previously released as Supernatural Chronicles: The Necromancers Novella #7)

JAX: The Doppelgänger (A Shadow Realm Novella 2)

WILLOW (A Shadow Realm Novella 3) (Coming soon!)

SOLANGE (A Shadow Realm Novella 4) (Coming soon!)

NA/ADULT PARANORMAL ROMANCE

RYLEN (The Tangled Web Book 1)

MATHER (The Tangled Web Book 2)

JET (A Tangled Web Novella)

HAVENWOOD FALLS

Reawakened (A Havenwood Falls High Novella)

Dawn of the Witch Hunters (A Legends of Havenwood Falls Novella)

Redefined (A Havenwood Falls Novella)

Rise of the Witch Hunters (A Legends of Havenwood Falls Novella)
(Coming Fall 2019)

To anyone who needs a second chance. To anyone who needs to redefine who they are. You got this!

CHAPTER 1

*H*ollis Blackstone stared at herself in her bedroom mirror, seeing only the assassin she had been created to be, wondering if there was anything else she might ever become. She had quickly gained the position as one of the lead assassins for her father, Dante Blackstone. Being a witch hunter was more than her job; it was her entire life, day and night. Hollis had been training to be the best since she could remember. On nights when the teams ransacked home after home, she caught a rare glimpse of him smiling at her—at what she'd accomplished—and she believed him to be proud of her. The teams liked to make a mess of each witch's home they attacked, but Hollis preferred her team to be stealthy, more deadly. The lack of interruption to one's home seemed to send a greater message than a tantrum of violent proportions.

Her room was nothing more than an empty shell, a cavern of unrealized possibilities. Hollis didn't waste time decorating her rooms, for there would always be another, in another town. Her father's organization—her family—moved around more often than they stayed in one place, or so it seemed the past year or so. Plus it was just one more thing to have to worry about, to take her focus away from her job—her obsession.

Pulling on her black leather jacket, despite the early May warm weather, she covered the multiple tattoos on her shoulders stretching down toward her elbows. Hollis fluffed her long dark hair in the mirror, checking to ensure the scar at her hairline was hidden, and made sure she was presentable. She had been called in to see her father, and he didn't tolerate sloppiness or tardiness. Dante always dressed impeccably to impress and to intimidate, and he expected nothing less from his teams. An inept capability to be present when requested was unacceptable to Dante.

They had only recently set up this home, and Hollis didn't even remember what city they were in this time, but she knew they were somewhere near Santa Fe, New Mexico. Dear old dad had been chasing a lead in his lifelong obsession to track down the other Blackstones—those he considered lost and in need of his guidance —and the secret place in which they lived. About a year and a half ago, they had almost found it, but somehow it mysteriously—most likely magically—slipped through their fingers, and they couldn't remember anything about where they had been or where they were trying to get. Her father had been infuriated.

He had been on a rampage ever since they had let Macy Blackstone—who'd been staying with them—get away. Macy had been the biggest lead they'd had in a long time. Her father received slight pulls in the right direction, which he could never describe other than to say he "sensed the spirit of his sister Marie and the rest of his family who *should* be with him." At other times, Dante would utter vague accounts of being so close to the name of the town in his mind only to have it slip away like a lost memory he tried to force to the surface. Somehow they still mysteriously received secret letters from Aunt Letti to Grace and the other old gals no matter where they were, but her teams could never trace the letters' origins.

Hollis strode down the hall with purpose and ownership, stopping only when she arrived at her dad's office. Knocking twice, she didn't wait long. He was straight to business as he called through the door.

"Come in, daughter mine," Dante called through the door, his

8

voice strong and sure. It could have been one of several of the Blackstones who lived with them at the door, but he seemed to always know when Hollis was near. Dante had lived a long time and been quite prolific with reproduction over the span. Even Grace, who appeared to be in her seventies and was half hunter and half human, was one of his descendants. Hollis refused to consider them all siblings since the ages varied so drastically, but they were family just the same. Right as Hollis turned the handle, a young girl in her early teen years with golden blond hair skipped around the corner.

"Have fun, Hollis!" Sunny called with a singsong voice and a big smile.

Hollis didn't let anyone close, but if anyone could get under her skin and attach themselves to her, it was Sunny. Sunny had a way about her that would disarm the most hardened criminal. The family referred to her as their "little ray of caffeinated sunshine." Hollis reached out and tugged on one of Sunny's pigtails.

"Thanks, kid. See ya 'round."

"Maybe, maybe not," she continued in her singsong tone and shrugged. Sunny suddenly stopped and then frowned. Her expression sobered, then she stared into Hollis's eyes. "I'll miss you, but I'm happy for you." Sunny came in for a quick, unexpected hug, then turned without another word. She skipped down the hallway, leaving Hollis with a dumbfounded look on her face.

"What was that about?" Hollis wondered under her breath.

"Are you coming in, Hollis?" Dante asked with an edge in his voice. He didn't like to be kept waiting.

"Sorry, Father. Sunny stopped me," she offered as an excuse, the only excuse she would ever use, and the only one he would allow. He gave her a sharp nod.

"Come sit. I'm waiting on Nala and Rachel. And here they are now."

Hollis turned to find the two other hunters walk through the door. They sauntered in, their heads high and chins jutted out, proud to have been summoned. They were both exceptional hunters in their own rights, but Hollis was better. Their presence caused her to wonder why he wanted to see all three of them. Perhaps he had another mission for them, though they had each been out on a witch hunt last night.

"Take your seats," Dante directed as he stood, straightening his suit and refastening the bottom button. In his suits, he appeared dapper and put together like Pierce Brosnan in a James Bond movie, even down to the silver streaking his otherwise black sideburns. "It has recently come to my attention through a reliable source—"

"You mean snitch," Rachel sarcastically snickered.

Dante inclined his head. "Such a crass term. I prefer 'source.' Anyway, this source confirmed what a separate source had previously supplied. The town we have been looking for is, in fact, in Colorado. It is called Havenwood Falls."

"Weren't we just in Colorado, like a year ago?" Nala impatiently asked. She had been one of the main hunters first tailing, then keeping watch, on Macy Blackstone when she had inadvertently stumbled upon them.

"Indeed, but my memory of it has remained maddeningly elusive. No doubt a side effect of those damned witches the *other* Blackstones associate with."

"They shouldn't be allowed to use the name Blackstone," Rachel spat with disgust. Nala and Hollis both agreed.

"No, no. They are of our blood. Though they are misguided, we can bring them back into the fold, into our family, and redirect their purpose—help them see the error of their ways, so to speak," Dante clarified, looking each girl in the eye to ensure they understood.

"Do you know where in Colorado?" Hollis cut to the chase.

"No. That is the frustrating part. However, we know it is somewhere in the middle of the state. Most likely somewhere with a significant area of land where they could hide an entire town."

"How do we know your 'sources' aren't sending us on a wild goose chase?" Nala asked as she whipped her long blond hair behind her shoulder.

Dante sneered, and an evil glint entered his eyes. "I extracted the information from the witch myself. She couldn't help but tell me."

Nala and Rachel each swallowed hard. They knew what kind of methods the source would have had to endure for Dante to get the information he wanted. Hollis didn't flinch. She knew he did what he had to, to get what he needed.

"Well, it's about damn time. When do we go?" Rachel asked, readjusting in her seat as if she wasn't afraid of Dante's tactics. They all feared him. The ones like Hollis had the ability to hide their fear, which separated them from the others.

"No." Dante surveyed the girls slowly, taking measure of something they weren't aware of. "For this mission, I need to be able to completely trust the person I send. She would have to be able to go undercover, be skilled at listening, and have the ability to not act on instinct—to conceal her hunter side for the greater good. For this mission, I choose Hollis. She is the best suited."

Without reaction, Hollis simply nodded her acceptance. The other girls groaned.

"Then why are we here?" Rachel asked. She had a tendency to speak out of turn. Dante put up with it to a point. He had reached that point. The look he gave her had her shrinking back into her seat. Hollis couldn't help the glow of approval she kept hidden in her chest. Rachel got on her nerves the most.

"*That* is exactly why I chose her. Hollis can control her reactions and simply observe. Also, not to mention, Macy has seen you both and most likely would recognize you right away. She never met Hollis during her stay, as Hollis was out on an extended mission." Hollis realized he had called the other girls in to teach them a lesson and to, once more, instill competition amongst them by elevating one over the other. She didn't agree with his tactics for camaraderie amongst teams, but he did get results. He turned and looked to her. "Will you go, daughter?"

"Of course, Father. When should I be ready to leave for Colorado?"

"Tomorrow morning. I will have Grace get flights prepared. Pack light. Disguise yourself. I want you to blend in. Be a tourist, if need be. I want specific information on the town and certain people within it. I'll get a list together while you pack."

Hollis inclined her head in a half nod and half bow, ready to serve.

"How are you so sure she'll find it based on 'somewhere in the middle of Colorado'?" Nala asked, but Hollis could hear the tinge of jealousy behind her tone.

"Can you find it, Hollis?" Dante pointedly asked.

"I won't come home until I do."

Dante smiled. "That's my girl."

And that was how Hollis found herself at the private airport in Grand Junction, waiting for a shuttle to take her to Montrose, yet another small city in the middle of the Colorado mountains.

CHAPTER 2

*H*ollis searched the small cities and towns of Colorado for over a month with nothing to show for her work. Until one afternoon, in the middle of May, she found herself wandering the small town of Durango. About to give up her search for the day, she overheard a middle-aged couple talking in aggravated hushed tones.

"We'll miss the bus up the mountain," the woman huffed with her hands on her hips, clearly frustrated with the man beside her. She shot a reproachful gaze at him.

"Don't get in a tizzy. We'll make it just fine," the man attempted to placate her.

"A *tizzy?* The special instructions we were given by the Havenwood Falls Tourism Bureau said the bus doesn't wait for anyone. It'll be your fault if we miss it," she rebutted with a harsh whisper. The woman cast eyes full of blame on the man, obviously willing him to feel her subtle wrath.

Hollis, excited about the potential lead, stayed several strides behind them, but continued to follow. She had very little in the way of clothes with her, but she always took everything in her small backpack every time she left the motel room in anticipation of an occasion such as this one. She never knew when luck would strike, and she would need to follow a lead.

Hollis continued to follow the couple behind a truck stop. Sure enough, a small bus, more like a shuttle, had its front doors open and passengers loading into it. Hollis had never seen a bus completely wrapped with images such as the beautiful scenery of trees and mountains as this one did. The imagery evolved from one season to the next: winter to spring to summer and then to fall around the outside. But no words indicated where the bus was headed. Hollis wondered how anyone would know this bus went to their destination. She might never have found it had she not been following the couple who obviously knew where they were headed. Hollis moved in close and casually examined the shuttle while awaiting her turn to board.

Out of the corner of her eye, the words *Havenwood Falls* shimmered as if by magic across the side of the bus. Hollis knew witches were involved, so it most likely was magic, but either way she had to admit it was a cool effect.

"Miss, will you be joining us on our journey up the mountain today?" the shuttle driver asked, breaking Hollis out of her entrancement. She cleared her throat.

"Yes. Yes, I will."

"Well, come on then." He waved her on and looked at his watch. "It's about time to be on the road before dark. The roads get mighty difficult in the best of times, but at night they can be a mite treacherous."

At Hollis's frown, the little man supplied a hearty laugh. "But I know my way around these parts like the back of my hand."

He examined the back of his hands, then winked at her. He moved inside the shuttle and to his seat, allowing her to climb aboard.

Hollis found an empty bench a couple rows from the front. Quickly, she surveyed the impeccable inside of the shuttle, located the emergency exit windows, and noted the couple who joined right before her and the three others previously seated. Everyone seemed to mind their own business except for one man in the back who eyed her suspiciously. She took the seat next to the window and tossed her backpack on the seat beside her, preventing anyone from taking it. Tugging at the collar of her new striped button-down shirt while simultaneously attempting not to retch at the sight of her bright white tennis shoes, she lamented the tourist look she had donned for the sake of the mission. Hollis sighed and hoped all her efforts would be worth it in the end. The shuttle waited another minute, then the driver closed the doors and started the engine.

"Buckle up!" the driver announced. "These roads have their twists and turns. Wouldn't want you falling out of your seat and giving the town another meaning to its name—Havenwood *Falls*." He chuckled, finding himself and his cheesy joke humorous, and pulled out of the lot. After several minutes of silence, the driver shouted, looking into the rearview mirror, startling several of the riders.

"Just a couple of announcements I've been asked to give." He cleared his throat as if reciting from memory. "If you're returning home, then welcome back. If you are here for the local fun, May 25, the annual Moons in the Mist Bonfire will be happening in Danzan Park by the lake. We have a farmers market every Saturday morning in Cook's Corner Park, First Friday Art Walk in the square, Second Saturday Movies in the Park also in Danzan Park, and Third Thursday Music in the Square. There is always something fun going on in Havenwood Falls!"

"Small towns . . . how quaint," Hollis muttered under her breath. She sat back and thought over how boring life must be in such a small, secluded place to have so many events. Once the bus ascended through the trees, the road curved back and forth. The monotony of the forest scenery, the hum of the shuttle engine, and the rocking with every curve eventually lulled Hollis to sleep. But just before her eyes closed, she saw the glow of several pairs of eyes peering out from the now darkened forest. Then she drifted into peaceful nothing.

"Welcome to Havenwood Falls!" the driver shouted, startling Hollis awake.

"I can't believe I fell asleep," she whispered with near panic as she looked around, taking stock of her possessions and her surroundings. She couldn't believe she let her guard down in such a way. Never before had she fallen asleep in public—on a job, no less. The false security of the bus ride shocked her to a fully awakened state. The bus passed a large sign made of layered stone and metalwork complete with a spotlight, welcoming them to the town of Havenwood Falls. The road crested a ridge and finally opened up to reveal a fantasy hidden amidst the mountains, a small world lighting the darkening sky. Hollis couldn't help but absorb everything on a first impression basis. She could understand why people might want to visit a small town like this quaint postcard-esque oasis, but not her. She preferred the anonymity a larger city provided. It's harder to stealthily move about when your neighbors watch your every move, or when the town's gossip shares your private moments.

No, a small town was not for her.

Yet something undeniably alluring was at work within Havenwood Falls. The draw had to be part of the magic—she just didn't know if it was witch-made or natural.

"All right, folks, I'll be pulling in at Whisper Falls Inn. If you have reservations or need somewhere to stay, I highly recommend this inn. However, there are a few other options for lodging if Whisper Falls doesn't suit you. If you want to be dropped off elsewhere, let me know and stay in the shuttle."

Hollis followed a guy off the bus. The sound of Whisper Falls Inn was appealing—not to mention close—and Hollis figured she'd make first contact and learn more about the town in the morning.

She acknowledged the driver and offered him a tip. When her hand touched his, something sparked in his eyes. Not romantic, but more . . . *other*.

"You may find your stay has more to offer than you planned on. Enjoy Havenwood Falls, miss."

And with his random words and the slightly creepy encounter, Hollis tightly smiled and then proceeded to practically run into the guy who had stared at her on the bus and who continued to do so. His eyes perused her person from head to toe, and he cocked his head as if deciding something, then darted without a trace into the town square.

"Creepy! What are they drinking in the water here?" she said under her breath, shaking off the effects of the weirdo, then followed the same couple she had trailed onto the bus up the steps of the nicely refurbished three-story Victorian manor. The inn looked straight out of the 1800s, complete with a charming wraparound porch, tall turrets, and beautifully painted gingerbread trim. She followed the couple all the way in, through the lobby area to the front desk, tugging at her shirt positioned just right to cover most of the ink on her shoulders and adjusting the plain straight-legged jeans she would never choose to wear.

"Welcome to Havenwood Falls and Whisper Falls Inn," a teenage girl said. "Are you checking in with a reservation tonight?" she professionally asked the couple in front of her.

While Hollis waited her turn, she admired the inn's original woodwork and decor while she stretched out her witch hunter senses, but she didn't pick up any witches or other hunters in the inn. She relaxed. At least there was that. Perhaps the inn was a place she could hide in peace while she staked out the town.

"Hi! I'm Aurelia Petran. How can I help you? Do you have a reservation with us?" the girl at the desk asked Hollis with a partial smile. She was a little on the thin side with medium-dark brown hair and large brown eyes.

"No, I don't have one. I have cash if you have a room available for tonight. Or if not, could you point me to another place?"

"No, no, don't go anywhere else. We have a room available. Do you have a preference of view—perhaps the town square?"

Hollis didn't have to think about it. "Yes, the town square." She hesitated, then remembered she had a part to play and added, "Please."

"This your first time in Havenwood Falls, then?" the teen pried.

"It is."

The young girl bit her lip when it was obvious Hollis wasn't going to give her much more, then rolled her eyes.

"Your name?" she asked, then snarkily tacked on, "please." Obviously not missing Hollis's awkward response.

"Why?" Hollis suspiciously asked.

The girl frowned and pointed at the computer. "For your reservation. I need to know what name to put it under."

Not wanting to draw more attention to herself, Hollis complied. "Hollis."

Aurelia narrowed her eyes for a moment before proceeding. "And your last name?"

"Blacks—" She stopped herself. Man, something about this town had her off her covert game. "Black. Hollis Black."

The girl lifted a skeptical brow. "Okay then, Hollis Black. Here is your key. Second floor, up those stairs." She pointed over Hollis's shoulder, across the lobby to the grand staircase, and smiled with a lot of attitude and teenage angst.

"Thank you."

"Hey, guys!" Aurelia greeted someone behind Hollis. "Nice timing. You missed the shuttle drop-off." The young girl rolled her eyes again then shrugged. "But never fear, I was here and checked everybody in," she sarcastically told the two newcomers who entered the room from the other side of the inn.

"Sorry, Aurelia, but we needed to help"—the woman shot a quick look to the man next to her before continuing—"Mammie in the kitchen."

"Meet our newest guest." Aurelia gestured toward Hollis who was quietly padding up the steps already, hoping to avoid small talk with the hotel locals. "This is Hollis Black. She's going to stay with us tonight."

"Hello, Hollis, welcome to our inn. I'm Michaela, the owner, and you met my sister. This is Xandru, my fiancé." She sighed when she looked over at the large handsome man who playfully grabbed

Michaela around the waist and pulled her back against his chest. "My permanent fiancé, it seems. Maybe someday I'll be able to call you husband," she privately grumbled to him.

"Hello," Hollis said as the extent of her pleasantries, awkward with the new turn of events.

"Do you know how long you plan on staying?" Michaela asked while she swatted away advances from Xandru so she could talk. He clearly had other things on his mind than stopping to chat with a new guest.

"I'm not sure yet. Perhaps a few days."

"Oh, you must stay at least through the weekend for the big town bonfire. It's so much fun!" The young girl practically bounced with excitement.

"Maybe I can. I look forward to seeing your town tomorrow in daylight."

"Well, let us know if you need anything while you're here," Xandru added, more distracted with Michaela.

"Goodnight, Hollis," Michaela added as she turned to Xandru and kissed his chin.

"Goodnight." Hollis quickly moved up the steps before anyone could ask her anything else. Though they seemed friendly enough, she had no idea if they were anything supernatural—as their strange greenish-gray eye color seemed to indicate—or simply human pawns in the witch's world in Havenwood Falls. Her gift only allowed her to discern witches, their magic, and other witch hunters. Something about watching the two relate stirred a longing she hadn't felt in a long time.

"Just another reason to not stay longer than necessary," Hollis whispered. She resolved to find other lodging sites and keep moving after a day or two so no one got to know her or her business.

CHAPTER 3

*T*he morning light streaked through the window as Hollis covered her head with the blankets, groaned, and turned away.

"Shit, could it be any brighter here? It's going to be one of those days. I can already tell." Stretching, she realized she slept all night for the first time in . . . well, she couldn't remember when. Often the hunters had evening drills, or she simply couldn't sleep. Rolling out of bed, she grumbled expletives as she got dressed.

Once the initial shock of morning wore off, Hollis quietly snuck down the staircase, hoping to leave unnoticed, in search of coffee.

"Morning, Hollis!" a chipper female voice called out.

She turned to the counter to see not Michaela but a tall beautiful redhead with the palest skin and blue eyes.

"Morning," she replied with less enthusiasm. "I don't think I met you last night." Hollis wasn't even sure why she cared to try. She wouldn't be in Havenwood Falls long.

"I'm Sindi Scott. I work the morning shift. Michaela is probably still in bed. Coffee?"

"Mind reader?" Hollis asked with a playful smile, yet her eyebrow lifted in silent question.

Sindi cocked her head and looked at Hollis strangely, like she wasn't sure if she was truly asking or not. Only in Havenwood Falls apparently would someone not consider that a cheesy joke.

Apparently Sindi decided Hollis was joking and offered a smile. "Nope, just have worn that same expression myself plenty of days."

"Where would I find some? Coffee, that is."

"There is breakfast and beverages in the dining room," Sindi answered, pointing in the opposite direction. "Or straight out the door and about half a block west is Coffee Haven, which is usually the more bustling café. But if you're looking for quiet, there's also Broastful Brew. It's on the opposite side of the square from here. Just cut across the square diagonally and you'll find it."

"Coffee Haven it is. Thanks," Hollis said and offered a slight smile. She didn't want to come off as too rude; that would draw a different type of attention. Her goal today: blend in. Thus the need for wearing plain jeans, a black plain T-shirt, her long unruly dark hair up in a ponytail, and boring gray tennis shoes. She didn't do tennis shoes. It was only to play the tourist role her father chose for her, that she wore them.

"I wouldn't have pegged you as a sneakers kinda girl," Sindi randomly offered. Her comment caught Hollis off guard.

"Excuse me?" Hollis asked, looking down at her new tennis shoes—she had even attempted to scuff them up to look worn.

Sindi shrugged. "You just struck me as a shit-kicker or boots with buckles kinda girl. No offense."

"None taken." Hollis smirked, then turned to go. Observant girl. She'd need to remember that. Moving to another inn might need to be in her near future.

Hollis jogged down the front steps and paused, taking in the scene before her. The town literally surrounded a big square, the center being green like a park, complete with walking paths and a fountain. Connected buildings filled with businesses and restaurants ran along each side of the square except for the north end. There stood a large official-looking brick building with a clock tower—

had to be City Hall—and the local police station resided adjacent to it.

"The square can wait for coffee," she muttered to herself.

"Everything can wait for coffee." The male voice came out of nowhere from her left. She hadn't even heard him approach and frowned at the distracting effect the town so quickly had on her.

Hollis gave him a curt smile and a nod. "True."

"You must be new here. You look lost, plus you're coming out of the inn." The nosy man had the audacity to approach her.

Do people in small towns not mind their own business? Hollis wondered to herself.

"Are you headed into Coffee Haven? I can show you the way. I was headed there myself." The man gave her a big toothy grin highlighting his pearly whites. His hands stayed in his pockets, apparently trying to make himself appear smaller and nonthreatening. Hollis had studied people and their mannerisms; she could read most people with ease. This one wasn't creepy, just overly friendly. Plus Hollis could handle herself in a fight if she needed to fend him off for any reason.

"You're a lot to take in, aren't you?" Hollis raised an eyebrow. About to brush him off, she couldn't help but notice that the nosy man was a big piece of gorgeous man-meat—olive skin, defined muscles, dark hair, and dark gray eyes. She also couldn't miss the low-frequency vibration that emanated from him. Witch. Or at least half witch and half something else. His frequency caused her to think of Grace back home; hers was similar.

"I've been told that before. I'm Ryne Calloway. And you are . . . ?" He let the end of his word hang in the air, waiting for her to respond.

"A stranger. Didn't your mama tell you not to talk to strangers, Ryne Calloway?" Hollis turned to leave, but not before catching the brief pain that registered on his face. The look was gone almost the instant it had occurred. Hollis wondered what pain he endured.

"If you told me your name, you wouldn't be a stranger, now would you?" He moved along next to her and smiled confidently, knowing his line was cheesy. He had an endearing quality about him. Hollis knew better but decided to make nice in Havenwood Falls. If nothing else, she might get some information out of him.

"Hollis Black." She smiled, then kept trying to walk away.

"Wait! Where you goin', Hollis Black?" Ryne moved to catch up to her, and with his long strides, it didn't take him long.

"Coffee." She pointed toward the shop with the sign that read *Coffee Haven* on the outside, while simultaneously glancing in the window of a fun-looking vintage clothing shop called Callie's Consignments. She told herself to duck in there later as her wardrobe now seriously lacked.

"Right. Do you mind if I tag along? I don't have to sit with you. I was headed there anyway when I saw you standing in front of the inn looking lost and in need of a guide."

"I'm not lost." Hollis glared at him.

"Not anymore, because I'm here to show you around." He smiled again, unfazed by her attitude.

"No thanks."

"Why not?" Ryne's expression softened, and he took on a puppy-dog-like quality in his pout.

"First of all, I don't know you. Second, I like to be alone. Third, don't you have a job or somewhere to be?" Hollis ticked off her reasons with her fingers.

"You do know me—we just met. Alone is so boring. And yes, I do have a job, but I have today off." He, too, ticked off his responses with his fingers. "So I can be your personal tour guide and show you all the cool places around town."

Suddenly what he said made sense to Hollis. And why not? "Okay. It would be helpful to have someone show me around and tell me about the people—the town, I mean."

"But first coffee?" he asked, his face lit up like a kid at Christmas.

"Right." She gave him a funny look. Was he for real?

He opened the door for her, and the fresh smell of coffee beans rushed out, assaulting her senses, shocking her into a fully awakened state. "Mmmm."

Ryne indicated Hollis should order her coffee first, then he sneakily interjected himself and ordered his drink as well, his wallet already out and ready to pay the bill.

"Can I interest you in today's scone? There aren't too many left," the girl behind the counter said with a wide smile. She took Hollis off guard with her silvery-blond hair and her bright turquoise eyes. She tried not to stare, but the woman was beyond intriguing.

"Morning, Willow! We'll take two please." Ryne turned to Hollis. "Her scones are the best ever."

"Here you go, Ryne. The coffees will be ready in just a moment." Willow turned to Hollis and stared at her a second longer than necessary, almost as if she'd slipped into a trance, then smiled. "Stick with this guy. He'll show you what our little town is all about. Have fun!"

Hollis, slightly unsettled by the barista's words, followed Ryne to an open table for two near the wall in the middle of the shop.

"Who was that?" Hollis inclined her head in Willow's direction.

"That is Willow Fairchild. She owns the joint and bakes the best scones—did I already mention that?" Ryne set their coffees down, winked at her, and pulled out a chair for Hollis, which she looked at, dumbfounded. "It's a chair. You sit in it."

Snapping out of her haze, she frowned and sat abruptly. "I know what a fucking chair is. I've never had anyone pull one out for me before."

Ryne was silent for a moment, then with a puzzled look, added, "Really? Not even on a date?"

"I don't date much. I'm busy with"—she hesitated, looking for the right words—"education and work."

"Oh, you're one of those types."

She frowned. "One of what types?"

"Focused. Motivated. Studious . . . that type." Ryne shrugged, leaned back, and stretched out his legs, crossing them at the ankles.

Taken aback, Hollis had never thought about the "type" she

might be, but those were as good as any. She shrugged and reached for her coffee and the plate with the blueberry scone on it. "Thank you."

"You have to try your scone," Ryne said around a mouthful of his own. His eyes practically rolled back into his head with sheer ecstasy. "Like right now."

Hollis couldn't help but laugh. Right there in public it looked like the man she shared a table with was having a private moment with a pastry.

"Would you and your scone like a room?"

But it was too late. Ryne had shoved the entire scone into his mouth and smiled a big crumbly smile full of blueberries and flaky goodness. Still he nodded and raised his eyebrows suggestively.

Hollis snorted and practically choked on her coffee. She had never made such a sound before. Slightly embarrassed, she righted herself and took a bite of her scone.

She nearly groaned herself, now understanding. "You're right. This is the best scone."

"You don't laugh much, do you?" Ryne asked, suddenly serious as he watched her eat her small controlled bite.

She cleared her throat and turned to observe the customers of the café. Other than coffee, observation was, in fact, why she now sat at Coffee Haven.

"Tell me about the town," she prompted him as she took another bite.

Ryne leaned back in his chair and crossed an ankle over his opposite knee. "What would you like to know?"

"How big is it? What do people do here? Why is it way up in these mountains? Who's in charge?" She shrugged around another bite. "You pick."

"Well, all right. I'm not originally from here. I've only lived here about a year, so I'll do my best to answer your questions. We get a lot of tourists, especially during the winter for our great skiing, but we also have a lot of town events that many out-of-towners find fun to participate in." Ryne sipped his coffee. "Let's see . . . Why is it in the mountains? From the stories I've heard, the founding families—the original townspeople—were looking for a quiet secluded place to settle down in the late 1800s, and this is where they ended up."

"Who's in charge? Do you have like a government or elected officials?" Hollis asked, absorbing all he said.

Ryne shrugged. "Mayor, city council, sheriff . . ." He paused in mid-sentence. "You know, all the typical stuff . . ." He quickly took another sip of coffee.

Hollis noted his pause, as if he wanted to say more but stopped himself. She wondered about the secrecy of the town and how it all worked. What would he do if she outright asked? Did he even know he was part witch? Would she scare him off if she were to be so blunt? She'd consider asking, but not today.

"So what do you do for work?"

Ryne almost looked relieved when she moved on to something else. "I work construction with McCabe & Sons Construction and a little bit at the ski lift this past winter."

"What else do you do?" Hollis kept him talking not because she was interested in him or what he did, but because she was able to listen to more around the room when she didn't have to talk. However, something about the ring of his voice, the low timbre of it, drew her in, and she found she wanted him to keep talking.

Suddenly Ryne's voice faded into the background as her senses kicked in, alerting her to not only one witch's presence, but two. She watched out of the corner of her eye as a woman perhaps in her forties walked in with a teenage girl and happily chatted with Willow and another girl at the counter. Both of the newcomers registered to her as witches.

"Have Gallad and Macy set a wedding date yet?" Willow asked the woman with a smile.

Macy? Macy Blackstone? Hollis completely tuned in.

"Not yet. They've decided to move slow. Which I, for one, am pleased with. I adore Macy, but I think they're still young and more time isn't going to hurt them," the woman said matter-of-factly.

"Well, you are Gallad's mom. You're entitled to think that. Do the Blackstones agree?" Willow's question confirmed they did indeed speak of Macy Blackstone.

"Oh yes, Lilith and I seem to be on the same page. And I think the kids are, too, now that hormones have settled down." The woman with long curly dark hair flippantly gestured with her hand at Willow, clearly not embarrassed.

"Oh, Mom, really!" The teenager with the same curly dark hair rolled her eyes, clearly embarrassed.

"Ronya, you're terrible," Willow said with a wink, and handed them their drinks in to-go cups.

"I have to take this one to the dentist, or we'd stay for a bit," the woman named Ronya explained.

"We'll see you soon! Bye, Ronya. Good luck at the dentist, Gianna." Willow waved and welcomed the next customer.

Hollis tuned back to Ryne just as he was saying something about the bonfire party.

"Will you be staying for it? It's this Saturday. I haven't been, but heard it's pretty epic."

"The bonfire?" Hollis clarified. At his nod, she continued, "I was thinking about it. Can tourists just show up?"

"Of course! You can go with me, then you won't be a tourist." He smiled at her and took a big gulp, draining the last of his mug.

"Where to next?" Hollis looked at him with a question in her eyes.

"A pretty tourist such as yourself needs an experienced guide to show her around so as not to be taken advantage of by the local riffraff. And I have volunteered myself to give you my time today." He placed his hand over his chest and bowed his head. "Out of the goodness of my heart and concern for your well-being, of course."

"Wow, that's so generous of you," Hollis began with sarcasm. "But I'm good. Thank you for the coffee and amazing scone, but I am fine on my own."

"I bet you are, but do you have fun on your own? Just a thought," Ryne said with a raised eyebrow. He returned his mug to the counter and strolled out the door.

"Did he really just leave me sitting here?" Hollis sat stunned with her mouth open and her gaze toward the door.

"Honey, if you don't recognize a keeper when one is right in front of your face, you don't deserve him." A tiny and frail-looking elderly woman at the table next to her offered her opinion without guilt or shame. Clearly one of the town's busybodies, Hollis noted.

"Oh, Irene, don't scare off the new girl," Willow whispered from the table she was cleaning nearby. "Enjoy your day, Hollis." Willow went back to the table she was bussing, Irene went back to her breakfast, and Hollis stood up with nothing else to do but leave.

CHAPTER 4

"*Y*ou don't scare easily, do you?" Hollis asked with an eyebrow raised, her stance widened and her arms crossed over her chest. A very cool and collected Ryne leaned against a vintage streetlamp, waiting for her.

"You're not as scary as you think you are," he replied as he pushed himself off the lamp and moved toward her. "Plus, you didn't think I would give up my new tour guide gig that quick did you?"

"Well . . ."

"Come on, you want to see the town, don't you?" Ryne held out his hand.

"I'm not taking your hand. I just met you." Hollis kept her arms crossed and strode by him, heading straight for a shop with a peculiar name. She cocked her head and peered up at the sign. "Does that really say *Hey, Nice Glass?*"

"Sure does. There's a lot of shops and some restaurants. We've got Backwoods for outdoor wear and equipment, and even a wine-tasting storefront for the vineyard at the edge of town. Anywhere you want to go in particular?" Ryne asked, strolling along beside her as if he had nowhere better to be.

"The vineyard sounds cool. What's that like?" Hollis asked,

curious if it could perhaps be associated with the Blackstones. Her father had told her stories of his youth back in the mid-1800s and his family's tobacco farm and vineyard—it wouldn't be much of a leap to think the Blackstones of Havenwood Falls would start something similar. She tipped her head up, closed her eyes for a second, and simply enjoyed the feel of the warm May sunshine on her face. The sounds of water splashing from the fountain at the center of the square offered her a brief sensation of peace.

"The Stone Falls Winery. It's a small vineyard owned by a family named the Blackstones. There's also some cabins called NamaStays Inn on the property, and they do yoga or some shit like that." Ryne clapped his hand over his mouth like he forgot he was trying to impress a lady and be on his best behavior. Hollis almost choked on a laugh.

"Interesting. And you said they have a storefront here in the square too?" She had been right, but remained casual.

"It's called Soothing Sips, and it's just a little farther." He pointed ahead of them.

Hollis suddenly stopped. She hadn't sensed the presence of another hunter nearby. Though she was still a slight distance away, she would have. Ryne gave her a quizzical expression.

"I just remembered I wanted to go into Callie's Consignment after coffee and look for clothes. It's back that way, right?" She pointed behind them. Most likely none of the Blackstones were present at Soothing Sips, but she couldn't risk their sudden appearance. The last people she needed to see right now or even get close to were the Blackstones. They would recognize her as a fellow hunter, and her mission would be over before it even began.

"Well yeah, but there's more to see this way." He thumbed behind him as he faced her. "We can make our way back around," Ryne suggested.

"New plan," Hollis countered. "I want to walk through the park. We don't need to walk by—what is that? City Hall?" She pointed to the larger buildings at the north end of the square.

"Yeah, the big one in the middle is City Hall. The police station and the chamber of commerce on either sides." He inhaled, then shrugged. "Sure, we could do that." Ryne's face lit up with a genuine smile, completely content. They cut across the street and entered the beautiful park-like setting at one of the paved, bench-lined walkways leading toward the fountain in the middle.

Hollis and Ryne spent the next couple hours walking in and out of several shops. Hollis chose to skip Howe's Herbal Shoppe with the excuse she had allergies to a lot of plants, but truthfully she could feel several powerful witches inside, and her skin practically crawled with the tingling sensation up and down her arms—her hunter instincts alerting her. Inside Backwoods Sport & Ski, she purchased hiking boots, claiming she wanted to hike the trails to the falls the next day. After circling back around, she found herself genuinely excited to visit Callie's Consignments.

"Hey, thank you for the tour, but I'd like to hit this next shop on my own. You know, try on clothes, take my time. I'd rather not put on a show." She shrugged sheepishly, pretending to be shy all of a sudden.

Ryne actually blushed and stammered. "Oh, of course. I didn't mean to overstep my boundaries. It's been fun showing you around. I like to remember all the things I came to love about this town when I moved here."

Hollis studied his face and noticed the minute lines of tension around his eyes that hadn't been there all day, and the essence that made him witch flared at his sudden unease. "Ryne, how did you come to move here?"

He shifted on his feet, suddenly uncomfortable. "Well, I came here with my mom about a year ago. She loves it here. We had to . . . She needed a new start, and I felt responsible for her after my dad died. I couldn't just let her go off to a new place alone. We ended up here." He shrugged. "That's it. Pretty simple."

But Hollis had the feeling it was anything but simple. It wasn't her business. And she didn't want to get involved. So why was she even asking?

"Cool."

He seemed relieved she didn't press for more information. Which, of course, made her want to press further. But not now.

"Hey! Would you like to meet up for lunch after you're done shopping?" he asked, like he'd had the greatest idea.

"Why?" She suspiciously narrowed her eyes and cocked her head.

"Because I enjoyed spending time with you; you're new and don't know anyone; and everybody's got to eat, right?" He was grasping at straws. Hollis might've found it cute under other circumstances. But she was on a mission to reveal all the witches of Havenwood Falls, not go on a date with one.

"I don't think so. Thanks, though," she responded, suddenly wanting to soften the blow for him.

He scrunched his face. "Okay, then how about dinner? I could show you the town at night. We have some nice places to eat. Plus I think it's the third Thursday tonight, so there should be live music in the square." His eyes lit up with remembrance of the local event. She couldn't deny that.

"All right. Dinner. I'll be ready at the inn. Six?" Her arms crossed over her chest suggested she wasn't too happy about it, but deep inside, if she was honest with herself, an excitement bubbled at the prospect of the personal attention and the possibility of fun.

Ryne smiled from ear to ear. He mock bowed and backed away. "Until then, my lady."

Hollis smirked at his silly antics. Why was this playful guy even remotely interested in her? Granted, she wasn't half bad in appearance—she had used her looks in her favor a time or two on a hunt—but she wasn't even trying. In fact, she was doing the opposite of trying—she had been trying to get rid of him most of the morning. He just wouldn't take no for an answer. Hollis chuckled to herself, then opened the door into the vintage wonderland that was Callie's Consignments and unexpectedly got hit with a wave of toxicity that almost had her doubling over.

A young woman rushed past her and out the door, taking the

toxic magic stench with her. Hollis had encountered that feeling too many times to mistake it for anything else.

Black magic.

But who was the witch, and what was she doing here? Did the council in Havenwood Falls allow such behavior from their witches?

No. She shook herself out of the effects it had on her. Hollis didn't care if a witch practiced black magic in Havenwood Falls. That wasn't her purpose this time. Though everything within her wanted to go after the woman and punish her for her participation in the dark arts. It didn't matter who she was or why she did it. The witch deserved to die.

But what about a half witch? The unwelcome question floated through her mind.

One with warm, inviting gray eyes who made me feel things I didn't realize were a part of me? She had never questioned herself or her instincts before. What was it about this town that caused her to do so only one day in?

"You shopping or getting out of the sunshine?" a woman yelled from behind the counter. She was reminiscent of a young gypsy with a flowy top, colorful skirt, and enough bracelets to stock a store. The woman looked expectantly at Hollis with a wild eyes.

"You Callie?" Hollis ventured a guess.

The woman squinted at her with cynicism. "Maybe. Who wants to know?"

"Just a guess. I like your shop. I'm Hollis. I'm just visiting your town and need to pick up a few new things."

"These are not mere *things*. These"—Callie stretched her arms wide across her store with pride—"these are artwork, amazing vintage pieces of art."

Hollis cocked an eyebrow. She had never heard anyone speak of clothing in such a manner. As if it mattered. As if it could be a part of you, or rather an extension of you. "Got it. What would you show to me, without knowing me?"

Callie moved toward Hollis, pursed her lips, and frowned, taking her in from head to toe—noting her tennis shoes with a cocked eyebrow of her own. "That's not your everyday look, is it?" But her question was really more of a statement, needing no answer. "Luckily for you, I like a challenge. Let's go find you, and not whomever this is wearing tennis shoes." She waved a hand in a circle in front of her, indicating all of Hollis. "Whatever suppressed thing you have going on is radiating off you, making me, and most likely the entire town, sick."

Hollis's eyes grew wide. Who did she just engage herself with? Not a witch—she would have felt that. But Callie was definitely something. Hollis wondered how many *somethings* other than witches could live in a small town.

"Don't look surprised. I'm good at reading people." Callie waved her off and shook her bangles. "Gypsy. Magical balls. Tarot cards. Fortune telling," she ticked off with a wink. But Hollis wasn't sure if Callie was telling her she was a real gypsy or if she portrayed the stereotype of one for fun.

"You definitely play the part well," Hollis returned.

"It's not a part. And you have a lot to learn, don't you?" Callie spun around and headed toward a rack of a variety of different types of "pieces," as she called them. "We'll start here."

After an hour or two, Hollis had tried on a multitude of clothes and had just put her uncomfortable "tourist clothes" back in place when she felt tingles like electricity shoot up her arms. Then she heard something that stopped her cold.

"Hey, Macy! Perfect timing. A new batch of vintage jewelry was delivered this week. I want to show you," Callie called out from across the room.

"Hi, Callie! I was hoping you would say that. I've been jonesing for . . ." She paused. "Something new," she said slowly, as if searching.

Hollis pulled back the dressing room fabric the tiniest bit to spy out. Sure enough, a girl just out of high school with white-blond hair and bright blue eyes matching the description her family had given her of Macy Blackstone stood in the center of the store, looking around with a confused expression.

"Macy? What the hell is wrong with you? Did you see a ghost?" Callie asked, half joking.

"Is anyone else here?" Macy whispered, moving closer to Callie. Callie frowned at her and nodded.

"There's a new girl in the dressing room," she whispered back. Hollis had a hard time hearing them, but by reading their lips she was able to make out most of what they said.

Macy frowned. Hollis knew Macy could sense a fellow hunter's presence just as Hollis could sense hers, but Macy wouldn't know Hollis was of her own kin.

"What? Is she dangerous?" Callie whispered, but didn't appear afraid.

Macy shrugged her shoulders. She leaned in and whispered something in Callie's ear, then backed up and said more loudly, "I'm sorry, I only have a few minutes, but I can come back to look later, too."

"Sure. The necklaces and bracelets are over here." Callie led Macy to the stands of jewelry. Macy did a quick perusal, then left the store.

Hollis breathed a sigh of relief and gathered the items she wanted to keep. She wasn't going to let a potential encounter with Macy take away from the fantastic new clothes—pieces—she found. Her father would be disappointed if he knew her train of thought preferred fashion over her mission. The absurdity of the thought almost made her laugh. She would still try to follow Macy; it was a win-win in her book. Good thing her father wasn't there.

She stepped out with her items and went to the counter. Callie paid attention to her, but didn't seem any different. She gathered the clothes from the counter and rang Hollis up with efficiency. The last item she handed to Hollis personally and happened to touch her hand.

"Thanks for your business." She paused, and her eyes quickly flashed as if she had a momentary blackout. Then as if nothing had happened, she smiled. "I hope you'll come back. If you ever want to take that leap, you'll fit in just fine. Maybe you'd even find it fun to come to a girls' night out sometime with me and my friends. You belong, Hollis. Especially now that you have cute shoes. I'd better not see those damn tennis sneakers again."

Hollis smiled shakily, slightly taken aback by Callie's bold intuitions. "Um, sure . . . okay, thanks." Hollis took the bag from Callie and gave her an odd look. "A gypsy, huh?"

Callie shrugged. "Gypsy," she replied. "You never know around here. See ya 'round!"

Hollis headed for the door with a lot more new things than clothes to consider.

Now to try to find Macy.

CHAPTER 5

*A*fter several minutes of searching for the direction Macy went, Hollis gave up and took her bag of new "pieces" back to her room at Whisper Falls Inn. On her way up the stairs, she was greeted by Michaela coming out of the parlor.

"Oh, hey, Hollis. How was your first day in Havenwood Falls?"

"It was . . . interesting. But I got some fun things at Callie's." Hollis held up her shopping bag.

"I love Callie. She's a good friend. Didn't you just love her store?" Michaela asked as she rounded the desk to take her position behind the computer. "Did she make you try on other shoes?"

"It was great. And, yeah, how did you know?" Hollis asked, looking down at the tennis shoes that made her skin itch with a desire to burn them.

"She has a thing against tennis shoes," Michaela said with a chuckle. "Especially if the person wearing them doesn't seem to fit them."

Hollis squinted. Did she really just say that? "What is with people and my shoes in this town?" she spat with frustrated irritation as she headed for the stairs.

"It's not your shoes, Hollis. It's what they're hiding," Michaela boldly stated as if she knew something.

"Whatever. I have a dinner thing to get ready for."

"A date? With Ryne? He's such a sweetheart. Don't break him, Hollis." Michaela approved and warned her all in one breath.

"Not a date. Just dinner. He doesn't take no for an answer." Hollis frowned. Too many people were keeping tabs on her already in this tiny town. Time to move.

"Oh, Michaela? Could you tell me which way to the vineyard? I thought I might like to see it and get some wine to take back with me."

"Of course. I'll draw you a map and have it sent up to your room."

"Thanks."

Hollis jogged the steps two at a time up to her room on the second floor, but just before she exited the stairwell, she overheard Michaela on the phone. "Hey, Addie, it's me. I have a guest by the name of Hollis Black. I think she's up to something or is more than she seems, if you know what I mean. I'll keep an eye out for the Court, but maybe you can check her out. She probably needs to register as a visitor." She paused. "Yeah, I think she's something other than . . . Just a hunch. Bye." She hung up the phone.

Hollis couldn't believe her ears. They'd discovered her faster than she thought. She didn't know who Addie was, but they were keeping their eyes on her.

They must have a way to keep track of supernaturals. I wonder how that works, Hollis questioned mentally with concern after she entered her room. Her jig might be up before she got much more than clothing.

Some time later, a folded map of the town slipped under her door. True to her word, Michaela circled the Stone Falls Winery and drew a path from the inn, making it an easy route to follow. Hollis knew it was a risk going somewhere the Blackstones were sure to be, but she wanted to see what she could find out, especially now the leash of her disguise grew shorter. Unfortunately, she didn't have time before dinner, but perhaps she could slip away after.

At six o'clock on the dot, Ryne pulled up in front of the inn, but Hollis already waited outside for him. She didn't want him to come into the inn, knowing the town was full of busybodies. Earlier Hollis had decided to use her time with Ryne to her advantage and make it part of her cover: she had come to visit and spend time with her friend, Ryne.

"Well, don't you clean up nice?" Ryne smiled and started to reach out for her, then stopped himself, suddenly awkward.

To both their surprise, Hollis reached out in response to him and grabbed his hand. The smile that boy sported could have melted the hardest woman's heart. And if Hollis wasn't careful, she would be no exception.

"What can you show me tonight?" she asked, alleviating the awkward moment.

"We can eat on the square and enjoy the evening music by the gazebo—grab Napoli's pizza or something else close by." He pointed to where several townsfolk were setting up folding lawn chairs and spreading blankets on the grass, settling in for an evening of music. "Or we could go somewhere a little off the beaten path. There's a restaurant at the top of the falls—it's a little nicer but has a great view of the town—or we could . . ."

"Pizza. Napoli's sounds amazing. Not sure about the sitting around kumbaya-style with a bunch of strangers part."

"Pizza it is. We can eat inside and then decide on the music after we hear how it is. If it's a high school band practicing then . . ." He shrugged his shoulders and scrunched his face in distaste.

"Lead the way, then." She gestured for him to take the lead.

Napoli's was a nice family-run establishment. The inside boasted a darkened, cozy Italian flare. They found a table off to the side and away from a larger group of high school kids, probably headed out to hear the band. One boy in particular caught Hollis's eye. He looked about seventeen, lean and lanky with dark hair. The crowd he hung with looked about the same age and sported various skateboard gear. His bright blue eyes struck her. She had seen those eyes not only in the mirror, but on her father. If she tuned in to him, she could feel the energy of a fellow hunter, but just barely, as if he hadn't been awakened yet into his powers. Interesting. *He must be a Blackstone.* She had heard they slowed the awakening with Macy, too.

"Here it comes!" Ryne said with the excitement of a young boy.

Hollis watched with amusement. When he caught her looking, he didn't even blush.

"What? I love their pizza. It makes my mouth water just thinking about it." He pointed his fork at her. Hollis held her hands up in supplication. "You just wait. You are going to love it, too."

Hollis wasn't so sure, but his confidence in it alone made her want to try it.

An hour and an entire pizza later, Hollis and Ryne walked out of Napoli's. People of all ages now covered the green of town square. Music blared out into the four corners, and to Hollis's ear, the band didn't sound too bad. Children danced with each other and ran around while grandparents and older folk sat in folded chairs chatting and watching the young ones play. People listened, but most used it as a social opportunity. The sight was quaint and joyful, and the warmth of the moment caught Hollis off guard. She didn't see witches and witch hunters, vampires and werewolves, or any other supernatural race who might be hiding out in this small town. She simply saw people being people, and she found that refreshing.

"Would you like to find a seat and listen to the music? They don't sound half bad," Ryne said, slightly impressed.

"Actually, I was thinking I'd like to see the Stone Falls Winery and enjoy a glass of wine. Would you like to join me?" she asked hesitantly, as if she had never asked anyone out.

Ryne smiled and gave her a single nod. "That sounds like the perfect end to a perfect day."

"Are you always this cheesy?" Hollis asked.

Ryne feigned shock. "I'm hurt. I am not cheesy." He gently nudged her, but Hollis staggered under his strength. She had to fight her instinct to shove him back and realized he was playing with her. "But in all seriousness, I had a nice time today. You are a breath of fresh air in this town. And there is just something about you that draws me in," he said honestly.

"Really?" Hollis asked with confusion. She had never been described as a breath of fresh anything. And thinking over the day, she hadn't even been that nice to the guy. "I . . . I don't know what to say. Thank you?" she guessed.

Ryne laughed out loud. "That'll do."

He reached for her hand, and she let him take it as they walked up one side of the square, past the storefronts, and strolled into a residential part of the town she hadn't yet seen.

Hollis ignored the constant tingling she felt race up her arm at his contact, but considering he was only half witch, the sensation seemed dulled.

"The vineyard is through a neighborhood?" Hollis asked, taking in all the different types of houses.

"It's just up this road a few blocks, at the base of Mt. Alexa." Ryne pointed straight ahead of them. "See, just there you can see the white lights from the patio."

"That's pretty," Hollis caught herself saying. She frowned, then closed her mouth, confused at her own treacherous reactions.

"Sure is. The Blackstones are real nice people, and they've got a nice place here. Granted, I've only been here a few times, but I've enjoyed it every time."

Hollis considered what he said. "Would you say they are friends of yours?"

"We're not that close, but I've hung out some with their oldest son, Brock. And I know Gallad Augustine—he's engaged to their daughter Macy. They're a nice couple, though a bit unorthodox." Ryne frowned as if he wished he hadn't said that last part.

"What do you mean, unorthodox?" Hollis wasn't about to let it go.

"Well . . . I just mean . . . he's . . . and she's . . ." Ryne looked pained. "They're still young is all."

"Oh, I'm sure if they've got family and friends like you, they'll be in good hands." She decided to throw him a bone. He was obviously not used to hiding things.

His shoulders relaxed. "Oh look, they've got a fire going in the back. Let's head to the back patio."

Hollis looked up. The mountain towered above, a formidable shadow, reflecting what little daylight remained in combination with the glare from the town lights. Humbled and small was how she felt in its presence.

"Pretty amazing, isn't it?" Ryne asked, coming back to where she stood in awe. "It never gets old, looking at it."

"I have never seen anything quite as magical, and I've seen a lot," she admitted.

Lowering her gaze, she observed the vineyard establishment. The main building was a mixture of dark wood, clean lines, and a rustic modern vibe. Aspens dotted the landscape as well as large barrels of potted florals with trailing greenery. Small lanterns guided their steps from the graveled parking area up to the main walkway, leading them around to the back of the building where a concrete patio was brought to life with overhanging white lightbulbs and simple wooden table-and-chair sets. Modern garage doors opened into what appeared to be the main tasting area. But out past the patio was the vineyard—rows and rows of meticulously lined grape vines of various kinds. Hollis noted other buildings off to the right.

"What's over there?" she asked Ryne quietly, not wanting to disturb the other patrons enjoying their quiet evening.

"I think those are mainly barns for storage and making the wine. This smaller but nice two-story building is the NamaStays Inn. It's the main check in area. They have several small cabins you can rent, then come inside here for meals . . . like a B&B, I think. My mom and I stayed in one when we first arrived, but I didn't really partake of all its amenities. I'm sure we could ask at the bar, if you're interested."

"No." Hollis almost panicked. "I mean, no thanks, not right now anyway." She wasn't quite ready to encounter a Blackstone yet.

Thinking of that, she stretched out her hunter senses but only felt the faint hum of someone off in the distance.

Ryne frowned, but moved into the patio area anyway. "Let's sit and have some wine. Enjoy the music and ambiance here."

Hollis nodded and followed him into a large room, rustic and modern from floor to ceiling with concrete floors and horizontal wood paneling on the walls and ceiling. Fantastic yet simple light fixtures hung at various points in the room, sliced barrels hung on the walls with names of different wines, and the back of the concrete bar top area was a chalkboard filled with the season's flavors along with some town favorites.

The man behind the counter turned around. He had dark brown hair and green eyes, and he didn't give off a witch hunter's vibe. Not a Blackstone. Hollis relaxed.

CHAPTER 6

"*H*ow can I help you two?" He looked up and noticed Ryne with a smile. "Hey, Ryne! Good to see you, buddy. Who's your friend?"

"Brock, how are you, man?" He pulled Hollis next to him. "This is Hollis Black. She's in from out of town, and I thought I'd show her a few of the town's finest establishments." He winked at Brock, who seemed to be caught on Hollis's face.

Quickly Brock recovered and stuck out his hand. "Nice to meet you, Hollis. Welcome to Stone Falls Winery. Would you both like to try our newest bottle for this summer?"

Brock pulled out two clean wine glasses and placed them in front of Ryne and Hollis. At their consent, he expertly poured a small amount into each glass for them to taste. He went on to describe the flavor and what went into the production.

"Would you like to try some of our other wines?" Brock asked.

Hollis shook her head. "This one. This is the one I want," she said with a smile of satisfaction on her face. Brock nodded and poured her a full glass.

"Ryne? How about you? Want to try a deeper red?"

Ryne squished his mouth to the side. "In all honesty, I'm not much of a wine guy. You all don't have anything else available here, do ya?" he asked sheepishly.

Brock's eyes lit up, and his expression took on one of secrecy and mischief. He leaned in close and whispered, "Actually, I've been working on some micros in the basement. Wanna try what I've got cookin'?"

At Ryne's sly smile, Brock slammed his hand on the counter with excitement. "Give me a sec. I'll go grab you something."

"No worries, I'm going to the men's room." Ryne turned to Hollis. "Will you be all right here? I'll be right back. If you want to grab a table out by one of the fire barrels, I'll join you."

She smiled and lifted her wine glass. "That's where I'll be."

She ambled over to a small table and sat. With her glass of heaven, and the warmth of fire at her side, she gazed up at the mountain again and allowed herself to imagine what her life might be like if she weren't who she was but instead a normal townsperson. Perhaps she'd have a Friday night ritual where she would meet up with Callie, Michaela, and their friends for a quick glass of wine. The pretend life made her smile.

But that wasn't her life. And she wasn't a normal girl who could simply move to a new town and settle down, maybe try a real relationship with Ryne and grow old . . . older.

"Girl, you are in over your head. What in the name of all that is holy are you doing in Havenwood Falls?" a woman's voice harshly whispered as she took the seat across from Hollis, startling her back into her reality.

Hollis's eyes grew wide as saucers. "Letitia?"

She was uncertain the woman before her was the same one she had once known as a little girl. The woman had aged since the last time Hollis had seen her. Witch hunters—full hunters—aged at a slow rate if they took the lives of witches on the regular, but even if not, they still aged slower than the average human. Her father, Dante, was somewhere close to two hundred, she thought.

"Hollis Blacks—"

"Shhh, Letti. It's Black. Hollis Black." Hollis stared intently at

Letti, willing her to hear her out. Of all the Blackstones she could have run into, Letti might be the only one to lend a sympathetic ear, having spent time with Dante's rogues herself once upon a time.

The older Blackstone raised an eyebrow. "Why are you here?"

"I'm visiting a friend, Ryne Calloway. I'm not hunting."

Letitia narrowed her eyes in disbelief. "How did you even find us?" Letti asked with growing concern. "Is your father on his way?"

"Like I said, I'm here with Ryne." Hollis expertly evaded the truth with a truth of her own. "And no, he isn't on his way."

Letitia frowned. "Hollis. If your dad finds us, all we know and love here will be destroyed. Do you not see that?"

Hollis paused and looked around. "Maybe. But if he could only see what I'm beginning to, maybe he could grow to love it, too." She said the last as an unconvinced question.

"I thought that once, too. But I'm sorry, he won't change." She paused and leaned into Hollis. "Does the Court know you're here?"

"I knew there had to be some kind of leadership council. No. And I don't want them to. Can't we keep this between just us, Aunt Letti?"

Letitia scowled. "I'm sorry, dear, but I will have to inform them, especially as a former member. Your presence here brings danger to us all. You need to talk to the Blackstones and announce your arrival to Lilith. She's on the Court."

"Please, Letti, I just need a little time. I'm . . . I'm having fu—"

"Hi, Ms. Blackstone," Ryne said pleasantly as he approached the table. "I see you met Hollis."

Letti hesitated, then a small smile grew on her face. "I did indeed. I couldn't have one of our fine customers sitting all alone."

Hollis visibly relaxed and offered Letti the briefest smile.

"How did you two meet?"

"Fate," Ryne jumped in before Hollis could say anything. He winked at Letti, and she laughed.

"I'd say so. Well, I'll let you kids enjoy your evening." She got up from the table and reached for Hollis's hand. "Don't be a stranger, dear. You really should meet the rest of my family and the owners of this vineyard while you're here."

Hollis heard the message loud and clear. Tell the Blackstones she was in town or she would do it for her. Letti wouldn't have a choice.

"I would like that, thank you."

Just then, Brock brought out a pilsner glass filled with a dark microbrew with a thick froth of purple-tinted foam at the top.

"Oh man, you delivered!" Ryne rubbed his hands together. "What do you have for me?"

"You'll have to tell me what you think. It's a porter. I presented it last month at the plate-painting event, so it's been dubbed the Purple Pig Porter."

Ryne took the glass and sipped off the top.

"I see you've met my nephew, Brock Blackstone, already." Letti bored the words into Hollis's eyes. Then she turned to Brock. "I was just telling this young woman she would need to meet the rest of our family soon."

Brock looked at her again. "You look so familiar. Are you sure you haven't been here before?"

"Positive. I've been told I have a familiar face." Hollis gave a shaky smile.

"Excellent beer, man! This I can definitely enjoy. Thanks," Ryne said, taking his seat. Brock put his arm around Letti and escorted her away.

"Have a nice evening," she called over her shoulder. "Remember what I told you, dear."

Hollis's hand shook with a slight tremor. She hoped Ryne couldn't see it. She sipped on her wine to calm her nerves. Her timeline just got bumped up even further.

CHAPTER 7

*A*fter, Ryne walked her back to Whisper Falls Inn and said good night. They made a plan to meet up late the next morning for a hike to see the famous falls for which the town was named. But Hollis couldn't shake the feeling that if she didn't do something right away, her time in Havenwood Falls would come to an abrupt end.

And she wasn't ready for her time to end—for more reasons now than only her mission.

Before she and Ryne had left the vineyard, she ducked her head into the main office at NamaStays to ask Letitia for directions, which she followed as she walked up to Blackstone Road and then west to Havenwood Heights—the old money part of town, if the mansions and large iron gate had anything to say about it. Letti had given her the address to the Blackstones' house.

Hollis found herself standing in front of the Blackstone family home, tingles climbing up her neck at the presence of hunters, with her hand outstretched to ring the doorbell. It proved unnecessary as the door flung open with four Blackstone faces staring back at her, their mouths about to land on the floor.

"It was you!" Macy gasped. "In Callie's earlier, I sensed you."

Hollis nodded. "You did. I wasn't ready to meet you. I was afraid you would jump to conclusions and not give me the chance to explain myself."

"Come in off the street. We don't need the gossiping neighbors finding more to talk about." The petite woman with a fierce blond bob and blue eyes had to be Lilith, according to Hollis's limited knowledge. They moved aside and allowed her to enter. She could tell each of them had their guard up. Hollis couldn't get a read on the older man, so she assumed he was human like Brock, but the younger boy—the same boy she saw earlier at Napoli's—she got a different energy reading from. His hunter essence repeatedly fluctuated and dampened.

"Welcome to our home. I'm Reggie, this is my wife Lilith, our daughter Macy, and our youngest son Brice." Reggie's words were kind enough, but she could hear the strength in his tone. This was his home, and he would do what was necessary to protect his family, even if he was not powerful enough to take out a hunter.

"I'm Hollis Black. I met Letitia and Brock earlier tonight, and they suggested I come introduce myself to you."

"Why are you here?" Lilith asked, straight to the point, her stature tall and unmoved.

"I'm on vacation. I have been spending time with a friend, Ryne Calloway. I mean no harm while I am here. I wanted to respect your territory, though, and let you know I am temporarily in town."

Macy didn't say much, but she watched Hollis intently, making her uncomfortable. But what the little girl didn't know was Hollis had been around the block for longer than Macy had, and she could hold her own. Lilith, on the other hand, would be a fight if it came down to it, but she seemed distracted.

"Hey, I saw you with Ryne at Napoli's tonight," Brice mentioned.

"I saw you as well. You like to skateboard?" she asked, trying to make nice. He nodded and flicked the hair out of his eyes that continued to find its way back.

"Well, Hollis, we appreciate you announcing your arrival to us. You will have to officially check in with the Court of the Sun and the Moon and let them know you're here. You have twenty-four hours from when you first arrived. Addie will register you as a temporary visitor. They like to keep track of all supernaturals who come into and out of Havenwood Falls."

"Mom, don't you think you should do that—inform the Court, I mean," Macy protested. Her frown indicated she wasn't happy with her mother at the moment. Lilith glared at Macy with a quick flash of her eyes—a look that said *don't question me in front of strangers.*

"You know I will, dear—I have an obligation after all—but I wanted to give Hollis here the chance to prove herself," Lilith countered.

"You'll have to forgive us, Hollis. We were in the middle of a family . . . conversation when you showed up," Reggie explained. Just then the front door opened and shut, and Brock entered the great room.

"Are you a member of the group of witch hunters associated with Dante Blackstone?" Lilith asked straight out.

"I used to be, but left them some time ago in hopes of a newer way. Their methods are so archaic and harsh. I wanted to see if there was more for me out in the world. A more peaceful coexistence, you know?" Hollis explained, her words full of lies, and yet . . . there might have actually been more truth to them than she had ever realized.

Lilith's gaze caught Macy's with a question. Hollis only caught the look because she happened to notice at the right moment. Macy spoke blatantly. "No, I don't recognize her from my time there. But . . . several hunters were away on missions, too."

"Hey, guys, you'll never guess who I met at the vineyard today . . ." Brock stopped in his tracks, and his eyes lingered on Hollis before quickly surveying each of his family members. "Hollis Black—who is now in our living room." He seemed deflated his news was no longer pertinent. "I didn't realize she was a hunter, of course. Aunt Letti informed me of a strange hunter in town, and I put it together." He sheepishly looked over to Hollis. "Sorry, I didn't mean you were strange . . . more a stranger though." He sighed. "I'm going to shut up now."

Macy snorted, and Brice elbowed Brock playfully and whispered, "Smooth, bro."

"It's all right. I am a stranger, and perhaps a bit strange too." She attempted to laugh it off, but even to her own ears it sounded hollow and wrong. She'd never had trouble playing a part before, but she unexpectedly had trouble playing this part with these people. Something in Hollis wanted to burst out with the truth and be done with it.

"I won't keep you. It's already late. I just wanted to come by before too much time went by. I didn't want any misunderstandings." Hollis turned to go.

"How long will you be staying?" Macy asked before she got to the door.

"Not much longer. Probably through the bonfire—I've heard a lot about that. It sounds magical." Hollis winked and walked out the front door. After she shut the door, she could hear Macy loud and clear.

"I don't trust her, or believe her for that matter."

"Remember, Macy, where would we be now if someone hadn't given your ancestor, Marie Blackstone, the benefit of the doubt and taken the risk of friendship? We need to give her a chance first," Reggie said.

"What if someone gets hurt because of it?" Brice maturely asked.

"Is that our risk to take?" Macy added in agreement.

Hollis didn't want to hear anymore. They were hesitant, as they should be, but they were going to give her a short leash with a limited amount of time. Now she had to be on her guard and walk on eggshells even more. For all intents and purposes, they appeared to be a regular family with regular faults and shortcomings, but they also cared for one another and their town. Even in her brief encounter, she could see the siblings love and the parents' protectiveness. She still needed to figure out how they participated in the town. Were they the pawns her father believed they were, under the control and brainwashing of the witches? She needed to find out the truth now more than ever.

CHAPTER 8

*T*he next day, Hollis met Ryne at the gazebo in the town square. He leaned against one of its sides, waiting for her with a big smile on his face. It was another lovely day in Havenwood Falls, and it being Friday, the townsfolk seemed to be out in full force, even more than the day before.

"What's going on? Are there always this many people hanging out?" Hollis asked, watching people coming and going with bags and boxes filled with plants, vegetables, and crafts.

"In the summer, we have a farmers' market in Cook's Corner Park. It's tomorrow, so they're setting up for it. It's just west of the square about six blocks, by the cemetery and the schools. Do you want to see?"

Hollis thought about it. The cemetery sounded intriguing. Another day. "No. I want to stick with the plan. See the falls." She stuck out one of her feet. "See? Even wore my new hiking boots."

Ryne tried not to laugh. "Okay, but we'll take it easy since they aren't broken in yet."

"Why?" She scrunched up her face.

"You'll get the mother of all blisters if you hike all day in shoes not previously broken in."

She could actually feel her face start to heat. Was she blushing? "I didn't think of that."

"No worries. We'll take a leisurely stroll to the falls and not go too far up. It will still be a sight to see from any angle."

She smiled, pleased he wasn't upset his plans were changed. Hollis relaxed and found she actually looked forward to spending the time with Ryne.

"We'll take my car since it's still a bit of a walk to the trailhead. That'll save your feet a bit. I'm parked right over there." He pointed to a spot along the side of the road in front of Madame Tahini's and, of course, Coffee Haven. Noting where her gaze went, he added, "I thought we could grab a coffee to go, too."

Hollis smiled. The boy knew all the right moves. "Definitely."

They leisurely walked in that direction, but Ryne suddenly stiffened. Hollis noted the change and under the guise of shielding her eyes from the sun, she followed his gaze across the street. He stared at a man who looked to be in his late twenties, tall and lean, wearing a flannel shirt, jeans, and work boots. And though he had on a hat and sunglasses, from the way he paused and turned toward them, Hollis had no doubt the guy stared right back at Ryne.

"He a friend of yours?" Hollis nodded toward the man.

Ryne snapped out of it and rubbed his eyes, but Hollis caught a quick glimpse of red rings around his irises. Whoa.

He huffed out a harsh laugh. "Uh. No, not with Orlon Laroc."

"Do you have a problem with him?" Something in Hollis rose up in defense of Ryne. She would introduce that Laroc fellow to her double-edged blade if Ryne wanted her to.

"Don't worry about him. Come on, let's get our coffee."

After quickly grabbing the coffee, they took Ryne's beat-up Ford pickup and drove straight up Eleventh and took a left on Blackstone Road, following it past Havenwood Heights to Alverson Road.

"Where we get out is just up here!" Ryne looked at her with excitement. "You're going to love this, Hollis."

Hollis watched him with a fascination unlike any other she had felt before. "I don't get you. You're excited about so many things. Is it real? Are you truly that happy with life?"

Ryne paused and looked at her, really looked at her. "I am. I've had reasons not to be, but in the end, I'm grateful for life."

"Why?" she prodded with genuine curiosity.

Ryne seemed to think about it, then made a decision, nodding to himself. "The place I grew up was very harsh and demanding. It wasn't easy for us where we used to live, especially for my mom. It crushed my spirit. And after my father died, my mom and I took our chance—the opportunity—and left, looking for a new life. A safer, more personable life."

"It sounds like you lived in a community or something, maybe not so unlike this one?" Hollis ventured a guess.

He laughed again. "Way different than this one. Here the people care about this town and each other. Everyone is allowed to be themselves as long as they don't hurt anyone else. My mom and I are free to be ourselves here." A sadness crept into Ryne's eyes at the mention of his mom.

Hollis listened and took in everything he said and didn't say, trying to read between the lines. She so wished she could figure out what his other half was; then maybe what he said would make more sense. The more curious thing? She actually was interested in finding out more about him. Her heart smiled a little.

She hadn't even realized how much they had walked until Ryne stopped.

With arms outstretched, Ryne revealed the most breathtaking sight Hollis had ever seen before her. "There she is. The falls."

Directly in front of her was a large glistening pool of the most refreshing-looking water. Casting her gaze up along the edges of the shore, she saw the source of the sound. Water cascaded from several stories above them at an intense rate, creating a power and energy all its own.

"Wow." Hollis couldn't bring herself to say anything else. The sight was awe-inspiring. She understood why her ancestors, and anyone from Havenwood Falls, would be drawn there. She crouched down onto her knees and bent over to peer into the crystalline pool. Reflected back at her was her image, warbled and wavy. The water smoothed to a flat glass, reflecting her face as she always saw herself in the mirror. As she looked again, the water warbled and smoothed again then showed her another version of herself—not too different from how she looked now, only softer and filled with joy and peace. Her heart ached with longing to know that person, what she was like, and how she was different than who she knew now. Hollis dipped her hand into the cool water and swirled her fingers through the reflection.

"I wouldn't touch—" Ryne started to say, but he was too late.

"The water?" Hollis looked up at him with curious eyes, but ended up having to squint with the sun in her eyes. Ryne, however, seemed to be staring at her with just as curious, if not skeptical, eyes in return. "What's wrong?" she asked, standing again.

"Nothing." He took a step back then inhaled slowly, absorbing the air around him. "It's so peaceful here. It's really a sanctuary for all kinds, you know?"

Hollis found his response strange and wondered if she had done something.

"Hey, can we hike around a bit? You know, before my feet blister." She smiled and held out one of her feet.

He smiled, shook off whatever strangeness had just happened, and reached for her hand.

"Absolutely."

They hiked around for the better part of the day then decided to call it quits. Hollis took her shoes off and rubbed her feet.

"Hey, do you want to go to the Moons in the Mist Bonfire with me tomorrow?" Ryne asked.

Hollis hesitated.

"Unless you already have someone to go with, then it's not a big deal. I just thought with the whole not knowing anyone thing you might be available." Ryne shrugged as if it were no biggie.

Hollis playfully slugged him in the upper arm. She caught

herself and actually looked at her fist. She had never done anything playful like that before.

"Yes. I'll go with you."

Ryne smiled and grabbed her hand unexpectedly. It was nothing more than a simple hand hold, but it warmed Hollis deep within her chest. She couldn't stop staring at her hand in his.

Ryne started to pull away. "Sorry, I should've asked first. I know you're not one for affection."

"I . . . I like it." Choosing not to think, but only to feel, she squeezed his hand and laced her fingers between his. When her gaze found his eyes, the depth of joy and sincerity of heart she saw in his face almost floored her. How could anyone like him be a bad thing? He obviously wasn't doing bad things with his magic, if he even knew he had it at all.

Maybe not all witches needed to be extinguished.

Maybe her father was wrong on that front. What if he was wrong on all fronts? Her chest tightened, and her heart rate sped up. Hollis could barely breathe. What was happening to her? She'd feel it if Ryne had put some kind of spell on her—at least one of a magical sort.

"I'll drop you off at the inn," Ryne started to say. His words snapped Hollis out of the life-altering state she'd been in.

"Oh, wait. I'm not staying there anymore." She quickly remembered she had checked out that morning.

"You're not? Everything okay?"

"Sure. I just felt it was time to move on." She looked out the window as they approached the Stone Falls Winery. "Actually, you can drop me off at the vineyard. I'm renting one of the cabins. I thought it might be nice to see different parts of the town." She shrugged. Plus, she subscribed to the adage "Keep your friends close and your enemies closer." She'd also been avoiding a run-in with Addie Beaumont, despite Michaela Petran's efforts to see her registered as a visitor.

"Well, I guess we're here then." Ryne pulled into the small

gravel parking lot in front of the building with a sign indicating NamaStays Inn.

"Yep, this is me." Hollis didn't move except to pick her boots up off the ground. She hesitated and turned back to Ryne, who looked like he was searching for something else to say. "Thank you for showing me the falls. I had a good time." Hollis frowned, unsure if that was what she should say. Truthfully, she had never been on a real date before. She had always been too busy and focused on killing witches. She'd never tried to date one. If her father could see her now.

"I'd like to see you again, Hollis. I feel this deep pull in"—he thumped his hand on his chest—"in here when I'm with you. I don't really know what it means, but I want to see where this could go. I know it's fast, and I don't really know anything about you than the little glimpses you let me see, but—"

Hollis cut him off, planting her lips onto his. He moaned and tried to return her kiss, but her position in the truck was less than ideal and a little awkward. She quickly pulled back, and as embarrassment flooded her cheeks, she clutched the handle to open her door. Ryne grabbed her elbow and gently turned her back to him. He slowly moved toward her face, guiding her chin close to him with his outside hand while his other hand reached behind her head. His mouth found hers and gently started moving over her lips. Hollis couldn't help the groan of pleasure erupting from her chest like a damn cat. He teased her lips, and she found herself wanting more from him. Emboldened by his kiss, Hollis readjusted her position and climbed onto his lap. The intensity of their kiss grew, and the oxygen in the car diminished. Hollis's chest grew unexpectedly hot . . . too hot. She leaned back to find Ryne's eyes not only rimmed again with red, but also his normal gray electrified.

"Wow . . ." She leaned in to say something about his eyes, then caught herself. She breathed deep. "I mean, I've done that before, but . . . with you . . . I don't know, it was different." Hollis was at a loss for words as she caught her breath. Her stomach erupted with damn butterflies. She felt giddy like a teenager, which she was most definitely not. Why had kissing Ryne felt different? A little voice whispered to her in the back of her mind, *"Because you have feelings for him—half witch and all."*

Ryne's gaze roamed from the top of her head, over her face, and further south, studying everything about her. No man had ever looked at her before like that. When she peered deep into his eyes, now back to their normal soft gray, she could still see magic, but only what was naturally him. Or perhaps his witch side and his man side were not exclusive. Perhaps all of it was what made him who he was. And she liked who he was.

Ryne tenderly swiped a piece of hair out of her face, sliding his fingers across her forehead. A sudden vibration in her back pocket arrested Hollis out of her little bubble of happiness—happiness! She wondered if that was what happiness felt like. She pulled out her cell phone, surprised to find all of a sudden it had service, when previously it had been pretty spotty since she'd arrived. Reading the screen, her heart plummeted to her feet.

Her screen read: Dante Blackstone. Her father. The infamous witch hunter who had sent her to Havenwood Falls on a mission. And here she was not only with a witch but KISSING one.

Scrambling off Ryne and back to her seat, Hollis grabbed her boots. "I . . . I have to go. I'm sorry, Ryne."

"Is everything okay? Was that too fast?" His expression looked worried as she hurried out of the door.

"Yes, no, I mean, I'm sorry. I have to go." She held up her phone. "It's my dad, and if I don't answer, he'll worry."

Understanding dawned on his face. "Gotcha. Go take your call. Maybe later?"

She nodded and waved, then ran around the inn entrance, following the path to her private little cabin in the back of the vineyard.

CHAPTER 9

"Hello? . . . Dad? Can you hear me? The reception isn't good here." Hollis answered her phone after the third time in a row her father had called. She could practically hear the irritation ringing through her phone.

"Where am I? I'm here. I made it." She paused, and a weak smile emerged on her face based on some praise her father had said, even though he mentioned he didn't catch all her words. "I found the other Blackstones and am learning about the dynamics of the town with the witches," she explained. He said more, and she was quiet as she walked into her little cabin. But frustrated she kept losing the call again, she stepped back outside.

"Sorry Dad, I can't hear you well. Yes, the source was right. It's in Colorado in the mountains somewhere . . . What? Hello? Are you there? Oh, there you are. I don't know where exactly. I came on a bus in the dark." Hollis gazed up at the mountain and then out at the beautiful rows of vines filled with plump grapes ready to be harvested. She wondered what it would feel like to mash grapes within her hands and to work the land. Getting distracted, she almost dropped the phone when her dad yelled into the receiver.

"Yes, I'm here. Bad service, I told you," she lied. The last time she had lied to her father, she was little and had to stay in a dark room alone for an entire day, though it felt like several. She never did it again.

"Yes, I'm staying focused. What are you looking for with the witches? Plans? Organization? Magic? I don't know what I'm looking for." Listening, she kicked a rock from her path and felt her chest cavity close in on itself as her father listed the many things he wanted to know about, such as the hierarchy, who the leaders were, where their sacred circles were, what kind of weapons they had, what the procedure was if they were invaded, etc.

"I'll check back in a couple days with more information. Okay. Bye, Dad." She hung up. "Yeah, love you too," she muttered sarcastically under her breath.

"Not the affectionate one, is he?" Letti asked from the edge of the vineyard, far enough away to not be detected by her hunter vibes but not quite far enough to not overhear her conversation.

"No, never has been," Hollis answered her question with a previously unrealized hint of regret.

"Neither was mine. I turned out okay." Letti consoled her with a wink.

Hollis smiled. Still unnerved, she asked, "How long have you been there?"

"Oh, not long." Letti waved her concern off. "I just came to see how you were faring."

Hollis crossed her arms over her chest. "You mean you were checking up on me."

Letti smiled but didn't correct her. "Have you had a chance to chat with the Blackstones yet?"

"I did, actually. They were quite . . . welcoming."

Letti laughed. "In their own way, I'm sure."

Hollis also laughed. "They don't know who I am yet, Letti. I need a little more time."

Letti frowned and bit her lower lip. "I can't be an accomplice to this, Hollis."

"No one will know you knew. I'll keep your part a secret."

"Only because I'm hoping you can see what I see in this town."

"I'm afraid your wish may bring me consequences." She sighed. "The Blackstones want me to check in with the Court. Where do I find them?"

"Oh I'm sure they will find you. Addie Beaumont has been on the search already. She's a powerful witch and will want to register you as a visitor."

Well, Hollis couldn't take the chance of Addie Beaumont reading her with magic or temporarily registering her and being able to trace her or her heritage. She wasn't sure how registering worked, but she couldn't risk it. She would lie and tell the Blackstones she had an appointment to meet with Addie—and if they followed up to see if she met with her? Well, plans get changed, don't they? Hollis planned on not staying in one location long enough to be found.

"Have a nice night, dear. Looked like you were having one before your phone call." Letti pursed her lips and chuckled, then turned to leave.

"Why, you little spy," Hollis teased, slightly offended she got caught. Then she remembered that no one truly knew her. They weren't going to tell her father on her. She could be whomever she wanted to be in Havenwood Falls; the thought caused her to think.

"Good night, Hollis." Letti had told Hollis she didn't live on site, and she left every night promptly at six unless she had an evening Yoga in the Vines class, which only happened a couple nights a week. At least that's what the sign had announced.

"Right. A good night. You too," Hollis said, distracted as she went into her cabin for the evening. At the door, she stopped and looked up at the mountains with fresh perspective, inhaling deep and slow. "I could be whoever I want to be here."

~

Ryne had told her he had to go to work at McCabe & Sons Construction. So the next day Hollis decided to try her hand at roaming the town on her own. She had been bombarded with

Ryne's presence since she first arrived in the small town. Then he started to grow on her. Hollis still couldn't understand why he wanted to hang around her. She thought of their kiss with a smile, and her body heated all over again.

A jarring thought suddenly occurred to her: he could be a spy. What if he was a part of the town Court she kept hearing about, and he had been keeping his eye on her since the beginning? The thought didn't sit well with her. He hadn't come off suspicious at all, and she'd been trained to be a good reader of people and intentions. Plus she had pretty good natural instincts as a hunter. No, she didn't think he was anything but who he portrayed himself to be. She still didn't know what his other half was, but she found herself becoming lulled by his presence and not agitated by the witch essence that normally assaulted her on a constant basis. Instead it was like her body acclimated to his presence—only his. She still felt the same agitation climbing her arms into her neck, but she had been a hunter for so long, she knew how to control the sensations and not let the feelings control her. Hollis touched her neck at the mark she'd been born with, the mark that declared her a witch hunter; it had always been a part of her. With Ryne, she decided she would trust her instincts.

Hollis casually strolled from the vineyard toward the town square, weaving through neighborhoods to see parts of town tourists wouldn't normally see. The town, the places people lived, the strangers offering her a wave and a friendly hello on the street— it was a mix she thought existed only on television, and yet she found it genuine and endearing.

I wonder what kind of home I would live in if I lived here? Hollis wondered to herself, looking at the cute craftsman homes and then observing the nice well-kept apartment building as she headed into the square. She would never allow herself to even ponder such a question on a mission, but since she was playing the part of Hollis Black visiting a friend, and no one knew the difference, she figured she'd embrace it and see what it felt like to dream.

She passed Broastful Brew but sensed a heavy witch presence

and decided to keep going back to her new favorite, Coffee Haven. Plus, she couldn't forget the taste of those blueberry scones!

When she entered the café, the smell of roasted coffee beans and baking deliciousness hit her all at once. Her traitorous body wanted to close her eyes and swim in the magic of her olfactory senses; instead, she willed herself to stay present. Hollis sensed a couple of witches, but decided she couldn't avoid them all. Waiting in line, she took the time to observe the shop and the people in it. But as soon as she did, she regretted it.

At a table amongst the crowd sat Callie, the owner of Callie's Consignments, and two other women. One woman—the one with light brown hair, black-framed glasses, and tats running up and down her arms—she was pretty sure was Addie Beaumont, the witch whom she'd been avoiding. The other, a petite woman with long brown hair and green eyes, she hadn't seen before. There was a brief conversation between the three before Callie extended her hand and waved her over. Hollis hesitated. She could sense the one girl was a witch and a strong one at that. She wasn't sure what the other woman was, but she could sense dark magic surrounding her —not black witch magic, but something else entirely. If Hollis refused and left right then, she would be admitting guilt of some kind and cause a scene. So instead, she smiled and gave Callie a short wave in return.

"I'm going to order, then I'll come over," Hollis said, pointing that she was next in line. Callie gave her a curt nod and waved her to stay put, not rude but just to the point. That was why Hollis liked her. Callie showed you who she was—no games.

Not like the game Hollis now played. Regret bubbled in her chest. It shouldn't matter. She wouldn't see these people again after the mission. But what if she did? Hollis Black could even see them being friends, maybe.

"Hi, Hollis, what can I get you this morning?" Willow asked with a smile. Taken aback at first that Willow remembered her name, Hollis paused, then smiled. She realized she liked it.

"Morning. Just coffee, black please. And a blueberry scone, if you have any?"

Willow smiled. "Of course I do. Your coffee will be right up if you want to wait a second." Willow was suddenly pushed forward with a slight burst of shock, then she laughed and looked down behind her. A little girl with hair so blond it was almost white clung onto Willow's leg. "Hang on, sweetie. Mommy's working."

"She's yours? How old is she?" Hollis asked. The little girl looked up at her with big, surprisingly golden eyes and gave her a toothy grin. No hesitation. No judgment. Just joy. Hollis couldn't help but smile back at her and wave.

"She is. This is Arabella. She's just over one and a half. I thought she was playing in the office with Harlow."

"Sorry, Willow. I opened the door for a second, and she escaped. You're a little escape artist, aren't you?" the other woman, who must have been Harlow, said with a playful tone as she scooped up the little girl, kissed her cheek, and held her. Hollis watched with interest as the tingling sensations climbed her arms. Harlow, too, was a witch.

But Willow watched Hollis instead. "Maybe someday you'll have this too. You could, you know."

The spell was broken, and Hollis cocked her head. "Can you read minds or something?" Hollis whispered.

"Something like that," Willow cheekily responded with a wink. "Here's your coffee and scone to go, Hollis. Have a good day."

Hollis grabbed her coffee off the counter and her scone in a paper bag. She turned back to the little girl staring intently at her just as her mama had—as if she knew too much.

Walking around a couple tables filled with people, she made her way to Callie and the others. "Morning, Callie."

"Hollis, these are my friends Harper Sinclair and Addie Beaumont," she introduced.

Addie. Witch. The one Michaela had already warned about her. Confirmed. Great, now Addie knew what she looked like. There'd be no hiding after this.

"I'm Hollis Black," she said with a forced smile.

"Would you like to sit?" Addie asked, pulling out the fourth chair at their table.

"Thank you, but I'm not staying." She held up her paper bag as if that proved it.

Harper was quiet and smiled but she kept looking around Hollis as if she was seeing more than what was right in front of her. It was unnerving, to say the least. Hollis needed to get out of there.

"Will you be around much longer?" Callie asked.

"Not too much. I'm staying for the bonfire tonight, then I'm not sure."

"Going with Ryne?" Callie asked suggestively. Addie slugged her with her elbow, but Callie shrugged, unconcerned. "What? I saw them together."

"I am, yes." Hollis grew more uncomfortable.

"Is Ryne who you know here in town?" Addie questioned, her eyes tightening, as though scrutinizing her.

Hollis hesitated. Aside from the witch vibes Hollis felt up her arms, she also got the impression Addie wasn't happy with her, though she seemed nice enough on the outside.

Hollis nodded. "He's my friend."

"But maybe more than that?" Callie slyly added.

Hollis's gaze flickered around the room, unsure of who was listening. She cleared her throat. "I don't know what you mean."

Callie smirked wickedly. "I like you, Hollis."

But Harper didn't look so sure.

"I need to take off, but you ladies have a good one. Nice to meet you." Hollis couldn't leave fast enough.

"You too," Addie and Harper both said.

"Hey, I like your shoes. They're much more . . . you," Callie said with an appreciative nod at Hollis's feet. Instead of the tennis shoes she had first seen her in, Hollis wore her black buckle-up boots over gray skinny jeans. Something about Callie's approval made Hollis feel more like herself than the tourist she pretended to be. Perhaps she was someone in the middle of the two. Hollis wished she knew. Life was simpler before she arrived.

As she left the table and reached the door, she heard Harper whisper, "A lot of darkness surrounds that girl . . . a lot of death."

Goosebumps erupted down Hollis's spine. How could she know that? Is that what she was seeing—ghosts? The thought made Hollis want to run until she couldn't run anymore. Instead she casually walked away from Coffee Haven, not willing to let Harper's words or the type of people in the town rattle her. But that was exactly how she felt—rattled.

CHAPTER 10

*a*fter Hollis's encounter at the coffee shop, she needed to walk off the strangeness she was seeing more of in Havenwood Falls. At first it appeared so serene and tranquil. But she had the feeling a storm of supernaturals and their darkness and secrets percolated beneath. That thought alone comforted her to know she wasn't the worst being who might be in town. Perhaps the darkness she carried, the monster she was, could fit in a place like this.

Unaware of where she'd been heading, she was surprised to find herself in front of the town cemetery. Slowly Hollis wandered inside. She had always liked cemeteries and would often find the oldest one in the various towns and cities they ended up in. She could find peace there and take a few minutes to herself—unless she had hunted in that particular area. She was afraid one day she would be haunted by the ghosts of those witches she had removed from the world. The thought hadn't bothered her too much until now. Grateful she had never been in Havenwood Falls before, she felt safe to stay for a few minutes. Rows and rows of precisely placed headstones dotted the ground, and evenly distributed benches were accompanied by clusters of trimmed trees. For the age of

Havenwood Falls, Hollis expected older graves and wondered where those were.

As she continued to walk, the thought occurred to her that Blackstones in their final rest should reside there. Wandering around for several minutes, she discovered there oddly weren't any. Something shimmered and caught her eye. Hollis walked to where pretty crystals hung on a tree. Out of the corner of her eye another path revealed itself to her, as if beckoning her to follow. Curiosity struck her, and she continued on the path, which mysteriously led her to a stone-pillared arched tunnel that traversed under Blackstone Road.

"What's on the other side?" she whispered, not expecting a response. She looked around to ensure she was alone and bravely strode through the tunnel. To her surprise, the tunnel opened to another section—a hidden section—revealing the type of cemetery Hollis had originally been expecting. Pausing at the entrance, she reverently absorbed the scene. These plots were much older, less pristine and orderly, but also held a serenity and beauty all their own. She wondered why the separation, unless this section was reserved for supernatural families. Hollis wondered if anyone could wander into this section or if she found it because she was herself not entirely human.

This section hummed with magic—witch magic, mixed with magic she couldn't place. Witch magic essence thrummed through her veins from her fingers to her shoulder blades, crawling up her arms. The magic was powerful and old—very old. Hollis hesitated. She had never felt the harmony of such magic working together in one place. She sensed the warning and the danger, but also the protection and the symbiosis of it. This was sacred ground.

"I mean you no harm. I'm looking for my ancestors," she whispered to the magic, in case it listened. Lightly she stepped, staying on an invisible path, guided by an invisible arm drawing her in one direction. This portion of the cemetery felt alive, not only from the strength of the magic, but actually alive. When she didn't look directly at something, she saw vines grow and twist, flowers bloom and release petals over the dead, branches bend and sway out of the corner of her eye.

Hollis gingerly walked by much older graves. Bending down, without touching them, she noticed many held runes or other magical symbols.

"I wonder what those are for," she whispered out loud. Continuing her curious meandering, she came across what appeared to be possibly the oldest graves she had seen yet. They were oddly covered with metal cages. Hollis frowned and steered herself away from those. She couldn't fathom what they were for, unless . . . Nope, she didn't want to think about horror movie–style scenarios involving zombies.

She kept on in her search. One in particular she looked for: Marie Blackstone, her father's youngest sister. The one who started the separation between the Blackstones back in the 1800s. When Macy had stayed with Dante's hunters after leaving Havenwood Falls almost two years ago, she informed Dante of Marie's passing at the turn of the century.

Noting the names on headstones, she recognized some of them from names she had heard in town: Beaumont, Fairchild, Augustine —and some she hadn't heard yet: Bishop, Mills, among others.

Finally she found the name she'd been seeking: Blackstone. Several were familiar, but others must have been Blackstone hunters from Marie's line. Finally she saw Judson Carter Blackstone, and right next to him was his wife, Marie Marcella Blackstone. Hollis walked right up next to it and placed her hand on top of the headstone. She couldn't see or hear ghosts, but the stone warmed under her hand, and she felt welcomed. She hadn't expected that.

"You know who I am?" she whispered, not at all feeling strange speaking to a gravesite. "Your brother sends his love." Hollis laughed darkly as she said the words, sure Marie knew the truth of it. "I found my way here. I'm sure you know why. But I have all these conflicting emotions and thoughts. Part of me sees what you were seeking when you left my father and the others all those years ago. I see the camaraderie this town has no matter the races, no matter the secrets. I'm sure they have their conflicts like any family, but that's what it feels like—family. And I just figured that out." Hollis huffed, struck by the absurdity of her mission and essentially her whole life.

"My life is a sham. What I thought was family has been an organization intent on using whoever they can to advance the one ideal of a madman—my father. He doesn't care about me, not really. I can't believe it took me talking to a dead person to figure that out."

Rocking back on her heels, Hollis simply stayed and absorbed the love she suddenly felt emanating from Marie's headstone. She closed her eyes, and though she knew it had to simply be the magic of the place, she allowed it and even craved it. One by one she felt additional warmth coming from Judson and then each of the other Blackstones nearby. The feeling was overwhelming.

Hollis cried. She never cried, but there in a magical cemetery, surrounded by dead ancestors freely offering her love with no judgment or stipulation, she broke down, and the tears flowed.

Several minutes passed, though to Hollis it felt like a lifetime had come and gone. A gentle stroke ran up and down her arm. Startled, she looked around, searching for the source until landing on a vine reaching down to her from a nearby tree. It was suddenly in full bloom, whereas it had only buds minutes before. The vine grew downward and stroked her arm once again, as if coaxing her to rise. She stood and felt her moment was finished. It was time for her to go.

"Thank you," she quietly said, looking at each of the Blackstone graves. "I know what I need to do."

Hollis left with renewed spirit and a new mission. She stood tall, her inner badass coming out to play, but this time tempered and softened by a redefining moment. She didn't have to be who she was trained to be.

Her phone rang. Her father's ringtone blared, as if he somehow sensed her change of heart. Quickly she left the sacred space of the old cemetery, not wanting to taint it with opening a channel to her father. Once outside the cemetery, she wiped her pants off and straightened her jacket. She steeled her shoulders and stiffened her spine.

"Dad, I was just about to call you—" She paused mid-sentence. "What? You're where? On your way to Colorado? Oh, I had no idea you were coming so soon. Why didn't you tell me?" Again she listened. "I told you the reception up here is crazy."

In her chest, Hollis felt the panic start to throw her off, but she planted her feet and deeply inhaled. He wasn't there yet. And he didn't know where to go past the city of Montrose, as far as she knew. She needed more time in the town. She *wanted* more time in the town and with Ryne. Her heart sped up at the thought of Ryne and what he'd think of her when he found out the truth. She needed to tell him right away.

"I don't have all the information you need yet. I need more time. How far away are you?" She listened and nodded as if he could see her. "I'll get it for you by then. Call me when you're in a nearby town." She hung up and squeezed her phone. She'd throw it if she didn't need it.

"Think, Hollis. He's on his way, but not here yet. Your new mission hasn't changed. What are you going to do?" Hollis paced right outside the cemetery then abruptly stopped. "I need to find the Court. I could ask Cállie to call Addie. Aunt Letti said they would find me. Well, now would be a good time."

Chills went up her spine, warming at her neck, and she felt eyes on her. A hunter was near. She stormed back toward the town square and figured she'd know her next step when she saw it.

CHAPTER 11

*H*ollis strode up to the intersection of Eighth and Stuart Streets, at the corner of the town square, her stride full of focused intent with renewed purpose. The little witch hunter followed her, but she wasn't about to let Macy stop her yet. Hollis had a plan, and she needed to see it through in her own way.

Hollis was ready to march straight into either Whisper Falls Inn for Michaela or over to Callie's Consignments for Callie—either could get her in touch with Addie, so she could finally register.

Lucky for Hollis, she didn't have to go that far. Gathered right in front of City Hall stood Callie, Michaela, and Addie chatting on the grass side of the street. She swerved and made a beeline for them.

"Callie! Michaela!" Hollis called and raised her hand to get their attention. Their heads all swiveled in her direction, surprise written on their faces. Michaela smiled and waved back. Callie cocked her head, and Addie lowered her sunglasses to peer over them.

"I was just looking for you—all of you, actually," Hollis admitted as she approached closer. "I have to say something. I'm not who I said I was."

"We know," Michaela confirmed, unsurprised.

"We were waiting for you to do the right thing," Callie admonished.

"You've been dodging me, but these two—and Lilith, by the way—convinced me and the Court that you'd figure out on your own that we're not the enemy, and to give you a little more time." Addie shrugged. "I guess my girls here can read people pretty well."

"Stop!" a female voice yelled from a block away. All four of them turned to find Macy Blackstone with her phone up to her ear, running straight for them. Simultaneously, a black car pulled up right along the opposite side of the street. Letitia, Brock, and Lilith Blackstone got out of the car, followed by an older woman, who most definitely carried the Blackstone trademark look of blond hair and blue eyes.

"Shit," Hollis muttered under her breath.

"Hello, Lilith, Brock, Letti, and Eva. What brings you here together on this lovely day?" Addie asked, trying to defuse the sudden tension crackling in the air.

"Macy told us to get here right away," Lilith answered.

"Hunter business, dear. Hollis, this is Eva, Lilith's mother," Letti added, regarding the other woman.

"There's Macy now," Eva noted. Macy caught up to where they were, out of breath but quickly recovering.

"Hey, Hollis!" Ryne shouted from the other direction, getting out of his truck. He ran over with a big smile on his face.

"Oh, what a shitshow," Hollis mumbled and looked to the sky in defeat. This was going to hurt him. Her heart broke at how he might be affected by this turn of events.

"Hey, everybody!" Ryne took everyone in, along with their expressions, as he approached Hollis's side. "What's going on?" he added with suspicion.

"How is he involved?" Eva asked, confusion etched on her slightly wrinkled face. "He shouldn't be here."

"He's my friend," Hollis defended him, to her own surprise. "None of you should be here. I came to talk to Addie on my own."

"She's not who she says she is," Macy blurted out.

"She's a hunter, dear. They already know that," Letitia confirmed for the benefit of the others present.

Addie and Michaela didn't look surprised.

"Lilith already told us," Addie supplied for Macy's benefit. However, the expression on Ryne's face told her he had suspected nothing of the sort.

"*What?*" he expelled with a rush of air. Hollis couldn't bear to see his face. She refused to look at him until she had said her bit.

"No, there's more," Macy added. "I kept thinking there was something more familiar to her. But I saw her leaving the sacred part of the cemetery after spending time at the family plots. I can't believe I didn't see it sooner. And her phony name. It was so close, how did we not suspect it?" Macy deeply inhaled to replenish the air she had used rushing out the last bit of information. Then she blurted, "She's a Blackstone."

Gasps of surprise were uttered from within the group.

"We're too exposed here," Addie said quietly, looking around at those on the streets surrounding them. The afternoon sunlight was high and bright in the sky, and townspeople went about their business none the wiser. They needed to keep it that way and not cause a scene. "We need to get to the bottom of this, but not here."

"We can take her inside and call the rest of the Court," Lilith directed.

"Are you on the council? I was trying to find them," Hollis said, directing her question to Michaela.

"You don't get to speak. Not yet," Macy spat. Anger shone in her eyes as she pointed her finger at Hollis's chest. "You lied. You deceived us about who you were and why you were here."

"Why are you here?" came a low and quiet man's voice. Ryne. He had been quiet up until then. The softness of his voice, the undercurrent of pain she could hear, broke her heart. She may have lost him before she even had him.

"Addie's right. We can't do this out here. Inside, everyone," Letti said, and ushered them toward the back of the City Hall building.

"I was coming to tell you the truth, to come clean about

everything," Hollis admitted as they walked across the street and to the side of the building. She crossed her arms, frustrated but not surprised it would go down in chaos and consequences.

"This should be rich, coming from you," Macy vehemently said.

Hollis snapped her head toward her with a glare that would intimidate most men. "What is your problem? You haven't even heard what I have to say."

"You're related to Dante, and a part of the rogues. That's all I need to know." Macy crossed her arms but didn't take her eyes off Hollis.

"No, it's not. You're all in danger, and I might be the only one who can help," Hollis countered.

"Not here," Addie said through clenched teeth. "We've had enough trouble lately. We don't need any of the town in a frenzy over something we don't even know about yet." She moved ahead of the group and led them around the back of City Hall to a secret door. She uttered a spell and opened the door. Hollis could feel the magic hum over her skin and glanced at the other hunters in the group. She noted the slight strain at the corners of their eyes as they, too, felt the magic flow, but there was hardly even a flinch among them. She wondered how they had perfected their control over the years, being around so many witches.

"I'm not sure I need to be here for this," Brock mentioned casually to his mom. She patted his arm.

"It's up to you. We can fill you in if you need to man Soothing Sips. Depending on what transpires here, we might need the basement ready to access," she whispered in return. Brock nodded and turned to leave. Before he passed Hollis, he stopped and looked her in the eye.

"I'm not a hunter, but I do know how to protect my family and my town. I hope I don't have to against you. You could be a great addition to our family." Then he left.

Hollis cocked her head in confusion. It sounded as if he hoped she stayed and didn't hold who she was against her. Even after she lied. Too bad Macy wasn't going to be so easy to convince, but then again, she had spent time with her father, so Hollis almost didn't blame the girl.

"You can go, too, if you want, Callie," Michaela offered.

Callie crossed her arms over her chest. "No way. I'm not missing out. Plus, aren't I an eyewitness or something?"

Michaela rolled her eyes but nodded. Hollis didn't even mind they might be talking about a hearing for her. She liked their connection and mutual respect for each other and their town. She envied that.

They entered the building and immediately descended a flight of stairs into the basement under City Hall. After a long hallway, they entered into a large room. Addie flicked her fingers, and candles erupted with flames of light within large glass globes hanging from the ceiling. Addie threw a notebook and her bag onto the desk at the back of the room. Hollis absently noted the murals of what must be a timeline of Havenwood Falls history painted on the walls. An aisle up the middle of the room with rows of chairs on either side led up to a raised dais with a space for each member of the elusive Court of the Sun and the Moon. Hollis was about to find out who made up the council.

"I texted the members, Lilith," Addie announced.

Lilith nodded, "Very good. They will be here shortly, then." She turned to Hollis. "Please have a seat at the front table facing the Court's seats."

Hollis confidently strode to the front and took the seat Lilith indicated. Lilith and Michaela continued on up to seats on the dais. Hollis was surprised to see Michaela—someone so young and so cool—was a member of the Court. Perhaps she would be willing to listen. The others sat in chairs randomly behind her. She looked to Ryne, but he sat and kept his head down. Just as she was about to turn back to the front, he lifted his head and glared directly at her. She swore she saw an orange spark erupt in his eyes, then ring his irises once more with red. It seemed to happen whenever he experienced intense emotion. She didn't think a witch could do that and wondered not for the first time what his other half was. Then he turned his head away.

She deserved that. And more. She could argue he kept his own secret from her, but this was about more than hurt feelings. She had to own what she did.

CHAPTER 12

$\mathcal{M}$embers of the Court Hollis kept hearing about began to file into the room and make their way onto the raised dais right in front of where she sat. No one spoke to her. They barely even spoke to each other. Other than Lilith Blackstone and Michaela from the inn, she didn't know any of the other members. Addie must have been more of a secretary, since she sat and pulled out notes from the desk they passed at the back.

"Explain for the Court why have we been summoned here, Michaela." A woman with silvery-white hair in a French twist and wearing a navy blue business suit sat herself in the center, her eyes shifting from Michaela to Hollis and back again. She exuded a lot of power. Hollis had to keep herself from shivering from the effects of the woman's magic.

"Saundra, this is Hollis Blackstone," Michaela introduced. "She has been in town for two and a half days under the name Hollis Black. Lilith asked us all to give the witch hunter a chance to do the right thing and come to us. It took her a little bit, but she did."

"Yes. The coven has been on edge since she arrived." The witch named Saundra gave Hollis a pointed stare. Hollis could feel the magic seep from her pores. The witch's power was so immense, she must have been high up, if not the head of her coven. "So you did the right thing. That's good to know. But why the summons, Michaela?" She turned her sharp gaze back to her fellow Court member.

"Well," Michaela continued, "she had just come clean to Addie, Callie, and myself when Macy and the Blackstones arrived on the scene to out her as a Blackstone—one of the *rogue* Blackstones. We do not know her intentions for being in town, but—"

"I could—" Hollis began, but was quickly cut off by Saundra, who seemed to be the one in charge, glaring at her with a lifted brow.

"Hollis, you will get your chance," Michaela said before turning back to Saundra. "I was about to give her credit for coming to us. She was trying to tell us of a danger coming. She stayed at the inn and is now at NamaStays. We have observed her, as we all discussed with Lilith, and Ryne Calloway has spent time with her as well. I've not personally witnessed any ill will toward the town thus far." Michaela tilted her head, indicating she was finished, and all eyes swiveled to Saundra.

"First off, Hollis, I am Saundra Beaumont, and this is the Court of the Sun and the Moon. You are not officially on trial, but are on very thin ice. This is an opportunity for you to speak your side, and we will decide from that point. This is our town, and we protect it against all threats. Our job is to determine if you are, or bring to us, a threat."

Hollis nodded. "I understand."

She gave away nothing in her demeanor. Sitting tall and confident, she studied the Court and chose her words. She knew she hadn't done anything wrong, not really. Lied maybe, but she hadn't hurt anyone and truthfully had tried to keep to herself. This was her making a change.

"Hollis, please tell us why you are here and what danger you spoke of to Michaela, Callie, and my granddaughter, Addie," Saundra directed.

Granddaughter. Right, that would explain the witch power Addie exuded.

Hollis started from the beginning, sharing how she came to find Havenwood Falls up to her experience in the cemetery and her phone call with Dante. She even included her brief encounter at Callie's with a witch practitioner of black magic. She figured this was the place to inform them, then they could deal with it or not. It wasn't her job.

"So he's coming. I haven't told him where I am yet. Reception has been, thankfully, bad. But he knew up until the small town of Montrose. I have no doubts he'll find a way to seek out Havenwood Falls. He says you put a spell on him to keep him from it, but he has ways around things eventually." Hollis lowered her eyes momentarily. "But I've come to love your town and the potential to find out who I am outside of being a witch hunter. I've never really felt like I belonged anywhere, but this feels like it could be somewhere. I'm sorry. I didn't know he would come. This was supposed to only be an information-gathering mission."

"Unless he never planned that all along, dear, and was just using you to get here," Letitia spoke up from her seat in the audience, though no one seemed to mind.

Hollis opened her mouth to say something, to rebut her suggestion, but deep down, she knew the truth. Her father had set her up, and she didn't know to what extent.

"She used to be on the Court before Lilith," someone whispered from behind her. Hollis nodded, not caring who it was.

"He's going to call when he gets to Montrose. I'll be there to meet him when he does," Hollis said as quickly as she had decided it. Leaving Havenwood Falls was the right thing for her to do. No one would get hurt that way. She glanced with a heavy heart at Ryne out the corner of her eye. At least, no one else would get hurt.

"You're offering to leave?" Michaela asked from the platform.

Hollis looked up at her with confusion. "Isn't that what you would have me do? If I'm gone, then he won't be able to find you."

"What will he do to you, Hollis?" Lilith asked, her voice oddly low. Hollis had heard her name mentioned by her father. Apparently they had made contact years ago and again more recently, when he followed Macy back as far as he could. She wondered how much Lilith knew of her father and his ways. Judging by the pale complexion and the brief flash of fear she saw in the woman's eyes, Lilith knew more than she let on.

Hollis shrugged and turned her head. "I'll be fine. I'm his daughter." Her voice was weak, and she wouldn't have believed herself either. "I deserve whatever I get. I'm not blameless in the lifestyle he's lived. After all, I've been a lead witch hunter for several years. I'm good at my job." Hollis felt her blood run cold, and her eyes go flat. She had to convince the Court she was indeed dangerous and they needed her to go.

"If you change your mind, there are alternatives we could explore," another older woman suggested. She, too, exuded strong witch powers, but she carried herself more like the grandmotherly type. But Hollis bet she was much more than that.

"Mathilde, the girl has already made her decision. Let her go and see what comes of it," a distinguished-looking man said as he gazed at his fingernails, as if bored with the entire event. The witch magic coming from him was not only powerful and old, but almost convoluted—not quite black but definitely dangerous. She wondered why the Court kept him around.

"Roman, I was merely pointing out she didn't have to leave. But yes, I understand she made her decision."

"She will have to see it through as far as her heart will allow her," a different man said. This one was older, wiser, and ornery-looking. He simply stared at her as if reading her beginning to end like an open book. His vibe unnerved Hollis when not much did.

"Elsmed, what does that even mean?" Lilith asked, practically rolling her eyes with the tone she used.

The one she addressed as Elsmed turned and shrugged. "She will have to decide."

Hollis pinched the bridge of her nose. The Court talked in circles, and it gave her a headache. She just wanted to leave already. She didn't even know why she still sat there. Hollis stood and gave a last look at the Court, especially Michaela and Lilith, and nodded.

She turned and strode out of the room back the way she came. She heard shouting suddenly erupt behind her, and the voice initiating it pinched her heart.

"Are you just going to let her leave? Her father is dangerous," Ryne shouted.

"Are you?" Callie questioned. Hollis smiled. They weren't even friends, and yet she wished they were.

As soon as she reached the street, she found she couldn't breathe and had to run. She ran all the way back to Stone Falls Winery and NamaStays Inn. Except once she was almost there, she veered left on Blackstone Road and kept running until she reached the falls.

CHAPTER 13

*H*ollis ran up to the lake where Ryne had taken her. The water was as sparkling and clear as it was then. She watched the falls flow down from the highest point she could see. Closing her eyes, she felt the rush of power freely offered and felt the spray of the water as it kissed her face. Tingles ran up her arm as she felt another hunter approach.

She turned as Macy Blackstone emerged up the path. "You're fast," she huffed as she caught her breath.

"You could be, too, if you let yourself embrace all your gifts—you know, except the killing of witches part." Hollis shrugged, critically eyeing Macy.

Macy frowned. "After I spent time with your dad and the others, I was afraid but also determined to not let my hunter side control me. But I'm always on guard and always extra careful because my boyfriend—fiancé now"—Macy blushed, obviously not yet used to saying it out loud—"is a witch, so I don't let myself fully embrace that side of me. I don't know how."

"I could help you . . . Well, if I were staying, that is," Hollis quietly said. "You wouldn't trust me anyway, though."

Macy bit her lip in consternation. "I don't. It's true."

"Why are you here? Making sure I leave?" Hollis turned her

back to Macy and bent down to the cool pool of water, cupping some in her palm.

"I wouldn't—"

Hollis brought the water to her mouth and drank it all. She raised an eyebrow to Macy. "You wouldn't what?"

"Well, at least I know the falls are okay with you." Macy frowned at the traitorous waters.

"What?"

"The water . . . Well, the magic in the water. Supposedly it'll harm those who intend to threaten our town." She shrugged, as if that was something in everyday conversation.

"The water?" Hollis whispered and cocked her head in thought, remembering Ryne having the same reaction. "The water is the source of power for the town." She looked at Macy. "And for you all? Somehow it empowers or binds you to the town, is that it?"

"Something like that." Macy suddenly looked uncomfortable, as if she had accidentally told a traitor the biggest secret the town had. Perhaps she did.

"I want you to trust me. I won't let Dante know about Havenwood Falls." Hollis stared deep into Macy's eyes, pleading with her to believe her.

"I'm here because Aunt Letti reminded me everyone deserves a second chance." She sighed. "I want to believe your change of heart, but you need to understand how it appears to us and how I am holding it loosely in my hands based on what I know of your father and his organization of rogue hunters."

"I understand. I'm leaving anyway, so you won't have to worry about it."

"Don't go to him. Go anywhere else, but don't go back to him, Hollis," Macy begged of her.

"If I don't, he might still try to find you. At least if I go to him, I have a chance at distracting him from Havenwood Falls." Hollis placed her hands on her hips and looked out behind them at the fantastic view of the town and the surrounding mountains. "This place is special, and it, and you, deserve the chance to be free from Dante Blackstone."

"So do you," a male voice said.

"Ryne," Hollis breathed with surprise and a tinge of hope as he approached them.

Hollis noted Macy standing uncomfortably to the side, her eyes shifting to each of them and back again. "I'm going to check in with my parents. Come say goodbye when you're ready, Hollis. They'll want to see you out of town."

Hollis nodded but didn't take her eyes from Ryne's. She hesitated. She'd hurt him, and she didn't know how to fix it. She'd never had a friendship like his, never had feelings for anyone she wanted to get close to before. As she studied him and looked deep into his eyes, she felt within herself something she'd never thought she could have. She wanted what the other Blackstones had—family, friends, and a home. She wanted a new life, and she wanted to redefine herself. Hollis wanted that life with Ryne.

"I think I love you," she blurted out. Then quickly she backpedaled with her hand over her mouth and shock on her face. "I thought that was in my head. I mean, I want you. I want this." She gestured out at the town behind them. "I want a home where I can get closer to you. I do . . . I love you." Her voice grew in confidence the more she spoke and the more she felt as she allowed herself.

"Hollis—"

"I've never felt this way before. I've never felt the way *you* make me feel. Being around you makes me happy." She smiled as she spoke.

"Hollis." Ryne's voice grew strong and stern, causing Hollis to stop. She noticed him, truly noticed him, and realized he wasn't reciprocating.

"Oh god, you don't feel the same." She put her hands to her head and turned away from him. Her heart sunk like a lead weight to her feet. "I need to go. I'm sorry, Ryne. So sorry for all I put you through. I didn't mean to hurt you. I wanted to tell you everything, but was afraid you'd hate me."

Hollis stormed past him. He reached out and grabbed her arm, stopping her, but she refused to look at him.

"Hollis." His voice was low, pained but filled with desire just the same. Hollis stared at him straight on then, seeking something worth fighting for in his eyes. When she found it, she couldn't turn away from him.

"Hollis," he whispered once more. "I can't deny the powerful pull I feel to you. It's almost like . . ." He frowned and shook his head.

"Like what?"

"It's not possible, but it's almost like I'm responding to you like you're my mate."

"Mate?" Hollis reared her head back, confused by the terminology. "Witches don't have mates," she said out loud, forgetting they hadn't talked about that part of him yet.

"You know?" Ryne's face widened with surprise, then he remembered. "Right. You're a witch hunter, so you can, what . . . sense witches?"

Hollis nodded, uncertain about saying anything more. She didn't want to break the tenuous connection they had at the moment.

"You knew and you still hung out with me. Did it not bother you? I heard it can be painful."

Hollis gave him a snarky smile. "I have excellent control."

Ryne laughed, alleviating some of the tension between them. "Truth?"

"It's true I have been trained to control all my hunter instincts. But with you, I didn't feel compelled to even try to control it. I mean, I can sense you're only half witch, so the magical energy wasn't as strong as, say, Addie's. But even so, what I did feel seemed to bring me closer to you. I wanted to be with you. I've never felt that way before, Ryne. With who I am . . . it shouldn't be possible either."

"Maybe it's true. You could be my mate," Ryne wondered aloud. He pulled her in closer to his chest and gently touched her forehead, tracing his finger over the scar she had hidden beneath her hair, and frowned.

"Ryne, what is your other half? I mean, I don't have any right to ask . . ." Hollis had the decency to look sheepish.

"Phoenix. I'm half witch and half phoenix, Hollis. Have you ever heard of such a thing?" He laughed, but it wasn't one of humor, instead more of the exasperation of an old topic of discussion he'd grown tired of. "I'm a phoenix witch who can't control either side of my powers."

Hollis hadn't ever heard of that combination of supernatural, but as she thought of it, it made sense. "I could see that. I've seen sparks of fire in your eyes when you didn't know I was looking. I'm not able to discern more than witch magic, but I knew there was more to you than human."

Ryne reached for her hand and clasped it. "Will you sit with me by the water and talk?"

She nodded, and he pulled her toward a large boulder they could both fit on.

"I'm sorry, Ryne. I'm sorry for lying to you. I'm used to keeping to the shadows and hiding, to playing a part so much, I don't even truly know who I am anymore . . . if I ever did." Hollis gazed longingly up at the falls. "I wish I did. Maybe I could be someone you deserve, someone you could love in time."

Ryne laughed and shook his head.

"What the hell are you laughing at?" Hollis frowned at him with a glare. *How dare he laugh when I'm being my most vulnerable.* This was why she shouldn't be vulnerable.

"Don't be sore, Hollis. You owe it to me to hear me out." He squeezed her hand and wouldn't let go when she tried to pull away.

"Fine."

"I'm only laughing because you are so blind." His words were almost rough, frustrated he had to spell it out. "I fell in love with you the first time we hung out. I was instantly attracted to you. I felt an undeniable pull to be near you. I even tried to stay away but I couldn't, even when you tried so hard to push me away." He laughed again. "I knew from the beginning you were hiding something, but most of all I knew you needed me." He winked at her, and she punched him in the shoulder, at which he laughed more. "You needed someone to push you and pull you out of yourself to see the bigger picture . . . to see who you could be without all the constraints you put on yourself . . . to see you the way I see you can be." Ryne turned her toward him, and with his other hand, he gently brushed some of her dark hair out of her face. "It only hurt so much to find out the way I did about your secret and your lies because I love you."

He gazed at her face, waiting for the words to sink in. When they did, Hollis's eyes brightened, and she even dared to smile.

"You love me? Even after everything you found out? Even knowing who I really am and why I came?" She couldn't help the hope that snuck into her voice.

"I do." He leaned forward and tenderly kissed the tip of her nose. She closed her eyes and leaned her head forward, touching his forehead, simply breathing him in for the moment . . . knowing the moment wouldn't last.

"Tell me about you, Ryne. How are you half witch and half phoenix? I want to know everything."

"Well, it started with my father being full phoenix and my mother being full witch. Do I really need to go into how that all happened?"

She slugged his arm again and pulled back, crossing her legs and getting more comfortable on the boulder. "Ha. Ha. No, I think I got that part figured out."

"Well, it's pretty simple. My mother was the only witch in the phoenix clan my father was from. The clans are usually pretty small. Many years ago, the clan leader had found a way to harness a witch's power to enhance his phoenix powers, thus raising him above all the others to keep his status as leader. Over time it became a clan secret to keep a witch around, but they were not to touch her. She was sacred, though a captive held against her will. My father was the clan leader's son, and he fell in love with the witch."

Hollis gasped, entranced by his story.

"He wasn't supposed to, but he did. There were grave consequences, even for the leader's son, if anyone took the witch either against her will or even with her consent. She, in turn, fell in love with him. They had a secret affair for many years until she could no longer hide she was with child—me—and my father tried to secret her away from the clan, but they found out."

"Oh no!" Hollis covered her mouth with her hand.

"My grandfather, the clan leader, put my father in solitary confinement as a punishment until I was born. He could have had him killed, but thankfully he didn't. My mother was punished as well. After she had me, she was expected to fulfill more than her duties to the clan and had to give more and more magic. It wore her down. My father noticed and tried to plead with the clan leader to back off. They weren't allowed to marry, but my father took care of her the best he could. A few years ago, my father was making another appeal to his father to free my mom, and several of the other members got riled up and even challenged my father. It was fair to do this, but he never made it to the fight. Phoenix aren't known for controlling their tempers, and several lashed out and challenged my father. If he had made it to the fight, he would have won. He was the next strongest in the clan. But they trapped him and turned him over to a group of rocs who killed him."

Hollis' eyes filled with emotion. She placed her hand on his knee. "What happened? What's a roc?"

"I'll get to the rocs. My grandfather protected us for a while, but he was getting on in years even though phoenix live a long time. I was technically next in line, but I wasn't ready to take over. My phoenix power and my witch power were in conflict, and I messed up a lot of things. Phoenix powers are connected to emotions, and mine were all over the place. In general I was a more laid-back guy than I should have been, according to the others. I had a dream they were going to kill my mom, and the next day, I left my grandfather a note and packed us up. We left. That was a couple years ago. We traveled around for a time, but eventually found our way here the end of last summer. The guy you saw me reacting to in the square the other day was a roc. A roc is essentially a giant eagle. A single flap of its enormous wing can create cyclone-type gusts of wind, and his tongue is long and forked like a snake. His kind are enemies with the phoenix because they've been jealous they don't have healing abilities or immortality, and it's tough to overcome such ingrained ancient prejudices. They are the only creatures known who can kill a phoenix."

"Wow, I had no idea phoenix, and now these roc people, were so violent. I had only heard of phoenix in stories," Hollis commented.

"Make no mistake, this is not phoenix across the board. From what I understand, other clans aren't like that. In fact, there's another phoenix in town I'd like you to meet sometime; she's a bit younger than us, and I've come to think of her like a little sister. I met her shortly after I moved here. Her name is Ember, and she's a pistol—I think you'd like her. She didn't know any others like us even existed." He paused for some air. "Anyway, I think my clan corrupted their powers by taking advantage of witch magic, and the power made them unstable and aggravated."

After a moment, he turned his gaze up at the falls. His eyes filled with emotion, and he pulled in a tight breath. "My mom was finally able to refresh her powers and be rejuvenated by the other witches in town. Havenwood Falls saved her life, and I suppose mine as well. I don't think our clan would have let us survive much longer. But she left a few months ago and hasn't checked in for quite some time. The last I heard from her, she mentioned meeting someone, which I found odd because she's never been interested in another relationship since my father. I'm a little worried something's wrong, but with her powers restored, I know she can take care of herself. Plus she's not too good with cell phones, and you've experienced the kind of reception we get up here." Ryne chuckled but added, "I miss her though. I hope she comes home soon. I'd love for you to meet her."

"Ryne! I'm so sorry. Here I've been so concerned with myself. If there's anything I can do, let me know."

He placed his hand on her knee. "Thank you," he said quietly.

Hollis was suddenly struck. "You haven't learned to use your phoenix powers because you're afraid you're corrupted, aren't you?"

Ryne looked away, shame coloring his expression, and a fire sparked in his eye. He gave her a curt nod and confirmed her suspicion. "I tried once to combine the two, and it went very wrong. I'm able to separate the witch side more easily because my mother was able to teach me, but the phoenix side is unpredictable. It tends to erupt more when my temper rises or due to fear."

"You are more powerful than you know. I can sense that much and see it in your eyes. Because you care." Hollis moved away from the boulder and sighed.

"What is it?"

"I have to leave, Ryne. I wish now more than ever before that I didn't. But I do."

Ryne slid his body up against hers and pulled her close to his chest. He inhaled in the crook of her neck, sending chills down to her toes. "Don't go, Hollis. We can find a way to protect you and misdirect your father. Please, don't go."

She turned into him and let him claim her lips. Passion grew between them. Hollis had never felt such closeness and such instant heat. She'd been caught up in the moment before, had even used her wiles to get what she needed done on a job, but never before had she felt connected with another person like their souls belonged together. Ryne kissed her like he would never see her again. His mouth roamed from hers and moved down her jawline to her neck.

"Can we go somewhere? I just want to be with you before I go," Hollis said with a breathy tone between his kisses.

He grabbed her hand, and they walked away from the falls. They didn't get far before the phone in Hollis's back pocket rang. She frowned. "You've got to be kidding. It's like he knows."

"Who?"

"My father."

CHAPTER 14

"*D*ad, have you arrived already?" Hollis asked, straight to the point. She stopped moving. "You are? Why lie to me?" Hollis frowned. Then a vacant expression crossed her face. "*What?* Why did you never tell me about this?" Looking down at her wrist, she touched the underside, then poked and prodded at it.

Ryne moved in close to her, concern written on his face. He reached for her wrist and examined it himself. Hollis could feel the color in her face drain completely out. "Why the game if you knew where I was the whole time?"

Ryne stood straight and crossed his arms, pushing his chest out. His eyes ringed with red. She wanted to smile at his show of concern, but she knew he was no match for her father . . . at least not yet.

"I'll meet you in town when you arrive and show you myself." She paused and breathed in slowly through her nose, as if trying not to lose her patience. "It's no big deal at all, Dad. I'll just meet you." Another pause. "See you then. Bye." She hung up.

Ryne gripped her elbow, probably attempting to steady her. Hollis felt light on her feet.

"What was that about?" he asked.

"He knows. Somehow he knows." Hollis studied her wrist and poked and prodded a part of it.

He moved his head in closer to see what she looked at. "What are you doing?"

"I can't even see it."

"Hollis! What?"

"A tracker. He put a damn tracker in my wrist. He's known where I was or at least approximately, since signal up here is spotty, where I—or Havenwood Falls—was this whole time. I can't believe he fucking tracked me!" Her voice grew as did her eyes with each statement she made. "Do you have a knife?" She looked up at Ryne with panic.

"No way in hell am I giving you a knife! You want to cut it out of you? You don't even know where it is or how big it is." Ryne tried for a voice of reason when he realized she wasn't even listening. "We should ask the Blackstones and the Luna Coven. Maybe they can find it with magic, see what we're dealing with."

Hollis nodded absently. "Yeah, okay. Good idea."

Hollis didn't even remember Ryne putting her into his truck and taking her to the Blackstone home in Havenwood Heights. Luckily, they didn't have far to go from the falls.

"Are you ready to leave?" Macy asked as she came out the manor's front door, followed closely by Lilith and Letitia.

"She's not leaving. At least not yet," Ryne supplied for her.

"Why not?" Lilith asked, crossing her arms over her chest. Her blond hair whipped in her face as she swung around, accentuating the tightness in the lines of her face.

No one said anything, and the tension grew.

"Do you want me to tell them?" Ryne asked her quietly.

"Well, for the goddess's sake, someone tell us what's going on," Lilith demanded.

Hollis stepped forward. "He's getting closer."

"Then you should be on your way," Lilith dryly suggested.

"Perhaps there is more to this story, dear," Letitia said, paying closer attention.

Hollis stuck out her arm. "He tracked me. I didn't know about it, I swear. I don't know how well it's worked up here in the mountains, but it has at least given him a good idea where we are. He played me the whole time. I think he knows . . . knew I would switch . . . I don't know. I don't know anything anymore."

"I see," was all Lilith said, staring at Hollis's bared wrist.

Macy approached her. "I'll call Gallad and see if his grandmother has a way to magically find the tracker or stop it or get it out? I'm not sure what she can do, but I'll ask."

Hollis nodded and offered a small smile to Macy. "Thank you." She would have been embarrassed by how weak her voice sounded, but she was still in too much shock to care.

"We'll wait for the Augustines inside." Letti ushered them all into the house and out of view of the neighbors.

Not more than ten minutes later, a knock sounded at the door.

A tall, handsome young man walked in like he owned the place with a crooked smile on his face as soon as he saw Macy. She ran into his arms, and he planted a big kiss on her cheek.

"Thank you for coming." She looked to the older woman, whom Hollis had seen at the Court—Mathilde, she thought the woman's name was. "Thank you, Mathilde," Macy supplied.

"Of course, dear. Now what seems to be the trouble?" She looked from Macy to Hollis.

"Dante placed a tracker in my wrist. I didn't know about it, and the reception seems to be spotty based on the way he spoke—he didn't seem to have an exact location yet. But then again, he could be lying about that too, and maybe he's on his way up the mountain now." Hollis rushed her words out with frustration and defeat.

Mathilde held out her hand. "Let me see, Hollis."

"Can't we just cut it out and be done with it?" she impatiently asked.

Mathilde's eyes went wide, but then considered what she said. "Even with magic, that wouldn't be our best option. Let's save that for a last resort."

She patted Hollis's hand then clasped it between her own. She closed her eyes and hummed something low and indecipherable. The room grew heavy with anticipation. Gallad moved up next to them and, keeping his hands in the air, he positioned one below and one above his grandmother's hands, adding his own energy and magic to her spell.

Quickly glancing around, Hollis noted the Blackstones stepped back, allowing the witches to do their work but also preventing the magic from bothering them too much. Hollis could feel the magical energy building around her to the point it began to do more than agitate her. Just before she closed her eyes to shut out the room and focus her breathing on the pain, she noticed a ring on Mathilde's finger—a shiny opalescent stone that illuminated with the increase of power.

Hollis cried out and practically collapsed with the surge of power as it flooded her body. She felt hands behind her, holding her up. Macy and Letti both uttered soft words of encouragement and strength. She knew the power must cause them pain as well, but they still joined to help her.

"I can do no more," Mathilde breathed heavily, and beads of sweat shimmered at the sides of her face. She grasped Gallad's offered arm to steady herself. "I'm afraid it has been bound by another witch's spell. It's not that I'm not powerful enough, but the spell is complicated and twisted. Like a labyrinth of layers entangled together. It would take a tremendous amount of energy and time, which we do not have."

Hollis breathed in deep and nodded. "Thank you for trying. I'll leave right away and hope the connection has been spotty."

"Wait, just a moment, dear," Mathilde continued. "What I did do was put a spell around it that should work like a shield and buy us some more time to find a more permanent solution." Her eyes, aged and wise, peered into Hollis's eyes. "I'm assuming you want to stay?"

Hollis looked around the room at each of the Blackstones, the witches, and finally Ryne. She did want to stay.

"I won't put you all in danger. This is on me. Thank you for shielding the tracker. That will give me time to relocate far away in the event it comes back online. Dante will find me somewhere else, far from here."

"No," Ryne interjects. "That's not good enough! There has to be another option so you can stay."

"I don't deserve to stay here and build a life like nothing ever happened. I—" Hollis was cut off by the shrill ring of someone's phone.

Mathilde answered her phone and frowned. "I'm with them now. We'll get prepared. Thank you, Sheriff." She hung up and looked to Lilith.

"Dante has been spotted in Durango. We need access below Soothing Sips, Lilith. Is Brock there now?"

Lilith placed her hands on her waist and nodded. "I'll get him prepared."

Lilith took out her own phone and walked out of the room.

"See, even more reason for me to go to him now," Hollis pleaded. "There will be others with Dante. They're not all bad and shouldn't be included. They've been my family this far, and I don't want them hurt. I'll go to him and try to get them to turn back." She took a deep breath. "If he won't, then you can intervene."

"I'll go with you, then," Ryne said with determination.

"Why don't you use the magical dust you used before to confuse their minds and send them away from the mountain like last time when he followed me back?" Macy asked. It was at that moment Hollis realized why Macy had been so hard on her: because she still carried her own guilt for almost bringing Dante to the borders of Havenwood Falls.

Letti shook her head. "He'll be expecting that possibility and probably come prepared to combat it." Letti frowned, then looked to Mathilde. "Seems Dante may be using witch magic to fight witch magic."

Mathilde also frowned but nodded in agreement. "I was considering the same thing. For him to have such magic around the tracker, and to be so close so fast, he would have to be working with or somehow harnessing a witch's magic. And that is an entirely different concern."

"Indeed," Letti concurred. She turned to Hollis. "Do you know of any witches who would work with your father?"

"With his reputation for killing them all? No way. I've never seen a witch with him or even felt one at any of our homes." Hollis frowned in thought. "There have been times more recently when he wouldn't let any of us go with him to 'check on something'," she said, using air quotes. "I suppose it's possible he keeps one somewhere. It would have to be against their will, though. No way any witch would voluntarily work with him unless he held something pretty big over their heads."

"That's what I was afraid of," Letti said sadly.

"Time to go," Lilith directed as she re-entered the room. She had even taken a moment to change from her business attire into dark cargo pants with plenty of pockets, a tight black T-shirt, and a jacket. With her bright blond hair in its sharp A-line cut, Lilith looked the part of a badass ready to battle. "Everyone meet at the armory."

"You have an armory?" Hollis offered a fierce smile. She could appreciate someone ready for a fight at a moment's notice. To protect this town, she assumed the supernatural residents had to be prepared for anything that may come their way.

Lilith turned her head toward Hollis and gave her a smile that sent chills down her back. "You know it. We protect our own, Hollis." She walked out the door.

Macy sidled up to Hollis. "If you stick around, that includes you, Hollis. I'm sorry I was so hard on you before. I hope you stay."

CHAPTER 15

*B*ack on the east side of the town square, just a half block away from Whisper Falls Inn, Hollis watched several people enter Soothing Sips. She recognized a couple from the Court, but even more had arrived. Hollis sat with Ryne in his truck, taking a moment for themselves.

"Ryne, I don't want you to join the fight."

"You've got to be kidding me! Is this because my power is weak?" he asked, suddenly dejected.

"Of course not!" She turned to look him straight in the eyes. "Your power is anything but weak. But you're part witch, and I don't want anything to happen to you. If there's any way for my father to know how I feel about you, he will target you to teach me a lesson." She paused. "It wouldn't be the first time."

Ryne grabbed her hand and brought it to his lips. He kissed each of her knuckles while watching her, his eyes boring into her own.

"Ryne." She started to say something but got lusciously distracted watching him kiss her skin. He chuckled, then stopped.

"I want more time with you," she whispered. "I just found you."

"We'll get that time, I promise. You're my mate, Hollis Blackstone, and I plan on keeping you."

Hollis offered him a small smile. She wished with all her heart that could be true. Unfortunately, she just didn't know if it would.

"Let's go inside before they plan this without me," Hollis said, and she reached for the door handle.

"I'm going with you, and I'll be by your side." He stared her down. "Don't even try to do this on your own, Hollis. You may be a badass fighter, but I can hold my own even without magic." He jokingly flexed his muscles.

"I believe you can." She smiled and nodded. "Together."

They entered Soothing Sips, a rustically modern tasting room for the Stone Falls Winery. Hollis couldn't help but appreciate the simple wood, metal, and concrete decor. Plentiful bottles of wine were expertly displayed against the wall, behind the long concrete countertop. She decided she'd come back with Ryne after whatever happened, happened. She hoped she would have the opportunity, but she had to consider the fact that even if they defeated Dante, she would have to still account for her crimes and face whatever punishment the Court might dish out.

Macy and Gallad stood behind the counter, waiting for them. "Follow us. We'll show you the secret armory."

Hollis rubbed her hands together, excitement lighting her eyes. No matter what, she was a born fighter, and nothing compared to the feel of a weapon in her hands. Ryne laughed as if he could read her mind.

Hollis raised an eyebrow at him. "What?"

"Nothing. Just picturing you gripping a powerful weapon between your hands and seeing the passion rise in your eyes."

A throat cleared. "Um, weapons now. Get a room later," Macy said with an embarrassed chuckle.

"Right." Hollis licked her upper lip and winked at Ryne, suddenly feeling more free than she ever had, with the weight of her secrets lifted.

"Shit, girl. You slay me," Ryne said, and slapped her ass as she walked in front of him to follow Macy and Gallad into a back room.

Through a door into a basement, they found themselves in a much larger space than what should be structurally available. Several people milled around and examined different weapons hanging from the wall. Hollis sucked in a sudden breath and gained control of her hunter side. Continuous tingles shot up her arms. Many of the people in the basement were powerful witches. Several were people she didn't even recognize. They all turned and stared when she walked into the room.

Mathilde got everyone's attention after Gallad whistled for them to listen up. She introduced Hollis to the room and explained that she, and the town, needed their help. She went on to explain how Dante, the rogue witch hunter, was closing in on Havenwood Falls with the intent to attack. His main objective was the witches, so they were to fight in pairs or groups.

"Lilith, direct them to the weapons, then Addie will explain the battle strategy."

Lilith stepped forward. "Many of you have been in here before. You've fought for Havenwood Falls before. Pick your weapon of choice and sign it out with Reggie at the table. He's also going to put a spelled bit of liquid magic on the tip for extra measure. Be very careful not to touch it yourself, or you'll be down for the count." She stepped back, finished.

Addie stepped forward. "Our objective is not to kill but to capture. But if killing is your last defense, by all means, protect yourself. We will be stealthy and hidden at first to assess his forces. We have reason to believe young hunters will be with him, and his way is all they know. We also have reason to believe he may have the assistance of witch magic, so be prepared for anything. This is not your usual witch hunter. He's been after our town since the 1800s, and I'd like nothing more than to put him in the Infernum for good." She paused as Sheriff Kasun approached behind her. He whispered something in her ear, and she nodded.

"Sheriff said his scouts have eyes on Dante. He's still in Montrose for now and doesn't appear to be in a hurry. Either he has a plan, or he doesn't know the direction to head in yet. This gives us a little time. Choose your weapons. Conceal them as you leave. Some of you go out the back door. We don't want to concern the rest of the town. Tonight is the Moons in the Mist Bonfire, and the perfect cover. It also means a lot of people will be out tonight, so be discreet. Meet after nightfall at the edge of town, by Cooley Creek. We'll spread out from there, covering all access points down Miles Mountain. We're seeking Dante and his people out before they can find us. When it's all over, be sure to return your borrowed weapons. Dismissed," Addie said with militant tone and direction.

Saundra Beaumont approached Hollis once her granddaughter was finished. "Mathilde has informed me of your other little problem." She pointed to Hollis's wrist. "We will work on a permanent solution if you wish us to. I can't decide for the Court if they will permit you to stay, but would you like me to proceed either way?"

Hollis didn't answer lightly. She glanced at Ryne, who simply watched her, letting her know the decision had to be hers. "Yes, I would like you to. I understand the Court may vote against me. That's something I'll have to accept. But if there is the possibility, I'd like to stay."

Saundra nodded and left the basement.

"I'm sure she'll come up with something. She's the most powerful witch and one of three leaders of the Luna Coven, alongside Mathilde and Roman Bishop," Ryne said with complete confidence, which in turn strengthened Hollis's confidence.

"Ryne, what's the Infernum?"

Ryne shivered. "It's a part of Hell for supernaturals. When bad supes die, that's where their souls go. And those who are impossible to kill get sent there, too. Havenwood Falls has its own portal there used by the hellhounds—"

"Wait. Hellhounds are real?" Hollis interrupted.

"Yes." Ryne nodded toward a couple of big, intimidating guys dressed as bikers, standing near the exit. "I'm sure others are probably out on Dante's trail right now. They escort souls to Hell, and the Luna Coven traps others there, in like their own little slice of the Infernum. I've only heard stories about what kind of creatures have gotten themselves locked up there."

Hollis frowned. The thought of her father being locked up in an impenetrable prison in Hell sounded to be about what he deserved, but he was still her father, and she wasn't sure she could be a part of entrapping him.

"Take your pick, Hollis and Ryne," Macy said, bringing Hollis out of her thoughts. Her arms gestured wide as if the armory was an all you could eat buffet.

Hollis smiled greedily and went shopping.

CHAPTER 16

J ust before Hollis and Ryne were to meet the hunting party, they had a date to carry out. Ryne picked Hollis up in his truck in front of NamaStays Inn. Garbed in her tall black buckled boots, black leather pants, and black leather jacket, she felt more like her old self. However, she wore a couple new additions—new pieces—she had acquired from Callie's: a vintage V-neck Journey T-shirt that allowed her tattoos to peek out from her neck and a narrow piece of silver metal stamped with the word *Redefined* on a strip of suede hung from her neck. With her long dark hair down and blowing in the breeze, she felt wild and free, even knowing she would be hunting her own father later that night.

"Wow, you look . . . electrified!" Ryne said with hunger in his eyes, which were rimmed with red.

"Ha! You're one to talk. Do you know your eyes do that red circle thing sometimes?" she asked as she climbed in the truck.

Ryne's mouth fell open, then quickly closed before he sheepishly explained, "It happens at heightened emotional states."

"I noticed."

"You ready to see some fire?" Ryne teasingly asked.

"Let's see what your town's got!"

Ryne parked his truck along the side of the road wherever he could find a spot. It appeared the Moons in the Mist Bonfire was a town favorite. Ryne had explained the event was a way to celebrate the coming of summer, and apparently everyone was excited to bring on the new season. As they entered the large park, they were greeted by a wave of heat wafting from the largest of the bonfires. Scattered about, several smaller barrels filled with wood were being lit as well. The sun continued its descent while the moon rose high in the darkening sky. Stars, too, peeked out early from the tapestry above, hesitant still to reveal their full glory until darkness had arrived.

"This is really cool," Hollis said. Townspeople set up smaller fires for barbecues and additional heat. High schoolers threw random burnable items into the insatiable blaze of the main fire, music blared from some unseen source, and others strung beautiful white lights through the trees for a magical ambiance.

Ryne grinned from ear to ear. "It is, isn't it? I wasn't in town yet for it last year."

Hollis could see the appreciation and even desire for the fire glow in Ryne's eyes. Being a phoenix, he had told her he had an affinity for fire, but she wasn't sure to what extent.

"How does it work? Could you touch the fire and not get burned?" she whispered to him in secrecy.

Ryne glanced at those around them to be sure. "I can feel it, but yeah, I could hold it for a short bit. I played with it once when I was younger, and I think maybe my primary element as a witch is fire. But I can't engulf myself in natural fire like a full phoenix could."

"Good to know. Stay out of fires." Hollis playfully smiled.

"Come on, let's get some food before it's gone," Ryne said and grabbed her hand, tugging her toward a food table with a line of people already forming. They stayed at the bonfire, and Ryne introduced her to several of his friends, until darkness had fully fallen.

"Well, time to go," Hollis said, noting a few people from the armory already leaving the party with a nod in their direction.

"Shit," Ryne spat. "I don't want this part of tonight to end. I'm having fun with you."

Hollis reached up on her tiptoes and kissed his chin. "Me too. After it's all over, we'll have fun. I have a lifetime without fun to make up for." She winked and pulled him along behind her as they headed for his truck.

When they arrived at a trailhead by Cooley Creek, Ryne parked the truck and got out. The Blackstones were there waiting for them and accompanied Hollis and Ryne on foot to the meeting spot. Hollis was about to confront Dante, and protect the borders of Havenwood Falls—such a one-eighty from her original mission. She walked beside Lilith, who had been eerily quiet since they arrived. Brock joined the group and quietly chatted with Ryne.

"Something I'm wondering," Macy began as she jogged up in between her mother and Hollis.

"What's that, Macy?" Lilith asked almost indulgently.

"Why does Hollis have dark hair and not the typical white-blond of the witch hunters? Actually, I remember many of the rogue hunters did also. Did you dye it, Hollis?"

Hollis noticed Lilith stiffen next to her.

"Macy, this is hardly the time to talk hair," her mother reprimanded.

"No, it's always been this color," Hollis admitted. She was surprised at Macy's question, however. "Many of our hunters have dark hair. It has to do with the parents and their—" Hollis was cut off, seeing Lilith's glare of death behind Macy's head. She wondered what Lilith could be hiding, but decided to play along until a better time. "I suppose it could be due to having both parents be hunters. Which I realize is somewhat rare, as there aren't that many non-related hunters."

Hollis noted Lilith's apparent ease in the barest lowering of her shoulders. When this was over, she had questions of her own for the matriarch of the Havenwood Falls hunters. Hollis's reason seemed to appease Macy for the moment, but from what she'd observed of Macy so far, she wasn't one to let things go.

"But my brother Brice has only one hunter parent." Macy chewed over the information for a minute but didn't get the chance to continue.

The group had stopped in a darkened, quiet area just off the road on the edge of town and the forest heading down the mountain.

"Thank you all for coming," Saundra Beaumont announced. "Sheriff Kasun has been keeping me apprised of Dante's whereabouts with use of his patrols and members of the Blaekthorn pack who have pitched in, as well as Rusty Higgins and the forest services. He and a large group have spread out below Miles Mountain. We're going to split up. A leader in each group will have communication links to the leaders of the other groups and with headquarters back here, which will be myself, Mathilde Augustine, and Letitia Blackstone. The following are leaders of the groups: Addie and Tase, Michaela and Xandru, Lilith Blackstone and Roman Bishop, Brock and Reggie Blackstone, and finally Tate Kasun and Shade StormIron. Each of you will join a group. Time is of the essence."

Hollis was struck by how many people had turned out for the witch hunters' hunt. Even more than those who came to the armory showed up. Hollis couldn't understand why these people would risk their lives and be willing to fight for her mistake. But she remembered their cause was something bigger and more precious—their town.

Everyone moved quickly into what seemed like already predetermined groups. Lilith and the man Hollis had seen on the Court—Roman—approached them.

"Hollis and Ryne, you will join our group along with Macy, Gallad, and several others from the Luna Coven," Lilith directed.

Hollis nodded, willing to comply for the moment, but she had no intention of letting the newest members of her family get caught in the crossfire with her other family. She glanced up at the tall, commanding Roman Bishop. She cocked her head and studied him unabashedly. He simply stared back at her with a challenging gleam in his ocean eyes, then gave her a one-sided smile that was more sinister than cocky.

"What's your deal?" she stupidly asked.

Roman raised an eyebrow at her insipid question.

"Why are you helping me, a witch hunter? I mean, you're obviously a mage—a very powerful one—but your magic is different. It's not quite black, but it's not on the pure side either. How is it you are on the Court here?"

Roman looked down at her, his expression stony. "I have my reasons for helping. I am powerful. That's all you need to know. As for my Court position, that is for me to know."

"And me to find out?" Hollis snarkily asked.

Without answering, he turned and walked away, expecting the group to follow him. Hollis frowned after him.

"Don't poke the beast," Macy whispered. "No one truly knows —well, I'm sure Saundra or someone knows—but nobody else knows the truth about the Bishop boys. They are mysterious, and their actions border on illegal, reprehensible, and dangerous, but it's never fully proven and somehow overlooked."

"Yeah, you don't want to be on his bad side," Gallad chimed in, then smiled as if it were just another night filled with pleasant conversation.

"You all take strange to a new level here," Hollis playfully responded.

"And proud of it." Gallad stuck out his chest and beat on it like a Neanderthal.

There was something so natural about walking and talking with Macy and Gallad; it warmed her heart. Hollis was beginning to feel like she might belong.

"Keep up," Roman barked as they took a hiking path down the middle of Mount Mae.

They hiked for hours with nothing and no one in sight who shouldn't be.

"No one is out here," Roman was saying, then stopped abruptly. Hollis and the other witch hunters all froze. The place at the base of her neck that warned her when a witch hunter neared practically electrified her with how many she abruptly registered.

"He's here," Hollis whispered, looking slowly around their group. "Where is he?"

"You don't have to whisper." Roman sighed. "I've placed a silencing spell around us, and cloaked us in a shield of invisibility," he dryly supplied.

Hollis nodded in appreciation. "Nice." She peered out into the darkness of the forest. The chirps and sounds of the nightlife had silenced. Her father's presence deafened even the creatures of the night. "I don't see him yet, but he's out there. I can feel him."

They continued a bit farther. Ryne held Hollis's hand and squeezed it every time she paused to listen or send out her hunter senses. She squeezed his back, though she couldn't look him in the eyes. Her most recent decision weighed heavily upon her heart. She only waited for the right opportunity.

Lilith continuously glanced her way out of the corner of her eye. She had to know. Hollis tried not to catch her eye, but kept her gaze outward into the forest. A twig snapped behind them, and they all spun around. Several of Dante's rogues approached them from behind. She sucked in a sharp gust of air. She hadn't realized how it might affect her to see Nala, Rachel, and Charlie—people she grew up with and considered family—hunting *her*, or at least the people she had become fond of. Macy came up alongside her and threaded her arm through Hollis's in what she could only assume was a show of solidarity. Hollis patted Macy's hand, but pulled away as the rogues moved closer.

Vaguely she heard Lilith talking to someone on her phone, letting them know how many they found in their area and they suspected Dante wasn't far behind them.

Hollis tuned all the excess noise out when she saw her father come out from behind a large tree. Though his back was to her, the air rushed out of her lungs. Hollis's hand flew to her chest as she steadied her breathing. Even knowing he couldn't see them, the thought of him being so close to Ryne and the other witches, especially, caused her to realize just how much she had grown to love them in such a short amount of time. Anger rose in her chest and colored her cheeks. Her fists clenched at her sides. She had to do something.

Hollis stepped forward, about to cross the boundary of Roman's magic shield protecting them from sight. Someone grabbed her elbow and kept her from advancing. Ryne. She knew he wouldn't understand.

"Wait." But the voice didn't belong to Ryne. It belonged to Lilith Blackstone. Hollis turned and frowned.

"I know you want to let me go," Hollis whispered under her breath. "You're hiding something, and I am someone who could shed light. So just let me go."

Lilith tugged harder, pulling Hollis back into her shoulder. "You don't know what you're doing. I know the power Dante can wield against your mind even without magic. I can't let you." Hollis shot a look at Lilith's face and was surprised to see guilt and shame and even fear in the woman's eyes. Lilith held up her phone. "Plus Saundra called. They have a solution to your tracker issue and an idea to send Dante away. But she needs a little more time."

Hollis bit her lip and nodded in understanding. "Okay. I can give her a little more time." She looked into Lilith's blue eyes, silently pleading with her. "Can you trust me?"

Lilith hesitated, then nodded. She glanced to the side, where the others stood studying the advancing rogue hunters with weapons out, ready for anything to happen, including Ryne. "He's not going to like it."

"No, he's not." And with that, Hollis didn't hesitate. She turned from Lilith and the team and took a step beyond the protection of Roman's spell. Ryne yelled for her to stop. She glanced back at him just barely in time to see Roman and Gallad holding him back.

Ryne's eyes rimmed red and started to glow, just as she felt the snap of magic against her skin as she fully crossed the line.

Hollis quickly pulled herself together and sauntered toward the man she called father. After all, she was a badass assassin, trained by one of the best.

"Hello, Father."

CHAPTER 17

"*I* thought you were going to let me know when you arrived, Father. Let me give you the info I collected." Hollis stood behind him with her arms crossed, looking every bit the part of the assassin he would have last seen her as.

Dante slowly turned around with a closed smile on his face. "Hollis, you don't seem too surprised to see me." He scanned the area surrounding her. "In fact, I'm willing to wager you brought some new friends with you. Though how you are concealing them . . ." Then his face lit up sarcastically. "Witches, is it? So you've turned against me, have you? And I thought you were the one I could trust."

"Yet, you didn't really, did you?" Hollis held out her wrist, fury filling her eyes.

Dante shrugged, unconcerned at her outburst. "I need to keep track of my assets." He pulled down the edges of his black leather jacket and straightened his collar. "I'm guessing Lilith is with you around here somewhere . . . and perhaps even young Macy. I had high hopes for her once, too. Oh well." Again he shrugged.

"Leave them out of this," Hollis said, keeping up a casual façade on the outside, though inside a storm brewed. "Dad, I just wanted to tell you you're wrong about the other Blackstones and about the witches—at least most witches. They aren't all bad, and they don't deserve to die just because they were born with extra gifts they didn't ask for."

Dante's face was a mask of apathy except for his eyes. His eyes grew flat and filled with the prospect of death. "So then, you've chosen them over me."

Hollis almost felt sorry for him. "No, Dad. I've chosen a different way of life for myself. I don't want to be an assassin anymore. I want to settle down and have a family of my own. I can't do that with the life I have with you."

"Of course you can. Don't be stupid," he spat, taking a step toward her. "I did. I had you and others, didn't I?"

Hollis pursed her lips in frustration. "I don't want to hunt witches. I don't want to kill witches anymore."

"After everything I have done for you? After everything I gave you, you're going to throw it all away, just like that?" His voice remained the same level the entire time. The tactic was more intimidating than if he had been yelling.

"I need to try something different. I hope you can let me go." Hollis began slowly taking one step at a time backward the way she came, hoping to reach the shield barrier—if it was even still there. If they left her to deal with Dante on her own, she was as good as dead. And she wouldn't even blame them.

Dante advanced toward her, malicious intent now deeply etched into his face. She hadn't seen him truly angry in a long time. His calm demeanor hiding anger underneath the surface terrified most of them, but when he teetered on the verge of an unstable burst of rage, he was truly scary.

Hollis took several more steps in retreat. She knew better than to run from a predator; she refused to be the prey. She knew better than to run from her father; her lessons had taught her to hold her own. She had to stand up to him, but she didn't think she could handle his rage on her own this time.

"Dad, please let this go. It's time to move on. Let the

Blackstones alone and leave it in the past. Marie is dead and gone. I saw her grave."

"I won't ever let this go!" His eyes glossed over as he shouted. "My sister betrayed our family! She turned her back on who we are —who she was supposed to be! Don't you get it? Her descendants need the chance to experience the fullness of being witch hunters! They've been deceived and lied to, kept hidden from their gifts and denied their power." He beat his fists against his chest as he continued to advance. "I can give that to them!" He looked wildly about. "Do you hear me, Lilith Blackstone? You are holding your children back." He turned in a circle with his arms spread wide as if taunting her to face him. "It's their birthright to experience the power killing a witch gives them! You know better!"

Hollis took advantage of his rage-induced distraction and felt the sizzle of the magical shield border behind her, but he spun to see her face. His own was a sudden mask of indifference except for the glimpse of cold hatred in his eyes.

"Goodbye, Father. I've found a place and a people with whom I can be loved for who I am. Don't look for me."

She took the final step and disappeared behind the magical shield. A relief she didn't know existed lifted off her shoulders and she stood taller. Lighter. And though she smiled, a single tear for the loss of her past trickled down her cheek. She would allow no more than that; she made her choice.

On the other side of the shield, Dante held his head up and jutted out his chin. He would not be made a fool, and Hollis knew it.

"Kill anyone you find," he instructed his rogues now closing in around him. Dante didn't take his eyes off the place Hollis had just stood. She could feel the hatred within his eyes bore straight into her soul. Hollis turned from the edge and found the loving eyes of Ryne searching her face. And she ran to him and let him embrace her like no one ever had. He escorted her away from the space.

"You shouldn't have gone out there alone. We were supposed to do this together," he whispered roughly in her ear. She could feel the frustrated fear in his tone and laid her head on his shoulder.

"I'm sorry," she whispered in return, "I needed to face him first on my own." The others moved in behind her, surrounding her with support. She knew Lilith stood at the edge, staring Dante down, could feel her energy spiking as if Lilith wanted to run out and fight Dante herself.

Only a moment later, she watched Roman grip Lilith's elbow and tug her along with the rest, out of the vicinity of the rogue Blackstones. Saundra Beaumont, Mathilde Augustine, a man and a woman about Hollis's age, and a young witch barely out of high school crested the hillside above them. Saundra and Mathilde, though both getting on in their years, looked fierce, and the essence of magic surged powerfully in and around them. Hollis could feel it creep along her skin like electricity. The man and woman in their twenties felt human for all Hollis could tell, and the other witch, though young in years, had a powerful streak to her magic she had not yet learned how to fully temper, based on the vibes of energy Hollis received. They stepped inside the protective shield with an audible *snap*. Saundra spotted Dante over their shoulders and then swiveled to pierce Hollis with her all-too-knowing gaze.

"Hollis, we have found a solution to your tracker," she said.

Hollis held out her wrist. "Anything. What can you do?"

Saundra gestured back to the man behind her. He was tall though of a slight build, dark, and handsome, complete with a scruffy beard. Hollis wondered if he was supposed to be some kind of bodyguard, though he was casual in appearance with his denim jacket, ripped jeans, and boots.

"This is Montezuma Tayute." The man stepped up next to the witch. "He is also a technological master among other things. And he has an idea that might work, since your tracker involves magic and high tech machinery."

Hollis listened as Montezuma quickly explained the gist of what he would do.

"Call me Monte. First, we can try to remove it, but based on what Mathilde told me, it is tied to your essence."

At Hollis's look of confusion, Saundra cut in. "If we remove it, there's a chance it could kill you."

Hollis's eyes grew wide with surprise. "Oh."

"With a little tech and a little magic provided by Saundra, I can hack into the device and reroute the signal to bounce from satellite to satellite and confuse the signal so it's always in a different location around the world while she is prying into the other spell surrounding the tracker."

"Wow, you can do that?" Hollis was afraid to hope the idea was possible.

"I can." Monte confidently stated, though his demeanor was almost too relaxed for Hollis's comfort.

"I'll be assisting Montezuma with magic to enhance his technical skills. The Luna Coven has also agreed to offer you a spell to conceal your life's essence, but you'd be bound to Havenwood Falls," Saundra explained with grave sincerity. "Or you could walk away and go anywhere you want, but I fear your father could still trace your essence eventually."

Hollis paused. She looked up into Ryne's hopeful eyes and knew she was home. "I choose to stay here."

Saundra nodded. "Montezuma will disable the tracker right here so your signal doesn't give anything away." She gestured with her head toward Dante and the others, who still scoured the mountainside. Even though they moved farther away, time was of the essence. "The rest we will take care of tomorrow with the Court of the Sun and the Moon."

Hollis followed Saundra's gaze, watching as Dante hiked up an incline just on the other side of where they stood. "How will we get him to leave? Do we fight?"

"No, dear, I think that won't be necessary tonight," Mathilde explained. "That's what Liberty Veitch and Circe Alexander are here for. Liberty is a distraction, and Circe is skilled with illusions."

Hollis frowned, but nodded at the women, accepting their help.

She imagined Liberty was a distraction in most settings with her generous curves snug as a glove in her tight leathers. She was otherworldly beautiful, but Hollis didn't think that the woman's appearance would be an appropriate distraction for what they were doing.

Dante held out his phone and looked at what Hollis guessed was her tracking signal, and he turned back toward them.

"Hurry! Do it, Monte!" She held out her wrist to him, not caring what he had to do to her.

He simply held her wrist, lowering them both to the ground so he could crouch down with his bag. He pulled out some kind of tablet and a small device hooked to a cable he connected to the tablet. Monte looked up at her. "Okay, this might sting a bit."

Hollis looked him in the eyes, daring him to continue warning her. "Do it."

Monte gave her a toothy grin. "Yes, ma'am."

He placed his thumb over the place where the tracker supposedly was and held the small device against her skin. Saundra came up behind him and placed her hand on his shoulder. Hollis could feel the magic flow from the witch while Monte's other hand flew over the tablet, tapping and sliding across the screen. He then mumbled something under his breath Hollis thought sounded like "Please work."

She felt a prick in her skin and then a flood of intensely local energy pierce through her wrist. She struggled not to cry out, it was so intense. Ryne came up behind her and placed his hands on her shoulders, giving her a squeeze.

"All done," Monte abruptly said and packed up his stuff.

Hollis held her wrist to her chest then pulled away to examine her arm. She was sure there would be blood or something, but her skin didn't even look marred. Not even a scratch.

"Wow. A sting, huh?" She looked up at Monte with a raised eyebrow.

He winked at her and shrugged. "Knew you could handle it."

"All done then?" Ryne asked, helping her to her feet then also examining her wrist, though there was nothing to see.

"All done."

Hollis watched as Dante tossed his phone with frustration to one of his rogues next to him. His eyes scanned the area around them, sure he could see something else. Unexpectedly, he turned around and walked away. Though confused at how easily he was giving up, Hollis breathed a sigh of relief and turned to Saundra.

"Thank you. And thank you, Monte."

"Hollis! Look out!" Macy screamed.

Time seemed to stand still as Hollis turned. A dagger flew toward her in what felt like slow motion. Directly behind it stood her father with his arm extended, having released the dagger, with a cruel sneer on his face. She knew it would be a direct hit. While the magical barrier they stood behind shielded their location and muted their voices, it would do nothing against a physical weapon striking through it.

"NO!" Ryne yelled. He threw himself in front of Hollis and across the magical barrier. Ryne took the hit, having knocked her to the ground in the process, partially across the barrier. Hollis screamed but could see nothing but a burst of light combined with sparks of red and orange before she and everyone else was plunged into the darkness of night.

CHAPTER 18

"*R*yne!" Hollis called out in a panic, jumping up off the ground. She had no idea if he was hit or how bad it was. Just as quickly as the light had erupted then left, an orange glow surrounded the figure of a man hunched over.

"Ryne?" Hollis whispered, half in awe and half in concern for him. He'd accessed his power, and she knew he didn't think he could control it. He seemed pretty in control at the moment to her. In fact, he seemed powerful and even stronger than before. He stood forcefully up with power rushing through him. Throwing his arms back, he released a transparent image of a phoenix that hovered above him. From her position behind him, she watched in awe as magical fiery red wings transposed over his back. He hadn't become the phoenix—he had embodied the spirit of one; maybe the result of his combined heritage.

Dante stared at Ryne with a dawning familiarity and possibly a hint of fear. "You must be Ryne Calloway."

"I am," Ryne growled with an inhuman sound.

"Does she belong to you?" Dante asked, looking nowhere but at Ryne. Hollis wanted to rebuke her father, to say that she belonged to no one but herself, but out from behind a tree Nala brought forward a disheveled woman—a witch from the tingles racing up Hollis's arms—with her wrists bound as if a prisoner. Oh no.

"Mom? Mom!" Ryne shouted with a tremor to his voice, barely containing the power he held.

"Dad? A witch? What are you doing?" Hollis asked as all the air fled her lungs. She couldn't believe what she was seeing. The culmination of everything she had believed about her father shattered before her eyes with this final revelation. Her father had not only consorted with a witch, but he kidnapped Ryne's mother.

Dante shrugged. "She was easy and unassuming prey. I needed her power to accomplish a few things, and her knowledge of Havenwood Falls came in handy too."

Hollis felt sick. She knew her father well and was sure he had tortured the poor woman for information, or at the very least had threatened her son in order to gain her cooperation. "Oh, Ryne, I had no idea. I'm so sorry."

From behind Ryne, she could only guess his eyes glowed orange. And in his hands he held what looked like white glowing orbs of light.

"Ryne, you have to believe me. I had no idea."

Ryne crossed his arms in an "X" at his chest then flung them outward, releasing the white light as it extended behind him in a line in front of the others. It erupted in flames, creating a protective barrier behind him, keeping Hollis contained with the others and out of harm's reach. Ryne stepped forward so nothing stood between him and Dante but space.

"No one hurts my family!" Ryne shouted, the pain of his past combined with the hope of his future filtering through. Ryne cocked back his hand, filled once more with orbs of crackling white light, ready to launch his attack back at Dante.

"Ryne," Hollis called to him. She couldn't let him follow through. She would find a way to rescue his mom. When he didn't respond, she called again louder. "Ryne," she pleaded, "we'll find a way!"

She wanted to see Dante punished just as much as the rest of them after he tried to kill her, but she didn't want him dead at Ryne's hand. Plus, if Ryne made a move, Dante would kill his mom. Ryne didn't need to carry that guilt into their relationship—if he still wanted one.

Ryne screamed in frustrated rage. He let loose both orbs of white light, exploding two trees on either side of Dante's head. To Dante's credit, he didn't flinch as the rest of the team had.

Ryne extinguished everything glowing about him and shook his head to regain his bearings. His chest heaved as he caught his breath. He looked at his mom, guilt obvious in his gaze, but at her encouraging nod, he rushed through the line of fire to Hollis, picked her up, and threw her over his shoulder. He carried her back across Roman's magical barrier and gently set her on the ground.

She leaned her forehead against his, both breathing heavily. "I'm so sorry, Ryne. We'll get your mom back, I promise." With her eyes she pleaded with him to believe her.

He gave her a curt nod in agreement. "We will."

Ryne gently grabbed her ankle and tried to examine her.

"I'm fine. It's just a scratch. I'll live, thanks to you."

"Let me fix it."

"Really, it's fine. I've had worse." She tried to bat his hand away.

Ryne's head snapped up, his eyes rimmed with red and filled with emotion, but his words remained gentle. "Let me . . . please."

Hollis acknowledged his need to do something—anything—and nodded.

"Are you going to cry tears on me?" Hollis cheekily asked.

Ryne laughed out loud. "No. I don't need to cry on you. I simply need to touch you with my blood or water from my body, and I can transfer some of that healing power to another."

"So like spit? You're going to spit on me? Well, what are you waiting for?" She winked at him. Finding humor in the moment seemed to help take her mind off the fact her own father had just tried to take her life and kidnapped her future boyfriend's mom.

He mischievously smiled, spat in one hand and rubbed it together with the other one, then placed his hand over her wound.

Concentrating, Ryne looked into her eyes. The outer edges of his were ringed with red once more, but this time he controlled it. When they both looked back at her ankle, the skin was healed and back to normal.

"Thank you," Hollis said. Her words were simple, but she pushed so much feeling and heart into them, he couldn't help but feel what she felt in that moment. "You saved me."

"I love you."

"Time to break it up. We're not done here yet," Macy warned as she and the others watched Dante and his group attempt to regroup and pull out weapons of their own. Nala pulled Ryne's mom back away from the potential action.

Hollis saw knives and a few other weapons, but when she saw one of the hunter's weapons, she started to panic again. "Gun! I see a gun!"

"You're up, Liberty. Move fast, Circe. I need you ready as soon as Liberty distracts them," Saundra directed. "Gallad, I want you to assist Circe's magic when she's ready. That line of fire won't hold for long."

"Not full force, dear. Just enough to bring them to their knees or distract them for what Circe will show their minds," Mathilde said, patting Liberty's hand before she stepped out. Liberty sashayed gracefully in front of the magical barrier still held intact by Roman. He and Lilith waited at the side. Roman ready with his magic, and she with a dagger in each hand. Without pause, Liberty opened her mouth and began to sing a beautiful song that grew in strength and sound as it traveled through the air. The benefit to being behind Roman's barrier was it protected the rest from the powers of her song. Dante and his team immediately covered their ears. Some fell to their knees, and by their reactions, Hollis would guess some were in various kinds of pain.

"Is she a siren?" Hollis whispered to Macy, who crouched by them.

"Not really. She's called a xana. She's a type of fae, but her song can affect evildoers like a siren's song would," she explained.

Just when the flames Ryne had set ablaze began to fade out, Hollis observed as Circe moved out of the protective barrier with Gallad at her back. Circe was petite with shoulder-length chestnut brown hair. Hollis took note how slight she was, but her size had nothing to do with the power she was about to unleash. She began to chant something under her breath, and the air around her shimmered in waves extending from her. Circe's magic was peaceful but powerful. Gallad came up beside her and placed a hand on one of her shoulders, lending her an extra push of his magic. The scenery changed as her magic pushed out farther and farther away from her. The sight was unreal as rocks and hillsides turned to plains and lakes surrounded by trees. The mountainous cliffs turned to hills in the distance. The scene looked like something from an entirely different location. Hollis could see Dante and the others become confused and disoriented. She heard their shouts of discord and frustration as they looked at compasses and GPS signals.

Hollis knew they had been spared—for now. It was only a matter of time before he tried again. Dante wouldn't let his vendetta drop. It would consume him until he died. He looked one last time in the general area Hollis and the others stood, watching. Then he rounded up his team and signaled them to head out.

Ryne started to follow after them, but Roman and Gallad held him back. The sight broke Hollis's heart. She stood and watched her father and his team go until they couldn't be seen as they disappeared into the small forest of the new landscape they saw.

Once they were gone, Circe dropped her spell, and the scenery changed back to the regular Colorado forest at the base of Mt. Sousa. Everyone breathed a sigh of relief. Roman, too, dropped his barrier, but Lilith refused to put away her weapons.

"Thank you, all of you," Hollis said with a rush of emotion-filled words. She couldn't believe it worked without them having to actually fight.

"Letitia's husband Tranner will follow them from the sky." She turned to Ryne, steely determination in her eyes. "We will not give up your mom without a fight, I promise you that." Saundra sighed.

"For now, it's time to go. I have vehicles waiting," she called out, and everyone followed her back to the road.

Ryne acknowledged her words with an appreciative nod, but couldn't take his eyes away from the last spot he saw his mom being yanked back into the forest with the rogue hunters.

"What is Tranner?" Hollis asked Macy with a confused whisper as she watched Ryne with concern.

"He's a dragon shifter," she explained.

"Of course he is." She let the others get ahead of her as she slowed down in thought. But before Hollis got too far, she saw a shock of blond, curly hair peek out from behind a large tree trunk. She hissed in a breath of surprise.

"Sunny!"

The bright blue-eyed girl about the age of thirteen or fourteen —no one knew for certain—came out from behind the tree with a big smile on her face. She innocently skipped over to Hollis like nothing had just happened.

Hollis's gaze shot all around them to make sure no one else was there. She reached out with her hunter senses, but they were the only ones left.

"Don't worry. They're gone," Sunny confirmed.

"You shouldn't be out here all alone," Hollis chastised. The girl just smiled at her.

"Macy said that to me once before, too. Someday you will all learn, I'm fine." She rolled her eyes as if having to explain things to adults was exasperating.

"What are you doing here?" Hollis asked.

The girl's eyes roved over to see Ryne standing next to Hollis, a flame of fire hovering in his hands, ready to protect her if needed. Sunny smiled even bigger than before. "I wanted to meet him!"

The flames in his hands died out, and he inclined his head. "I'm Ryne."

"I'm Sunny, but you knew that by now." She turned to Hollis and stared into her eyes. "You're happy now. So I'm happy. He'll take care of you."

With emotion in her eyes, Hollis couldn't help but smile up at Ryne. She knew Sunny's words were true. Turning back to the girl, Hollis had an idea that lit up her eyes. "Sunny, come back with us. You don't need to stay with Dante. You can live with me."

Sunny gave Hollis a big hug. "It's not my time yet."

She turned and left. A young, seemingly innocent girl in a yellow dress skipped unafraid through the dangerous forest all alone at night. Hollis shook her head and chuckled at the absurdity of the sight.

"Whoa! Is she for real?" Ryne asked with surprise.

Hollis nodded. "She's special. No one knows her true story. She's a hunter, but she's something else as well. I don't think she even knows. But for some reason, and I'm betting it's not good, Dante keeps her around and humors her childlike innocence. She was the only one I really ever felt connected to."

"Should we go after her?"

Hollis watched Sunny turn around and wave in the distance before she could no longer be seen.

"No. She'll be fine. We'll see her again someday. She runs on her own timetable." Hollis laughed at her own words. It was true but to anyone else she would sound crazy.

Ryne put his arm around Hollis's waist. Everyone else had gone. "Ryne, he won't kill her. She proved her value to him in finding Havenwood Falls. And now she's leverage. I promise you we will find her—and Dante will pay."

He kissed the top of her head. "Let's go home."

"Home." She sighed contentedly for the first time ever. "I like the sound of that."

Hollis snuggled into his side. Ryne tossed a fireball in his free hand like it was nothing. She laughed. "Look at you! Figured out how to merge your magic with your phoenix and just like that, you're an expert."

"It was because of you. I have never done what I did tonight before. I can't wait to tell Ember about it. She won't believe I did it."

Then growing a bit cocky, Ryne tossed a fireball a little too high and almost missed catching it.

Hollis laughed deep from her gut. "Don't burn down the forest or we'll be kicked out of town for sure!"

He extinguished the fire, and they walked hand in hand back to the car. Saundra, Roman, Lilith, and the others waited for them.

"We'll be shortly behind you," Saundra said as she closed the car door. "Be at Court chambers tomorrow morning."

Hollis and Ryne joined the others and were driven back to Havenwood Falls, back to their home.

"I wonder where the elders are going," Gallad said, staring out the car window after them with a pinched expression on his face.

"I don't know. I'm sure they'll tell us later. We're safe again for now," Macy said with relief.

"For now," Hollis echoed. Concern for what would happen next with her father and also with Ryne's mother weighed heavy on her chest. The night hadn't been a victory, but they were able to buy some time, at least.

EPILOGUE

"*H*ave a seat, Hollis," a stodgy older man with pale green eyes and wild white hair directed the next morning in Court chambers. He hadn't been present the last time she had been in front of the Court, but his name plate said *Lawrence Mills*. She took the seat she had sat in before, and Ryne sat behind her. Hollis immediately found Macy and Gallad seated in the audience. Addie sat in what must be her usual seat in the back, ready to take notes. Letitia and Eva Blackstone were also present.

Roman Bishop and Lilith were mysteriously absent from their Court seats, but Mathilde, Michaela, and Saundra were familiar faces, as well as Elsmed—who she came to understand was fae— and another woman whom she didn't recognize with a name plate indicating her as Barbie Stuart. Ryne told her Barbie was the mayor of the town and the only human on the Court.

"Let's begin," Saundra said, unnecessarily striking her gavel. "I hold Lilith's vote. Elsmed, you have Roman's?" Elsmed slowly nodded. "Mathilde, you have Odette's, and Michaela, you have Siobhan's vote."

Mathilde turned to Hollis. "Hollis Blackstone, you came to Havenwood Falls under false pretenses. You have since then selflessly helped to protect the town from danger. As for Dante

Blackstone, he has been dealt with, thanks to you. This is a small trial to test your true intentions as of this moment. Will you agree to this test?"

Hollis paused at Mathilde's comment regarding Dante but figured she could wait for another time to ask her about it. She looked them each in the eye. "I will."

"Do you plan to harm the people of this town?" Saundra began.

"No."

"Do you intend to divulge the location or secrets of this town and its people?" the grumpy man, Lawrence Mills asked with a gravelly voice.

"No."

"Will you continue to protect this town and our people?" Michaela took her turn.

"Yes. I will."

"Why are you choosing to stay here?" Mathilde then asked.

Hollis took a deep breath and looked over at Ryne then smiled. "I have found where I belong. My heart has chosen Havenwood Falls and Ryne Calloway."

Hollis turned back to the Court and winked at Michaela, who was smiling at her. Mathilde cleared her throat. "Elsmed, what say you?"

Elsmed nodded. "She passed."

Hollis figured he must have some kind of lie-detecting gifts, being fae.

The gavel struck the wood. "Time to vote. All in favor?" Saundra called and noted the hands raised. "All opposed?" Saundra looked to the Court.

Saundra struck the gavel once more. "Congratulations, you are now a member of Havenwood Falls, providing you agree to our final stipulations. The first being the spell we spoke of last night to ensure your life essence is disguised from Dante. And the second, you receive your registered tattoo completed by Addie at the close of this meeting. Do you agree to our terms?"

"Yes, I do," Hollis answered. She glanced out at the audience and noted Lilith sneaking into the audience late. Her usual uptight, put-together self was lacking, and there were dark circles under her eyes. Hollis wondered what she got up to the rest of the night.

Mathilde, Saundra, Addie, Gallad, and other witches Hollis had felt hiding in the shadows stood up. Even Ryne stood up behind her. He was after all, half witch. "The spell is simple but requires a great deal of magical energy. We have invited members of the Luna Coven to assist us. It will not only bind you to Havenwood Falls unless provided with a leave of absence by the Court, but will also sever your tie to your old life."

"What do I need to do?" Hollis asked. Her skin practically crawled with all the witch energy flooding the room. She felt herself on the edge of control, but miraculously held it together.

"Nothing. Just allow the spell to take root in your soul," Addie interjected with a reassuring smile.

"What you feel is your raw hunter side emerging because of the power. Once Addie completes your tattoo, it will provide an extra cushion of protection from the effects witch magic has on you," Mathilde explained. Hollis couldn't speak; she could barely nod, the feeling was so intense.

"Just do it," she chattered out between her teeth.

The witches chanted in unison. Their voices grew louder with each new phrase. The power was intoxicating and overwhelming. Hollis felt the spell circling her body, seeking entrance. She closed her eyes and opened her soul, coaxing her body to accept it. She thought of Ryne, and her heart swelled with love. The spell took root, and she gasped at the instant connection.

As soon as it started, it was over. She sighed with relief and took a moment to catch her breath.

"And now, Addie, please do your part," Saundra instructed. "This concludes today's session." She struck the gavel once more. On cue, the rest of the coven filtered out of the room, and the Court stood and gathered their things to leave.

"Go ahead and sit, Hollis. We can take this part a bit slower," Addie said as she sat next to her and got out her tools.

"We just do this right here?"

Addie smiled. "I can do it anywhere. Do you know what tattoo you'd like?"

"I get to pick?" she asked with a smile.

"You bet! So make it a good one," she said with a wink. "But if you don't know, I can come up with something. It's my specialty."

Hollis shook her head. "I know what I want."

"I figured you might."

The tattoo only took Addie about an hour, and when she was finished, Ryne was waiting for her.

"What did you get?" Ryne asked, rubbing his hands together in excitement.

She peeled back the gauze from her wrist and held it out for Ryne to see. It wasn't big, but it covered her entire wrist, over the place where her tracker was embedded. Ryne couldn't take his gaze away from where he gently held her wrist.

"Ryne? What do you think?" Hollis asked, trying to see into his eyes. When he didn't respond, she looked to Addie for help. Addie only shrugged as she packed up her tools.

"Ryne?" she asked again more softly.

He lifted his head, and with tears in his eyes, he said, "You got a phoenix with magical sparks. For me?"

Hollis nodded, suddenly unsure of her choice.

Ryne grabbed her face with both hands and brought her in for a kiss that took her breath away. When he pulled back, she laughed. "So does that mean you like it?"

"I love it. It's beautiful with its feathers and the flames shooting out from it. And the magic sparks actually shimmer." He looked to Addie. "You did an amazing job as usual, Addie."

"She knew exactly what she wanted, which always helps the artist, but thank you."

"What's this word? Is that Latin?" Ryne grabbed her wrist again and studied it.

"It is. It says: *redefined*. It means I get to decide who I want to be from now on," Hollis quietly said, touching the necklace at her neck that inspired her.

"Perfect," Ryne whispered and kissed her hand.

Addie walked with them as they all left the chamber.

Roman Bishop, Lilith Blackstone, and Saundra Beaumont stood outside, apparently waiting for them.

"I trust your registration is all taken care of?" Saundra asked, looking between Hollis and Addie. Hollis nodded and held up her wrist with the bandage back in place. Saundra nodded.

"Mrs. Beaumont? What did you mean when you said Dante had been dealt with in there today?" Hollis dared ask.

Lilith stepped forward at Saundra's gesture. "Hollis, with the help of Tranner last night, we tracked Dante back to where they were staying and apprehended him. We now have him in custody, in preparation to have him sent to the Infernum."

Hollis knew they all watched her for a reaction, but she didn't give one. Instead she deeply inhaled and briefly closed her eyes. Upon opening her eyes, she offered a sharp accepting nod.

"If you would like to say goodbye, we could arrange that for you," Saundra offered.

"That won't be necessary," Hollis replied. "I said all I needed to say last night."

Ryne cleared his throat while eyeing Roman suspiciously. "What about my mom?"

"Did you find her? That would be the only reason I'd talk to Dante," Hollis interjected.

Roman and Lilith glanced at each other for a suspenseful moment, then moved apart, revealing Ryne's mother. She appeared exhausted, drained, and disheveled, but she wore the brightest smile on her face with tears of happiness trickling down her cheeks.

"Mom!" Ryne rushed in, picking her up in a big bear hug and swinging her carefully around. "You're here! Are you all right?" He didn't let her go so she could answer, but Hollis smiled at her tiny nods compared to how big he looked holding her. Once he finally put her down on her feet, he looked to

Roman, then to each of the women there. "Thank you for saving my mom. You don't know us well and yet you treated us like family, like we mattered, more than any of our actual family ever did. Thank you."

"In Havenwood Falls, you are family," Saundra said with a smile.

"Welcome home, Hollis," Lilith said. "We expect to see you at the house for dinner on Tuesdays with the family, and I'm pretty sure Letti is going to put you to work at NamaStays."

Hollis smiled. "I'll be there, thank you."

Lilith turned and departed to the waiting car across the street, where Reggie stuck his hand out and waved at Hollis.

Roman, too, turned to leave, but before he did, he stepped back to Hollis. "Remember this favor in the future, witch hunter. I will collect."

Hollis gave him a curt nod and he left. She knew he was only invested for something he might need in the future. But today she didn't care.

"Come on, Mom, I'll take you home," Ryne said, with his hand steadying his mother's elbow. "But first I want you to meet someone." He brought her toward Hollis with a big cheesy grin on his face.

"We can do this later, Ryne," Hollis offered. His mom looked like she could use a long nap, a feast, and several showers.

"Nonsense," his mother interjected. "I've been waiting a long time for this day. You were very brave last night to stand up to your daddy like that, young lady. My Ryne is a good judge of character. I'm Jessica Calloway."

"I'm Hollis." Hollis actually blushed. She had never met a guy's mother before.

"Well, that made my job easy." Ryne chuckled. His mom swatted him in the chest.

"Ryne, you stay with Hollis. Saundra has offered to take me home and inspect me to see if I need healing. Come by later, both of you, when I've rested."

Saundra took Nina's other arm and helped her into a car. Ryne watched as they drove off.

"She'll be fine, Ryne. I could see her already growing stronger the longer she's been in Havenwood Falls," Addie supplied. "I'm off too. See you both around."

"Bye, Addie, and thank you," Hollis said with a smile.

"Ryne, get her a new phone and then give her my number. I'll get Callie and Michaela, and we'll go out for drinks some night."

Hollis stopped in her tracks and smiled. "I'd like that."

"Wow, you already have friends," Ryne said, smiling at her.

"And a boyfriend too." She winked at him.

"Shit, you work fast, woman!"

"Today is a good day. Your mom is safe and home. Dante has been stopped. And I get to start my life fresh."

Before she could say anything to continue their banter, Ryne scooped her up in his arms and carried her to his truck.

"Put me down! Where are we going?" she said, laughing the whole way.

"Well, I figure if I've got a girlfriend, I'd better take her on a proper date." Ryne smiled and leaned in toward Hollis's face staring up at him from his passenger seat.

"I guess so," Hollis said as she pulled Ryne down toward her and threaded her fingers through his dark hair. Hollis kissed him slow and sensual, biting and nibbling his lip. Ryne groaned and deepened the kiss.

"But first take me home."

～

You might also enjoy Morgan's other stories in the Havenwood Falls universe, about the Blackstone witch hunters:
Reawakened
Dawn of the Witch Hunters
Rise of the Witch Hunters
Rediscovered

ABOUT THE AUTHOR

Morgan Wylie is an award-winning and *USA Today* Bestselling Author with several genres published from YA fantasy to adult paranormal romance, as well as other stories in between. Morgan published her first novel, *Silent Orchids,* one year after moving across the country with her family on a journey of new discovery. After an amazing three years in Nashville, Tennessee, and the release of two more books, Morgan and her family found their way back to the Northwest, where they now reside. With a collection of twelve-plus titles, she passionately pursues working every day with great optimism. Daily, Morgan continues to embrace all things: Mama, wife, teacher, and mediator to the many voices and muses constantly chattering inside her head, where it gets pretty loud!

You can find her and news on her books at the following:
MorganWylie.net
Morgan Wylie Books on Facebook
@MWylieBooks on Twitter and Instagram

ACKNOWLEDGMENTS

I have loved every minute I get to spend in Havenwood Falls! Not only has it been an amazing place to write and create for, but it's been such a fantastic experience to work with so many amazing and talented authors. Thank you to Kristie Cook for following your heart and creating such a magical place for us as mere humans, and for the characters we've grown with, to hang out. Thank you to all the authors involved with Havenwood Falls even if I didn't have the opportunity to collaborate with you on this story specifically. You are all an inspiration to me.

Specifically I want to thank Kristie Cook for letting me hang out with Michaela, Aurelia, Xandru, Addie, Tase and Saundra Beaumont. Thank you to Randi Cooley Wilson for letting me hang out with Callie, her consignment shop, and Roman Bishop. Thank you to E.J. Fechenda for the use of Willow Fairchild, her daughter Arabella, Harlow, Coffee Haven, and Elsmed. Thank you to Amy Hale for Lawrence Mills, Melissa Wright for Circe Alexander, Victoria Escobar for Liberty Veitch, Justine Winter for Shade StormIron, Nadirah Foxx for Montezuma "Monte" Tayute, Kallie Ross for Sheriff Ric Kasun, Tate Kasun, and the pack, Susan Burdorf for Rusty, R.K. Ryals for Harper, Amy Miles for Orlon Laroc, Ember Ramsey, and the rocs, and to anyone else I may be missing . . . Thank you!

Thank you to Liz Ferry for catching all the little things that slipped through, and helping my words flow smooth.

And thank you to the readers! You give our little town wings to fly and a voice to be heard. Thank you and keep reading!

BETRAYAL AMONG THE FROST

AMY HALE

A Havenwood Falls New Adult Novella

HAVENWOOD FALLS

BETRAYAL AMONG THE FROST

AMY HALE

ALSO BY AMY HALE

Ulterior Motives

THE SHADOWS TRILOGY
Shadows of Jane
Shadows of Deception
Shadows of Deliverance
Overshadowed (A Shadows Trilogy Novella)

Catching Whitney

Letters From Jayson

HAVENWOOD FALLS HIGH
Somewhere Within
Blood & Iron

HAVENWOOD FALLS
Flames Among the Frost
Betrayal Among the Frost

To my sister Lana, who's a badass even when she doesn't realize it.
I love you, Sis!

PROLOGUE

J walked into the disgustingly ornate room my father called an office and plopped myself into one of his overstuffed chairs. He didn't even glance up from his desk. Not that his blatant dismissal of my existence particularly surprised me. It's been this way since I hit my late teens. I once made the mistake of asking about my birth parents, and the old man blew a gasket. He couldn't believe I had the audacity to inquire about my origins. He'd since labeled me an ungrateful freeloader that needed to learn her place.

Fuck that noise.

I'd since made it my mission to annoy the piss out of him. And the news I'd just walked in with was likely to send him reeling. Since the chair I'd chosen was close to his desk, I stretched out my legs and rested my black boots on the edge.

"Jetta Mills, kindly get your repulsive shoes off my desk," he muttered without looking up from the paperwork he was writing on.

"Aren't you even a little curious why I'm here?" My feet stayed where they were.

He raised his pale green eyes to mine. "Do I want to know?" He looked at my boots. "I'm guessing I don't. Now move your feet, you insolent spawn." Lawrence Mills was never one to mince words. I took in his appearance. Today he wore a brown pinstriped suit that probably cost more than most people made in year. Wild white hair normally covered his head in more of an Albert Einstein fashion, but today he'd actually tried to tame it. It was combed back and almost looked mismatched with his crazy white eyebrows that still appeared to have a mind of their own. His skin was pale and creased with the wrinkles everyone expected from an eighty-something-year-old man. He looks good for his age, considering he's really one hundred and ninety-seven.

I chuckled. "Insolent spawn. I like that one. Your names for me are becoming more creative."

I sat up, placing my feet firmly on the hardwood floor.

He sighed.

"What do you want? I'm busy." The annoyed tone in his voice made me somewhat giddy. We were definitely heading for an argument.

"I'm getting married," I announced.

He dropped his pen. "You're what?"

"Married. You know, where you stand before a bunch of people and say vows, then fly off to Bora Bora to bump uglies."

He scrunched up his face in disgust. "Of all the . . . do you always have to be so crass?"

"Do you always have to be so cranky?" I tossed back.

"Whom do you think you're marrying?" He leaned his forearms on his desk and inspected me as if I were a nasty stain he couldn't vanquish.

"I *know* I'm marrying Conrad Monroe." I couldn't help the slight edge to my voice. It always pissed me off when he tried to run my life. I was a hundred and three years old, and he still thought he could tell me what to do.

"The lava dragon? You barely know him!" he bellowed as he got to his feet.

"We've been together for a few months now. I know enough," I stated calmly. I would not to let him get to me, and as a bonus, my lack of emotional response always made him angrier.

"Jetta Mills, I forbid you to marry that stranger." He started to pace the area behind his desk.

I rolled my eyes at him.

"I accepted his proposal shortly after we'd gotten rid of Brandt. I've been engaged for weeks now." I stood and put my hands on my hips. "It's happening. You don't have to like it, and I don't want or need your approval. I'm giving you notice as a courtesy."

"Damn it!" He grabbed his cane and pointed it in my direction. "Why can't you just be normal and obedient? You owe this family!"

"Because I'm not a dog. I don't live for your praise, nor do I want to be normal." I shuddered at that last word. Normal was so boring. "As for owing you, I'm sure I paid my penance years ago."

"Isn't there someone else you'd rather be with?" He stepped toward me.

"Like who? There aren't many dragons in town. And you know damn well you'd be having a fit if I were contemplating marriage to a vampire or fae."

"I've never forbid you to date either." He stuck his nose up in the air like a petulant child.

"No, you only forbade humans. But date is the key word there. You don't care so much when it's nothing serious, but the minute it looked like I might commit to someone, you worked to sabotage the relationship." I crossed my arms. "I'm not a fool. I knew what you were up to with past boyfriends."

He shrugged. "I was hoping you'd get all that wildness out of your system before you settled down with a good, respectable frost dragon."

I laughed. "All this wildness, as you call it, is who I am. Accept it or don't. But quit meddling in my business. I'm marrying Conrad, and you can't change my mind."

He took a deep breath and frowned.

"At least you're marrying a dragon," he grumbled.

"But you still hate him," I said with a matter-of-fact tone that didn't require an answer.

"I do. He's not Turner," he snapped.

"Not this again. Turner is the last person you should want me to be with." I felt my temper rising, and I took a deep breath to calm myself. I hated it when he brought up my ex. The guy was useless.

"Turner is a frost dragon and a proper mate for you!" Lawrence shouted.

"And the only boyfriend I've ever had that you liked. He's also an asshole and full of himself. If things had worked out between us, I'd be miserable." I looked at my father. "Not that you really care if I'm happy or not."

He harrumphed. "Marriage has nothing to do with happiness. It's about keeping the species going and our bloodlines pure."

"Well, shit. If that's all it is, I should have already been sleeping with every frost dragon I meet. I could just wander the town popping out babies and making more," I deadpanned.

"I didn't say you should be a whore." He growled, his pale green eyes almost glowing as he glared at me.

"You could have fooled me. Marrying for any other reason than love is whoring yourself." I moved to the doorway, fully prepared to leave. "I have too much self-respect to marry for less."

His cane wobbled as he leaned his weight into it. "If you had an ounce of self-respect, you'd be a different person than you are today. You don't look or act like a lady. You have the mouth of a sailor. And your choice of acquaintances leaves much to be desired."

"You don't like my friends?" I raised my eyebrows in mock surprise. "Well, pardon the fuck out of me."

"Watch your mouth, young lady!" he shouted.

I laughed. "Wait, you said I wasn't a lady. Make up your mind, old man. Am I a lady or a disgrace? You can't have it both ways."

He squinted his eyes at me and pointed a bony finger in my

direction. "Mark my words, girl. You'll regret the decisions you've made. One day it'll all come back to haunt you."

"Uh huh," I said, as I brushed a piece of lint off my black T-shirt. "What are you gonna do? Cut me out of the will?"

He studied me a moment. "I just might."

"Well, there's a surprise. I honestly thought you'd already done that years ago." I smiled sweetly. "What'd you leave me, daddy dearest? A stick of gum?"

His bushy white brows drew together, and his pale lips puckered up in frustration. "I don't know why I bother talking to you. It's like trying to converse with a tombstone."

"I don't know. I only talk to you when I must. You seem to be the one that likes to keep it going."

He frowned as he hobbled past me and out the door, waving his hand in disgust as he left.

"Bah," he muttered, as he disappeared down the hall and around the corner.

CHAPTER 1

J sat at a small table in the back of Coffee Haven and looked at the pile of invitations stacked in front of me. A deep sigh escaped as I tried to clear my thoughts. How did I get myself into this mess? Many have never considered me the marrying kind of girl. I certainly wasn't the type you brought home to meet the parents. But there I was, stuffing wedding invitations into envelopes and contemplating the implications of just eloping. My fiancé Conrad wouldn't mind, but our friends and family would kill us. Not to mention it would be worth all the hassle to watch my frost dragon father bite his tongue as I said my vows. My father was a species snob and only approved of like marrying like. While Conrad was a dragon, he wasn't the right kind of dragon in my father's eyes.

Conrad's deep, masculine voice shook me from my thoughts. "You're smiling. What are you thinking about?"

"Hey there." I stood and kissed him. "I was just imagining the look on my father's face as we tie the knot."

He chuckled. "You do love pissing him off."

I sat back down and picked up another invitation.

"You know what they say—if you're passionate about something, do it. And I'm good at making that old man see red." I smiled wickedly.

Conrad chuckled. "You enjoy harassing him way more than you probably should."

I pointed an envelope in his direction. "You didn't grow up with the old turd, so no judgment out of you."

He held his hands up in surrender. "Nothing but love and respect here, babe."

I smiled up at him. "You're sexy when you're bending to my will, you know that?"

I took a sip of my coffee.

He smirked as he looked at his watch. "Is that so? I wonder if that works the other way around. I'll make a list of ways I'd like you to bend later."

I choked on my coffee at his double entendre. Every patron in the shop turned to look at me.

I took a moment to catch my breath. "You may be the death of me. You love to catch me off guard."

He leaned down in front of me, placing his palms flat on the table. His eyes were level with mine.

"That's part of the fun." His gaze traveled to my lips. "You missed a spot." He leaned forward and sucked my bottom lip into his mouth, removing any coffee that remained.

My will to become a respectable citizen in Havenwood Falls was quickly slipping away. I pulled back just enough to look into his eyes once more and whispered, "How much would it destroy our reputations if I tossed you on this table and proved to everyone that internet porn isn't nearly as interesting as we are?"

His smile was wide. "It would probably totally decimate any chance we had of a fresh start. Not that we really care, but . . ."

His eyes blazed with heat, as if he were challenging me to go through with it.

Temptation was staring me in the face.

Closing my eyes for just a second, I took a deep breath. I planted a quick kiss on his lips, then sat back. "It'll have to wait. I promised I'd meet Bianca here to discuss wedding plans."

The thought made the butterflies in my stomach return.

He made a pouty face. The kind that looks utterly ridiculous on a man. "I'm heartbroken. I never thought I'd see the day when flowers and invitations would be more important than me."

I shook my head. "I don't really care about that stuff, but Bianca does, so I'm doing this for her."

He stood and smiled. "I've got to meet Ms. Collins anyway. She's wanting a bid on repairing her kitchen cabinets. Don't let Bianca talk you into any pink shit."

I snorted. "Never."

He stepped behind my chair, then leaned down where his lips brushed my left ear. "I love you. Enjoy your time with your sister-in-law, and I'll enjoy you later."

He placed a hot kiss just behind my ear, and a shiver ran down my spine.

"I love you too," I whispered.

As he walked away, I focused my gaze back to the invitations. I had most of them stuffed and ready to mail. I loved him. I wasn't lying about that. I wanted to spend the rest of my life with him. But the closer the wedding came, the more uneasy I grew. I needed to figure this out before I did something that would ruin Conrad's life.

I was afraid of destroying his future. He deserved every happiness—a loving wife, a house full of kids, the whole nine yards. It worried me that I might not be able to offer him that. What did I know about family life? Someone had left me on Lawrence Mills's doorstep when I was too young to remember my real parents. Lawrence's wife Christine Mills passed away years before I was even born, which meant someone left my upbringing to a very cranky old frost dragon and a sweet but somewhat distant older brother. I had no role model to mold my idea of a wife or a mother. My sister-in-law Bianca was fantastic at both positions, but I'd only known her as a wife and mother for a short time, since she and my brother ran from Havenwood Falls shortly after they married. Another absence in my life I can attribute to my father. Thankfully that loss was only temporary, and they'd come back home several years later.

The idea of being a mother terrified me. I couldn't imagine myself in charge of assuring another being stayed alive, let alone thrived. And Conrad wanted kids. His life up to this point had been devoid of family connections, and he wanted to change that. Surrounding himself with people he loved and who loved him was a goal. I understood that, but I worried I wasn't the right one to give it to him. What if I screwed it all up?

Being a wife wasn't quite as scary, but I still worried I'd disappoint. What if I didn't meet his expectations? I often fell far below the standards of many. Expectations were a lot of pressure.

I looked up from the table to see Bianca heading my way. I pasted on a smile I didn't quite feel. "Hey there. Glad you made it."

She blew out a frustrated breath. "Yeah, sorry I'm late. Zoey had a minor teenage meltdown about her plans with Jordan for July fourth, and I had to keep her from losing it. The last thing I need is her shifting in the living room and then trying to explain to the neighbors why a large dragon was destroying my house."

I chuckled. "Yeah, that'd make for interesting gossip in the HOA meetings."

She shook her head. "I love that girl to the ends of the earth, but she knows how to try my patience."

I swallowed hard. Bianca had the patience of a saint. If she struggled with motherhood, how would a hothead like me ever make it work?

"Anyway, enough about that. Are you ready to pick out flowers?" The excitement in her voice helped me forget my worries momentarily. Bianca's eyes lit up when I originally asked for her help to plan the wedding. I had no idea what I was doing.

"I am. What are you thinking?" I took another sip of my now cold coffee.

"I was thinking—" She froze. "Oh my god."

"What?" I frowned at the expression of disbelief on her face. Her eyes looked past me, focusing on something in the background. I was about to turn and look when I heard a voice I hadn't heard in years.

"Hello, Jetta. It's been a long time."

Turner Ireland stood beside our table. He looked just as I remembered him all those years ago, with only a slight hint of maturity aging his features. And it appeared he'd spent some time in the sun, which was odd since frost dragons didn't tan. He had to be spray tanning. He smiled down at me, and all I could do was stare in response. He pulled a chair up, flipped it around backwards, and sat down. Blond hair sprinkled his lean, muscular arms that he crossed over the back of the chair as he leaned forward.

"Nice to see you again, Bianca." He glanced her way.

She nodded. "You too."

He smirked, a small chuckle escaping his lips. "You never could lie well."

Bianca looked at me and blinked rapidly. Her confused face echoed the thoughts racing through my mind. What the hell was Turner doing back in town?

He turned his gaze back to me, and I could almost feel his bright blue eyes roaming over me. "You look amazing, Jetta."

I opened my mouth, willing anything remotely intelligent to come out. "Oh. Thanks," was all I managed. I frowned. "What are you doing back in Havenwood Falls, Turner?"

He shrugged, the motion causing his blue button-up shirt to pop open at the neck, revealing more tan skin beneath. "I needed a change of scenery."

I raised one eyebrow. "When you left twenty years ago, you said you hated it here."

"I thought I did. But time changes a person's perspective. I've very recently realized that I've never really been happy anywhere but here."

I chewed on the inside of my cheek, a nervous habit I hadn't had in years. *Damn you, Turner.* "Well, welcome back. Bianca and I have some important things to discuss, so if you would excuse us, we need to get back to it."

He stood. "Absolutely. I just wanted to come over and say hello. It's good to see you again, Jetta." He glanced at the pile of envelopes on the table but made no comment other than "I'll see you around." He walked to the counter, picked up an order to go, and left.

Bianca sighed. "Wow. He's just as hot as he was when you two were together."

I stared at her. "Really? That's all you can say?"

"Sorry, I'm still in shock, I think."

I glanced back at the door, assuring myself that he had left. "I can't believe that just happened."

She reached out and put her hand over mine in a comforting gesture. "Are you okay?"

"Sure. Why wouldn't I be?" I tried to brush off her concern.

"Hello? Because Turner was the love of your life once. You were together for years."

I stacked the invitations into a neat pile. "I'm fine. I'm just surprised, that's all. He means nothing to me anymore."

Deep down I prayed that was true. When he left, it crushed me. Seeing him again drudged up a lot of uncomfortable emotions and issues I'd just as soon forget forever. And it appeared those issues were staying in town for a while.

CHAPTER 2

I walked through the door of the rental house Conrad and I shared and tossed my keys on the hall table. My head was pounding. After my run-in with Turner, I'd spent the rest of the afternoon trying to prep for my evening set at Fallview Tavern & Grille, but I just wasn't feeling the music. Tonight would suck if I couldn't get my heart behind the sound.

It didn't happen often, because I loved my job, but my music suffered when I lost that part of my soul. The crowd may not notice so much, but I always did. I always left feeling like I'd somehow cheated them. And I felt cheated. My music was therapy. Normally I could walk through those doors with trouble on my mind, sit behind the mic and play my guitar for a couple of hours, then leave feeling clear and refreshed. My emotions gave a rawness to my songs that often touched the audience in profound ways. But now and then even a melody couldn't soothe my soul. This was one of those times.

I walked to the kitchen and grabbed a bottle of ibuprofen. A frown formed on my face as I squinted to read the directions.

"What's wrong?" Conrad's voice carried down the hall.

I turned to see him walk in behind me.

"I have a headache." I glanced at the bottle again. "Two capsules every six hours for ages twelve and up." I held the bottle up and shook it. "I wonder what the dosage is if you're over a hundred? It feels like an atomic bomb went off in my skull. Think I should take the whole damn bottle?" I rubbed the bridge of my nose.

It was Conrad's turn to frown. "Are you okay?"

He stepped close and put his arms around me.

"Yeah, I just need to make this pounding stop and get a little rest before tonight." I huffed. Turner frustrated me, and I had to be sure I didn't take it out on Conrad. It wasn't his fault my ex came back to town and upended my composure.

"Think you should cancel? Simon would understand." He tucked a lock of silver hair behind my ear.

I reached up and felt the length of my hair. "Should I let it grow out more, or go back to the pixie cut again?"

He looked into my eyes. "You're changing the subject."

I sighed. "I really want your opinion on this." I held a few strands of my hair to the side. "Long or short?"

He kissed my forehead. "You know I love it either way. I'd love you bald. Do what makes you happy, baby."

"That's no help at all." I shook my head, then winced as that small motion set off a fresh wave of pain.

"Seriously, call in tonight. The tavern won't fall apart without entertainment for the evening."

I sighed. "If it's not better after my nap, I promise I'll call Simon."

He nodded. "Good. Let me know if you're hungry when you wake up. I'll take care of dinner."

"Thanks." I blew him a kiss as I took the bottle of ibuprofen and my throbbing head to bed.

～

My head was remarkably better when I awoke, but I couldn't say the same for the rest of me. Not that I was sick, but I had this horrible sense of dread that had settled in the pit of my stomach. My entire body was on edge. I'd been fighting my own nerves off and on, but this was more than wedding jitters. It was unsettling to feel so not like myself. I considered myself levelheaded about most things.

I stretched as I slowly moved from the bed to the closet to choose my clothing for the evening's gig. It was early July, but Colorado could still get a little cool in the evenings, not that the cold was an issue for a frost dragon. I preferred the cooler climate most of the time. Most people dressed in layers in the evenings in case they needed to adjust for changing temperatures.

My work outfits were often much more elaborate than my daytime clothing, which was usually whatever was comfortable. That often meant jeans and a T-shirt. Tonight I chose a pair of red leather pants with black metal studs that lined the outer seam. Between each stud was a slit exposing the skin. It gave the illusion that my pants were riveted together. They were Conrad's favorite pair. I'd often had to make him promise to let me remove them so he wouldn't rip them off me after a show.

I paired these with a black sequined off-the-shoulder crop top. It bared my midriff and my shoulders, with a hint of cleavage to boot. It was the perfect accent to the studs on my pants. And it showed off all my tattoos. I added a red choker, some large diamond stud earrings, my black four-inch heels, and I was ready to rock.

I stepped out of the bedroom, and Conrad let out a slow wolf whistle. "I'm not sure I should let you out of the house looking like that."

I grinned at him. "Like you could stop me."

He stepped in front of me and braced his arms on the wall on either side of me, caging me in. "Might be fun to try."

His smile was wicked.

I poked his chest. "Oh no. Not in my favorite outfit."

He let his gaze travel down my body. "Yeah, it's one of my favorites too."

I raised an eyebrow and smirked. "I look way better in it than you do."

He lifted his eyes back to mine. "You sure as hell do."

I laughed and planted a kiss on his lips as I wrapped my arms around his neck. He deepened the kiss, and when his tongue met mine, I momentarily forgot that I'd been heading to work.

I pushed him away. "Really, babe, I gotta get to work. I didn't get a lot done earlier with the way my head was hurting. I want to double-check I tuned my guitar and do another sound check."

"Promise we can pick up where we left off when you get home?" He wasn't budging.

"I promise." It wasn't like he had to beg.

He stepped aside. "I'm glad you're feeling better. I'll stop in after I've finished helping Tristan fix the garage door."

Conrad's new handyman business was keeping him busy. Even my brother preferred to hire him than deal with repairs himself.

"Sounds good." I kissed him one last time and grabbed my keys.

I fired up the Jeep and drove the familiar route to Fallview Tavern & Grille I'd driven so many times before. It was so automatic I sometimes barely remembered getting there. Tonight was one of those times. My mind was all over the place. I walked in and waved to Simon.

"Hey, Jetta. Ready to roll?" He poured a beer for a customer at the bar.

I gave him the thumbs up as I continued walking toward the area we called the stage.

He smiled and continued with his work as I concentrated on the scene ahead of me. Earlier I'd positioned my barstool in front of the microphone stand as it should be. My new guitar sat nearby, propped up in its case and ready for a final sound check. I rounded the right side and stepped up the small steps to the platform. I still had about thirty minutes before my set, so I had time to tune, do a mic check, and grab a drink before we got going.

"So you're still doing this, huh?" Turner's voice floated up from the floor area directly in front of the platform.

My stomach turned sour, and I refused to look at him. "Yep."

I draped the guitar strap over my neck.

"I figured you'd have moved on to something more . . ." He searched for a word he couldn't seem to find.

I whirled on him. "What? More what, Turner?"

Anger raged through my veins. How dare he suggest anything I do be beneath me?

"Something more in line with finance, like your father did. You've always had a mind for numbers. Or at the least that you'd be running his pawn shop." He smiled as if he were just making a simple inquiry and not asking something personal.

"No, I do what I want. My father has no influence in my life anymore." The anger had left my voice, but I was far from apologetic.

"Good for you."

I looked directly into his eyes. His words sounded sincere, but it was hard to tell with Turner. What he said and what he meant weren't always the same and sometimes required digging deeper. He stuffed his hands in the pockets of his blue jeans and smiled at me, a wavy blond lock of hair falling in front of one eye.

"Yeah, well, I decided years ago that it was time I did things for me instead of trying to please everyone else." I stood straighter and adjusted my shirt to ensure my boobs were still in their proper place in relation to the neckline. Turner watched the movement with interest.

"I gotta get to work, so if you'll excuse me." I plugged my guitar into the amplifier, happy that I was finally mixing my usual acoustic gig up with some electric.

"Sure. I'm looking forward to your set. It's been too long since I've heard your music."

"You're staying?" My mouth suddenly went dry.

"I gotta eat. And the beer here is great. So why not enjoy the entertainment too?" He shrugged as if it were a perfectly logical conclusion. And I guess if I was being honest, it was. I just found it unsettling to suddenly see him everywhere after not hearing a peep from him in twenty years.

I put my guitar pick between my lips and made a minor alteration to my strap.

"Do what you gotta do," I said between pursed lips.

I moved my stool back so I could sit down and spent a few more minutes making adjustments to my equipment, all the while trying not to notice that Turner had taken a seat at a table near the front of the stage. I could do this. I could pretend he wasn't there and work normally. I knew I could. I sighed. It would be a long night.

I finished my last song of the night, after dedicating it to a lovely couple in the back of the grille. Jerina and Thane Beltaine were celebrating their seventy-fifth wedding anniversary. The general public didn't know that, as one was fae and one was vila, which made them practically immortal, and both looked to be in their twenties. The common assumption was that this was a five- or ten-year anniversary. The Beltaines loved being vague. I thought it was sweet, and the song I'd chosen to end the night was perfect for them. I sang about an enduring love, through all the trials of life, and how the word forever had been invented for a bond like theirs.

After a heartwarming round of applause, I set aside my guitar, and the small light over the stage went dark. Once my equipment was off and put away, I made a beeline for the bar and my regular after-set drink. Conrad was sitting at one end chatting with Simon, and I couldn't wait to get him back home. We had some very enjoyable unfinished business ahead of us.

Turner stepped in front of me and blocked my path. "Hey, that was amazing. I didn't think it was possible, but you've gotten even better than you were before."

I assumed he was trying to compliment me. "Thanks."

I stepped around him. Turner blocked my path once again, and I released a deep sigh.

"What do you want?"

He put his hands on his hips. "Nothing specific. I just wanted to catch up, see how you've been. That kinda thing." He gestured toward the bar. "Maybe buy you a beer?"

"I'm covered, but thanks." I nodded toward Simon, and he held up a bottle of Jack Daniels.

Turner frowned. "You're drinking whiskey?"

I cocked my head and gave him an insincere smile. "I'm doing a lot of things different these days. But you know what I'm not doing?"

He smiled, trying to turn on a charm that once held me captive. "No, what's that?"

I put my hand on his chest. "I'm not doing this . . . with you."

I gave him a shove and stomped past him to where Conrad and my waiting bottle of Jack sat. Putting the bottle to my lips, I took a huge swig.

"Who's that?" Conrad asked, his eyes narrowing as he glared at Turner.

"No one important," I muttered. I took another swig just before I pulled Conrad close and kissed him.

CHAPTER 3

The following day was a busy one. I'd spent the morning doing some chores around the house, then I went dress shopping with Bianca. I wasn't sure how this would go, considering Bianca's idea of the perfect wedding included a big white billowing dress.

"What about this one?" She held out a bright white mermaid-style gown covered in delicate beads. And while I'd admit it was a gorgeous dress, it wasn't me.

"You do know I'm not a virgin, right?" I laughed.

Bianca looked around and blushed. "Shhhh! You don't have to announce it to everyone in the store."

"You're such a prude." I chuckled again, and she put the dress back on the rack.

"I'm not a prude. I just don't think everyone in Dress Perfect needs to hear about your sex life." She walked over to a rack of material and pulled out a bolt of white satin.

"I'm pretty sure everyone in town already has opinions on my sexual prowess."

Bianca put the material back and pulled out another bolt. This one was all lace. "Well, it doesn't matter anymore, because Conrad is making an honest woman of you."

"An honest woman?" I frowned. "Are you suggesting I'm something else?"

Bianca's face fell. "Oh, honey, I'm so sorry. I didn't mean that the way it sounded." She stepped toward me and took one of my hands in hers. "Lord, I sounded just like your father, didn't I? I'm so very sorry. You have every right to punch me in the face for that."

I shook my head. "Don't be silly."

"I just meant that gossip wouldn't matter anymore because you'd be married and . . . and . . ." She trailed off and dropped my hand.

"Is there a lot of gossip about me now? I mean, more than usual?" I asked. I wasn't sure why I cared. That kind of talk hadn't bothered me in years. I supposed the problem was that Conrad's name and mine were now linked. Gossip about me was gossip about him too. He didn't deserve that.

"No, not really." She looked at the floor. "I think people have just always associated you with . . . Well, you know people think you live a wild lifestyle, which is no one's business. You know I love you no matter how you live. But you know how small towns are—busybodies and all."

I nodded. She was trying to make me feel better, and I appreciated the effort. "It's okay. I understand what you mean. I was just giving you a hard time about choosing white. I don't think anyone is going to fault me for not wearing a virginal color."

She smiled. "True."

"So how about we look for something less traditional and more . . . Jetta Mills?" I gave her a wink, working to get back the fun, less somber mood we'd had earlier.

"Absolutely. I don't know what I'm thinking with all this." She shoved the material back on the rack, and we walked over to another small display of custom dresses that were more for cocktail parties and nights out.

We both shuffled through the rack, looking for anything that stood out. I found what I was looking for within a couple of minutes.

"This is it." I smiled, pulling a black floor-length sheath cocktail dress out and holding it up to myself.

Bianca's expression changed to one of uncertainty. "Black?"

I peeked at the tag. "Well, technically it's a very dark blue."

She studied it a moment, then nodded. "Actually, I can see it."

I jumped up and down in excitement. "I can't wait to alter it!"

Bianca's eyes went wide. "Alter?"

"Oh yeah, this is way too conservative for me. It needs some flair."

"Well, you're in the right store for custom work. Let's go see what Nina can do." She looped her arm through mine as we headed to the counter.

With the arrangements for the alterations out of the way, we met my niece Zoey and her best friend Miranda for lunch at Daily Knead. Zoey was to decorate the venue for the wedding—the venue being the gardens at Mills Mansion. My father insisted we have the ceremony at his house, which surprised the hell out of me. He still disliked that I was marrying Conrad, but I guess choosing the venue allowed him to feel he had some kind of say in the event. I'd let him keep that illusion as long as he didn't interfere otherwise.

We had agreed to meet them for lunch so they could tell us all about what they'd found on their shopping trip. Thankfully, Zoey had tastes similar to mine, and I didn't have to worry about an area full of doves or hearts. She knew I didn't want something traditional, and she and Miranda were having fun trying to find unusual decor.

People packed the restaurant, and we took the only available table along the right side wall. Miranda's cell phone kept buzzing, and she groaned.

"What's up with you?" I asked

"I'm helping with a float for tomorrow's parade, and I keep

getting texts about flowers falling out. I told them what they needed to do, and they aren't listening." She put her hands up in surrender. "I'm done. They can figure it out on their own if they're going to be stupid about it."

I raised my eyebrows and glanced from Zoey to Bianca. "Is there something going on here I don't know about?"

Miranda frowned. "I'm just tired, and I haven't seen Kai in almost a week. It's making me cranky."

"Ah, that makes more sense," I said. "You're not normally so short with people."

Zoey jabbed Miranda in the ribs. "There's more to it than that."

I looked at the teens. "Spill."

Miranda released a deep sigh. "Kai's parents are really putting on the pressure for him to come home and for us to break up. They harass him constantly, and if they can't find him to annoy, they move on to me."

I scowled. "Tell me exactly what they are doing."

Zoey grinned. "You can't eat them, Aunt Jetta."

"I didn't say I wanted to. Besides, they're vampires and prominent members of the community. Someone would notice if they go missing. But I do want to have a talk with them."

Miranda looked panicked. "No. Please. It'll only make it worse."

"These are adults bullying teens. It's not okay," I growled. I had far too much experience with this to allow it to happen to others. Especially someone I cared about.

Bianca tapped her finger on the table. "I agree. It's not okay."

"The Reynolds family can make things hard on my parents. I don't want that. They've been through enough." Miranda looked at her phone once more. "I promise I'll handle it. And if I can't, I'll let you know."

I nodded. "Be sure you do."

We spent the rest of our lunch discussing my dress and the various items they'd found for the wedding. I tried to focus on the excitement the other three women had about my upcoming vows and worry less over the troubling situation with Kai's parents. They were bullies of the highest caliber. They knew how to push buttons just far enough to make their point without implicating themselves in any wrongdoing. Eventually karma would catch up with them. I hoped I'd get to be a member of the chase party. I was looking forward to seeing those two taken down a notch.

Tomorrow was the big Independence Day Festival and Cookout Contest. Many people were focusing on preparations for that, and Conrad was busy helping businesses with last-minute repairs, additions, and whatever else people suddenly decided needed to be done before the celebration. He didn't mind. Those last-minute jobs paid well. And since I refused to take my father's money, we could use all we could get. My savings were starting to dwindle. Thankfully Firestorm Handyman and Repair was a rapidly growing business and Conrad had a steady stream of work.

I allowed myself a few moments to walk around the square and observe all the activity that filled the area. Some citizens were planning where they'd set up in the morning. Others were talking about the upcoming parade. Then there were those that were just out enjoying the beautiful day. One family in particular caught my eye. They sat on a blanket they'd spread out on the ground. The mom was pulling sandwiches out of a basket, while the dad handed each of the three children a plate. I watched with interest as they loaded up their plates, then bowed their heads to say grace. It wasn't something I ever remember doing at our house. Being thankful for something meant expressing our undying gratitude to Lawrence Mills. Anything short of worshiping the ground he walked on was heresy.

For a moment, I envisioned Conrad and me on that blanket, three beautiful children surrounding us, ready to enjoy the picnic. But my imagination was such a skeptic. Instead of children enjoying sandwiches, I saw the oldest one tossing it at me and yelling, "I hate that kind!" The youngest was entertaining himself by setting the blanket on fire as he blew flames in tiny streams, while the middle child breathed frost on it to put it out. The process repeated itself over and over. I shivered, shaking off the image.

"Nope. Absolutely not," I muttered. Maybe it was time I talked my fears over with Conrad.

CHAPTER 4

I chickened out. I had totally planned to have a discussion with Conrad about all my anxieties. But when I came home and saw how happy he was, I couldn't do it.

He held up his suit. "So what do you think?"

I nodded. "Impressive. You'll be the hottest groom ever."

He looked in the mirror again, holding the suit up to him. "You don't think it looks stupid?"

I walked up behind him and put my arms around his waist, giving him a squeeze. "You could never look stupid."

He grinned. "You didn't see me in my teen years."

"I doubt you looked bad even then." I hugged him again.

"Thank God we didn't have social media back then. I'd have gone viral for being the biggest dork on the planet."

"So you're saying you were king of the dorks?"

He tossed the suit on the bed and turned to face me. "Yes, I was king of the dorks. Now I'm king of the bedroom."

He kissed me, and all other thoughts fled my mind. I decided it wasn't so bad if I waited and talked to him in the morning.

That conversation didn't happen.

July fourth was the craziest morning ever. Conrad got several calls for help, and I spent the day running errands for friends setting up in the square.

The Independence Day Festival was in full swing, starting with the parade. It was always a favorite part of the day with the little kids. Pretty floats, candy, and music filled the streets. The cookoff contest in Danzan Park was Conrad's favorite part of the day. He sampled every food available. And unlike the human participants, he didn't get sick despite eating a ridiculous amount. The perks of being a dragon.

My favorite part of the celebration was the dance, which started directly after the fireworks. Most everyone joined in moving to the beat. Conrad wasn't a dancer and made that clear when we first dated, but he said he enjoyed watching me dance. I was a bit of a free spirit when the music took over, and I just went with whatever felt good. It earned me more than a few odd looks, but I always had fun so I brushed them off.

I stood near the gazebo and bobbed to the latest dance remix blaring from the DJ's speakers. I caught a glimpse of Zoey and Jordan and smiled. They were laughing as they moved to the music. Next to them were Miranda and a reluctant looking Kai. It was obvious Miranda was enjoying badgering Kai. He kept glancing around as if he were afraid his fellow SIN members would see him. I chuckled and raised my bottle of beer to my lips.

The music changed tempo, and a ballad took the place of the remix. Kai had no problem pulling Miranda into his arms, and Zoey and Jordan were giving each other that gooey puppy love smile that often accompanied being with your first love. In Zoey's eyes, Jordan could do no wrong. He was her happy ever after.

I frowned, remembering when I once felt that way. I had all the same ideas about the perfect relationship. Those died years ago. Not that I didn't expect to be stupidly happy with Conrad. We were already happy together. More than I probably deserved. But I was no longer that naïve young woman who believed relationships were perfect, or that people were perfect.

I glanced back up, and my niece and her boyfriend were now

dancing with their foreheads touching, staring into each other's eyes. I'd have gagged if it weren't so damn adorable.

My eyes shifted to the right slightly and landed on Turner. He was on the opposite side of the dance area and staring at me. He walked my way. *Shit.*

I downed the rest of my beer with the full intention of hurrying away to find the nearest trash can. Turner reached me before I could escape.

"Hey, Jetta." He smiled, his blue eyes intense beneath thick lashes.

"Hey." I didn't bother to pretend with niceties.

"Would you like to dance?" He held out one hand.

I stared at that hand as if it were an alien appendage. "You've got to be shitting me."

He frowned. "No, I'm dead serious. Why can't two old friends dance? If I remember correctly, this is your favorite part of the day."

"No, thanks." I looked away from him and refocused on the teens dancing.

"Where's your guy?" The disgust in his voice was easy to spot.

I turned to face him. "What does it matter to you?"

He shrugged. "Just seems sad that you're here. Not dancing. Not doing something you love. And he's goodness knows where? Doing what?"

I closed my eyes. "You know nothing about him, Turner."

"I know he's not here with you, and he should be." I felt Turner's hand slide down my back.

I stepped out of reach. "Listen, Conrad and I are getting married soon. So whatever game you're playing, cut it out. I'm not interested."

I moved to walk away, and he grabbed my upper arm. "Jetta, you need to listen to me."

"I don't need to do anything but stay away from you." I peeled his fingers from my bicep. "Like I said, not interested. Getting married."

"You're not married yet." He grinned.

I blinked at the sheer gall this man had. Shaking my head, I walked past him and found a trash can, deposited my bottle, and made my way toward the stand where the alcohol was being served. There wasn't enough booze in town to deal with Turner tonight.

Conrad walked toward me as I paid for another beer. He had lawn chairs under his arms. "Hey, I thought we could sit and enjoy the music."

"Sounds good." I followed him to an area near the fountain and we sat down.

"Did I miss you dancing yet?" he asked with a smirk.

"Nah, I don't feel like it tonight." I picked at the label on my bottle.

Creases formed on his forehead. "Are you okay?"

He leaned into me, draping one arm behind me on the chair.

I nodded. "Yeah, I'm just a little tired. All this last-minute wedding stuff is draining."

He chuckled. "Everything is last minute. That's what happens when you postpone picking a date, then suddenly decide to get married a month out."

I playfully shoved at his chest, enjoying the feel of his muscles under my palm. "I have to keep you on your toes."

"I'm not the one running around like a crazed person trying to do six months' worth of planning and preparations in three weeks." He kissed my temple.

"Yeah, that kinda backfired, didn't it?" I grinned.

"I get to make you mine forever in a matter of days. That's all I care about." He lifted my chin so my eyes met his, then planted a kiss on my lips.

For a moment I felt that gooey romantic idealism I'd once had as a younger woman. I gave myself a reality check. "You sure you want to do this? Being saddled to a Mills for a century or more might be more than you bargained for."

His smile widened. "Oh, I'm counting on it."

I laughed, letting any self-doubts temporarily wash away. "You brave, brave man."

CHAPTER 5

$\mathcal{I}$t was roughly a week after the Independence Day
Festival when my father invited us to dinner at his
house. While I disliked the idea of spending an evening in his
presence, I was trying to be civil for the sake of peace at the
wedding. And he'd mentioned working on the wedding layout after
the meal. Knowing my brother Tristan and his family would be
there, we agreed. Unfortunately, Conrad got a call for an
emergency window repair at a residence in the Havenstone
development.

Alone, I walked up the stone steps of my father's mansion and
rang the doorbell. My eyes shifted to the granite dragon statues that
flanked the door.

"You guys don't get paid enough to hang out here," I muttered.

The door opened, and Bianca flashed me an odd-looking smile.
"Hey, you're here. Come on in."

"Sorry I'm late. I tried to help Conrad finish up some work so
he could join us, but he got a call last minute anyway, so he couldn't
come. It's just me."

Bianca cleared her throat. "Yeah, that's too bad."

I narrowed my eyes. "What's going on? You're sending out weird
vibes."

Tristan entered the foyer. "Hey, sis. Dinner is being served. Come and eat."

Bianca nodded and hurried over to Tristan's side. Something was definitely up.

I entered the double doors of the dining room and noted the guests already at the table. My father sat in his usual spot at the head. To his right was the place where Tristan and Bianca were seating themselves, with Zoey next to them. To my father's left sat Turner Ireland.

"What the hell? Why is he here?" I growled.

My father bristled. "It's my house. I can invite anyone I please."

I crossed my arms. "This was supposed to be a family dinner, then planning in the garden for the wedding."

The old man shrugged. "Turner's practically family. It's fine."

I shook my head. "How do you figure that?"

"He was almost the one you married." My father had no shame.

I felt my anger grow, and my vision clouded as my irises began to change.

"Aunt Jetta," Zoey interrupted my fuming. "Don't shift here!"

I turned to look at her and steadied my breathing. I nodded. She was right. Shifting wouldn't help the situation. I nodded and noticed that my place setting was conveniently next to Turner's. I considered picking up my plate and moving over one spot, putting a space between us, but I decided that was childish. I was a grown woman. I could tolerate sitting next to the man for an hour.

I moved toward my seat, and Turner stood and pulled out my chair.

"Thanks," I said, with no real gratitude.

Once I was seated, Turner sat back down, and I thought I caught a small smile cross his lips. I had to resist the urge to stomp his foot under the table.

"So now that we're all here, let's enjoy our dinner." My father smiled, and I almost dropped my fork. I couldn't remember the last time I saw a genuine smile on his face.

"So . . . Jetta, did Nina get the alterations done? I know we didn't give her much time." Bianca was trying to keep the subject light, and I appreciated her effort. I snuck another glance at my father, expecting a scowl.

"Yes, dear, how is that going?" He took a bite of a ridiculously large steak.

My mouth fell open. "Excuse me. Did I just walk into the twilight zone?"

Turner chuckled. "Why would you say that?"

"Because Pops over there called me dear, and he's still smiling as he asks me about wedding preparations. Shit, he's smiling. That alone should be a red flag for everyone."

Dad shrugged his shoulders as he stabbed another hunk of meat. "You're the only daughter I have. I've realized that I need to enjoy my time with you. What makes you happy makes me happy."

"Okay, now I know I'm not in Kansas anymore." I placed my fork on my plate. "What is happening here? We both know damn well that you don't give two shits about my happiness."

He frowned. "Jetta, you wound me. I know I've not been forthcoming with my affection, but please believe me when I say I love you and want you to be well cared for."

I squinted my eyes as I studied him. "Forgive me if I don't gush over your sudden declaration of parental concern. My skepticism has been well honed over the years, as has my bullshit meter."

Turner laughed. "Ah, Jetta, you are so honest. That's refreshing."

"Well then, you'll love this." I scooted in my seat to face him full on. "I think you're easily the most narcissistic and selfish asshole I've ever met."

He chewed a bite of his vegetables and nodded. "Fair enough. Can you take what you dish out?"

"Bring it." I raised one eyebrow in challenge.

"You used to be such a timid, malleable little thing. It was boring. Now you're this amazing, independent woman with a strong will. I like you much better this way."

I released a humorless laugh. "Well, that's ironic, since you're the one who made me this way." I turned back to my plate and forcefully stabbed a bite of my own steak.

Bianca and Zoey stared at us with wide eyes. Tristan looked frustrated as he glanced from our father to Turner.

My father sat there with that absurd grin on his face during the rest of the meal. I ate in silence and kept my eyes forward, ignoring Turner as much as possible. His leg brushed mine a couple of times, and I couldn't tell if it was intentional or not, but I decided if any other part of him touched me, he was going face first into his mashed potatoes, just after I stabbed him with my fork.

Most of us moved to the garden once we had cleared away the dishes. Bianca and Zoey showed me where they thought the black candelabras should go, and where we could place the chairs, creating an aisle for me to walk down. For a moment I could envision it all—Conrad waiting for me at the end of a red-carpeted path, his suit fitting him perfectly. Pastor Leandros standing there with that cheesy grin he always wore. The song we'd chosen to replace the traditional march playing over the garden speakers. It would be perfect. I smiled.

Turner stepped up beside me. "You still have a gorgeous smile, but now there's something more there. Something confident that spills out with it."

"It's called happiness, dumbass. Something I never had cause to show you." I looked down at my engagement ring, the small diamond set in white gold shining up at me.

"Jetta, we really should talk. I have a lot of explaining to do. I'd like the chance to set things straight." He took my hand in his and looked into my eyes. "I hate that we're at odds all the time."

"Well, I see I arrived too late for dinner." Conrad stood in the ballroom's doorway with his hands on the handles of both doors as he'd pushed them open.

I pulled my hand from Turner's. "Hey, you made it."

I rushed toward Conrad and threw my arms around his neck.

He wrapped his arms around me in a tight hug, his hands caressing my lower back before letting go. "I couldn't miss the planning of the most important day of my life." He moved his gaze to Turner. "I don't think we've met. I'm Jetta's fiancé, Conrad."

Turner stepped forward and put out his hand. "It's nice to meet you. Turner Ireland. I'm an old family friend."

Conrad shook his hand, and it seemed like the men held their grasps just a few moments longer than necessary. I had to refrain from rolling my eyes. The testosterone was going to choke me if it got any thicker.

I pulled Conrad with me. "So Bianca thinks we should put the chairs here and here, with the carpet for the aisle here." I pointed to the areas she'd shown me moments earlier.

He nodded. "Yeah, that'll work great."

Zoey ran over to us. "Uncle Conrad, wait until you see the candelabras we've picked out! They're very old-school Gothic." She bounced in excitement.

He high-fived her. "I knew you'd find all the cool stuff."

Turner cleared his throat. "Do you have a backup plan in case it rains?"

All eyes turned to him.

"Yes," said Bianca. "The ballroom is plenty big enough, should the weather not cooperate."

"Turner, my father and Tristan are having a drink in the den. Maybe you'd like to join them. This wedding stuff must be boring you." I prayed he'd take the hint.

"I'm enjoying it, actually. This garden has always been one of my favorite places." If he was hoping to make me blush, I would disappoint him. I knew what he was referring to. He'd done some naughty things to me in that garden. But I'd prefer that everyone around us not pick up on that bit of information. It wouldn't be hard to figure out, with the way he was looking at me. Although we'd shared some intimate moments in this garden, it had been so long ago that I really hadn't thought about them until now.

"Well, I think we've covered enough for tonight." I shot Bianca a pleading look. "Conrad, are you ready to go home?"

He put his hands on his hips. "In a moment." He stepped closer to Turner, putting them face to face. "So just what is your history with this family?"

Oh God. Not here. Not now.

Turner stared Conrad in the eyes. "I was once a very important person to the Mills. Jetta in particular." He smirked as if he had some kind of advantage over Conrad.

"*Once* being the keyword there," I interjected. "Conrad, let's go home. A hot shower sounds divine." I needed to end this before it escalated.

Conrad glared at Turner a moment more before he turned his attention to me. "A shower."

I gave him a flirty smile. "I'll let you wash my back."

His frown transformed into a smile. "Sounds fun."

He glanced at Turner one last time, then picked me up and threw me over his shoulder just before slapping my ass.

I laughed. "What are you, a Neanderthal?"

"The faster I get you home, the faster I get you naked," he stated, making sure everyone in the garden heard him.

CHAPTER 6

We hadn't been home more than five minutes before Conrad asked the question I knew was coming.

"What's the story with that guy?" He stood with his hands on his hips, his posture stiff.

I sat on the sofa and reached out to him. "Come here."

Conrad joined me, and I held his hands in mine. "Turner is an ex-boyfriend." I took a breath. "No, that's not accurate. He is *the* ex-boyfriend. The one I thought was forever."

He nodded in understanding. "So what happened?"

I squeezed his hand. "Well, it's not a pretty story. I think I'll need a drink to go down that road again."

I stood and went to the cabinet where we kept the liquor. The whiskey bottle was just over half full. That would have to do. I poured a glass for each of us, then sat back down with the bottle in tow. I emptied the glass in one gulp.

"Turner and I dated for five years. I was head over heels. I was sure he was the man I'd marry. He was good to me, had the approval of my family, he was a frost dragon, and we seemed to be suited in every way." I laughed. "Believe it or not, I was a very quiet, mild young woman back then."

Conrad shook his head. "I don't believe it. I can't imagine you ever being mild . . . or quiet."

I gave him a playful shove. "Well, I was. I followed him around like a puppy, doing everything he asked of me. Except sex." I shook my head. "I didn't understand it at the time, although I thought I did. I believed he was actually being a gentleman and wanted to wait until we'd married." I poured two fingers of whiskey in my glass and downed it again.

"So what was the truth?" He leaned back and stared into his own glass.

"He was getting laid elsewhere, with several other girls. I was the gullible girlfriend without a clue. But that's not the worst of it."

"It gets worse than him cheating on you with several girls?" Conrad shook his head. "What a dick."

I nodded. "One night we'd both had a little too much to drink, and our make-out session went much farther than I'd intended. After that, I was sure that he'd propose. It seemed like the natural progression. And to hear my father tell it, he had mentioned it to him a time or two."

"But," added Conrad.

"But the proposal never happened. And since we'd already had sex once, Turner expected it regularly. At first, I was fine with it. Like I said, I thought he'd propose soon. But then I missed my period. And the next month too. He became distant and made excuses for why he couldn't spend time with me. The next thing I knew, he'd packed his belongings and left town. He left me a note saying he hated Havenwood Falls and just couldn't do it anymore. That was it."

Conrad sat forward and put his glass on the table. He threaded his fingers through mine and looked at me. "What happened to the baby?"

"Well, this was twenty years ago, so the rumors spread like wildfire. Somehow it'd gotten around that I was a slut who let him get me pregnant and then ran him off. Many in town liked him. He was an upstanding citizen they were proud to have around, so to some I was the bad guy. When my period mysteriously showed back up the next month, and it turned out I wasn't pregnant after all, no one would believe me. I went to the doctor, and they confirmed I hadn't had a miscarriage. It was just one of those weird things. But someone accused me of getting rid of the baby."

He pulled me into his arms. "Damn, baby. That's rough."

"It sucked," I said. "But it also taught me a lot. And it made me who I am today. I decided that if I was going to be accused of all these things, I might as well live up to the reputation. I started out dressing wild and being mouthy just to be rebellious, but somewhere along the way, I learned that this feisty bitch is really who I am. The quiet, obedient Jetta never truly existed. I played the role expected of me. Since that revelation, I've been very happy with who I am and the choices I've made. Granted, I still didn't just sleep with anyone, despite what some people think. I'm also not a druggie, although that rumor spread for a while too, thanks to my short stint running with the wrong crowd."

Conrad swallowed hard. "Are you still in love with him?"

I shook my head. "No. I'll admit there are some unresolved anger issues there, but love is the last thing on my mind. I'd rather pants him in the town square and shove him in the fountain than speak with him again. But it's not because he broke my heart. I got over that. It's because of the wreckage he left behind. He didn't care what it looked like or how any of it affected me. He just callously packed and left."

Conrad kissed me. "I'm sorry he did all those things to you, but I'm grateful for who you turned out to be. I wouldn't want you any other way."

I ran a hand down his chest. "Are you sure there aren't other ways you could want me? I'm pretty flexible."

He moaned. "Hell yes, woman."

∼

The next morning was relaxing and a nice change of pace. Conrad and I both had the morning free, and we went to Eggstravaganza for an early breakfast. We were enjoying chatting about the wedding over a large serving of biscuits and gravy with a side of bacon.

The door opened, and I glanced up. In walked Zeke and Suzanna Reynolds. I felt my blood begin to boil.

Conrad looked at me and stopped eating. "What's wrong?"

I pointed my fork at them as a waitress sat them across from us.

"Kai's parents?" he whispered.

"They've turned up the heat on Kai and Miranda. Miranda's been a wreck over it lately." I glared at them as I took another bite.

"I don't know how they can't feel the hatred radiating off you right now." He chuckled. "And why are they even in here? Do they actually eat food?"

"Only on occasion, to keep up appearances," I said as I continued to glare at them. "But I'm gonna make sure they know how I feel." I put my fork on my plate and leaned toward their table.

"Hello, Zeke, Suzanna." I smiled.

Zeke nodded, and Suzanna shot me a snooty look.

"I've been hearing some interesting gossip about you both lately," I teased.

That got their attention.

"Oh?" said Suzanna. "And what is that?"

"I hear you guys love trying to scare the shit out of teens," I said loudly.

I glanced at Conrad out of the corner of my eye. He had his fork in one hand, and he strategically placed that hand to hide his laughter from the Reynolds.

Zeke glanced around nervously, his dark hair looking as if someone glued it into place. "Would you please keep your voice down?"

"Oh! You want me to be quiet?" I all but shouted at them. "Why is that? Is it because you're a pair of ass clowns?" While my voice was loud, I kept my tone sweet, making my questions sound sincere. Kind of.

Suzanna's cold blue eyes bored into mine. "How dare you?" She spoke through her teeth, practically hissing at me.

I pointed my fork at them. "I'll make you both a deal," I said in a quieter voice. "You stop trying to run Kai's life, and leave everyone he cares about alone, and I'll make sure rumors about you two don't circulate."

"Rumors? What rumors?" Zeke frowned.

"Oh, the kind that connect you with Unseelie fae and a lot of the underground illegal activities we all know happen in this town." I took another bite of my biscuit.

He scoffed. "You couldn't pull that off. No one would believe you."

I chuckled. "Oh, Zeke. You have no idea what I'm capable of. If you remember certain rumors about me from years back, you know I have some connections in that area myself. But unlike you, some of them like me. So despite your friends in high places, I have some in low places. Very low places. Places that can drag you right down with them if the right individuals tell everyone how well they know you."

Suzanna frowned. "You wouldn't."

Conrad laughed out loud then. "She sure as hell would."

They both looked at each other. When the waitress came around to get their order, they declined. "No thanks. I think we'll be leaving."

I smiled at them. "So do I get to spend today minding my own business? Or will I be contacting my old friends and setting you up?"

Suzanna started to speak but Zeke shushed her. "We'll allow Kai to live his own life."

I wasn't sure I bought it, but I felt it'd make them back off a little for the time being.

"Sounds like a good life choice." I gave them a small wave. "Have a good day."

They stormed out, and Conrad grinned. "That was impressive. Who would you have to contact to get that ball rolling if they break your deal?"

I shrugged. "I have no idea. The few unscrupulous fae I knew are pretty well gone." I nodded to the door the Reynolds had just exited through. "But they believed all those stupid rumors back then, so they don't know that." I flashed him a large smile before I took another bite of bacon.

"My god. I love you, woman."

I reached across and took his last piece of bacon. "Do you still love me?"

He nodded. "I'd follow you to the ends of the earth."

CHAPTER 7

I walked into Napoli's intending to pick up a pizza for lunch and ran into Lyra Beaumont. She lived on the Beaumont estate near my father's mansion, and I'd always liked her. We'd gotten along well over the years.

"Hello, Jetta. How are you?" She placed a hand on my arm in a friendly gesture.

"I'm doing okay. How about you?" I asked.

She smiled. "I'm doing well." She glanced around, then cleared her throat. "Is everything going well on the wedding planning?"

I nodded slowly, sensing something was off. "So far so good."

She let out a little breath that almost seemed like relief. "I'm happy to hear that."

I frowned. "Why did you ask?"

She shrugged. "I was just curious how it was going. I've heard the horror stories of trying to put a wedding together."

"*And,*" I pressed further.

"And." She paused. "There have been some rumors that there may be a little trouble in paradise." Her face crumpled in an *I'm sorry* expression.

"Has there? I wasn't aware." I was trying to figure out what kind of bullshit was circulating about me now.

Lyra nodded. "It had me worried, but now you've said it's all going well, I'm relieved. I couldn't imagine you dumping Conrad for Turner."

"Thank you. It's all good." I flashed her a genuine smile. I knew whatever was being whispered behind my back hadn't started with her. She wasn't that type.

She held up her pizza. "I'd better get home. You have a great day."

"You too," I replied.

I'd suddenly lost my appetite. I left Napoli's without ordering our food and drove straight to the Dirty Knuckle. If anyone had heard the whispers, it was likely Casten. He was the bartender there, and while he wasn't an overly social guy, he was very observant.

I walked in and allowed my eyes to adjust to the dim interior lighting. It was almost two, so only a few patrons were occupying the small bar. I saw Casten pouring a drink for a guy at the bar, and I walked his direction.

Casten was Seelie fae, and I knew I could trust him to tell me the truth, since fae couldn't lie. He stood behind the bar in his usual attire of black pants, a white button-down shirt, and an apron to protect his clothing.

"Hey, Casten. How've you been?" I took a seat on one of the empty barstools.

He shrugged. "Okay. You?"

"Well, I was doing okay until just a bit ago. Can I get a beer?"

Casten nodded and filled a mug from the tap.

I slapped some money on the bar just before I took a long drink. "Hey, maybe you could help improve my day?" I said casually.

He raised his eyebrows. "How can I help?"

I leaned in conspiratorially. "I know you aren't a gossiper, but you do hear half the crap that goes on in this town. Would you be willing to give me some information if I asked you about some gossip about me?"

He studied me a moment. "Yes, if that's what you truly want."

I smiled at him and took another drink of my beer. "That's what I truly want. So what's the latest? Something to do with trouble in paradise."

I grabbed a handful of peanuts sitting in a bowl and tossed them back.

He leaned in close. "Well, I've heard some say that Turner's return to town spells trouble for your relationship with Conrad. A few have said they've seen him touching you and that it's just a matter of time before one of you calls off your wedding.

I closed my eyes. "Shit."

Casten looked concerned. "Sorry to bear bad news, but you asked."

I nodded. "I did. And I appreciate your honesty. Thank you."

I threw another few bills on the bar. "You've earned a bigger tip," I said, as I downed the last of my beer and put the empty mug on the bar.

He put the bills in the tip jar and nodded. "Glad I could assist you."

"Have a good one, man." I threw those final words over my shoulder as I walked out the front door and into the street. I had to get this situation under control before the gossip became a reality and it ruined the wedding. I called Conrad once I got back in the Jeep.

"Hey, babe. I hit some complications and didn't get the pizza," I said.

"Only you could go out to get food and run into complications." He laughed.

I smirked. "You know me. Drama queen always looking for trouble."

"That's my girl." He paused a moment. "So what happened?"

"I ran into a friend. She reminded me I had forgotten to take care of a couple of things." I didn't know how to deal with these rumors just yet, and I didn't want to go down that road with Conrad until I had a plan. "I'll be home soon, though. I'm gonna run by the grille. Want me to bring you something back?"

"Sure. You, and a full rack of ribs." I could almost hear his smile.

"You got it." I pulled out of the parking spot and pointed my vehicle toward work.

~

I'd just returned with Conrad's food when I noticed we had company. A black Volkswagen was sitting in the driveway. Two people I didn't recognize sat in the back seat. I had to stop and collect my composure. I wasn't in the mood for visitors.

I opened the door to see Turner standing in my living room and Conrad clenching his fists. I shut the door behind me. "What's going on?"

I sat the ribs on the end table.

Conrad stepped up to face Turner. "I don't know what you think you know, but I suggest you check your facts before you make accusations."

Turner's lip curled up in a snarl. "If you're innocent, there is nothing to worry about."

"My past is just that, the past. I'm warning you to leave it there, beach boy." Conrad's voice was calm, but I could detect his barely restrained anger.

"What the hell is happening here?" I insisted again.

"Turner showed up and accused me of keeping some kind of secret from you." He glared at him.

"Turner, you should leave." I pushed him toward the door.

He turned. "No, you need to know the truth."

"I know I love Conrad and he loves me. There are no secrets between us." I pushed him once more, but he didn't budge.

"So you know all about his wife and son?" Turner crossed his arms.

I froze. What the hell was he talking about?

Conrad's posture went rigid, and he stepped forward. "You are delusional."

"Conrad's never been married." I knew this was a desperate attempt on Turner's part.

"Oh, but he was, and legally still is. And to make matters worse, he up and left her to care for their son by herself." Turner wore a smug, self-satisfied smirk. I assumed it was because I couldn't keep the shocked expression off my face.

"There's no way." I shook my head.

Conrad chuckled. "And just who is it I'm supposed to have married?"

"How about I bring her in?" Turner walked to the door and opened it, motioning for someone to come in. He moved his attention back to us. I caught a glimpse out the front window of those two people getting out of Turner's car.

A woman who appeared to be in her late twenties entered the house, a young boy holding her hand. She had long blond hair about level with her elbows. Her hazel eyes landed on me for a moment, then focused on Conrad. The boy with her couldn't have been more than seven or eight years old. He had the same color hair as Conrad, with the current popular style of short on the sides and long in front so it could be spiked. On the other hand, his eyes were a bright blue, unlike Conrad's chocolate brown irises.

"Hello, Conrad. It's good to see you again." Her smile was nervous.

Conrad's face was total confusion. "Kira, what are you doing here?"

"I'm here to hopefully fix our marriage." She looked down at the young boy beside her. "At the least, Oliver should get to know his daddy."

Conrad's eyes looked as if they were ready to fall out of his head. "Have you lost your mind? We aren't married, and I don't have a son."

She sniffed, a hurt look marring her otherwise lovely features. "I can't believe you still stick to that story, when you know darn well we got married at the courthouse in St. Louis. I was very pregnant, and you were so sweet to take care of everything so all I had to do was show up. It wasn't the church wedding I would have liked, but I know how much you dislike all that frivolous ceremony stuff." She tugged on Oliver's hand, and he stood in front of her. She placed her hands on his shoulders. "Oliver was too young to remember when you left, but he deserves to know the truth."

Conrad looked at the boy and scratched his beard. "When were you born, Oliver?"

Oliver looked up at his mother, and she nodded.

"I was born on February sixteenth," he stated clearly.

"What year?" Conrad eyed him cautiously.

"2011, sir," he replied.

Conrad frowned. "We did not get married, and you were not visibly pregnant when I left St. Louis. I don't know why you're going along with these lies, Kira, but it's beneath you." He looked at Oliver again. "And if this is my son, why didn't you contact me earlier?"

Kira shrugged. "It's been difficult to find you. You just kept moving from place to place, job to job. Last I heard, you were in Atlanta, then by the time I got ahold of my contact there, you'd moved on again. Thankfully Turner found me and brought us here."

I felt tears fill my eyes. While I wasn't sure I believed she was Conrad's wife, it seemed plausible that this child could be his son. He'd told me about some of his past travels, including a two-year stint in St. Louis from 2009 to 2011. He'd never mentioned Kira though, or Oliver.

I looked at the man I intended to marry in a few short days. "Conrad, it seems you two have some talking to do. I'll give you some privacy."

I stepped toward the door.

Conrad grabbed my arm. "Jetta, baby, this is not what they are making it out to be."

I nodded. "I know. But it's obvious there is something here you need to work out. I don't need to be here for that conversation." I kissed his cheek. "I'll be back later."

Turner walked to the door. "I'll give you some time together. Kira, let me know when you're ready to go home. You can text me."

I walked out the door, with Turner close behind. I glanced back and just before the door closed, I saw Kira approach Conrad and throw her arms around him.

"You're gonna take her all the way back to St. Louis tonight?" I asked, remembering Turner's parting words.

He shook his head. "No, she's staying here for the time being."

A nagging suspicion crept up my spine. "And where is that?"

"Your father was kind enough to offer her a room at Mills Mansion, as he did for me." He put his hands in his pockets and glanced up at me from under his lashes. "Jetta, I'm not happy about this situation. But when I learned the truth, I had to tell you. I couldn't stand back and watch him lie to you. I care about you too much to allow that to happen."

I frowned. "Yeah, you look real broken up over it."

I walked to my Jeep.

Turner fell in step beside me. "I know you hate me, but I honestly only want to be sure you're cared for properly."

I rolled my eyes. "Sure you do."

"I do. I know I screwed up all those years ago. I don't deserve a second chance, but I do hope we can be friends." He put his hands behind his back.

"I don't want your friendship," I snapped. My mind was going in several directions, and the last thing I needed was Turner throwing another complication in the mix. I could not be friends with him.

We made it to my Jeep, and I unlocked the door. "I would appreciate it if you just left me alone."

He put his hand on my door to keep me from closing it. "I'm sorry, Jetta. I should have called. I should have written. But you know how the memory ward works. After a few weeks, I didn't know Havenwood Falls even existed. I couldn't remember you or us . . . anything."

I turned to face him fully. "You also know how the memory

ward works, but you left anyway. Now here you are. How did that happen, by the way?"

He shrugged. "You know how things happen sometimes. I kept getting clues that eventually led me here. The town must have wanted me back here."

I bit the inside of my cheek. He noticed and ran the back of his fingers over the spot I absentmindedly chewed on. "I see you still have that nervous habit."

I slapped his hand away. "Don't touch me."

"Jetta," he sighed. "How can I make things right between us?"

I laughed. "You can't. That opportunity passed shortly after you left town. You left me here with wild rumors and a ruined reputation. Did you know that?"

He shook his head. "I'm so sorry. I didn't realize."

"Everyone heard the news I was pregnant, except it turned out I actually wasn't. It was just one of those freak things that happens now and then. But no one believed me on that either. More gossip flew about how I'd gotten rid of the baby so I wouldn't have to be a responsible adult." I felt the anger build in my chest. A combination of my father's meddling, Turner's presence, and this bombshell with Conrad formed a pain in my heart I couldn't deal with. "They branded me a slut, irresponsible, and untrustworthy thanks to you. I caught most of the flak from the self-righteous humans who lived here at the time. But the accusations that hurt the most came from my father. And you didn't even know or care. You believed I was pregnant, and instead of marrying me or staying to deal with things, you ran like a coward."

He closed his eyes a moment. "God, Jetta. I'm so very sorry. That was never my intention. I just freaked out. Leaving you was the biggest mistake I've ever made. You were the most important thing in my life, and I threw it away the day I drove away. I wasn't thinking straight when I left." He pressed his lips into a thin line. "Much like what Conrad did to Kira and Oliver. But what he did was worse, because he was legally responsible for their well-being. They were married, and he knew he had a child, but he left them to struggle on their own without a word or a dime from him in over seven years. They barely survived at times. And where was he? Out riding his motorcycle from town to town, taking odd jobs and living a life of freedom from worry and responsibility."

"It's not really worse than what you did to me. And you don't know Conrad's side of the situation." I couldn't believe I was having this conversation.

"Neither do you. I mean hell, your entire relationship started out based on lies and deceit. How can you be so sure he's not still lying to you now? That he's not been lying this entire time?"

He had a point, and I hated him for it. I also hated that he'd somehow found out about my situation in Atlanta and how I met Conrad.

Tears built behind my eyes. "I can't talk about this right now."

I sat down and slammed the door shut, almost smashing Turner's fingers. I backed out of my parking space and peeled out as I drove away.

CHAPTER 8

The tears fell like steady rain as I followed the winding road that took me to Smalls Falls. That little cave was always a place where I could think and be myself. I needed clarity. I needed to shift. And maybe afterward to fly.

The drive was a blur, and I battled to keep my emotions in check. I needed to get to the safety of our cave. Once I parked in the small cutout next to the trail that led into the trees, I followed the path until I reached the dirt trail that veered off toward Smalls Falls.

It wasn't long before I heard the comforting sound of rushing water. It had three areas where water rushed over the rocks to the lake below. None of them were tall waterfalls, but they had enough of a drop that when the water was plentiful, all three falls were a beautiful sight.

The natural stone steps that led down to the cave next to the falls were damp, but not too treacherous. I reached the cave and stared into the small void that fooled everyone but dragons. Stepping through the inky darkness, I came out the other side into the warded lair that kept our humongous and plentiful cave a secret from all other life forms.

I took a moment to breathe in the scent of damp earth before the flood of emotions overwhelmed me. My knees hit the dirt as I crumpled to the cavern floor. My hands clutched at the soil as I fought for composure. Grief, anger, shock—it all coursed through me at once. I sobbed uncontrollably for a few moments before I felt my entire body tremble. I hadn't stripped down before I shifted into my dragon form.

My vision cleared, and I now looked at the cave from the vantage point of my twenty-foot-high body. I usually waited until I was in the larger room before I shifted, so now I'd have to squeeze myself through the opening between the two rooms to get to the waterfall. It wasn't bad, but the opening was a bit smaller than most full size dragons.

I carefully shuffled my large body through to the largest of the caverns and then closed my eyes, listening to the sounds of the triple falls. After taking a moment to just exist in the quiet, I lumbered over and pushed my head through the rushing water. I activated my camouflage as my face crested the water's surface. The pressure of the spray felt like a shower jet on the back of my neck, and I rolled my head around to enjoy the sensation. Little by little I moved the rest of my body past the falls and into the lake.

The area was empty, so I allowed my camouflage to drop, and I studied myself in the water's reflection. I hadn't really changed a lot in the years since I'd fully matured. A few scales had changed color slightly, but mostly I looked as I did a few decades ago.

My damp scales were white with a bluish tint, the water droplets shining as they clung to them. My forty-foot long body was still lean and muscular. Long dark talons jutted from large paws, and my huge white serrated teeth gleamed when the light hit them. Horns the height of most men made a crown around the back of my head, their tips pointing backward. My normally ice-blue eyes were now a more vivid bright blue, with the expected reptilian slit for a pupil. As dragons went, I was kind of spectacular.

Footsteps pulled my attention away from my reflection, and I instantly went back into camouflage mode.

Turner walked out of the trees and stood on the bank. "Please don't hide from me. I've always thought you were one of the most beautiful dragons I've ever seen."

I assured myself he was alone, then resumed my visibility.

He began to undress. I shook my head to indicate I'd prefer he didn't.

He smiled at me as he continued to disrobe.

Turner shifted, and for a moment, I forgot about everything that had happened as I looked at the dragon I'd once considered my mate. He was much the same size and build as me, with only a couple of feet difference in height. His scales were more of a bone white and were consistent in color until you reached his crown. The horns were that same off white, but each had a black tip. I'd always thought it was a beautiful pattern. His blue eyes were almost the same hue as mine.

He used our telepathic connection to relay his excitement. "It feels so good to be back in my natural body."

"Yeah," I agreed. I said nothing else as I stood and lumbered my way past the falls and started up the side of the hill. I hoped he wouldn't follow me, but I should have known better. Turner never did anything I wanted him to do.

His steps echoed mine as we made our way up the mountain and to my favorite peak. The outcropping gave a beautiful vantage point above our lovely little canyon. When we reached the edge, I perched myself comfortably and took in the view. Majestic trees, mountain peaks, and some of the most unique creatures the average person would never believe surrounded Havenwood Falls as it lay nestled in the canyon.

Normally this view caused me to smile, but today I just saw the town I'd felt so trapped in all those years ago. The one I'd tried to finally escape more than a year ago. The escape that led me to Conrad.

I felt a tear run down my face.

"Why are you crying, Jetta?" Turner perched beside me and looked at me before turning his attention to the view below.

It was a stupid question. He knew exactly why I cried. And if he didn't, he was dumber than I thought.

I shook off my melancholy and pushed myself off the rocky ledge, clumps of dirt and gravel falling as I glided forward. I flapped my wings and allowed myself to revel in the feeling of the wind in my face.

I could feel Turner behind me, his flight clumsy and out of practice. It was obvious it'd been a long time since he'd used these skills.

"Jetta, wait!" His voice was urgent.

I refused to let him ruin my personal time, so I pushed myself harder and faster, outrunning Turner easily. I dived, then soared, going higher each time. I used each dive to pick up speed until the sheer exhilaration of flight had blocked out all other feelings. For a moment, I considered how easy it would be to just stay a dragon forever, but I knew that wasn't a realistic answer to my problems. I still had a family who loved and needed me. If I ever gave up my human form permanently, I needed to be sure those I loved knew of that decision.

I allowed myself time to enjoy being the dragon I truly was. And for those few moments, it was a welcome relief from my human sorrows.

CHAPTER 9

*A*fter my respite, I grabbed the remnants of my clothes and got to my Jeep without being seen by anyone on the road. I had no idea what happened to Turner, but I was glad I'd been able to ditch him. I grabbed my spare clothes from the back of my Jeep and quickly dressed.

I threw myself into my music for a while. The schedule didn't call for me to come in until much later, but I needed my guitar. There was a slight lull between the lunch and dinner crowd, so I just stayed on stage. I was lightly strumming a melody from my planned set list when Simon called my name from the bar.

"Jetta, you need to take this. He says it's important." He held up the phone that sat behind the bar.

I placed my guitar on the stool and walked toward him. "Why is someone calling me on this phone?" I muttered.

Simon handed me the phone, his expression grim.

"Hello?" I tried not to sound annoyed. Whoever this was, they interrupted my practice and my thinking.

"Jetta, it's Tristan."

"Why didn't you call my cell?" I asked.

"I tried. You never answered," he barked.

Wow, he was cranky. I pulled my phone from my pocket and

realized I'd missed several calls. "Shoot, sorry. I must have accidently turned off the ringer again."

"Listen, it's Dad. He's passed out, and we aren't sure what's wrong with him. You need to get to his house as soon as possible." The urgency I was picking up in his voice now made sense.

"Oh shit. Okay, I'm on my way." I handed the phone to Simon.

"What's up?" He frowned.

"My dad isn't well." I glanced back at the stage. "I'm gonna run and find out all the details. I'll be back when I know we've settled things."

Simon shook his head. "Don't you dare. I know he's not your favorite person, but he's still your father. Go be with him. Take as long as you need. We'll be fine here."

I climbed on the bar and gave him a huge hug. "You're the best, you know that?"

He hugged me back, then squirmed away. "Yes, I know. Now get your ass out of here."

I hopped down and jogged to the stage, grabbing my keys from their place on top of the amplifier. My mind raced as I rushed out the door and then quickly drove all the way down the mountain until I reached the street that led back up the hillside where my father's mansion stood.

I barely remembered turning off the Jeep. I pushed my way through the double doors and saw Zoey sitting in the foyer. She was crying.

"Sweetie, what happened?" I asked.

She ran and embraced me in a desperate hug. "He just collapsed. I think he's dying, Jetta." She sobbed as she relayed her last sentence.

I ran a hand over her hair, trying to soothe her. "It'll be okay, kiddo. He's a tough old dragon. It's gonna take more than this to bring him down."

She nodded and sniffled as she stepped back. "I know. It was just so scary. I've never seen him so helpless before."

I tucked a strand of her raven hair behind one ear. "Your grandpa has a way of keeping us on our toes."

She pulled a tissue from her pocket and blew her nose. "Yeah, he sure does. Old fart."

I laughed. "That's my girl. Now, where is he?"

She pointed up the stairs. "They've got him in his room. He refused to go to the hospital, so he's up there with Dr. Underwood."

I kissed the top of her head. "Great. You go find a snack in the kitchen, and I'll come join you once I get caught up on all the details, okay?"

She nodded again.

"All right, see you soon." I started up the stairs, taking them two at a time as Zoey walked to the hall that led to the kitchen.

In less than two minutes, I was at the door to my father's bedroom. It was a huge, ornately carved oak door on brass hinges. I pushed it open to find my father lying in bed. Tristan, Bianca, and Dr. Underwood were gathered around the bed.

"Dad?" I whispered as I approached the foot of his bed.

Tristan stood and walked over to give me a hug. "We aren't sure what happened, but we know he's weakened."

I glanced at the man I'd called father all of my life. His pallor was even paler than usual, and his breathing was uneven. "Is he gonna be okay?"

Dr. Underwood nodded. "In time, if he doesn't push himself. But at his age, I'm not sure he can handle too many episodes like this."

Tristan pulled me aside. "We need to talk."

I nodded. "Sure."

We left the room and walked down the hall to the bedroom that was once mine. I pushed open the door and stepped inside, noting that anything related to me and my childhood had long been removed.

Tristan shut the door behind him and took a seat on the bed. "Jetta, I don't know how to say this."

I shrugged. "Spit it out."

He sighed. "Dad was standing in the driveway when he collapsed. He'd gotten a call from someone on the Court. A couple of humans reported seeing a white dragon flying over Havenwood Falls."

My mouth popped open. "What?"

"Did you fly earlier today?" Disapproval marred his features.

"Yes, but . . ." I took a moment to think back. "Shit."

"Dad was livid. When the girls found him, he was all but foaming at the mouth."

I closed my eyes. I couldn't believe I'd been so careless. "I'm so sorry. I'll make it right."

He shook his head. "I think they have it handled, but they may call you in for a hearing."

"Who saw it?" I racked my brain, trying to remember when I'd let my camouflage fall.

"It was a visitor and her son. Kira something," he said.

I froze. "Kira Hubbard?" I asked.

He nodded. "Yes, that's it. Do you know her?"

I frowned. "Unfortunately." I crossed my arms. "Did you know this same Kira and her son Oliver are dad's latest houseguests?"

Tristan chuckled. "You're pulling my leg."

I shook my head. "I'm not. They are friends of Turner's and staying here too."

He scratched his chin. "Well, that seems off."

"Oh, it sure as hell is. And something about this whole situation has Turner's slimy stench all over it." My anger was building once again.

"Why would Turner bring a lady friend when it's obvious he's trying to win you back?"

"So you noticed that too? I was hoping I'd imagined things." I stared at the floor, trying to put all the pieces together.

"At first I didn't, but the more he's around you, the more it's obvious he'd like to pick up where he left off." Tristan frowned. "Also, it helps that he was one of my closest friends, once. I know him better than most."

"Well, to answer your question, Kira and Oliver aren't here for Turner. They are here for Conrad."

Tristan held up a hand. "Wait a minute. They know Conrad?"

"It appears they may know him much better than I do." I did my best to keep my voice calm, although the thought of Conrad being married to anyone other than me sent a pain through my chest.

"I don't understand." He must have sensed the pain I was feeling, as he moved close and gave me a hug. "What's going on?"

"It's a long story, and one I don't care to repeat. Feel free to ask Conrad. Or Turner." I hugged him and decided I needed air. "I'm gonna get some fresh air. Let me know any updates on Dad."

He nodded, and I made my way back down the hall. Turner was just walking up the stairs as I was going down.

"Hey, I just heard. How is he?" Turner looked concerned.

"He's weak. And pissed off," I added.

"Pissed off?" he asked.

I nodded, then continued down the stairs.

"Wait for me," he shouted as I hurried away.

I kept walking, determined to make it to the garden.

"Jetta, talk to me."

I pushed the double doors open that led to the garden and sat on one of the stone benches. "Leave me alone, Turner."

"Explain what's going on." He sat next to me.

"I don't know. Why don't you tell me?" I glared at him.

"What do you mean?" He had the nerve to smile at me.

"I mean a call from the Court brought on my father's episode. Your new friends Kira and Oliver conveniently saw a white dragon flying earlier today and reported it to someone who then reported it to the Court. Everyone assumes it was me." I pinned him with a stare. "Do they know about us? About this town?"

"No, I haven't said a word. I swear." He crossed his heart with his finger.

"I was sure I used my camouflage today. Did you?"

"Of course I did. I know the penalty for not staying hidden." He sounded offended that I'd even suggested he broke the rules.

"I'm sure I did as well, so what the hell did they see?" I snarled.

"I don't know. I'm sure it'll be fine, though. Just take a beat. Your dad will work it out."

"Dad? He's possibly on his deathbed. And even if he could work it out, that'd mean I owe him for something I'm sure I didn't do. I don't want or need to owe him anything." I stood and made my way through the hedges.

"Jetta, let me help then. I know a few people on the Court from when I lived here before. I might be able to pull some strings." He followed me.

"No!" I shouted. "I don't want to owe you either."

He grabbed my shoulders and turned me to face him. "Jetta, I'm not offering because I want you to owe me. I'm offering because I love you."

"You are so full of shit," I spat. "You've never loved me."

He frowned. "You're wrong. I love you more than I've ever loved anyone." He pulled me against him and kissed me hard.

I shoved at him. "What the fuck? Don't touch me!" I growled.

"You know we're meant to be together." He gripped me tighter.

"I'm warning you," I said in a low voice. "Let me go."

"Conrad is a liar and a fraud. I'm so much better for you." He tried to kiss me again.

I shoved him hard and started back for the house.

"I know you remember what we did in this garden." He was again right behind me. "All the ways I made you feel good. You loved me. I know you still love me."

I kept walking, feeling sick to my stomach at the thought of what I'd allowed him to do in my own backyard all those years ago.

I'd just stepped back into the house when I saw Conrad standing near the stairs. Kira and Oliver were with him.

"Jetta?" He seemed surprised to see me.

"Conrad," I said without emotion as I glanced at his supposed wife and child.

"Hold on, baby. What's wrong?" He held out his hand in a gesture that had always symbolized my safe space. I could let him hold me and all would be well. But not this time.

"What's *wrong*?" my voice cracked. "Everything. Everything is wrong."

Turner walked in at that moment. "Ah, Kira, glad you're back. We need to discuss something."

She smiled at Turner, then placed a hand on Conrad's arm. "Do you mind watching Oliver while we chat?"

She batted her eyelashes at him, and I wanted to rip her eyelids from her face.

"I don't think—" Conrad couldn't say more before she walked off with Turner.

He looked down at Oliver, seeming unsure what to do.

"Oliver," I said, "do you like video games?"

He nodded.

"There's a huge TV and an Xbox in the den there. Knock yourself out." I walked past Conrad. "You're welcome, Daddy."

I slammed the door behind me as I left the house. Conrad and I would talk later at home. For now, I didn't want to see him.

I heard the door open behind me, and I fought the urge to run.

"Jetta, wait just a damn minute," Conrad demanded.

I stopped and turned to face him. "You need to be in there with Oliver."

"He ran to the den the moment you shut the door. I'm sure he's fine. He's not a toddler."

"But he needs your attention, as his father." The words almost choked me.

"Holy shit, Jetta. We don't even know that he is mine. We've yet to see any real proof. All we have is Kira's word, and that clashes with what I know to be true." He stepped forward, taking my hands in his. "We will figure this mess out."

I sighed, trying to find the right words. I wasn't ready to have this talk, but since he was pushing the issue, now was as good a time as any. "Conrad, maybe you're better off with her and Oliver."

He drew his brows together. "Have you lost your mind? Of course I'm not."

"She's an experienced mother, maybe even the mother of your child. She could happily give you more children. She's likely spent time around women who have successfully run a home and family. She probably knows how to be a good wife."

He dropped my hands. "You're not making sense."

"I don't know how to do any of that. I had no mother, Conrad. I've little skill in any of those areas. I could totally ruin your life." I released a breath, willing the tears not to fall. "You deserve to be happy and have all the things you want in life. I don't want you to one day look at me with resentment and disappointment."

"How could I possibly be happy with a woman I don't love?" He pulled me into his arms.

I felt a tear slip down my cheek.

"Please, don't give up on us. This is just a blip." His face dropped. "Unless you've changed your mind about me."

I wiped my face with my hands and stepped back.

He shrugged. "I've heard the stories going around. I've tried not to put any stock in them, but . . ." He looked me in the eye. "If you still love him, Jetta, I can't change that."

"I just heard about all those rumors myself. It's just nosy people speculating on something that happened years ago. I do not give two shits about Turner," I stated.

"Some said they saw him all over you at the Independence Day Festival." He kept his expression passive.

"All over me? Hardly. He asked me to dance, and I told him to fuck off. I think he grabbed my arm or something, but you know me. I would have broken his fingers before I let him touch me in any way that was inappropriate."

Conrad nodded. "What about dinner?"

"Dinner?" I asked, confused at his meaning.

"That emergency window I had to go help with. The one that caused me to miss dinner at your father's house. Someone had done it on purpose. I was talking to the homeowner when his kid accidentally blurted out something about buying a new bike with the money they got for the broken window."

"I honestly knew nothing about that." Was he accusing me of being in on it?

"I believe Turner set that up so I would be out of the way for the evening." He was angry, and I couldn't blame him.

I shook my head. "I knew the moment I saw him back in town he'd be a pain in my ass. But I have no intention of ever getting back together with that selfish prick."

"Okay, then let's slow down before we jump to any conclusions or make any decisions that change our current plans. We love each other, and we are getting married in eight days. Let's focus on that."

CHAPTER 10

I walked into my father's bedroom about an hour later and looked at the man sleeping peacefully. His breathing had evened out, so that was encouraging.

"Jetta? Is that you?" His raspy voice still sounded strained. I hadn't meant to wake him.

"I'm here," I said, as I walked closer to his bedside and took a seat next to him.

He reached for my hand. "I'm so glad you're here."

He coughed, and I wondered if he'd contracted a virus on top of his heart condition.

"I'm glad I can be here." And it surprised me to realize I meant it. I didn't like the old man, but I did still hold some affection for him. He was the one who took me in and cared for me when I had no one else. When I was defenseless. He could have left me on the street.

"Will you stay in the house? Just until I'm better?" He reached for my hand and gave it a faint squeeze.

"I'm not sure that's a good idea. Not with the other houseguests you already have." I did not want to socialize with Turner or Kira any more than I had to.

"I need you, Jetta." He wheezed again. "I know I've never really said it, but I need you. You are the only one I trust to assure I'll be properly cared for." He gave me a crooked smile. "You have that special touch that your brother and that blasted home care nurse don't have. I know I can heal with you here."

I sighed. "Sure, I'll stay for a few days." I prayed I wouldn't regret that decision. "Let me grab a few personal items, then I'll be back."

He gave my hand a light squeeze. "You're a wonderful daughter."

I'd wanted to hear those words from my father since I was little. Despite not wanting to care what he thought, deep down I still did. A little.

I hurried home to get the necessities. I was packing my bags when Conrad came home.

"Babe, what's going on?" His expression showed that what he saw alarmed him.

"I'm gonna stay with Dad for a few days. He wants me there to help take care of him."

"You're not leaving me?"

I stopped and turned to face him. "Should I?"

Conrad stepped forward. "Hell, no." He put a hand on my suitcase. "Like I said earlier, the situation with Kira and Oliver looks bad, but I promise you it's just a misunderstanding. Kira and I are not married, nor have we ever been."

I frowned. "And what about Oliver?"

He shook his head. "I don't know. He could be mine, but if she was pregnant when I left, she said nothing."

"And if he's yours?" I wasn't sure I was ready to think about those consequences just yet. I'd only allowed myself to accept that all of it was a lie.

"Then I'll figure it out. But no matter what happened then, it doesn't affect us now. I love you and only you." He pulled me close, wrapping his arms around me.

"It does affect us, Conrad. If Oliver is yours, then we have to take his needs into consideration too." I laid my head against his chest.

He put his chin on top of my head. "True, but it changes nothing about how I feel about you."

I closed my eyes, trying to keep the tears at bay. I was afraid of losing him, but I was also afraid of staying. The doubts I'd had earlier pushed their way back in. What if I really didn't know him? What if everything Turner said was true?

Conrad held me tighter. "I don't know what I'd do if I lost you, Jetta."

"Let's just focus on figuring out this Oliver situation." I tried to keep my voice soft and calm. "And get Dad better."

He let go of me and stepped back. "Yeah, sure. Do you think he'll be able to attend the wedding?"

I shrugged. "Not sure."

Conrad stared at me a moment. "Let me know if I can help."

"I will." I shoved the last of my essentials into the small suitcase. "I only plan to stay a few days. He mostly needs rest and someone to ensure he's eating and taking his vitamins." I zipped the case and pulled it to the floor.

Conrad stepped forward and picked it up. "I'll walk you to the Jeep."

We walked to my vehicle in silence, and he put my stuff in the back.

"Jetta . . ." He hesitated.

"Say what you need to, Conrad," I urged him.

"Where are we?" He looked vulnerable, and I wanted to reach out to him, but I also couldn't. Not until I straightened out my own feelings. "Are we good?"

I shook my head. "I don't really know. I'm pretty confused right now."

"Do you want to postpone the wedding?" His face had turned to stone, no emotions crossing his features.

I thought about it for a moment. "No. Unless you want to call it off."

He looked down at his shoes, then back up at me. "I'm not the one that's confused."

He turned and walked back into the house.

I felt the all too familiar sting of tears begin.

"Shit," I muttered as I climbed into the driver's seat.

My first full day at Dad's house was busy. I followed Nurse Freeman around, making sure I knew how everything was being done. I figured I could be the most help if I was useful in any area someone might need me. I learned almost everything about his care routine. As a bonus, I avoided Turner and Kira.

On day two, she gave me a list of things I needed to ensure were being done daily.

"These are the vitamins he should take every morning. And he needs lots of rest, so don't let anyone overtax him." She pushed a bottle of pills in my hand.

"Okay. But aren't you doing that? I'm just here as extra support." I smiled.

"No," she clipped out. "Your father has made it clear he doesn't want me here."

I sighed. It figured Dad would run her off. "Well, thank you for all you've done so far. I appreciate it, even if he doesn't."

She put a hand on my shoulder. "You've always been a kind soul, Jetta. I don't know how you stay so sweet with such a sour man for a father."

I shrugged. "I'm not sweet. I'm just great at lobbing his own bricks back at him. It's good stress relief."

She patted me on the back. "Well, I'm glad someone keeps that cranky old codger on his toes." She picked up her bag. "I'm heading out. If you have any questions, you know where to reach me."

"Thanks again," I said as I walked her to the door.

Once I saw her out, I worked down the list of recommendations. He'd already had his vitamins for the day. Lunch was over, and the next item was helping him walk up and down the hall. I scoffed at the list a bit, but I also knew this was a combination of human treatments and what we assumed an elderly dragon needed. This was new territory for all of us. Even Lawrence himself couldn't recommend a definitive treatment regimen, although some of these options came straight from his memories of caring for his own elderly father.

I checked my cell phone, hoping for a text from Conrad, but there was nothing. Maybe he was waiting on me to make the first move after our uncomfortable discussion the day before. But I just wasn't sure what to say. I was no less confused than when we last spoke.

I reached my father's room and knocked on his door.

"Come in." His voice lacked the conviction his normal speech held.

I stepped inside and closed the door behind me. "Ready for your walk?"

He pushed himself up. "Yes. I need to get out of this bed."

I stepped next to the bed and pulled back the covers. He slid his legs over the side, and I took hold of his arms as he pulled himself to a standing position. I didn't touch my father often, so I hadn't realized how thin he truly was. It was a shock.

I let him lean on me as he slipped his feet into his house shoes, then we slowly made our way to the hallway.

"How far have you been walking?" I asked.

"Oh, I usually make it to the end of this wing and back," he replied.

The west wing of the mansion wasn't excessively long, so it made sense he could make one lap. I nodded. "Let's get you moving then."

He took a wobbly step, and I steadied him. He'd grabbed his cane on the way out of his bedroom, so he leaned the bulk of his weight on that as he took small, careful steps. I stayed close enough I could catch him should he fall.

We made it halfway down the hall when one of the bedroom doors opened and Turner entered the hallway. I groaned inwardly.

"Well, good afternoon." He smiled widely.

"And to you, Turner," Dad replied.

I said nothing.

"I see you have a new nurse. She's much prettier than the last one." He winked at me.

I faked a gagging motion.

Turner laughed. "You are a fun one, Jetta."

Dad mumbled something I couldn't quite hear as we took another step.

"What was that?" I asked.

"Nothing," he replied, and returned his concentration to his steps.

Turner looked at his watch. "I have to run into town, but I'll be back soon. Maybe we can have dinner together tonight?" He directed his gaze to me.

"Sorry. Can't," I said, as I put my hand out to steady my father when he wavered.

"Why not?" Turner did not sound discouraged.

"Because I'm busy avoiding you. I expect it to keep my schedule full for days." I kept my attention on Lawrence's next steps.

"Jetta," Lawrence admonished. "Don't be rude. The boy simply wants to sit down to a meal with you." We turned at the end of the hall and started back to his room.

"And I said no." I refused to argue about this anymore with either of them.

Turner looked at Lawrence and shrugged. "Well, I tried. See you both later."

He disappeared down the stairs that led to the foyer.

"Jetta," Lawrence began.

"Not discussing it, Dad," I said as I once again steadied him.

He didn't say another word as we continued his walk and got him back into bed.

"How did that feel?" I asked, tucking him back in.

"Good. But I'm tired. I'd like to nap." He leaned his head back against the pillows and closed his eyes.

"Okay. I'll leave you to rest. I'll check back in later this afternoon."

He nodded, but didn't open his eyes.

I studied his face a moment before leaving. More conflicting emotions swirled in my heart. He could be such a vile man, but seeing him so frail made me sad. It was weird to dislike someone but also love them.

I worked on some new music, since I had some downtime. I'd brought my acoustic guitar with me, so I retired to my room and picked out the melody of my latest masterpiece.

It was getting close to bedtime a few nights later when I finally got a text notification on my phone. We had settled Dad in for the night, and I was just getting ready to put on my pajamas. I smiled, ready to see any communication from Conrad. I needed a boost of hope that maybe we were fixable. Instead, I saw a text from a number I didn't recognize.

MEET ME IN THE GARDEN

It was pretty cryptic, but never one to buck curiosity, I did as instructed.

Thankful I hadn't changed out of my jeans and tank top just jet, I made my way to the outer doors in the backyard. I stepped outside to see Turner standing under one of the garden lamps.

"I should have known it'd be you," I grumbled.

"I won't keep you long. I just have something you need to see." He held up a manila envelope.

I walked toward him. "Is this your secret mission? Please tell me you're being sent to Siberia."

He didn't crack a smile. "This is serious."

He held out the envelope.

I took it from him and sat in a chair next to a large patio table.

When I pulled back the flap, I saw there were photos and papers. I dumped them on the table and froze when my eyes landed on the first photo. It was a wedding photo of Conrad and Kira. She was all smiles, very pregnant, and holding a simple bouquet of carnations. Conrad's hand was in hers, and he too was smiling. A man in the background appeared to be a justice of the peace. He held a bible in his hand and was grinning at the happy couple.

I choked back a gasp as the next photo showed Conrad cuddling an infant in a hospital.

Turner stepped closer. "There's a copy of the wedding license and Oliver's birth certificate, if you require more proof."

I stuffed the contents back into the envelope. "No, I don't need to see anything else." I slid it toward him on the table and stood.

"Jetta, it pains me to have to be the one that exposes his lies. But I just couldn't stand back and watch you marry the wrong man."

I looked at him through the tears I could no longer hold back. "Just leave me alone, Turner."

He stepped forward. "Please. I know we will never be more than friends, but allow me to be here for you, in that capacity. I have more than adequate shoulders you can cry on."

I wiped away a tear, ashamed that I'd let him see me in a weak moment. "I'm fine, Turner. Have a good night."

I left him standing on the patio while I made a mad dash to reach my room. I wouldn't be able to hold back the flow of emotions that were beating me down. The dam was about to break.

I reached my room and shut the door, locking it behind me. I allowed the tears to flow. After a few minutes, my sadness gave way to anger. I glanced around the room I was sleeping in. I threw a pillow at the wall.

"Fucking Turner," I shouted. I threw a book, knocking a vase of flowers off the table and watching it crash to the floor. "Fucking Conrad," I shouted again.

I opened the window and looked down, considering making an escape. My dragon form would be a more comforting choice in that moment. But I knew that wasn't really an option. Running away from my problems had never solved them. That's a truth I'd learned the hard way.

"Fucking marriage," I growled as I slammed the window shut.

I needed a good night's rest before I confronted Conrad with what I'd seen. And he'd better have a fantastic and miraculous explanation. The shit was about to hit the fan.

Of course, sleep eluded me.

What little I got was full of dreams and images of Conrad's other life. Cranky didn't properly describe the way I felt when I awoke. I needed to deal with this as soon as possible. After checking on my father, I drove home. Conrad was just sitting down to breakfast.

"Hey," he said as he looked up from his plate of eggs.

"Hi." I couldn't force a smile, so I didn't try.

"Want some breakfast? I made plenty." He gestured to a pan on the stove.

"No, I'm not staying long." I sat next to him at the table.

He wiped his face with a napkin and gave me his full attention. "So why are you here?"

I could tell our last conversation still frustrated him.

"I'm here because I wanted to tell you I know the truth. I don't think we can get married."

He stood quickly, bumping the table and knocking his coffee over. "What truth?"

"I saw your marriage license and Oliver's birth certificate."

He frowned. "Those can be faked, Jetta. You know that."

I stood. "What about photos from your wedding? Photos of you holding baby Oliver?"

He shook his head. "All that takes is some photo editing knowledge. Why are you choosing to believe this shit over me?"

He was angry, but so was I.

"Damn it, Conrad. You know my history. Would you just take my word for it if the tables were turned?"

"I understand, and I'm sorry Turner lied and cheated and left you to suffer the way he did." He pounded on the table. "But I'm not him, Jetta. I'm not anything like him."

"I don't know what to think right now," I cried.

"Honestly, I don't know how I'd survive without you. I don't care about your lack of maternal experience. But I do know that I'm sure you are the only woman that could ever make me happy. And if being with you means things are a little crazy and our kids are wild, then so be it. Hell, even if we never have kids, I'll still be the luckiest man in the world as long as you're by my side." He sighed. "Please, Jetta. This is all a plot to get me out of the way. I know it."

I put my head in my hands.

"How did this all get so screwed up?" I moaned.

He put his arms around me. "Choose to trust me. I will prove it to you. Somehow." He kissed my temple. "I have to, because I don't want to spend another day of my life without you."

I nodded. "I'm sorry. I'm so sorry." I continued to cry.

"It's a bump in the road. We'll get over it, and it'll all be okay. I promise."

I hugged him and prayed it was true.

CHAPTER 11

*W*hen I returned to the mansion that afternoon, I saw Kira sitting outside, a book in her hand. I'd been debating having a talk with her since I learned she was staying at my father's house. I wasn't sure if now was really the time, but it might be my only opportunity. Neither Turner nor Oliver was at her side.

I sat next to her. "Hey, Kira, what are you reading?"

She smiled. "I found it in your dad's library. It's a parenting book."

I laughed. "My dad had a parenting book?"

She nodded. "It has some interesting information in here. I may try a few of these ideas with Oliver. He can be very obstinate sometimes."

I tamped down the previous worries I'd had about being a decent mother. The way things were going, I might never be a mother or wife, so why let it bother me now?

"But," she continued, "I'd have to run these methods by Conrad and get his approval." She sighed. "It'll be nice to co-parent again. It's been so hard on my own."

I nodded. "I'm sure it will."

She closed the book and set it next to her. "I hate that we've disrupted all your plans, but I know you understand how important it is that we reconnect our family."

"Oh, yeah," I said. "I totally get it."

She placed her hand on mine. "You are so understanding, Jetta. Oliver and I appreciate it very much."

I did my best to smile back. "Hey, I have a weird question."

"Okay." She looked hesitant.

"Turner was saying you saw something odd in the sky the other day."

She swallowed. "Yeah, it was unusual. I'm not sure if I want to talk about it."

I stood and pulled her with me. "Don't worry. You can trust me. Let's walk in the hedge maze. No one can bother us there."

She looked behind us. "Oh, I don't know . . ."

"It'll be fun. And it'll give me a chance to get to know the woman who holds Conrad's heart." I smiled as I tugged on her arm.

"Well, okay, I guess." She still looked alarmed.

We entered the front opening of the maze.

"So tell me, what did you see?" I pulled her in close.

"I'm not sure you'd believe me." She chewed on a fingernail.

I pulled her hand back down and clasped it in mine. "Don't be nervous. A lot of odd things happen here, so I promise you won't shock me."

She took a deep breath. "I saw something in the sky. It was huge and white and . . . it looked like a dragon, to be honest."

"Wow," I said. "Did you see it closely?"

She nodded. "I saw enough. It terrified me."

"I totally understand," I assured her. "I've seen it too, to be honest."

"Oh?" She turned to face me.

I nodded. "Like you said. Large. White. Flying across the sky." I glanced at her from the corner of my eye as I prodded her to walk deeper into the maze. "The one I saw had white horns with black tips. It was very clear. Did you see that too?"

She bit her lip a moment. "Yeah, I think I did."

I sighed. "Yeah, that dragon is a local legend, you might say."

"What, like bigfoot?" she asked.

"Kind of," I replied. "This particular creature is known for its deceit and betrayal."

"How can a dragon be deceitful or betray someone?"

I shrugged. "How can a dragon do anything? They shouldn't even exist," I said.

"True." She looked thoughtful.

"I don't like beings that lie, steal, cheat, or are disloyal. Do you?" We were almost near the middle now. It was a large area with a few small trees and a fountain.

She glanced at me. "No, of course not."

"So then explain to me why you are lying about seeing a dragon." I studied her reaction.

Her eyes went wide. "I'm not lying. I saw something in the air."

"And yet when I gave you an important detail, like the black-tipped horns, you conveniently remembered it. One you didn't remember before." I crossed my arms.

"I remembered everything. I just got a little confused." She searched for the way out.

"So going by the description you gave me, you saw Turner flying over the town."

She blinked rapidly. "Turner? No, it was a dragon."

I laughed. "It was Turner's dragon form. Or did he not tell you about that part?"

She shook her head. "You're crazy."

"Am I?" I stepped closer. "You're the one claiming to see dragons in the sky."

She stepped back.

"Or did Turner tell you what to say you saw, and you really saw nothing?"

She looked panicked. "Listen, I don't want trouble. I was just trying to help."

"Help? Help who?" I narrowed my eyes at her.

"Turner. He said if I reported a dragon, it would help him win you back. It doesn't make any sense to me at all, but I figured I owed him that much since he's helped me with Conrad."

I nodded. "Yeah, that makes more sense."

I was relieved to know I wasn't losing my mind. I had used my camouflage as usual. No one saw me.

"Let me help you make some sense of it all." I stripped.

"What are you doing?" Her eyes were wide as she watched me undress.

"I'm going to show you what Turner wanted you to describe." I tossed my clothes to the side, and she covered her eyes.

"You're a lunatic," she muttered.

"No," I stated. "I'm a dragon." Then I shifted.

My vision cleared quickly, and I saw Kira fall to the ground, scooting backward as quickly as possible. I pushed my head forward, making sure she saw my eyes. I narrowed them at her, as I had when I was human.

She froze in terror, then screamed. "No, get away!"

I pushed my nuzzle up against her and shot out a breath of frosty air.

She screamed again, and I noticed ice crystals now covered her. I gave her one more good snort before I stepped away and shifted back into my human form.

I stood naked before her. "Now you know the truth. Are you prepared for Oliver to become one of us? He's half dragon, you know."

She continued to cower and shiver against one of the hedges. "What? What are you talking about?"

"You can see what I'm capable of, so I'd like to have an honest conversation, if you don't mind."

She nodded quickly, her eyes still wide with fear.

"Turner brought you here to reconcile with Conrad, correct?" I walked toward her, not caring I was nude.

"Y-y-yes," she stammered.

"Are you and Conrad married?" I watched her closely, trying to gauge any signs of a lie.

She hesitated.

"Answer me," I yelled.

"No!" she shouted. "No, we were never married."

I sighed, relief washing through me. "Is Oliver really his son?"

She shook her head, keeping her lips tightly pressed together.

"So why would you come all this way, to break up a perfectly happy engagement, with these lies?"

Her entire body shook in fear, and I squatted in front of her. "Would it make you feel better if I promised not to shift again?"

She nodded. "And maybe put on your clothes?"

I laughed. "Sure. But while I'm dressing, I expect a full explanation."

She nodded again.

I stepped away and grabbed my T-shirt, underwear, and jeans. "Talk."

"Turner found Oliver and me living in a rundown apartment in St. Louis. Somehow he'd known about my history with Conrad. At first I thought he was nuts, but the more he explained his idea, the better it sounded. He said if we'd come with him to this little town and go along with the story he'd concocted, he'd pay us ten thousand dollars. All we had to do was lie about Oliver's origins and a marriage."

I frowned. "Did he explain why he wanted you to do this?"

"He"—she took a deep breath—"he said that he was trying to save you. That you belonged with him, and Conrad had stolen you from him. He said that I'd be helping him, you, and myself by going along with it." She frowned. "I guess I figured the ten thousand was a nice start, but having Conrad back in our lives—someone to provide and protect Oliver and me—that would be icing on the cake, ya know?"

I stared at her.

She stood. "I'm so sorry, Jetta. I did not understand how deep this all went. How . . ." She fumbled for the right words. "How out of my element I was here."

I believed her. "You were manipulated by a master, Kira.

Turner's been lying and scheming as long as I've known him." I finished putting on my shoes. "Here's what I need you to do to make it right."

She nodded. "Anything."

"I need you to admit to Conrad that Oliver is not his. In return for telling the truth on this whole sham, I'll send you home with more money than Turner promised you. You'll be in good shape for a while." It'd take all I had left in savings since I no longer wanted to rely on my father's money or diamonds, but it'd be worth it to get her out of our hair once and for all.

"That's very kind of you," she said softly.

I moved to give her a hug, and she quickly stepped back.

"Kira, I may look like a monster when I've shifted, but I'm not even close. I promise. Turner is the monster here. The dragon with the black tips is actually what he looks like when he shifts." I laughed. "And Conrad . . . well, that guy is one scary looking dragon, although he's really a big softy."

"Conrad is . . ." She clasped a hand over her mouth, then let it drop. "Oh, that's what you meant by Oliver being half dragon." She blew out a shaky breath. "For once I'm actually glad he's not Conrad's son."

I nodded. "Yes, that's what I meant. But Conrad is much more badass than I or Turner look. We are frost dragons. Conrad is a lava dragon. He's black and red. Leathery wings and a mane of fire. He looks like something out of hell itself."

She looked ready to hurl. "Oh. My. Well, that's unexpected."

"Like I said, you tell the truth, I'll be sure you're well cared for." I gave her a genuine smile.

"I feel like an idiot for asking, but how do you know I'll keep this secret to myself? Do you trust me that much? Or is the money hush money?"

"It's a good question," I replied. "In a sense it is hush money, but it's also not. After you've left town, you'll forget all about us here. This town has a memory ward on it to keep its secrets. I'll leave you with a reasonable explanation for the money. One you and everyone you know will believe. And you and Oliver can go on living your lives as you did before, hopefully a little better off. It'll be like you'd never met Turner, or us."

She nodded. "Okay. I don't understand it, but I'm okay with that. I don't think I want to remember any of this."

I smiled. "Well then, shall we go unmask the criminal?"

She nodded. "Yes."

We made our way back to the house and found Turner sitting in the den. He and Oliver were playing video games.

"Hey, Oliver," Kira said. "Would you do me a favor and get my vitamins from our suitcase? I forgot to bring them down for lunch."

"Sure, Mom." He put down his controller and took off for the stairs.

"Good kid," I said.

She smiled. "Thanks. I'm very proud of him."

"Speaking of pride. I bet you're pretty damn proud of yourself, aren't you, Turner?" I turned my gaze on him.

He sat his controller on the table. "I'm not sure what you mean."

"I'm sure you do." I crossed my arms.

"You're not making sense, Jetta." He stood.

"Well, I just had a fun chat with Kira. She's confirmed some things I've suspected about you for years."

He looked at Kira, and his expression was murderous.

"How much did it cost you to get those documents and photos made?" I smiled as his glare intensified.

"You're crazy. Why would I do that?" He stepped forward, and Kira quickly moved behind me.

"Don't even think about it. She knows the truth about us. And I'll protect her and Oliver long before I'll ever stand up for you," I growled. "Until they go home, they are guests in this house. If anyone treats them with anything other than respect, they will answer to me."

Turner left the room without another word.

CHAPTER 12

On July seventeenth, just three days before the wedding, I walked down the hall of the second floor, looking over the list of tasks I'd yet to accomplish for the day. The wedding was creeping up on us, and I'd not had a lot of time to devote to preparing since Dad had fallen ill.

As I approached my father's room, I heard voices. Instead of going in, I felt this nagging urge to stand outside the door for just a moment. Turner was in there with my father. After learning the truth from Kira, he was the last person I wanted to see.

"Did you show her the paperwork?" I heard my father ask.

"I did, Mr. Mills. But she somehow dragged the truth out of Kira. That plan has failed." Turner's voice held a note of frustration.

"Did we not offer Kira enough money?" My dad's voice was strong and clear. He sounded nothing like the weak man I'd been treating for several days.

"She said it wasn't about the money." Turner chuckled. "Stupid bitch developed a conscience I guess."

"Humans," grumbled my father. "Those documents were expensive."

I couldn't believe what I heard. My own father was conspiring with Turner to destroy my relationship with Conrad. I guess it shouldn't have surprised me, considering he'd rather see me with Turner, but it still hurt.

"What do you want me to do now?"

"You'd better figure it out. You're not getting a dime of her inheritance unless you successfully get her away from that lava dragon," Dad growled.

I'd heard enough. I stepped through the door.

"I don't even know what to say." I glared at them both.

"Jetta, daughter." Dad held out a shaky hand.

"Don't you daughter me, you deceitful old coot." I turned my wrath on Turner. "And you."

He stood. "Now, Jetta, you need to understand the circumstances."

I stepped close and grabbed his shirt with both hands. "No, you understand this, you lying, manipulative son of a bitch. Don't you ever come near me, Conrad, or anyone else in my family again." I pulled him close where I could look into his eyes. "And if I find out you've bothered Kira or Oliver, I'll hunt you down and kill you." I felt my irises shift for just a moment.

He put his hands over mine, covering them. "Sweetheart, you know I'm the right man for you. And don't send threats my way. You may be older, but I'm every bit as dangerous as you are." He smirked.

"I can't take you by myself, but teamed up with Conrad, we could rip you to pieces and feed you to the vultures before you knew what hit you." It was my turn to smile. "Have you ever seen Conrad's dragon? It's not a sight for the faint of heart."

Turner narrowed his eyes at me and pulled my hands from his shirt. "Neither of you scare me."

I laughed. "Then you're dumber than I thought."

He straightened his shirt. "I'll talk to you soon, Lawrence." He moved to leave the room.

"No, you won't," I countered.

"I can talk to Turner if I want, Jetta Mills. Don't you dare dictate what can and can't happen in my own home," Lawrence growled.

I turned to face my father, who looked suspiciously healthy now. "Was this all your idea?"

He said nothing.

"That's what I thought." I stomped out of the room and pulled out my cell phone. I pushed the quick dial for Conrad.

"Hey, babe." He sounded tired.

"I need you here, now," I said softly.

"You at the mansion?" he asked.

"Yes." Emotion was choking my ability to speak. The betrayal I felt in that moment overshadowed anything I'd ever felt in my life.

"I'm on my way." Conrad hung up.

When Conrad pulled up the drive on his Harley, the sight before him had to be a shock. I was on the second floor, the balcony doors that led to Turner's room wide open, violently throwing my ex's belongings on the front lawn and landscaping.

Turner stood below, ducking the objects I tossed out. Every time I missed hitting him, I cursed.

"Jetta, stop this now. You're being immature," Turner yelled up at me.

I'd run out of objects I knew belonged to him, so I found other things to chuck at his head. I picked up an old nightstand. It was probably worth a fortune, but I didn't care. I stepped back out on the balcony.

"You wouldn't know mature if it bit you on the ass," I shouted, then threw the nightstand. He must have assumed I wouldn't throw anything else, because this time he was unprepared, and the nightstand hit him in the head.

"Yes!" I shouted as the satisfying sound of wood splintering filled the air.

"You bitch!" Turner yelled, holding one side of his head.

I heard another thud and looked down to see Conrad standing over Turner. "You don't talk to her that way. Ever. Now apologize."

Kira appeared next to me. "Would you like some heavier objects? I could look for cast-iron pans or something."

I smiled. "I'm beginning to like you, Kira Hubbard."

She shrugged. "I'm not a fan of Turner's, so I'm happy to help." Then she returned my devious smile.

I looked down and saw Conrad in Turner's face, but I couldn't hear what was being said. I recognized the posture Conrad had taken, and I knew things were about to get ugly. "Kira, if you have a morbid curiosity about what it looks like to see a frost dragon and lava dragon fight, stick around. Otherwise, I suggest you find Oliver and keep him far away from the front of the house."

Her eyes went wide as she gazed down at the two men on the lawn. "I should probably find Oliver."

I nodded. "Good idea. I'll find you when it's over."

She disappeared from the room and back down the hall. I glanced down again and saw the chaos begin. I ran as fast as I could, trying to make it down the stairs and out the front doors before the fighting really began.

Once I pushed open the front doors, I saw Turner's large tail swing at Conrad. He jumped, and Turner's tail took out one of the large stone planters in front of the steps. I hit the landing, trying to avoid any debris that flew overhead.

Conrad's body shook the ground as it landed in front of Turner. He was a beautiful specimen. His black leathery wings were outstretched, and the two spiral horns that adorned the top of his head were just as black and menacing. His eyes glowed red as he focused on his foe, lava dripping from his chin and forming a beard of sorts. The grass below Conrad's head caught fire every time he moved. I made a mental note to get those small fires put out before the entire place went up in flames. I grinned a moment. Our children would be an amazing and unique breed of dragon.

Turner got in a blow with one of his paws, leaving a large wound from his talons on Conrad's back leg. I would not stand by and watch Turner hurt anyone else I loved. I ran down the steps, shifting as I moved. By the time I reached them, I had fully transformed. I screamed at Turner, channeling all my rage in his direction. He heard me say "I will not tolerate your bullshit anymore." Anyone else who witnessed this battle would have heard a deep, rumbling growl that turned into a loud reptilian screech.

I'd distracted Turner just enough that Conrad could sink his teeth into Turner's shoulder. A deafening howl escaped as he shoved himself away from us both.

"This isn't over," Turner screamed as he took flight and his camouflage kicked in.

"Coward!" I shouted. "You're running away again."

We watched the faint outline of Turner disappear into the sky. I turned and focused my attention on Conrad's wound. His back leg was bleeding.

He nudged me. "I'll be okay. It'll heal soon. If it hurts too much, we'll have Zoey come cry over her favorite uncle."

I rolled my huge eyes at him. "Just because her tears can heal you doesn't mean she should. You might deserve to suffer a little."

"I wasn't gonna sit back and listen to him insult you." He pushed his head to mine.

I nudged him back. "I know. And it's one of the many reasons I love you."

I stepped back and allowed myself to envision my human form. Once the transformation was complete, I looked around for something to cover myself with. Conrad was in the same position. We'd shifted without undressing, and now we were nude.

My father stepped out the front doors, his cane clicking on the stone. "You've destroyed my front yard." He frowned. "Put some clothes on. I do not want to see that."

Conrad grabbed a spare T-shirt from his saddlebag on the bike and handed it to me.

"I have clothes upstairs," I said.

"Use it until you get those, then I'll take it back." He turned and dug through his saddlebags again. This time pulling out a pair of chaps.

I laughed. "Is that all you've got in there? One T-shirt and a pair of assless chaps?"

He shrugged. "It appears I do. I guess it's better than nothing."

I shook my head. "Not really. The best parts are still exposed."

He looked down and chuckled. "It appears you are correct."

I cocked my head sideways and looked him over. "While I don't mind the view, we do still have a young lady and her impressionable son in the house. You'll need something better to cover up with."

He looked up at me. "Are you saying my manliness might intimidate them?"

I'd just pulled his T-shirt over my head. "No, that's not what I'm saying. But if it makes you feel better, you can believe that."

He stepped closer and pulled me toward him. "You've never complained."

I patted his cheek. "And I never will."

He kissed me. "Good. Now go find me some pants so I don't give that young man a complex about his anatomy."

I pushed him away. "So cocky."

He smirked. "That's what I was talking about."

I laughed as I passed my father and went back inside. He'd have to be happy with a pair of my sweatpants. It's not like he hadn't had to wear them before. The first time was when he'd shifted after regaining his memories, and I thought he'd looked dashing in my pink sweats that barely reached his knees.

My father followed me. "Jetta, we need to discuss what just happened."

I turned to face him. "Which part? The torn-up yard? The full-on dragon battle that thankfully no one was around to see? Or wait . . . maybe you mean the part where you promised my inheritance to the most despicable man I've ever met, present company excluded."

"I did it for you," he bellowed.

"So you keep saying." I clenched my fist, doing my best to

remain calm. "Every time you do something horrible to one of us, you follow it up with that excuse. You made Tristan so miserable, he ran off with his new wife almost two decades ago. You belittled me when you thought I was pregnant and Turner abandoned me. You gave me a hard time every time I wanted to learn about my birth parents. You finally meet your granddaughter Zoey and you try to destroy her relationship with Jordan." I glared at him. "Why is it every time you decide tough love is necessary, lots of people get hurt?"

He huffed. "I do what I think is best."

"No, you do what you want and to hell with everyone else." I jabbed an accusatory finger at him.

"Don't point that finger at me," he shouted.

I turned my hand, palm now facing me, and raised my middle finger. "How about this one?"

His face turned red, and I was sure he would have an aneurism.

"You were never as sick as you claimed, were you?" I put my hands on my hips.

He looked a little guilty.

"You faked the worst part of your illness to get Turner and me in the same house. You used my love for you as a chess piece. That's pretty low, even for you." I shook my head. "If you want to attend my wedding, then show up. If not, I don't care. But we are no longer having it here."

His bushy white brows drew together. "Don't be an idiot."

"I'm making the smartest decision I've made since I agreed to marry Conrad. The wedding will be where I want it, and you are not walking me down the aisle. That's an honor reserved for real fathers. You don't measure up."

He stared at me, but didn't say a word. I could see the anger in his eyes. But I knew it wasn't anger because I'd cut him out of the wedding. It was anger that the wedding to Conrad was still on.

CHAPTER 13

*W*e moved the wedding to Havenwood Falls Christian Church. I stood in one of the small classrooms and looked at my reflection in a full-length mirror. It was a weird sensation, seeing myself dressed for my own wedding. I never expected to get married. Turner had ruined that dream for me. But there I was, preparing to say I do to the most amazing man I'd ever met.

I turned sideways to view the way the black-laced veil draped down my back. I smiled. The skull-themed lace was my favorite part of the ensemble. The back of the dress was low cut and open except for the part that crossed my shoulder blades and wrapped around the front of my biceps to meet the rest of the material on my sleeves. My shoulders were bare, with the lace on the front of the dress moving up my chest in a triangular pattern until it reached my neck in a choker-style fashion. The hem was now just above the knee and would likely throw my father into a fit of apoplexy, if he bothered to show.

This dress was perfect. It was me. And I knew Conrad would love it too.

Bianca walked in and smiled. "You look gorgeous. I wasn't too sure about your plans for this dress, but I never should have doubted you. It's perfect."

"I was just thinking the same thing." I grinned at her.

She handed me a bouquet of red roses with black tips.

"I love this. I love all of this." I inhaled the scent of the roses and closed my eyes.

Bianca had tears in her eyes. "You deserve this wonderful day of happiness. And the lifetime you'll share afterward."

I pulled her in for a hug, careful not to crush my bouquet. "I couldn't have asked for a better wedding planner. Or a better sister-in-law."

She pulled back and looked at me. "Ditto on the sister-in-law thing."

A knock at the door caused both of us to turn our heads.

"Come in," I said.

Zoey poked her head through the door. "Um . . . we have a minor issue."

My eyebrows rose in surprise. "Minor?"

"Okay, it's a little bigger than minor." She frowned as she entered and shut the door behind her.

I gently placed the flowers on the table near the window.

"What happened?" I crossed my arms and braced myself for the worst.

"Well, you see . . . um . . . Conrad was standing near the candelabras and one must have been unsteady. It wobbled and then fell on him." She fidgeted.

"Is he hurt?" It felt like a silly question considering how quickly we usually healed, and that he's a lava dragon, but I felt the urge to ask.

"No, he's fine. Now. But . . ." Her words trailed off.

"But?" I sighed.

"Well, Conrad's suit wasn't so lucky." Zoey's face scrunched up in concern.

Bianca interrupted. "How bad is it?"

"The entire backside of his suit burnt up. There's not much left." She cringed as if waiting for a verbal assault.

I turned to look at Bianca, my face void of expression. "Of course it did. It appears he's destined to wear assless pants."

"What?" She shook her head. "Never mind. Don't worry. We'll figure it out. You just relax. I'll go take care of it." She hurried out the door.

"I'm so sorry, Aunt Jetta." Poor Zoey looked ready to cry.

"Aww, it wasn't your fault, sweetie. Stuff happens. It'll be fine." I attempted a reassuring smile, hoping I'd feel comfort in the process. It didn't work.

Zoey nodded. "I know, but I wanted today to be perfect for you. I chose the candelabras. If they weren't in the sanctuary, this wouldn't have happened."

"It'll be fine, kiddo. Don't worry about it. I love the candelabras."

She smiled through her tears. "Really?"

"Absolutely. I couldn't imagine the ceremony without them." It was mostly true. "Now, wipe your eyes and go see if your mom needs any help. We got this."

She nodded and promptly left me to my own thoughts. "Well," I muttered to myself, "if this is the worst that happens, I'll consider myself lucky."

I straightened my spine and stepped out into the hallway. I needed air. My nerves were getting the better of me. The sounds of upset voices floated from a room off to the side of the sanctuary, so I followed the commotion to see what was happening now.

My brother stood next to a confused-looking Seth Cooper from Daily Knead. "No, that is not what we ordered."

"Dude, I didn't make it. I'm just delivering it." Seth's amber eyes shifted from the object next to him and Tristan.

"I know. It's not your fault. I'm in shock about . . . this." Tristan gestured to something I couldn't see from my vantage point.

I walked toward them, wondering what I was in for now.

"I'm really sorry. I don't know how this happened." The teen was looking frustrated.

I rounded the corner and froze. The three-tier somewhat traditional cake I was expecting to see was instead a large, three-dimensional penis-shaped cake.

"What the fuck?" I asked as I stepped forward.

Tristan shook his head. "I don't know what happened. This certainly isn't what we ordered."

Seth glanced back down at the slip of paper in his hand, his dark hair peeking out from under his hoodie. "It says right here . . ." His eyes went wide. "Crap. I bet this was supposed to go to a different address."

"I'm guessing you're correct." I frowned.

"I'm so sorry. I must have delivered your cake to that other party instead." He scratched his head. "I took them to the right places, but somehow the addresses must have gotten mixed up."

Tristan crossed his arms. "What other party?"

"It was a bunch of older ladies. I think they were having one of those adult toy parties." He frowned. "I remember seeing a table with fuzzy handcuffs and other weird stuff."

I put my head into my hands and groaned.

"Is it possible to make a trade? We need that cake." Tristan's voice held a note of frustration.

"Yeah, I think so. Let me make a call." He stepped outside with his cell phone in hand.

I looked at Tristan. "What in the hell is happening here? Conrad's suit, now this?"

His frown deepened. "What happened to Conrad's suit?"

I shook my head. "Ask Zoey or Conrad. I didn't witness it."

Seth stepped back into the sanctuary a moment later. "I'm so sorry. Mrs. Preston said they opened the box, and her chihuahua saw the crow topper. He must have thought it was real, because he attacked it. The cake is now all over her living room, and her dog."

Tristan closed his eyes. "Oh, God."

"I can't deal with this," I muttered. "I'm going outside."

"Thanks anyway, Seth." Tristan slipped him a tip.

I stomped out the front doors, walked into the church's small flower garden, and sat on the stone bench. Breathing slowly, I brought my emotions under control.

"What's wrong, girl?" My father's voice interrupted my meditation.

I opened my eyes to see him standing in front of me, leaning on this cane. I looked up into his face. "Nothing concerning you."

He shifted his weight to the other leg. "Maybe I can help."

I laughed. "What in the ever-loving hell makes you think I'd want any help you can give? You've done nothing but sabotage this wedding from the beginning."

His bushy white eyebrows drew together. "I'm just looking out for you, Jetta."

I shook my head and felt tears trail down my cheeks. "Why?"

"Why what?" He sat down beside me and stretched his long, slender legs in front of him.

"Why have I never been good enough for you?" The question surprised me as much as it did him.

He opened his mouth to answer, then promptly closed it again.

"You don't even know, do you?" I wiped the tears from my cheeks. "All these years you've badgered me and talked down to me, and you don't even know why."

He cleared his throat. "I know why."

I turned on the bench to face him more. "Enlighten me."

"You've had everything handed to you on a silver platter. Then you decided that despite all I'd done for you, you needed to know who your real parents were."

"Why is that such a bad thing? Wouldn't you want to know?" I did not understand his reasoning at all.

"Maybe. Maybe not." He sat up a little straighter. "Not if I already had a perfectly good family," he corrected himself.

"I had no mother, a cranky father, and a mostly absent brother. I was often expected to fend for myself. How is that a good family?"

He bristled at my accusation. "Many have it worse. And you have other flaws, you know."

"What would those be?" I crossed my arms and glared at him.

"You had everything, including a mate who loved you and was a perfect fit for our family, and you ran him off!"

"I ran him . . ." I shook my head. "You have no fucking clue what really happened that day. None. You're only going off of the rumors you heard."

He growled. "I am not."

"Oh, really?" I asked. "So who gave you proof of my sins? Because it wasn't me. You never once asked me if I was okay or what happened. The only other person who could have given you firsthand information is Turner, and if he said I was the problem, he's lying."

"I haven't spoken to Turner until recently. But he said that you cheated on him and that's why he left town."

I stood, my limbs trembling from anger. "That's total bullshit. He was the one who cheated. And when I confronted him and tried to get an explanation, he skipped town. For twenty damn years. He's a coward."

He stood to face me. "It doesn't matter. You've done nothing but make a spectacle of yourself and smeared our family name since he left. I'm tired of cleaning up your messes, Jetta."

I stared at him for a moment before replying. "Well, that's not an issue you'll need to worry about anymore."

He raised one eyebrow at me. "And why is that?"

"Because my last name will soon be Monroe," I countered.

"So you'll ruin his name instead?" His words felt like a slap, but I knew it wasn't true. Conrad and I were a team. Anything that happened, good or bad, we were in this together.

"If you want to believe that, then go right ahead. But Conrad loves me, unlike you. He wants to help me and be by my side even when things get rough. All you've ever done is make matters worse. So consider this my withdrawal from the Mills family. I owe you nothing, and you owe me nothing. I will no longer be calling you father, and I'd appreciate it if you would refrain from calling me daughter."

His pale green eyes changed to a vivid emerald as his temper flared. "It doesn't work that way."

"It does now." I turned my back to him and reentered the church.

I marched back to the little room where I'd gotten dressed and slammed the door. I noticed my flowers had disappeared when I glanced at the table by the window. I searched the room but couldn't find them. Perfect.

Zoey knocked on the door and stepped inside before I answered. "Mom hasn't figured out the suit yet, but she will. Guests will arrive any moment."

I nodded. "Do you have any idea what happened to my bouquet?"

I pointed to the empty side table.

She shrugged. "No clue. I haven't seen them, so I don't know what they even look like. That was Mom's department."

"They were red roses with black tips."

"I'll go look for them." She put her hand on the doorknob. "Do you need anything else? You seem pretty calm considering the goof-ups."

It was my turn to shrug. "I'm dealing."

"Are you really okay? You seem . . . kinda sad."

"I am, kiddo, but it has nothing to do with the wedding. It'll be fine. Go find those flowers for me, okay?"

"Okay. I love you, Aunt Jetta. If you need me, I'm here." She approached quickly and wrapped her arms around me.

I hugged her back. "I love you too."

Zoey slipped out of the door, and I took a cleansing breath.

"What else could go wrong?" I whispered to myself.

I shouldn't have asked.

CHAPTER 14

Our wedding march began. It was an original instrumental I'd written and recorded myself. I peeked into the sanctuary. The church was full. I saw the faces of many of our friends in the community. Next to where my family would be seated sat our friends Addie Beaumont, Sindi Scott, Micheala Petran, Xandru Roca, and his brother Tase. On another bench I recognized Sedona Mathews, Micah Westbrook, Ryker Pride, and Harlow Augustine. I couldn't help but smile when I saw Conrad's biker friend Colton Shaw sitting on the same pew as my coworkers Simon and Maris, with Cameron DeSalle and Mavis LeGrand just another row back. Even my now ex-father was there near the front, which surprised the hell out of me after the conversation we'd had earlier. However, he hadn't queued up to walk me down the aisle. That was preferable. I didn't want him taking any part in what should be the happiest day of my life.

I still didn't have a bouquet, but that wasn't an important detail. I glanced toward the front and noticed that Conrad wasn't waiting up front. The butterflies in my stomach revolted. Where was he? Had he changed his mind?

I stepped back and noticed Bianca moving toward me swiftly, a cell phone in her hand. "It's for you."

I put the phone up to my ear. "Hello?"

"Hey, babe." Conrad's voice sounded frustrated.

"Hey, where are you?" The urgency in my voice was stronger than I'd intended.

"Sorry, I've been all over trying to find another suit. So far no luck." He sighed. "Nothing like what I had, anyway. Too last minute I guess."

"I don't care. Just get back here. We'll get married in our underwear if that's what it takes." I meant it. I was ready to do this and was tiring of all the distractions.

"Okay, I'll be there in a few minutes." He paused. "Are you sure?"

"Absolutely. Get your ass over here so I can make you miserable for eternity."

He laughed. "I'm so looking forward to eternity."

"Me too," I said, softening my tone.

"See you soon." He hung up.

I handed the phone back to Bianca. "He's on his way."

"No luck on the suit?" she asked.

I shook my head. "Doesn't matter. Anything will work."

She nodded, understanding I was ready to get this done.

Bianca pulled a Kleenex and mirror from her purse. "Here. You've got some tiny smudges under your eyes from your mascara."

I accepted both items and worked on making my eye makeup presentable again. It was obvious I'd been crying earlier, but I was thankful she didn't ask about it.

Conrad pulled up moments later and walked through the front doors. He was wearing black jeans and a white dress shirt. He stopped and stared at me. "You look amazing."

I smiled at him. "Thank you."

He glanced down at his own clothing. "I look very unworthy of you."

I stepped closer to him. "You look like everything I've ever wanted. Let's get married."

He looked at Bianca. "Is it against tradition if I kiss her now?"

She shrugged. "Like anything you two have done so far has been traditional."

I smirked. "Wait until he sees our wedding cake."

Bianca coughed.

"What about the cake?" His eyebrows drew together in concern.

"Just wait and see." I laughed.

Bianca pushed Conrad through the side door. "Go. Get in your place up front so we can start this thing."

He glanced at me one more time before obeying Bianca's order.

I handed the mirror back to her. "Better?" I asked.

She nodded.

Zoey came through the doors at that moment with an oversized bouquet of skinny purple flowers. "Aunt Jetta, will these work?"

"They sure will. Where did you find them?" I asked.

"Miranda saw them behind the church. There's a lot of them growing wild back there. She picked them and arranged them for you." She held them out.

I noticed they'd tied them together with the black ribbon that Zoey had worn in her hair earlier. "Thank you. I love them."

The wedding march began again, and I held them in front of me, as I would have my original bouquet.

Bianca and Zoey hurried to find their seats.

After a few beats, I pushed open the double doors and started down the aisle. Our guests stood and turned toward me. Most of them smiled. A few stood with their mouths hanging open. I assumed it was because of my dress choice.

Conrad stood up front, looking as handsome as ever. In that moment I didn't know why we'd worried about a suit. He looked amazing in anything he wore.

I made it to the front of the church without incident and breathed a sigh of relief. At least that had gone correctly.

Pastor Leandros smiled at us before addressing our guests. "Everyone please be seated."

Conrad and I faced each other and smiled. When I looked into his eyes, all my fears for the future disappeared. I knew I was doing the right thing.

"Jetta and Conrad have asked for a slightly different type of ceremony. While I would normally give a short talk about the sanctity of marriage, we will forgo that part today and go straight to the vows, which they have written themselves." He addressed Conrad. "We'll let the groom go first."

Conrad took my right hand in his while my left clutched the flowers. "Jetta, before I met you, my life had no purpose. I was wandering lost and alone. Odd circumstances brought us together, but I believe it was meant to be. I was born to be the man who stands before you now. To love you for eternity, and longer if possible. I vow to be by your side, no matter what happens. And to devote my life to making you happy."

I squeezed his hand.

"I object!" a loud voice sounded from the back of the church.

I closed my eyes, knowing who the voice belonged to. I was going to kill him.

"I didn't ask for objections," Pastor Leandros said. It was obvious this interruption surprised him.

"I still object," he shouted as he started down the aisle towards us.

I turned to glare at Turner. "Go away."

Conrad tensed up, and I knew he was ready to shift and destroy Turner, screw the consequences of doing such a thing in front of everyone.

I looked at him and handed him my flowers. "I've got this."

I faced Turner once more.

"You are supposed to be *my* wife. Conrad is a criminal and an imposter to our kind. He should be jailed!" Turner had almost reached the spot where we stood.

I took a few steps down the aisle to meet Turner. I could feel all eyes on me as I approached the man who'd left my reputation in tatters twenty years ago. I reached up and smiled, putting my hands on either side of his face.

"Dear Turner," I whispered.

He put a hand over one of mine and stared into my eyes.

I swiftly brought my knee to his groin, and he doubled over.

"I've told you more than once I never wanted to see you again. Is your brain so fried you can't comprehend that?" I asked loudly.

He tried to breathe through the pain, then attempted to speak. "You don't mean that. You love me. You need me." He stood again, although slightly hunched.

"What I need is this, and it's long overdue." I cocked my arm back, then brought it forward with all my strength. My fist connected with his face, and he went down like a sack of potatoes.

I shook my hand out a moment to relieve the sting in my knuckles. Turner was out cold in the middle of the aisle. I stepped back into place next to Conrad. "Let's continue."

Pastor Leandros looked concerned, but like a trooper, he tried to move past the moment and the fact that he had an unconscious man in the middle of his church. "Jetta, your vows."

I nodded and cleared my throat, then flashed my future husband a smile. "Conrad, you are the light that shines in the darkness. My smile when I fear I have no hope of finding joy. I give you myself—mind, body, heart, and soul for all time."

I felt a buzzing at my ear, and I absently waved it away.

"I vow to—" More buzzing and a pinching pain. "Ow!"

I glanced down to see a swarm of bees buzzing within my bouquet.

"You have got to be shitting me," I said as I dropped the bouquet.

Several more bees flew out, and for a moment, my mind envisioned a tiny bee-sized clown car with them piling out like a damn circus act. We heard a scream, then several people ran from the church as bees dive-bombed our guests.

The pastor ran out as well, yelling his apologies and that he was allergic to bees.

I stood in front, Conrad's hand in mine, as the church emptied of everyone but a still unconscious Turner.

Conrad's eyes met mine, and we both laughed at the same time. It wasn't really that funny, but somehow it seemed like the next logical step in the day's events.

He pulled me close and kissed me. "I now pronounce us man and wife."

He kissed me again. I threaded my fingers through his hair as he deepened the kiss. It was several moments before we separated.

"Should we go to the reception?" He chuckled.

I smiled knowingly as we started our walk back down the aisle arm in arm. "Oh yes, we should. Have you ever seen a three-foot dick before?"

He stumbled over his own feet.

CHAPTER 15

*W*e caught up with the pastor and got the marriage certificate signed to make everything official, then we met everyone in the small church gym for the reception we'd planned. After all we'd been through to get to this moment, I was kind of looking forward to seeing Conrad's face when he saw the cake.

We stepped into the room, and cheers and clapping boomed around us. Conrad smiled and pulled me close.

"We missed the kiss!" someone yelled.

Conrad pointed toward the back of the room. "Watch closely. You might learn something."

Then he tipped me backward and planted a kiss on me that would melt the sun. When we came up for air, I was just a bit lightheaded.

More cheers and a few wolf whistles continued.

Conrad looked at me, his eyes intense as he studied my face. "Mrs. Monroe, would you be opposed to repeating that kiss if we get further requests?"

Mrs. Monroe. I loved how it sounded. "I have no objections, Mr. Monroe."

Bianca came toward us with a look of purpose plastered to her face. I could tell she was on a mission and it involved us. "Time to cut the cake."

She shooed us toward the reception table. My eyes scanned the table for the monstrosity that would now be a part of our wedding memories forever. Disappointment hit me when I realized it wasn't there.

I leaned into Bianca. "Where is the cake?" I whispered.

She smiled at me. "It's right there."

I looked down to see two odd-shaped circles side by side. She had smoothed over the icing in the places where it had been modified. Someone had placed two plastic gold rings on top as a replacement for our crow that Mrs. Preston's dog destroyed earlier in the day.

I put my hand over my mouth, trying to hold in the laughter.

Bianca's face went from proud to concerned. "I thought I'd fixed the situation. Do you hate it?"

I couldn't hold it in any longer. I was laughing so hard I almost couldn't breathe. She put her hand on my back. "Are you okay?"

I nodded furiously, trying to relieve her discomfort.

Conrad put his arm around me and whispered in my ear. "What am I missing here?"

I snickered again.

"Let me in on the joke," Conrad hissed.

I nodded. "Let's do the toast and cut the cake, then I'll tell you."

He shrugged. "Okay." He picked up his champagne flute and tapped a spoon against the side, gaining everyone's attention. "I'd like to make a toast. To my beautiful wife. I'm the luckiest man on earth."

Everyone raised their glasses in agreement, and I smiled at all the faces I loved so much. I leaned in to Bianca. "Tell Tristan he can still do his official toast once we pass the cake around."

She nodded, then handed me the cake knife. Conrad and I both placed our fingers around the handle and made a small slice in one side. He raised one small bite and kindly, delicately put the cake in my mouth. I once again had to fight back giggles.

I took the remnants of that slice and gently fed it to him. Cameras flashed as we followed the old tradition so many couples had repeated for decades before us.

Bianca and Zoey gathered plates as I pulled Conrad to one side.

"Take a good look at that cake." I snickered.

He looked it over as they cut it into small slices. "Yeah, so?"

"That's the base of what used to be a very large penis shaped cake. I sort of mentioned it earlier."

He made a confused face, then realization dawned on him. "Our wedding cake is a pair of balls."

I laughed again.

He looked at the golden rings and said, "Oh, God."

We both were still laughing when Tristan began his best-man toast.

Later that night, as we lay wrapped in each other's arms, we discussed our favorite parts of the ceremony.

"Obviously," Conrad said, "the kiss was the best part."

I nodded. "Yeah, that was pretty hot."

He chuckled. "The rest was . . . unique."

"No shit," I said. "But you know what I really can't wait for?"

He turned to face me, pushing a stray hair behind my ear. "What's that?"

I once again fought back laughter. "When our kids are old enough to hear about the testicle cake with the cock rings."

Conrad howled with laughter. "Will they ever be old enough for that story?"

I smiled and pulled him to me for a kiss. "They will if we get started on our family right away."

His smile went from joyous to something more heated. "I'm more than happy to go along with that plan."

"As I said before, you're sexy when you bend to my will."

He rolled me where I sat straddled on top of him. "Then I plan to be sexy to you until the end of time."

And I had no doubt he'd follow through on that promise.

~

You might also enjoy Amy's other stories in the Havenwood Falls universe, about the Mills dragon shifters and their friends:

Somewhere Within
Flames Among the Frost
Blood & Iron
Betrayal Among the Frost

ABOUT THE AUTHOR

Since childhood, best-selling and award-winning author Amy Hale has been creating exceptional stories that summon a whirlwind of emotions and inspiration unto the reader. She loves creating characters and worlds from nothing but her imagination and a few glasses of wine. Her popular paranormal series The Shadows Trilogy has earned multiple awards, as have the Havenwood Falls books, in which she is a participating author. Her love of the written word has not only resulted in her writing some of her readers' favorite adventures, but has also manifested itself in the form of some seriously overloaded bookshelves. She's convinced it's not a sickness.

She debuted her first fiction novel in 2015 after retiring from thirteen years of nonfiction writing for various online entities. For the last couple of decades, she's also carried the titles of Laundry Goddess, Chef, Butt Wiper, Soother of Temper Tantrums, and in more recent years, Moderator of Sarcastic Eye-rolls and Sass. She resides in Illinois with her husband and two grown children, who claim they are never moving out. Regardless, they are the center of her universe, although her cat believes otherwise.

If she had any spare time, she'd love music, photography, watching Mystery Science Theater 3000 with her family, and long rides on the back of her husband's motorcycle.

ACKNOWLEDGMENTS

I don't know that my words can do justice to all those I have to thank for their help with this book. I work with an amazing team and am inspired daily by so many of the people in my life. Each person brings special meaning to the process as well as to my personal and professional growth. I'll do my best to name everyone, but if I miss someone please know it was unintentional and I adore you all.

I always have to start with my thanks to God and to my amazing husband John. Both keep me steady and pushing forward when I want to give up. Life can be hard at times, but it's bearable when you have those who love you helping you stand tall. My faith gives me strength. My husband gives me support unlike I've ever known. I love you John!

My grown children don't see me a lot when I'm in the depths of my own stories, but I appreciate their love, help, and patience while I work it all out. I am truly blessed by your presence in my life. I love you, Matt and Rachel!

This book would be nothing without the professional eyes of my editors Kristie Cook and Liz Ferry. You ladies wipe the mud off so we can see the beautiful, shiny chrome beneath. (Motorcycle metaphor for the win.) Thank you for your faith in my words.

Regina Wamba has once again rocked an amazing book cover. I bow at the feet of a true master. Thank you for giving my story a beautiful presentation.

I want to thank all my Havenwood Falls family for their generous lending of their characters. Jetta and Conrad are fun, but they need their community too! Thank you all for allowing your fascinating characters come play in this book.

A special thanks to my beta readers and my reader group Hale's Angels. Without you all I might still be wondering about specific parts of this story. Thank you so much for your amazing feedback!

As always, thank you, dearest reader, for giving my work and our world of Havenwood Falls a chance to entertain and thrill you. I pray this book met your every expectation.

FOREVER LOYAL

E.J. FECHENDA

HAVENWOOD FALLS

FOREVER LOYAL

E.J. FECHENDA

BOOKS BY E.J. FECHENDA

The New Mafia Trilogy

The Beautiful People

Clean Slate

Endings & Beginnings

Enforcer (a prequel novella)

The Ghost Stories Trilogy

End of the Road

Havoc

The Triangle (Coming Soon)

Havenwood Falls

Fate, Love & Loyalty

Forever Loyal

Havenwood Falls High

Fata Morgana

Legends of Havenwood Falls

Fated Beginnings

Havenwood Falls Sin & Silk

Stray With Me

Sun & Moon Academy

Book One: Fall Semester

For the Havenwood Falls fandom—you inspire me with your enthusiasm and love for this magical world.

CHAPTER 1

*A*ster stared at the note in her hand, with its bent edges and worn corners from repeatedly being touched. A photo album lay open on her lap, revealing happy images of a family she didn't remember. The only person she recognized was her sister Reeve, who was currently sitting next to her on the sofa. Aster tucked a stray hair behind her ear and read the note again, even though she'd known the words by heart for almost two years now.

Our Darling Daughters,

Your memories of us will fade, but know that our thoughts are constantly of you, for we remember. We can't explain why, but know that when we are finally allowed to, we will come for you. You were banished from our lives through no fault of your own but by laws established to protect the lives of many. The laws are tough but they have their purpose. This album is a touchstone and a way to keep our faces as part of your recollection.

Please know you are loved and you aren't forgotten. Love each other—always.

Love,
Mom & Dad

Aster traced the loops on the cursive "L" and peered at the family portrait. She and her sister, Reeve, sat in the front next to a guy who apparently was their brother, Braden, based on the handwritten caption below the picture. The resemblance was there —they all had varying shades of red hair. Reeve's and Braden's were more auburn, while Aster's had an orange gold hue. Their alleged parents stood behind them. Aster could see glimpses of herself in the mother's features: the straight nose, sharp cheekbones, and clear green eyes. Reeve had inherited her heart-shaped face and the auburn hair. Sometimes it was like looking at a catalogue of strangers, but not all the time.

"Every once in a while I'll feel this tug, like something is familiar, or a smell will resonate deeper and starts to call up a memory, but it never surfaces," Aster said, looking at her sister. "Does that ever happen to you?"

Reeve nodded and plucked her breast free of her daughter's mouth. Mina had fallen asleep while feeding, her eyelids fluttering as she slipped into dreams.

"I wish we knew more. The not knowing and the mystery of it all frustrates the hell out of me. What happened? Why can't we remember anything?" Reeve set her infant down on the middle cushion between her and Aster, placing a throw pillow on the outside, toward the edge, to keep the baby from rolling over and onto the floor.

"I don't know," Aster said with a sigh and tucked the note back into the photo album before closing it. She set it on the coffee table in front of her before gently caressing her niece's chunky cheek. "At least we have each other and the den. We're our own family now."

"Damn straight. You're stuck with me." With a yawn, Reeve stood up and stretched before disappearing into the kitchen. She returned moments later with a plate of brownies and two glasses of milk. "Alice dropped these off earlier. I was going to wait until Patrick came home, but who knows how long the guys will be gone."

Reeve's mate, Patrick, was beta of the Denver den of mountain lions. Aster's mate, Gage, was the alpha. The previous alpha, Damian Stone, had been part of a purist sect that had been growing within the den. He hadn't believed in interspecies breeding. Mountain lion shifters were becoming scarcer. Determined to create a dominant line, Damian believed that the offspring of an alpha and the daughters of other alphas would ensure the survival of the species. Reeve had been abducted by Damian, yet she escaped. That was where her recollection grew hazy. For Gage, too. He had been Damian's beta at the time. When he learned of the breeding house, where Damian kept a half dozen daughters of alphas captive as his personal breeding harem, Gage went after Damian, who was tracking an escapee: Reeve.

Gage remembers killing Damian in a vicious battle, just not where. Aster returned to Denver with her mate. Reeve and Patrick had come with them, too. Damian's corpse had arrived ahead of them, and he was laid to rest. His funeral turned into a ceremony where Gage assumed leadership.

It had been almost two years since Gage became alpha, and every day had been a battle to remove the members who were purists and had been poisoned by Damian's rhetoric.

Aster and Reeve spent many a night together while their mates were off dealing with issues. This was one of those nights. They put on a movie and ate brownies until Aster could barely keep her eyes open. Reeve tucked Mina into her crib, and the sisters called it a night.

Aster sluggishly made her way to the guest bedroom. Her legs felt like they were made of liquid concrete, each step a struggle. The room spun as she collapsed onto the bed. Awareness that something was wrong briefly flared right before sleep dragged her under—a warm, dark blanket snuffing out any thought.

She awoke the next morning, struggling to regain consciousness as Reeve's screams ricocheted through the townhouse, bouncing off every wall. Following the cries, Aster stumbled into the nursery to find her sister on her knees before the crib, hysterical and inconsolable. The crib was empty. Mina was gone.

CHAPTER 2

*M*ike McCabe's cell phone only rang once before he snatched it off his desk and answered.

"Ryker, how are my girls?" he asked. In addition to working for Mike at McCabe & Sons Construction, Ryker Pride was a member of the SIN motorcycle club, and occasionally he had to do runs to Denver for the MC. When Ryker made these trips, Mike asked him to check in on Aster and Reeve from a distance, since he couldn't do it himself or he'd be at risk of violating the terms of their punishment. The Court of the Sun and the Moon, the governing body of the supernatural community that lived in Havenwood Falls, had ruled that Aster be banished for two years, and sadly, Reeve had been permanently banned from town. They had shifted in public, fought in public, and Reeve had exposed the town to outside danger. The laws were harsh and the punishments severe, but they had kept Havenwood Falls a haven for supernaturals for close to two hundred years, unbeknownst to their human neighbors.

"Not good, Big Mike. Some serious shit has gone down."

Mike's hand clenched tightly around the phone as fear gripped his heart. "What happened?"

Mike listened impatiently as Ryker told him he had been working out at the Sweat Box, the gym Aster's mate owned, when he overheard two members of the Denver den talking. "Apparently your granddaughter has been abducted. Right out of Reeve and Patrick's house. Your girls were drugged. This wasn't a random kidnapping but planned."

"Fuck!" Mike slammed his fist into his desk, causing the wood to split along the grain and a pen holder to tip over, spilling pens and pencils onto the floor.

"Do you want me to do anything?" Ryker asked, his voice sounding distant, like he was underwater, as blood roared through Mike's ears. Mike looked at the calendar on the wall next to his desk and at the date circled. Only eight days remained before Aster's two-year banishment period was over. He planned on going to her then. If he approached her earlier, the consequences would be severe. Now that his granddaughter was missing, that week seemed like a lifetime.

"Stay there. I need eyes on the situation. I'll get there as soon as I can—I just need to make some arrangements." Mike ended the call. He ran a hand through his thick graying brown hair as he gathered his thoughts and prepared himself for what he needed to do. It was time to visit the Court, to beg and grovel. A child's life now hung in the balance.

Mike drove home, navigating through the winding streets of Creekwood Estates, the development his father had built. A red Land Rover was parked in the driveway, letting him know his wife, Anne, was home. She had been in the office earlier to process payroll but left at lunchtime to babysit their grandson and give their daughter-in-law a much-needed break. Jacob was five years old now and would be starting kindergarten in the fall. Until then, Kaitlyn relied on family for child care.

The house was quiet when he entered into the kitchen through the attached garage. The twins, Roxy and Remy, whom Mike and Anne had adopted, weren't home. Roxy was most likely working at Coffee Haven. Hopefully Remy was at summer school and not goofing off, or he was going to be held back a year. For being twins, they couldn't have been more opposite of each other. Their adjustment to structure at the McCabes' house and life in Havenwood Falls had been full of learning curves, and where Remy was concerned, a source of extra gray hair.

A loud squeal of laughter drew Mike's attention to the wall of windows that overlooked the backyard. Out there he saw his wife playing soccer with their grandson, who resembled his father more and more. Mike swallowed past the lump in his throat as he remembered Braden, his firstborn and only son. Braden was supposed to take over the den someday, but his life was cut short. He cleared his throat and took a deep breath before opening the French doors that led out to the deck. Anne looked up at him and smiled before she frowned, a crease forming between her eyebrows.

"What's wrong?" she asked, kicking the ball to Jacob before striding across the grass and climbing the steps. She stopped in front of him and placed her hand on his chest, over his heart. "I hear your heart racing. Are you okay? You're home way too early."

"We need to talk. It's about Aster and Reeve."

Anne's already fair skin paled. She licked her lips before they were cinched together in a tight line—a sign he knew after all their years of marriage. She was preparing for bad news, almost like her sealed lips would keep the fear at bay. After a few seconds, she nodded, and her lips parted, letting out a sharp exhale.

"I'll get Jacob settled in to watch a movie, and then we'll talk. I'll meet you in the office." Anne called their grandson, and he half ran, half skipped over to them.

"Grampa!" he cried out before wrapping his arms around Mike's legs in a big hug. Mike chuckled and scooped his grandson up in his arms, lifting him over his head as Jacob screeched with laughter. He carried the boy's wiggling body into the house and dumped him on the sofa in the television room. A few tickles left Jacob breathless, and Mike stood up, laughing along with his grandson. Anne shook her head with disapproval, but her lips twitched with amusement. Mike hated knowing the news he brought would douse any amusement. While Anne put a DVD on for Jacob, Mike walked across the hallway to his office. He stared out the window at the front lawn and flowers in full bloom. There had been a lot of snow the past winter, and everything was lush and green. He heard the door snick closed and moments later, Anne wrapped her arms around his waist and placed a kiss between his shoulder blades.

"What's going on, my mate, my love?" she asked.

Mike placed his hands over hers, enjoying her touch. He breathed in deeply. Her scent never failed to instill calm—it quieted his inner cat. From the first day they crossed paths she'd had that effect on him, which is how he knew she was his mate.

"Our granddaughter has been abducted."

"What?" He felt her tense behind him, and her voice was raised in alarm. "When? Oh my god! Honey, we have to go to them!" She started to pull away, but Mike held onto her hands, anchoring her to him.

"We will. Hear me out." He turned around in her arms and placed his hands on her hips, lowering his forehead so it was pressed against hers. "We're going to meet with the Court and petition for an early end to Aster's banishment. We'll ask them to remove Reeve's memory spell, but I doubt we can expect them to lift her banishment."

"Screw the Court!" Anne cried out, and stepped away from him. Tears streaked her flushed cheeks, and she held a hand against her stomach like she was going to be sick. "Our girls need us!"

"Don't you think I know that! But we have to do this right. We've built a life here. We have commitments. If we act rashly, we stand to lose everything."

"We've already lost so much!" Her tears turned into hiccupping sobs, and Mike watched her sag as the fight in her was replaced by renewed grief. Closing the gap between them, he pulled Anne into his arms and held her close. Slowly she calmed down, and when her sobbing stopped, he stepped back and placed a finger under her chin, tilting her head up so he could look into her swollen, watery eyes of the purest green.

"We do this together, and if we do it right, we can get our family back. Are you with me?"

"Yes, of course."

He sealed his mouth over her lips, which were salty, laced with tears. She parted her lips and welcomed his kiss. Her taste on his tongue awakened other feelings, and he growled, pulling his wife closer so she could feel the effect she was having on him. A throaty chuckle preceded a roll of her hips as she ground against his erection before she broke off the kiss.

"We save our granddaughter first, then sex, mister." She stepped out of his embrace, leaving him hanging.

"We've been together for over thirty years, and I'm as hot for you as the first time we met."

"I can see that, Big Mike," Anne said with a smirk, lowering her gaze to the bulge testing the confines of his jeans. "Call the Court and get us an appointment. I'm going to check on Jacob."

"So bossy," Mike teased, and smacked his mate on her ass before she left the room. Knowing his wife, that would be the last emotional outburst she was going to allow herself until they had succeeded with the task at hand. She'd roll her sleeves up and dig in, displaying nothing but stoicism and strength until she didn't need to be strong anymore. He loved that about her.

With a sigh, Mike crossed the room and sat down in the brown leather office chair before picking up the phone to call Elsmed directly. The Court elder and Mike's father had a long history together back when Elsmed helped his dad start McCabe & Sons Construction. He hoped that connection would work in his favor.

CHAPTER 3

ith their hands joined on the table, Mike and Anne faced the Court of the Sun and the Moon. It had been an agonizing two-day wait for their meeting—two days longer their granddaughter had been missing. Lack of sleep weighed heavily on Mike's face, and he noticed the visible strain on Anne's face, too. Mike knew the fact that the Court agreed to meet with them at all, and on such short notice, was a miracle.

The reception was lukewarm, and members of the Court sat on a raised dais so they loomed over whoever had to face them, forming an intimidating front. Torches flickered on the dark wood walls, and shadows played on the mural behind the dais, making it so the painted supernatural creatures appeared to be moving.

Almost all members were present. In addition to Elsmed, who represented the Fairchild family and managed fae affairs with Teeny Weeny Tahini, who sat to his left, Saundra Beaumont, Mathilde Augustine, and Roman Bishop (all witches), Lawrence Mills, and Michaela Petran were there. The only members missing were Sheriff Ric Kasun, Odette Alverson, and the town mayor, Barbie Stuart. Addie Beaumont, who wasn't on the Court but served as their business manager of sorts, sat off to the side, taking minutes.

"What you're asking for is highly unusual," Saundra Beaumont said. She was the first to speak after Mike and Anne explained their situation.

"We don't cut sentences short. All decisions are final," Lawrence Mills added, seeming personally affronted that the McCabes had the gall to ask.

"We know, but the circumstances are extenuating," Mike countered. "Aster's temporary banishment is up five days from today. It's not like we're asking it to be shortened by a year."

"Mike has a point," Michaela spoke up. "An innocent's life is also at stake here. What if Zoey were missing, Lawrence? Elsmed, your great-great-granddaughter is just as vulnerable."

Anne gripped Mike's hand at this unexpected show of support. Michaela hadn't been on the Court when their daughters were banished. The seat for the Petran family, a family of moroi vampires, had been empty at the time.

Lawrence scowled at the mention of his granddaughter's name, and Elsmed stroked his long chin, his expression thoughtful. There were some whisperings among the members. Teeny Weeny Tahini leaned over to talk to Mathilde Augustine. Roman Bishop spoke next, his voice commanding attention.

"So you're asking that Aster's banishment end early and for the memory spell to be restored for Reeve but not end her banishment, correct?"

Before Mike and Anne could respond, the heavy wooden doors burst open. Willow Fairchild and her cousin, Paisley Underwood, marched in, followed by Harlow Augustine.

"Harlow, what are you doing here? This is a private hearing!" Mathilde Augustine admonished her granddaughter.

"And I ask the same of you, Willow." Elsmed glowered at his great-granddaughter.

"We're here to support the McCabes and help our friend," Willow replied, tossing her long silvery blond hair over her shoulder. The three women came to stand behind Mike and Anne. Willow owned Coffee Haven, where Aster was a manager before being banished. Paisley and Aster had worked together there, too.

Harlow and Aster had been friends since they were little. The young Augustine witch placed a hand on Mike's shoulder and gave it a gentle squeeze.

"This is unacceptable!" Lawrence Mills sputtered, his face turning tomato red. "There are rules in place and a code of conduct. You can't just barge in here!" His pale green eyes briefly transformed into reptilian slits, indicating he was dangerously close to shifting into his dragon form. If he did shift, his dragon would burst apart the courtroom in seconds.

"Harlow?" Mathilde asked, her tone all business.

"Aster is one of my best friends, and when Ryker told me the McCabes were petitioning for an end to her banishment and the reason why—I couldn't stay away."

Mathilde pursed her lips and shook her head before letting out a heavy sigh that echoed off the chamber walls. "Fine. You can stay, but as a witness only."

Lawrence grumbled, his bushy eyebrows pulling together when he frowned, resembling a fuzzy white caterpillar perched on his forehead.

"As I was saying, before being so rudely interrupted," Roman Bishop said, looking down at Mike and Anne with disdain. "You're requesting an end to Aster's banishment and the memory spell lifted on Reeve for twenty-eight days. All of this to aid in the search for your granddaughter. Is this correct?"

"Yes," Mike answered.

"Is that all? You don't want to request anything else, since we're all here?" Roman smirked, raising a perfectly shaped eyebrow.

Anne gripped Mike's hand again, and he could feel the tension radiating off her. He returned the squeeze, hoping to convey reassurance. They knew going into this that it wouldn't be easy and that they might not walk away with the desired outcome.

"No. That's it. We know it's unreasonable to ask for Reeve's banishment to end early. All we want is to be there for our girls and to find our granddaughter."

Roman nodded, as if satisfied with his response. "Shall we

discuss this further or are you ready to vote?" he asked the other Court members.

The members conferred among themselves, and Mike started tapping his foot. The thick rubber sole of his work boot squeaked slightly on the polished hardwood floors.

"There's one problem," Saundra Beaumont said. "How do you propose the memory spell is lifted? We can't do it remotely. Your girls are in Denver."

"If I may," Harlow said from behind Mike. "I plan on going to Denver to help. Addie can teach me the spell. As a member of the Luna Coven, I am fully capable."

Mike whipped around to look at Harlow. Her brown eyes met his, and she smiled.

"Ryker is waiting for us. Paisley and Orion are going to come too," she whispered before turning her attention back to the Court, where the members were furiously discussing things again. With his sensitive hearing, Mike picked up most of what they were saying. Their concerns were what type of precedent would be set if they ended a banishment early and the risk of giving Harlow the spell to restore memories. Addie was called over to confer with her grandmother, Roman, and Mathilde, who in addition to being Court members, were leaders of the Luna Coven.

"Okay," Saundra announced, staring down at Mike and Anne. "We've discussed, and the majority of us have decided in your favor. Addie will give Harlow the spell, and Aster's banishment is over effective immediately. Reeve's banishment still stands. Not all of your daughters' memories will be restored, but it will be enough for them to know who you are and some details about their life. If Aster visits Havenwood Falls, all of her memories will be restored upon her return. You will have twenty-eight days before the memory spell takes effect again for your daughters, you, and anyone going with you. Both of you will be held accountable if Reeve returns to Havenwood Falls during this time period. Do you understand?"

"Yes," they answered in unison.

"Good. While the McCabe clan isn't one of the founding families, your family has been here since the 1950s and has been essential to the growth of our town. We do what we can to help and protect our own. No one deserves to have their child taken from them. I hope you're successful with finding your granddaughter."

A rap of the gavel ended the hearing, and they were dismissed. After standing up, Anne threw herself against Mike and hugged him hard. He wrapped his arms around her and kissed the top of her head. Her auburn hair smelled like a field of wildflowers that had been soaked in sunshine. He breathed in her scent, allowing himself to relax slightly for the first time since he'd learned of their granddaughter's abduction. Peering over Anne's head, he saw Addie approaching. Releasing Anne, he turned to face the young witch whom he had watched grow up to the confident woman standing before him. Her black-framed glasses drew attention to her brown eyes.

"Harlow, do you have a minute?" Addie gestured with a tattooed arm toward the left rear corner of the room. The numerous bracelets she wore clinked together when she lowered her arm, and the two witches walked away, their heads practically touching as they spoke quietly to each other.

"I'm glad everything went well," Willow said, coming to stand next to Mike and Anne. "Sorry we barged in like that, but when Harlow told me what was going on, I was inclined to help. Paisley, too." Willow looked over at her fair-haired cousin. Bright pink streaks highlighted the white-blond strands. While the two fae were cousins by marriage only, they shared traits common among the fae, like their petite builds and flawless pale skin. When they let their glamours drop, pointy ears and longer features showed their true species.

"Harlow said you plan on going to Denver with us?" Mike asked Paisley.

"You bet! We don't know what we will find, and my healing abilities could be of use."

"Healing abilities?" Anne asked, her eyebrow raised.

271

"Well, you know my dad is a healer, and I inherited the same ability. I want to come along and help in any way I can. I have the time, since I'm home from college for the summer. Aster was more like an older sister to me than my manager when we worked together."

"We'll take all the help we can get, but we're going to have to leave as soon as possible. I don't want to lose any more time, and it's at least a six-hour drive to Denver," Mike said, looking impatiently at his watch.

"I have that covered, and I'll fill you in outside," Harlow said, appearing next to Mike and Anne. She was holding two sheets of transfer paper in her hands with identical designs drawn on them. Harlow rolled the papers up and stuck them in her handbag. They all walked out together, and Mike reached for his wife's hand. She smiled up at him and moved in closer, their strides matching. They were so close to seeing their daughters and one step closer to finding their granddaughter. He wasn't going to stop searching until she was found. It was after nine at night, but they were a week away from the summer solstice, and the days already seemed longer; the town stayed busy later. People were out on the town square, and the smell of garlic drifted up the street from Napoli's. No one seemed to pay any attention to the group that had just left City Hall, which had technically been closed since five o'clock.

Ryker's younger brother, Orion, was waiting for them. He sat astride a motorcycle that was all silver and chrome. Even in the late evening it gleamed like a new nickel. Orion looked a lot like his brother, with golden brown hair and brown eyes ringed with gold. Physically, he wasn't as big, but he was close, maybe an inch shy of Ryker's six feet five. His build was a little leaner. One night, Mike was out at the Dirty Knuckle having a beer and overheard chatter that Orion was an agile fighter and when paired up with his brother, they were a force to be reckoned with.

Mike could hold his own and had the battle scars to prove it, but his brawling days were over. The last fight he was in had shaken his confidence. The mountain lion shifter that took his son's life,

Damian Stone, almost ended his as well. Knowing Orion and Ryker were joining the search provided some peace of mind. He had no idea what or who they were going to encounter.

Orion wore jeans, black boots, and a leather vest that was so new and stiff, it looked like it could stand up on its own. The last time Ryker had been over to the house to hang out with Roxy and Remy, he told Mike that Orion was prospecting. Remy's ears had perked up at that, and the young cougar shifter had since become obsessed with MC culture, much to Anne's dismay. Ryker had become a mentor of sorts for the twins, especially Remy, since the first time Mike introduced them.

"So what did you have to tell us?" Mike asked Harlow once they gathered in front of Orion's Harley.

Harlow looked over her shoulder first before leaning in. "I can make a portal that will take us directly to Denver. Ryker will meet us."

"Do you know where we're going to meet?"

"Yes. Ryker is just waiting for my call, and I know we have to hurry. If we meet in an hour at Smalls Falls, does that give you enough time to make arrangements and pack?" Harlow looked at everyone in the group, her eyes meeting Mike's last.

"Plenty of time. We had everything ready just in case. Our car is already packed."

"I can be ready," Paisley said. "Smalls Falls is like a fifteen-minute walk from my house."

"Paisley, since we all live in Creekwood, why don't you meet at our house, and we'll walk over together," Anne suggested, and Paisley agreed.

"Yeah, it won't take me long at all," Orion said.

"Great, see you all at Smalls Falls in an hour." Harlow fished around in her bag and pulled out a scrap of paper, which turned out to be an old receipt from Shelf Indulgence, the bookstore next to Coffee Haven. She scribbled her phone number on the back and handed it to Mike. "Call me if anything comes up."

"Good luck, you guys. I can tell you're all nervous, and it's literally making me vibrate," Willow said, and gave everyone a hug. Mike had no idea what it was like to be an empath, but if it meant feeling everyone else's emotions, he was grateful not to have that ability.

After that, they dispersed. Harlow climbed on the back of Orion's bike, and they took off with a growl, the Road King's exhaust echoing off the buildings surrounding the square. Willow and Paisley left in Willow's Subaru, which had been parked next to Anne's Land Rover. Mike drove home while Anne made phone calls from the passenger seat. They had made plans in case the Court ruled in their favor, and now it was time to put the plans in motion.

CHAPTER 4

$\mathcal{F}$irst Anne called Nicholas Jordan. He and his mate Audrey, the twins' half sister, were going to stay at the house to keep an eye on Roxy and Remy. Next, Anne called Mike's parents, Daniel and Colleen. Mike and Anne had taken over the construction business after his parents retired, but they helped out when needed. Even though they were in their eighties, Mike's parents were blessed with good health and seemed to have more energy than a room full of kindergartners. The day-to-day operations would run smoothly in his absence.

Mike listened as his wife went over a few details. "Ryker will be with us in Denver, so split his hours between Evan Grey—he's a fairly new hire—and Ryne Calloway. The payroll system Mom implemented before you retired is still in place, so payroll shouldn't be an issue." There was a pause, and Mike heard his dad ask some questions. "Uh-huh, yes, we're doing the greenhouse expansion at Fairy Tale Florists. Everett Weston is dropping the blueprints off tomorrow. He expedited them since he's going to be out of town next month. Oh, Irene Beckett is getting a new roof, and we're doing a slight remodel up at the Farnsworth Mining Co. Mine & Museum. Those are the new jobs starting next week. Thanks again, Dad," she said, and the call ended just as Mike was pulling into the driveway. Nicholas arrived as they were getting out of the car. He carried a duffel bag in one hand as he walked up the driveway to meet them.

"Thank you for coming on such short notice," Anne said, pulling Nicholas into a hug. "Where's Audrey?"

"No problem. Audrey is working tonight at Silk, and I just got off my shift."

"Busy night?" Mike asked, clapping Nicholas on his shoulder. He was wearing basketball shorts and a tank top that showed off his sleeve tattoo. His hair was wet and looked almost black instead of the usual brown. He smelled like mild soap. The obnoxious scented body washes were too strong for shifters who had an enhanced sense of smell.

"It's picking up. It always does around the full moon." Nicholas was an EMT, and in a town with a lot of supernaturals, things often came unhinged when the moon was full. Mike had already begun to feel the effects. Even though the magic Court-issued tattoo he had helped to control those urges, he suspected that having summer solstice riding on its coattails at the end of the week was exacerbating everything.

Maneuvering around the mountain bikes, ski gear, and other equipment that lined the wall by the car, they walked into the house. Anne was already launching into instructions, which Nicholas probably already knew by now, since this wasn't his first time housesitting and watching the twins. Stepping into the kitchen from the garage, Anne flipped on the lights over the island, which reflected off the dark gray granite counter. The aroma of garlic and tomato sauce lingered in the air, and a lasagna pan sat soaking in the sink. Mike watched as Anne walked over to the refrigerator that was covered with Jacob's colorful drawings. She opened the door and started shaking her head. She chuckled and closed the door. "I thought there might be leftovers, but nope. Remy polished off over half a lasagna."

"He's a growing boy," Mike said.

"Can't blame him, Mrs. M. Your lasagna is amazing—better

than Napoli's." He winked, his blue eyes sparkling when he smiled. "It was always Braden's favorite." At the mention of their son, Nicholas's smile faded, and he looked down at the gray tile floor.

"It's okay to talk about him," Mike said. "He was your best friend. You were like brothers. I find the memories more of a comfort now. At first, they were too painful, but it's getting easier." He looked over to see Anne nodding in agreement, but her eyes were shining as she held back tears.

"It's been nice having the twins here. Our house was too empty and quiet after—" She paused, taking a deep breath. "After everything."

It was true. The first year was unbearable. Mike hardly spent any time at home. Every room, every smell, was a reminder of everything they had lost. He immersed himself into work to avoid being consumed by grief. If it wasn't for the connection with his mate, he might have shifted and run off into the woods for the rest of his days. Anne was his anchor. His strong, brave, and resilient wife kept him from falling apart and held them together. The twins came along at just the right time. The twins needed a home, and they had a home to give.

Their grocery bill went up, along with their water and electricity bills, plus there were more shoes to trip over by the door and more clutter, but the house wasn't quiet and empty anymore. When the twins had their first sibling spat, Mike remembered looking over at Anne and a smile had lit up her face. That was a sound they hadn't heard since Reeve and Aster. Suddenly there was life and normalcy in their house again. It hadn't been perfect, and the twins were still adjusting, but a lot of healing had taken place over the past eight months—for everyone. Mike wondered about Roxy's upcoming trials for the new college the Court had created. If she was accepted, she'd be leaving. Life was like that, though—full of change and adjustments.

"So the Court agreed to end Aster's sentence early. What about Reeve?" Nicholas asked.

"No. She will get some of her memories back for twenty-eight days, but her banishment still stands," Mike answered.

"Damn. Well, at least you'll get to see her. That's better than nothing."

"We'll take whatever we can get," Anne said. "Now, let me go over a few things with you."

Mike left them in the kitchen and went upstairs. The twins had taken Reeve and Aster's old bedroom. Even though they could have had separate bedrooms, they wanted to be together. They had suffered through so much, and Remy was fiercely protective of his sister. The door was shut, and there was a strip of light at the bottom. Mike knocked twice before turning the knob and pushing the door open. Roxy was stretched out on her bed wearing leggings and a long-sleeved shirt, earbuds in and nose in a book. Remy was sitting up, his back supported by a mountain of pillows. He wore khaki cargo shorts and that's it. He had a game controller in his hands and was focused on the game displayed on the flat-screen television mounted on the wall. The twins shared the same features: sandy blond hair and honey-colored eyes that were set in narrow faces. But that was where the similarities ended.

Remy had a lot of energy and was prone to angry outbursts. Roxy was very quiet and contained. She had been severely scarred and hid her body with clothes, where Remy would probably be content running wild and free with clothing optional. Remy's side of the room looked like a dumpster fire. Dirty clothes littered the carpet, and a trail led to the wicker hamper, but never actually made it inside. Wrappers from Burger Bar and Tacos for Daze had formed a mountain of foil on his bedside table.

Roxy's side of the room was immaculate. The only thing on the floor were her flip-flops next to the bed. Her hair products and makeup were arranged on top of her dresser by size. Nothing was out of order.

"What's up, Uncle Mike?" Remy asked without taking his eyes off the screen. The twins had started referring to Mike and Anne as Aunt and Uncle a few months after they moved in. They had acclimated enough and decided calling them Mr. and Mrs. McCabe was too formal. They weren't ready for Mom and Dad, either. So, Aunt and Uncle stuck.

Mike sat down on the edge of Roxy's bed. She inserted a bookmark and closed her book, setting it down on her chest to give him her full attention. "Your Aunt Anne and I are going to Denver. Tonight."

Remy set his controller down and turned on the bed to face Mike. "Tonight?"

"Yes. Harlow is going to open a portal so we don't have to drive. Ryker is going to meet us. Nicholas is already here. He and Audrey will stay and watch you guys." One of the first things Mike learned about the twins was to be as transparent as possible. They had deep trust issues and were pretty adept at figuring out when someone was lying to them.

"Ryker's going to be there? Then I'm going too." Remy slid to the edge of his bed and bent over to pick up a rumpled T-shirt off the floor.

"No. I need you here to keep an eye on things, and you have classes. School is your number one priority right now."

His shoulders slumped, and he dropped the T-shirt. A scowl on the boy's narrow face told him Remy wasn't happy, but at least he was listening. That was an improvement.

"When will you be back?" Roxy's soft voice broke through the tension and changed the subject.

"I don't know. We have to be back within twenty-eight days. I hope it doesn't take that long." The idea of his granddaughter in the possession of strangers for that long sent his inner cat into a tizzy. He felt his skin ripple beneath his clothes and struggled to suppress the urge to shift.

Roxy nodded. "The memory spell."

"Yes, exactly. Are you two going to be okay while we're gone? I know Nicholas and Audrey are looking forward to spending more time with you." The question was directed toward Remy. Mike knew Roxy would be fine. She'd go about her routine and keep a low profile. Her brother on the other hand . . . Especially with Ryker away, well, that was a different story.

"We'll be fine, Uncle Mike. Just get back safely." Roxy's golden gaze met Mike's, and he saw the concern there. These kids had already lost so much. He promised to return and meant it. He didn't want to be the source of any more turmoil in their lives. He stood up and leaned over, kissing Roxy's forehead. "We'll definitely be back before your trials for the Academy," he assured her. Then he turned around and took the two steps that separated the twins' beds. He sat down next to Remy and ruffled his long hair before wrapping an arm around his shoulders and pulling him into a partial hug that Remy tolerated for a few seconds before shrugging him off.

"Enjoy your first Midsummer's Night Terrors and stick by Nicholas and Audrey, as it can get pretty wild. We'll check in when we can. Call us if you need anything," Mike said before leaving the room. The twins had already resumed their activities like he hadn't been there at all.

Anne was coming up the stairs when he stepped out into the hall.

"I'm just going to say goodbye," she said. Before she slipped into the room, Mike placed a hand on her arm, stopping her. She looked up at him, eyebrow raised in question. He brushed a stray curl away from her cheek, tucking it behind her ear. Words passed unspoken between them. They had been married so long they knew how to read each other's cues. Anne stepped closer to him and rose on her tiptoes to kiss him. Mike's hands circled around her waist. She was a little curvier now that she was older, and after bearing three children, but he liked that—he liked her softer curves and the way her ass fit in his hands. Her hands ran up his chest and around behind his neck before they were buried in his hair. She sank against him as he devoured her mouth, sucking on her full bottom lip, eliciting a soft, breathy moan. Movement on the other side of the door caused them to break apart, both breathless, and the longing Mike saw on his mate's face matched what he was feeling.

"What was that for?" Anne asked. "Not that I'm complaining." Her lips, glossy from their kiss, lifted with a saucy grin.

"Who knows when we'll be alone again next? I was seizing the moment." As if to prove his point, the bedroom door opened and Roxy stepped out at the same time the doorbell rang. Paisley had arrived. It was time to go.

From that point on, everything was a blur. Roxy went downstairs with them to greet Nicholas. After that, Nicholas drove Anne's Land Rover and dropped them off at the trailhead that led to Smalls Falls. They piled out, and Mike lifted the rear hatch, handing bags off. Paisley had a backpack stuffed full, and Ann carried a small duffel bag and a backpack. Mike carried the larger, heavier bag. They said goodbye to Nicholas and set off. It was less than a ten-minute walk from there, and the rush of water grew louder as they approached. The light from the almost full moon lit the narrow dirt path, but none of them needed it. Shifters and fae all had enhanced senses, and seeing at night wasn't an issue.

Harlow and Orion were already there, and Orion turned upon hearing their approach, instinctively taking a step so he stood in front of Harlow. When he recognized them, he relaxed, and Mike thought he moved away but realized Harlow had shoved him out of the way.

"Orion, chill out! I'm not some damsel in distress."

"Yeah, but you're my bro's old lady, and Crusher told me to watch out for you while he's gone."

"First of all, you know I hate being called an old lady. Secondly, I'm safe, and I can handle myself." She stood with her hands on her hips. Like Anne, Harlow had changed into more practical clothes. She wore jeans, hiking boots, and a T-shirt that said *Not Today*. A hoodie was tied around her waist. Anne was wearing an almost identical outfit, except she had on a polo that had the McCabe & Sons Construction logo over her left breast.

"Hey, Pinkie," Orion said to Paisley. He tossed his head so the hair hanging over his eyes flung back. He had his hands in the back pockets of his jeans, and he stood with a cocky, aloof coolness. With his distressed jeans, black T-shirt, leather vest, and black leather boots, he captured the stereotypical bad-boy look. Mike shook his head and chuckled to himself. It didn't seem like that long ago when he behaved that way around females, before he met his mate.

Paisley scowled at him. "Pinkie?"

"Yeah." Orion reached out, tugging on a section of Paisley's hair that was dyed pink. "Pinkie."

The petite fae rolled her eyes, and suddenly the pink streaks changed to blue, startling Orion, who dropped the section of hair he was holding. He examined his fingertips for any discoloration. "That's a neat trick, Blue."

"Ugh! What is it with guys and their nicknames? Your brother calls Harlow Country Club, and my cousin's boyfriend calls her Flannels. I don't get it." After her rant, Paisley's hair transformed into a rainbow.

Orion grinned, and his golden eyes flashed with amusement at the challenge. "Oh, I could do this all night, Goldie."

"Goldie?" Paisley's face crinkled with confusion. She walked to the edge of the pond and peered over to look at her reflection in the still water. "Explain," she demanded, turning back to Orion with her hands on her hips, practically mirroring Harlow.

"Because you're the pot of gold at the end of the rainbow." Orion winked, and Harlow groaned. Mike barked out a laugh, and he noticed Anne was shaking with laughter.

"That was sooo cheesy," Harlow said and stifled a laugh. "Come on, Lover Boy, leave poor Paisley alone. Your brother is waiting for us."

"I hope we're back in time for Midsummer's Night Terrors. I gotta know how the town puts all the humans to sleep."

"Magic, obviously," Harlow said. "I hope we're back in time, too, but who knows how long we're going to be gone."

Just like that, the antics were over and the group became focused on the task at hand. Harlow began to whisper a spell, chanting words under her breath. The wind began to stir, swirling around her and lifting her long dark hair. A faint vibration hummed beneath his feet, and Mike stared in wonder as the air before Harlow shimmered and then seemed to part, revealing a black hole that grew to the size and shape of a doorway within seconds.

"Go!" she commanded, and Orion stepped through first, followed by Paisley. Mike and Anne clasped hands and squeezed through together. Harlow came through last, closing the portal behind her.

Mike looked around at their surroundings. They were inside what appeared to be an abandoned warehouse or factory of sorts. Part of the roof was collapsed, and debris littered the cracked concrete floor. Weeds poked up through the cracks in the areas where sunlight would reach during the day. Rust-colored stains bloomed on the floor. He raised his nose in the air and sniffed. The metallic tang of blood lingered, and he suspected the stains on the floor weren't from chemicals. Broken bottles and glass from shattered windows sparkled in the moonlight.

"Where are we?" he asked, instantly on alert in the unfamiliar territory. "Why is there blood on the floor?" He surveyed the shadows, looking for any threats.

"The number one rule about the Supernatural Fight Club," Harlow said, slightly tweaking a well-known line from one of Mike's favorite movies. He understood, and it made sense. A remote location like this was the perfect spot for a fight club, especially a supernatural one. Even Havenwood Falls had a fight club that the MC hosted, though it had been years since he participated. Mike rubbed his right ear, running his finger along the divot where the top used to be. That had been bitten off by a member of the Blaekthorn wolf pack. Anne hadn't been too pleased when he came home that night covered in blood and missing half his ear.

"Seriously?" Paisley shuddered and looked around the room. Mike noticed she stepped closer to Orion and wondered if she even realized she had subconsciously sought out his protection.

"Yup, I've fought here before," the young lion shifter said.

"You have?" Her violet eyes were wide when she turned to look at him. "Who did you fight?"

"I've fought all kinds. My last fight was against a vampire. He was hopped up on faerie blood and almost killed me. Harlow saved my ass." Orion and Harlow exchanged a glance and Mike wondered what the real story was—it was obvious something significant had happened.

"Come on. Ryker's waiting for us outside," Harlow said, signaling an end to the conversation.

"Let's go get our family back," Anne said, sliding her fingers between Mike's and tugging. They walked together, hand in hand, a united front ready to face whatever challenges came their way.

CHAPTER 5

*T*he doorbell rang, and Aster looked across the room to Gage. He was standing in front of the window, arms crossed across his chest.

"He's here," he said, and turned to face the entrance to the living room. Reeve shifted from where she was sitting next to Aster on the sofa. Their hands were clenched together, and Reeve leaned against Patrick, who was sitting on her other side. She had finally stopped crying, but the blank, numb stare worried Aster. Seeing her sister shut down before her had her stomach in knots. She felt so helpless. Alice, the woman who had delivered the tainted brownies, was long gone. They had tracked her scent to a motel, and that's where it ended. If they were human, they could have gone to the police and reported the kidnapping, and an Amber alert would have been broadcast. Explaining to the cops that they suspected a group of rogue mountain lion shifters who had been exiled from their den would not go over well.

Instead, Gage had called a private investigator who handled supernatural cases. Asa Foster was a retired detective from Denver PD. He was also a bear shifter with connections to the criminal underworld as well as federal judges. The past four days had been excruciating as they waited for news on potential leads about Mina's whereabouts. They had basically shut themselves off from the den with the exception of a few soldiers who had been with Gage from when he had been Damian's beta. Since Alice's betrayal, trust was stretched thin.

While they were eating dinner, a solemn affair since none of them had any appetites, Asa called Gage and reported he had information and that he'd be by within the hour. That was the longest hour of Aster's life. Now Asa was here, and all attention turned to the hulking man that was escorted into the living room by Thorne, one of the few members Gage trusted at the moment.

The private investigator had to duck under the entryway, and he removed his straw-colored cowboy hat, revealing a thick head of brown hair graying at the temples. He palmed the top of his hat with a giant hand, and in his other hand he carried a manila folder. He wore a faded denim shirt, Western style, that stretched across broad shoulders. The shirt was tucked into tan Carhartt jeans, and the heels of his cowboy boots thudded on the hardwood floors. Aster's attention was drawn to his belt—not the large brass buckle, but the side holster on his hip that held a handgun.

Gage crossed the room and held out his hand. Asa met him halfway, limping slightly. He tucked the manila folder under his arm to complete the handshake. The bear shifter towered over Gage, which meant he had to be at least six and a half feet tall.

"Have a seat." Gage gestured to the upholstered chairs that faced the sofa, a coffee table in the middle. Asa sat down, the chair creaking beneath his weight, and opened up the manila folder on the table, spreading a series of grainy black-and-white photographs across the polished wood surface. Aster liked that he was getting right down to business, and she leaned forward to look at the images. Despite the poor quality, she recognized the one woman: Alice. She was holding a bundle in her arms, carrying it like one would carry a baby.

Patrick snatched up another image, his nostrils flaring. "Son of a bitch!" He handed the picture over to Gage. "See who she's with? Confirms exactly what we thought."

Gage studied the picture, and Aster noticed his hand shaking. Claws sprung from the ends of his fingers as his hand started to transform, slicing through the photo paper. He took a few deep breaths, and the claws receded.

"When was this taken?" he asked Asa.

"Three days ago, the day after your niece was abducted. They probably didn't realize the motel was under surveillance as part of a prostitution sting operation. A friend on the force let me review the footage. Your suspicions about Eben Brant are correct."

Aster sat up at the mention of that name. Eben was a purist. Part of Damian Stone's cult. He had been banished from the den almost two years earlier, after losing a challenge to Gage. She thought he had licked his wounds and moved on. She was wrong. Eben must have had Alice and who knew who else working for him from the inside. Spying, plotting, and taking revenge on the den's most vulnerable member: Mina.

"The Suburban they're seen getting into is registered to Eben. It was found abandoned yesterday, outside of Buena Vista. They torched it."

Gage pinched the bridge of his nose. "What else?"

"Coincidentally, I received a call yesterday from a small coven in Buena Vista. One of their witches was hired for some spellwork and never returned. She was only supposed to be gone half a day on Tuesday."

"Do you think this is connected?"

"I sure do. While the coven thinks a witch hunter is responsible, this witch was known for her cloaking and invisibility spells. Apparently, whoever hired her wanted to disappear."

"Eben fucking Brant." Gage stood up and started pacing, running a hand through his hair. "I should have fucking killed him!"

"Hey." Asa rose to his feet. "I don't want to hear that, so I'm going to go. What you do with the information from this point on is your business."

"No, I understand. Thanks, man." They shook hands again, and Gage walked Asa out.

Throughout this entire time, Reeve hadn't said one word. Aster glanced at her sister. She was staring so intently at the picture Gage had thrown down on the table, Aster thought her green eyes were going to burn holes through it. The picture showed Alice holding Mina, and Eben was grinning down at the baby, like a pirate who had found his long-lost treasure. Reeve's hands were curled into tight fists on her lap, the knuckles white from strain. She'd gone ghostly pale, except for hot red spots on her cheekbones. The grief that had been consuming her had been replaced—by rage.

"Patrick?" Reeve whispered.

"Yes, my love." He leaned forward and placed his hand over Reeve's fists.

"Once we get Mina back"—she pulled her gaze away from the picture and met Patrick's eyes—"he needs to die."

The cold, detached tone in Reeve's voice caused a shiver to run down Aster's spine. She agreed with her, one hundred percent, that kidnapping fucker needed to die. She knew Gage was shouldering the blame for this. He had let Eben live. He wouldn't make that mistake again.

Aster grabbed her phone off the coffee table and searched her maps app for Buena Vista. It was one of the larger towns southwest of Denver, sandwiched between the Pike and San Isabel National Forests and the Gunnison National Forest. The region was heavily forested and mountainous, which meant it offered a lot of places for mountain lion shifters to hide. If Eben did have a witch concealing their location, finding them was going to be even more difficult, and they had several days' head start. It was time to get a move on.

As soon as Gage returned to the living room, she broached the subject. Patrick and Reeve were just as eager to get started too.

"Hold on." Gage held his hand up, as they had all started speaking at once. "We can't all just rush in—we need a plan.

Patrick"—Gage looked across the coffee table at his beta—"I need you to stay here. You're going to be in charge while I'm gone." Patrick started to protest, but Gage held his hand up again. "If both of us are gone, things will go sideways here, and there's already too much instability. Leadership needs to be present and strong."

"Then you stay here! This is my daughter we're talking about! It should be me looking for her." Patrick got into Gage's face.

"And it's my fault she's been taken!" Gage sprung up from the chair to pace the room. "If I had killed Eben two years ago, we wouldn't be having this argument. It's my mess, and I have to be the one to clean it the fuck up!" He pounded his fist against his chest. "I did this."

"No, honey, no!" Aster went to Gage and pulled his fist away from his chest, holding it between her hands. "You gave Eben a chance to live and change. He chose to kidnap Mina. That's all him, not you."

"That's not how the den will see it. They'll see it as a weakness." He crossed the room to stare out the window. "I'm speaking as your alpha, bro. You need to stay here."

"Fuck you!" Patrick stormed out of the room, and a distraught Reeve followed him. Moments later, Aster heard the front door slam closed.

"Fuck!" Gage strode past Aster, and like her sister, she followed. He walked down the short hallway to the kitchen.

"I'm going with you," she said to his back.

He turned around to face her. "Not you, too. I'm your alpha, and you're staying here."

Aster balled her hands into fists, feeling her claws ready to come out. "Don't you dare pull that alpha bullshit with me! I'm your mate. Mina is our niece, and I'm coming with you."

"Damn it, Aster!" Gage ran a hand through his hair and exhaled sharply. "We don't have time for this. You stay here with your sister. She needs you. Plus, you'll be safer here."

This statement made Aster see red and fired her temper right up. "Oh, it's like that, then? Let the poor weak womenfolk stay behind?"

"No. That is not what I meant." Gage pinched the bridge of his nose and growled out of frustration. "Will you just listen to me?"

"Oh, I hear you loud and clear." She turned her back on her mate, so mad she couldn't look at him anymore. Reaching into the cabinet above the coffee maker, she grabbed a glass so she could get a drink of water. Once the glass was in her hand, her plans changed. With a scream, she threw it against the wall, where it exploded into a thousand shards, which scattered on the tile floor.

"Jesus Christ! What the fuck?" Gage yelled, stepping toward her and gripping her by the shoulders.

"That's better than punching you, which is what I really want to do." She stuck her chin out. Aster knew she was acting irrationally, but there was no way she would admit it. She wasn't going to back down until Gage agreed she could go with him. If she had her way, they'd already be gone. But no, Gage had to be a stubborn ass.

Thorne coughed loudly, interrupting their argument.

"What?" they both snapped at him.

"Sorry to interrupt, Alpha, but you have visitors." He kept his head down, a display of submission—or for personal safety to avoid flying glasses.

"Who?" Gage asked.

"Crusher from the gym is here, and he's not alone. He brought a witch, a fae, his brother, and apparently Aster and Reeve's parents?"

"Is this a joke? We don't have parents." This strange arrival, so soon after Mina's kidnapping, set Aster more on edge.

"That's all I know. Should I bring them in?"

Gage nodded. "Bring them into the living room. We'll be right there."

Thorne, always quick to follow orders, left the room. Aster, who had stepped away from Gage when they were interrupted, looked over at her mate. He was pinching the bridge of his nose again and had his eyes closed. His jaw was clenched, and her keen hearing picked up the grinding of teeth. She hadn't seen him stressed like this since he first took over as alpha.

"Are you okay?" she asked.

"Yeah. No." He shook his head and opened his eyes, locking his gaze on hers. "There's just a lot going on, and I don't want to fight with you. I need you by my side."

"And I will be by your side—when we go to find Mina." Before Gage could respond, she spun on her heel, her ponytail swinging against her back from the movement. "Now, let's go see who are claiming to be my parents," she called over her shoulder. A frustrated growl followed her down the hall, and she grinned, knowing she had won.

When Aster entered the living room, she froze mid-step, her eyes locked on the middle-aged couple sitting in the two chairs that faced the entryway. The couple stopped talking and seemed just as paralyzed. Gage came up behind her and placed his hand on the small of her back.

"What's wrong?" he whispered in her ear, his breath tickling the hairs on her neck.

"It's them."

"Them who?"

"From the photo album. You know that one with family pictures of Reeve and me. That's them."

"Are you sure?"

"Positive."

The other occupants in the room had turned around from where they were sitting on the sofa to look at Aster and Gage. A woman with long black hair and Asian features sat on the lap of Crusher, whom she had met once at Gage's gym. A petite woman with white-blond hair with purple streaks sat in the middle, next to another man who looked remarkably like Crusher.

"Crusher, explain," Gage said, focusing on the one person they knew.

Crusher stood, lifting the woman who was on his lap with him and setting her down where he had been sitting. "This is going to sound really strange, but it's the truth."

"Where's Reeve? Is she okay?" the red-haired woman blurted out. She started to rise out of the chair, but Gage growled and moved in front of Aster. The man sitting next to the woman pulled her back, causing her to sob. There was something so familiar about her voice that tugged at Aster, but she couldn't place why.

"This is Mike and Anne McCabe. They're Aster and Reeve's parents and they're from a town called Hickenbocker Springs. No, that's not right. Harlem Hollow. No. What the fuck is going on?" Ryker smacked his forehead with his hand and growled.

"Babe, let me." The black-haired woman stood up and faced Aster. "There's a reason why you can't remember them—can't remember me. I'm Harlow, by the way. We were best friends growing up, and that's Paisley Underwood, who you worked with at a place called Coffee Haven." Harlow pointed to the young blond-haired woman.

"What are you playing at, Crusher? Did Eben send you here?" Gage puffed up his chest and crossed his arms, still standing in front of Aster, who was busy processing all of the new scents in the room, which were familiar too. She isolated the scent of the red-haired woman, and her heart sped up as an association was made. *Home.*

"Who the fuck is Eben? No, dude, we're here to help find Reeve's baby. I'll try to explain. You see, when someone leaves Hollywood Fields. Damn it!" He let out another frustrated growl and turned to the woman who had introduced herself as Harlow. "You better explain, Country Club. I keep forgetting that I can't.

"As I started to say, there's a reason why Ryker can't explain, and I was temporarily given the ability to talk about it—your parents, too. See, there's a memory spell in place to protect the town where you grew up. Visitors forget the town almost immediately after they leave, and residents will forget the town and any memories made there after twenty-eight days. That's why you and your sister don't remember. You've been gone for almost two years."

"Two years?" Aster placed her hand on Gage's arm. "Remember how confused we were when we arrived in Denver two years ago? The doctor thought it was some strange form of amnesia." Aster stepped around Gage to examine the visitors more closely. She saw her own eyes on the older woman's face, which was heart-shaped like Reeve's. The man had a straight nose, like Aster's, and his scent had the same association. "I need to call Reeve."

Aster pulled her cell phone out from the back pocket of her jeans and dialed. The call went right to voicemail. Cursing under her breath, she typed out an urgent text message:

911! Get over here now! Bring that family photo album.

"No offense, Crusher, but after the past few days, I'm having a hard time trusting people," Gage said.

Crusher held his giant hands up in the air, indicating he didn't take offense. "I don't blame you. I trust very few people outside of the MC and about half of them are in this room." He nodded in the direction of the visitors.

Just then, Aster's phone vibrated in her hand, startling her. She looked down at the screen to see her sister's name and immediately answered.

"Sorry, I was pumping," Reeve said. "Now what is going on? What's the emergency?"

"You know that photo album with all of the family pictures that include us?"

"Yes, of course."

"The parents in all of those pictures just showed up here."

"What?" Reeve shrieked, and Aster had to hold the phone away from her ear. "Are you messing with me?"

"I wouldn't joke about this, Reeve. They're in the living room, and I'm looking right at them. Can you and Patrick get your asses over here, like yesterday?"

Reeve sighed. "Patrick is still pissed at Gage."

"Well, he needs to get over it and get over here. Both of you do." Aster ducked out of the room and quickly walked back to the kitchen. "I'm freaking the hell out! They say they want to help find Mina."

"Mina? How do they know she's missing?" Suspicion crept into Reeve's voice.

"That's a good question. We'll ask them when you get here. Hurry, please!"

"We'll be there in less than ten minutes. Longer if I have to tie Patrick up and drag his ass there."

CHAPTER 6

*A*n awkward silence filled the room as everyone waited for Reeve and Patrick to arrive. Aster couldn't stop staring at the couple who claimed to be her parents. Deep down inside, she sensed this was the truth because of the familiarity of their scents and the physical resemblance, plus the two-year timeline matched. Or maybe it was just wishful thinking and she wanted them to be her parents, so they could fill in all the blanks.

Less than ten minutes later, Reeve and Patrick came rushing into the living room. Just as Aster did earlier, Reeve froze like a deer in headlights.

"Oh my god," she said, her eyes fixed on the older couple. She held the photo album in her right arm, and Aster pried it free of her grip. Flipping through the pages, she stopped on the most recent family portrait. She looked to be about seventeen or eighteen years old, which made Reeve nineteen or twenty. Aster examined the picture, then looked up at the couple for comparison. They appeared to be the same people. She nudged Reeve to get her attention and showed her the picture.

"How did you know Mina is missing?" Reeve blurted out, her green eyes narrowing into slits. "Is this some sick game?"

"No, honey. Not at all. We're here to help," the older woman said. "This is so much harder than I thought it would be," she said to her husband. He reached for the woman's hand and clasped it tight.

"I told them about Mina," Crusher said. "I overheard some of your members at the gym talking about what happened." He directed this last part to Gage. "Big Mike, er, Mike McCabe is my boss, and he asked me to keep an eye on his daughters whenever I'm in town for club business."

"Why?" Reeve asked.

"Because if your mom and I tried to see you or make contact with you or your sister, it would have made things so much worse," the older man answered.

"Reeve, their scents. Are they familiar to you at all?" Aster whispered in her sister's ear. She watched her sister's nostrils flare on her delicate nose, very similar to their alleged mother's nose. Reeve closed her eyes as she inhaled but they suddenly popped open, and she looked at Aster.

"So familiar. Like—"

"Home?" Reeve nodded in response.

Aster handed the photo album to Gage. "I think they're telling the truth."

Gage looked doubtful, his eyebrows knitting together when he frowned at her.

"There's one way to know for sure," Harlow said. She stood up from where she was sitting on Crusher's lap and held a rolled-up piece of paper in her hand. "The town where you grew up is protected by wards and a memory spell. Each resident has a tattoo that works like an invisible fence. It registers you as a resident and offers certain benefits. Like your memories, these tattoos disappeared. I happen to be a member of the coven that controls these wards, and I have temporary tattoos that will restore some—not all, but some—of your memories. At least you'll know these lovely people are in fact your parents. Hopefully, Aster, you'll remember that I'm your favorite best friend."

Aster turned to look at her sister, stepping closer so they could have a more private conversation. "What do you think?"

Reeve chewed on her bottom lip. "I don't know."

Gage and Patrick joined them on each side.

"You can't be considering this," Patrick hissed.

"I want answers," Aster said, and Reeve agreed.

"But these people could be working with Eben. And witchcraft —what if it's dark magic?" Patrick countered.

Gage was surprisingly silent, and Aster peered up at him to see if his expression gave away his thoughts. He was looking at her, and when their eyes met, he leaned forward, placing a soft kiss on her lips. "I trust you."

She slipped her hand into his and gave it a squeeze.

"Reeve?" Aster turned to her sister. She wasn't doing this without her.

The woman who claimed to be their mom called across the room. "Girls, you don't remember this, but I taught you to always listen to your heart and your gut. Your instincts won't steer you wrong. Listen to them now. What are they telling you?"

Sound advice, something a parent would give. Tuning out everything else, Aster followed that advice and turned her focus inward. That feeling she had earlier was still there; something was telling her that these strangers weren't really strangers.

"Let's do this," Reeve said, having come to the same conclusion. She stepped away from them and approached Harlow. "What happens now?"

Harlow unrolled the paper in her hand, which turned out to be two sheets of paper with a variation of a Celtic knot drawn onto them.

"This is a symbol for family," she explained. "Once I transfer these temporary tattoos to your skin, the memory spell will be triggered. So where do you want them?"

Reeve didn't even hesitate. She was wearing a short-sleeved shirt and held her arm out so the creamy, smooth underside faced up. She pointed at her wrist. Patrick moved to stand beside her, and

Aster sensed the tension radiating off of him. His jaw was clenched tight, and his lips were pressed into an austere line. He stood with his knees soft and legs hip width apart, ready to jump into action if anything hinky happened once the tattoo was in place.

Aster watched every detail. Harlow set one of the sheets of paper over Reeve's wrist and placed her palm over the design.

"Restore but only memories that are pure. Family bonds that were lost are now found. For twenty-eight days, these terms shall be bound," she recited. Blue flames licked out from beneath her hand, and the edges of the paper turned black and curled before disintegrating into gray ash that disappeared before it could hit the floor. Harlow removed her hand, revealing the tattoo, the bold, black design a stark contrast against Reeve's pale skin.

Then it was Aster's turn. She held her right arm out, pointing at the same spot on her wrist as Reeve. Harlow repeated the process, and Aster braced for a burn, expecting the blue flames to cause some sort of pain, but they only emitted a soothing warmth that seeped into her skin and traveled through her veins like a dose of morphine. As the warmth moved into her brain, it was like something unlocked. This time, when she looked at the older couple, they weren't strangers.

"Mom? Dad?" Saying that came so naturally, and the knowledge was suddenly there that they were her parents, and she had only ever known them as Mom and Dad.

Her mom launched out of the chair, pulling Aster and her sister into a hug, which their dad immediately joined. Their combined scents along with the familiar comfort of their embrace was too much, and Aster started to cry. She wasn't the only one. They were all sobbing and holding onto each other.

Faint memories arose of sitting on her dad's lap in the cab of an excavator as he let her take the controls. A skinned knee being carefully cleaned with her mom's gentle touch. A field full of wildflowers almost as tall as Aster as she chased after her sister. Lying on her back and staring up at the sun, only to have it blocked out by an older boy as he stood over her laughing. Braden. Where was Braden? She pulled back as the void of her missing brother grew wider, heavier. Something horrible lurked in the recesses of her memories.

"Oh, my girls, we missed you so much!" Her mom sniffled, wiping tears from her cheeks. She smiled and cupped Aster's face and then Reeve's. Her hands were warm and soft.

"I don't understand. You knew where we were. Why did you let us go so long?" Reeve asked.

Their parents exchanged a look, and her dad's smile faded. "That's a long story, and it all starts with Damian Stone."

That name drop was as effective as throwing a live grenade in the room. Everyone was alert and on defense, Gage especially.

"What do you know about Damian?" he demanded.

"I know that he killed our son, and he's the reason why our girls were forced to leave their hometown. And I know you killed him to protect Aster. I'll never be able to thank you enough." Her dad clapped Gage on his shoulder.

"Braden is dead?" Aster gasped at the same time as Reeve. That explained the dread she felt earlier. Her mom pulled them into another hug and fresh tears fell as they mourned for their brother.

Gage stepped behind Aster and placed his hand on her back, using his thumb to rub small, soothing circles. "Damian was following Reeve. I remember tracking him. I remember killing him, but it's always been hazy. I couldn't remember all the details, especially where I killed him. Now it makes sense. The memory spell?"

"Yes. It's one of the most effective ways to protect our town," her dad said.

"Jesus Christ." Gage moved away, and Aster immediately missed his presence at her back. Pulling away from her mom and sister, she followed her mate across the room, where he stood looking out the window. She knew he was seeing beyond their neighborhood to where the woods beckoned. His inner cat was probably urging him to shift, to run and hunt to work out the problems he was facing in his human life. If only it were that easy.

Aster hugged him from behind, wrapping her arms around his waist and burying her face in the center of his broad back. Her mate was an alpha, through and through; a tough but fair leader and a masterful fighter who taught others to fight at his gym. He was kind, intelligent, and strong beyond measure, but the past two years, Mina's disappearance, and now this revelation that Damian had killed his mate's brother and that everything was connected was taking a toll. She felt it through their mate bond. He practically vibrated with frustration and anger. Gage placed a hand over hers and relaxed. She felt his muscles release, and he leaned back into her hug.

"I'm sorry about your brother," he said.

"Me too."

"Are you okay?"

"No," she admitted with a soft laugh. "This is a lot to process and there isn't time." Moving around so she stood in front of Gage, she looked up at him. Stubble grew along his strong jawline where he was normally clean shaven. There were shadows under his blue eyes, evidence of the sleepless nights they had both endured since Mina was taken. His hair was short on the sides, but where it was longer on the top, it stood in disarray from him constantly running his hands through it. She was surprised he hadn't started going bald from the repetitive motion, like when a path is worn in grass from people walking on it. She placed her hands on his arms and squeezed. "We can't fall apart now. We need to find Mina. I'll be damned if I let these purist fuckers take another member of my family away."

"Exactly," Reeve said from behind them. Aster and Gage turned to where she and Patrick stood. "As much as I want to go on the search, I'm still lactating and have to pump every few hours. I'll slow you down."

"You pissed me off suggesting I stay back," Patrick said to Gage. "But I've had time to think about it, and as much as I don't like it, you're right. I'll stay with Reeve, and we'll sniff out if there are any more traitors among us."

"Thanks, man," Gage said, and pulled Patrick into a bro hug. They clapped each other on the back, and when they separated, Aster thought she saw a glimmer of tears, but they'd never admit it.

"Just promise us you'll bring our daughter home." Reeve palmed her stomach, a habit she had developed when she was pregnant. She didn't have a baby bump anymore and in fact, had lost too much weight since Mina was taken. Reeve was usually pale, but always had a glow about her. That too had diminished.

"We promise," Aster said.

It was well past midnight before a plan was in place. Willing to trust relative strangers rather than members of his own den, Gage decided that Ryker, Orion, Harlow, Paisley, and Aster's parents were going to be part of the search party. Orion was a skilled tracker, and Ryker could fight. Paisley had healing abilities in case medical attention was required on their trip, and when Aster asked Harlow what she brought to the table, the witch flashed a mysterious smile and said, "I have skills. Don't you worry."

Before Reeve and Patrick left to go back to their townhouse, Reeve hugged Aster tight. "Please be careful," she pleaded. "I can't lose you too."

"I will. Take care of yourself. Hopefully we'll be back before you even notice we're gone. I love you."

"I love you too." They hugged again before Reeve went to their parents to say goodbye.

The group planned to leave at sunrise, giving them a few hours to sleep. Aster showed her parents to the guest bedroom, while Gage took Harlow and Ryker to the office, where there was a futon. Orion was happy to sleep outside on the back patio and stretched out on the chaise lounge underneath the stars. Paisley curled up on the sofa, and Aster turned off lights as their unexpected guests settled in. Gage had gone upstairs to their bedroom, but she couldn't sleep and only had a few hours to kill before sunrise, so she found herself in the kitchen, pulling out ingredients. She put a pot of coffee on to brew while she made a batch of blueberry scones. That's where Gage found her as the sky was beginning to lighten.

His eyes were bloodshot, so she didn't think he had slept much, if at all.

"Woman, you're killing me. I smelled these baking all the way upstairs!" He grabbed a scone and ate half in one bite, groaning as he chewed.

Paisley appeared next, yawning as she stumbled into the kitchen. "I thought I smelled your famous scones! Can I have one?"

"Help yourself. What do you mean, famous?"

"You won Best of Hickory Farms two years in a row. Wait, not Hickory Farms." She shook her head as if trying to shake sense into it. "These are award winning and my own personal addiction." She bit into one and sighed. "You left the recipe with Willow at Coffee Haven, and they're still amazing, but nothing like when you make them."

It was so weird having someone talk about parts of her life that she didn't remember. While she had memories of her parents and family, and there had been some vague recollections of her childhood, Paisley was still a stranger to her. They obviously had a history, though.

Soon, they were joined by everyone else, who all looked the worse for wear except for Orion, who bounced around with nervous energy. Coffee was poured and scones devoured. Aster packed up the rest to take with them on the road and cleaned the kitchen before going upstairs to take a quick shower, knowing it might be her last for a while.

At dawn, the group piled into the van Ryker had acquired and headed out to Buena Vista—the last probable location of Eben and his demented band of followers. All thoughts were on the mission: bring Mina home.

CHAPTER 7

*T*he van was like one a tour company or church group would use for an excursion: generic white exterior with a lot of windows and on the inside, three rows of bench seats with plenty of room in the rear for storage. Ryker was driving with Orion riding shotgun. Gage and Aster sat in the first row, Mike and Anne behind them, with Paisley and Harlow in the last row, both fast asleep. Mike held Anne's hand, and they both seemed content to sit there and watch Aster.

Physically, she hadn't changed much over the past two years. Her wavy red hair was still long, and she had the same athletic figure, but there were subtle differences. She'd always had this intensity about her, like she was ready for the day to be over with so she could move on to the next thing. Whether she grew out of it or Gage softened her edge, Mike didn't know, but he thought it was a good change. She hadn't lost her temper. He and Anne had heard the argument going on between their daughter and her mate while they waited outside their house. She hadn't backed down an inch, and that made Mike smile. He knew where Gage was coming from but learned a long time ago not to pull that kind of shit. He would have been disappointed if Aster had let him get away with it.

Now Aster slept, her head on Gage's shoulder, bobbing slightly with the motion of the van, and Mike knew it was because she'd stayed awake the night before. He had too. He'd lain in bed next to Anne and heard Aster moving around in the kitchen, which was directly below the guest room. He had been tempted to go down and spend time with her but knew her well enough to let her be. She usually baked to clear her head, the same way Reeve had to clean when she was mad.

They had mapped out a loose plan the night before. Once they were in Buena Vista, which was about a two-hour drive from Denver, Gage would call the coven leader about their witch who was missing. While Gage was meeting with the coven, the rest of the group was going to spread out and canvas shops to ask locals if they had seen Eben or Alice. Everyone had taken pictures of the surveillance images with their phones. Hopefully somebody in this town saw something.

The drive was beautiful and scenic. Highway 285 cut through valleys with trees rising on each side, fading away to rocky peaks, some still covered with patches of snow. They passed raging rivers, the rapids fed by melting snow pack, and the forest called to Mike, his inner cat itching to explore. They pulled into Buena Vista, a quaint old mining town with a main street that reminded him of Havenwood Falls. Storefronts lined each side, offering everything from coffee to gear rentals for rafting, fishing, and mountain biking. The town was just waking up, and the coffee shop's outdoor seating area was full. Ryker found parking on the street and expertly maneuvered the large van into the spot. Most of the vehicles parked along the street had either kayaks or canoes strapped to the roofs, or had bike racks on the back, loaded with mountain bikes. One Subaru had a bumper sticker that said *I'm fly and so is my fishing.*

Gage nudged Aster awake, and she sat up, blinking to clear her eyes. Mike watched as she stretched her neck and yawned. She had a sleepy disoriented and dazed look on her face when she glanced over her shoulder at him before climbing out of the van. She stretched again once she was standing on the sidewalk, a languid stretch that was very feline. Harlow and Paisley looked just as disoriented as they took in their new surroundings. Gage stayed inside the van and called the witch. Their conversation didn't last long before Gage climbed out of the van.

"I'm meeting her at a crystal shop in an hour." He looked at his watch. "How about we meet here at eleven o'clock. That should give us time to ask around."

They all split up, and Mike felt anxious watching his wife and daughter walk away. They weren't going far, but he had just gotten Aster back, and it was hard enough saying goodbye to Reeve, whom they had even less time with.

Since it was still early, not a lot of retail stores were open yet. Mike discovered the hardware store was open. It had a display out front of hanging plants with pink and purple blossoms. They swayed in the light breeze. Gardening tools and other summer essentials were on a rack by the front door, marked as perfect gifts for dad. This made Mike pause. He had forgotten that Sunday was Father's Day. It was a day he tried to forget, since that was the day Aster and Reeve left Havenwood Falls, just after he buried his son. Now he had his daughters back. Thinking of Reeve reminded him that Patrick was being robbed of celebrating his first Father's Day. This just added to his determination to find Mina. He opened the front door to the store, and a little bell chimed. He looked up to see a small brass bell attached to a hook, similar to the one at Coffee Haven. The shop had a resident dog that picked his head up from where it was lying on a dog bed soaked in a pool of sunshine. The dog sniffed the air and growled, baring its teeth at Mike. He almost started laughing, because the Chihuahua was not even a little bit intimidating. The poor thing would probably piss all over himself if he encountered Mike in his mountain lion form. He ignored the dog and approached the customer service desk at the center of the store. An older man was working the register, busy putting price tags on bottles of lighter fluid.

"Good morning, sir," Mike said cheerily, and leaned against the counter. "It sure is a beautiful one, isn't it?"

"Sure is, and it's about time. We had a cold, damp spring. What can I do for you?" The old man pushed his glasses up on his nose and peered at Mike.

"I have an odd request. My friend has a cousin who went off his antidepressants. He's not in his right mind and has gone missing. The police won't file a missing person report because he's an adult. Anyway, I'm helping my friend get the word out, and I'm wondering if you've seen this man—maybe he bought something here in the past week?" Mike held his phone up with the picture of Eben on display. The man squinted his eyes and pulled the phone closer with a liver-spotted hand before shaking his head. "How about this woman? He was last seen getting in a car with her. He was probably hitchhiking." Mike swiped to the picture of Alice and held his phone up again. This time recognition flickered in the old man's eyes.

"Yes. She was in here earlier this week. A fine-looking woman. I won't be forgetting that face anytime soon."

"Monday or Tuesday? Can you be more specific? And was she with anyone else?"

"Nope, she was alone. Let me think." The old man stared off into space for a few seconds before smacking the counter. "That's right. She was here Tuesday. I remember because that was the last day of our buy-one-get-one-free sale on solar-powered lanterns, and she bought the last four we had in stock."

"Thank you! Every little bit of information helps." Mike bought a bottle of water for the man's trouble and left. The Chihuahua raised his hackles at Mike when he walked by.

He texted the information to Gage and moved on to the next business. By the time eleven o'clock rolled around, he had visited ten businesses and received more tips. Eben and Alice were both busy on Monday buying camping supplies, increasing the odds they were preparing to disappear into the woods. This was the consensus with the group as they all exchanged their results. One of Alice's purchases had been diapers—evidence that Mina was still with them.

"So we're heading into the woods?" Aster asked.

"Yes. Eben's Suburban was found just outside of town on a back road near a youth camp. We'll go there and see if we can pick up a scent trail," Gage answered.

"I agree with Gage," Ryker said. "When I was younger and on the run, I went off the grid and hid in the mountains. We passed a Tractor Supply on the way in. We should stop and get camping supplies now. This way we don't lose time circling back."

"Agreed," Mike said. "Someday you'll have to tell me that story."

An hour later, the van was loaded up with camping supplies. They purchased the minimum since they'd have to carry it with them, and if all of the shifters shifted at one point, that would leave Harlow and Paisley with the burden. After a quick lunch in town, they arrived at the site where Eben had torched his vehicle. The Suburban was gone, but scorch marks remained on the ground, and there were discolorations where fluids had seeped into the dirt.

Gage had a sweater that belonged to the witch who had gone missing. He passed it around to the shifters in the group, so they could commit her scent to memory. They had already sniffed a blanket of Mina's and a hat that Alice left behind at the apartment she abandoned. As if on cue, all of the shifters lifted their noses in the air and started to sniff. Orion went one step further and stripped out of his clothes, shifting into his lion form seconds later. He was a sight to behold in the Colorado wilderness. His golden mane rippled in the light breeze, and his tail swished back and forth as he padded across the scorched earth. He chuffed once and pointed his nose toward the south.

"Unbelievable. He picked up a scent already?" Paisley's mouth hung open in shock.

"Told ya he's one of the best trackers," Ryker said with pride. He pulled out his phone and sent a text before opening the back of the van and unloading their supplies. "Load up. We'll follow Orion."

"What about the van? We can't just leave it here, can we?"

Ryker handed a backpack to Paisley. "I texted the coordinates to one of my brothers in the Denver chapter of SIN. It's their van, and they'll send a crew to retrieve it."

"Just like that?" Paisley's eyebrows lifted, and her violet eyes grew wide.

"Yup."

And just like that, they started hiking. Orion had shifted back to his human form and was in the lead, following the scent of the missing witch. They were still too close to civilization for him to be roaming the forest. An African lion sighting would garner attention, and they needed to keep a low profile. The men naturally flanked the women, Ryker picking up the rear while Mike and Gage each took a side.

They kept a steady pace, walking parallel with a creek and stopping occasionally to drink water. When their bottles became empty, they filled them up at the nearest source, and Harlow worked her magic, using a spell that purified the water. Breaks didn't last long, and there wasn't a lot of talking. Mike was focused on his surroundings. He didn't want to miss any sign or clue that would lead them to Mina.

As the shadows grew long and the sun began to dip below the tree line, they started looking for a place to camp for the night. Luck was on their side when they stumbled across an abandoned campsite with a fire pit ready to go: a circle of charred river rocks full of ashes with large logs for seating. Mike and Anne set up the tent while Harlow and Ryker went searching for firewood. Gage and Orion checked the perimeter while Aster and Paisley pulled out food for dinner. Collapsible bowls were set out with plastic spoons. The single pot they bought in Buena Vista was filled with water and dehydrated stew mix. As soon as Ryker and Harlow returned, logs were placed in the fire pit, and with a snap of her fingers, Harlow produced a flame and ignited the kindling. Aster set the pot in the flames, and it didn't take long for the soup to come to a boil. She reached in to grab the handle and hissed, pulling back, cradling her hand against her chest.

"Honey, let me see." Anne was by Aster's side in a second to inspect the damage. From where Mike was sitting across the way, he could see the ugly red mark, a blister already forming.

"I got this, Mrs. M.," Paisley announced, and sat down on Aster's other side. Anne released Aster's hand and watched as Paisley wrapped her fingers around Aster's wrist, then closed her eyes. Mike wasn't sure what was going on, and he thought maybe Paisley fell asleep or was in a trance, she remained so still except for the occasional flicker of movement beneath her eyelids. Aster's gasp drew his attention to her hand. The blister had burst, and the stretched skin sloughed off as the redness began to fade. Within seconds, Aster's hand was completely healed, and Paisley opened her eyes to inspect her work.

"That's amazing," Anne said in awe.

"What's going on? Babe, are you okay?" Gage dropped a dead rabbit on the ground and kneeled in front of his mate.

"I'm fine. I burned my hand, and Paisley healed me. She's a freaking miracle worker. You can't even tell." She flexed her hand and held it up to the firelight. Gage reached for her hand and kissed her palm, then thanked Paisley.

"It's what I do. I'm pre-med right now, but I don't think I want to study human medicine. I'm interested in supernatural healing. In fact, I'll be trying out next month for a new college. It's only for supernaturals. Supposedly there's a healing arts program. I hope I get accepted."

"Yes, Roxy is going through the trials, too," Mike added.

"Well, consider me your patient," Aster said to Paisley with a smile.

Then Paisley noticed the dead rabbit by her feet, and she squealed, lifting her feet off the ground. "I made soup. I am not cooking that! The poor bunny still has fur on it!"

Harlow whipped her head around in horror.

"Who did this?" she demanded, pointing at the body, tears starting to well in her eyes. Ryker rushed over, pulling her into his arms and turning her away from the dead rabbit.

"Her familiar is a snowshoe hare," he explained.

"Sorry, I didn't know," Gage apologized, picking up his kill.

"Paisley, I'll take care of this." Aster took the rabbit from Gage and grabbed a knife from one of the backpacks. She started walking toward the stream nearby, and Mike jogged after her to help.

"You know, I taught you how to clean rabbits and fish when you were little." He fell into step beside her, and she looked up at him with a grin.

Rocks crowded the riverbanks, and Aster chose a large, flat one to clean and skin the rabbit on. She tossed the skin and entrails in the water, the heavy current whisking them away. After rinsing the knife and her bloody hands in the water, she dried her hands on her jeans then sat back on the ground and looked at him. "Can I ask you a question?"

"Anything, baby girl." He sat on a nearby rock and stretched his legs out.

"This memory spell is for twenty-eight days only, right?"

He nodded and picked a pebble up off the ground and tossed it in the water.

"What happens after those days are up?"

Mike hesitated, and her eyes narrowed at him.

"What aren't you telling me?"

With a sigh, he leaned forward and wrapped his arms around his knees. "You can come back home, and as long as you visit once every twenty-eight days, you'll keep your memories. Your banishment was for two years only."

"Okay. Reeve, too?" He hesitated again, and Aster frowned. "Hers is longer, isn't it?"

"Yes, a lot longer. Reeve was permanently banished."

"What?" Aster was on her feet in a blur of motion, her red ponytail flying like a whip in the air when she rounded on him. "What the hell? That's beyond unfair. That's downright cruel! You mean to tell me she can never go back?"

Mike hung his head, his heart breaking all over again. "Yes, and your mother and I won't be able to contact her."

This brought her up short. "Which is why you never visited us."

She sat down on the rock next to him. "What horrid rules. Why didn't you leave?"

"We talked about it, but we have a lot invested in the town. Your nephew needs us, and the den needs us, too. Your mother and I knew you two would be okay. You're both adults, and we know we raised you right. Plus, you found your mates and had your own lives to live."

"So all of us got a pretty shitty deal, huh?" She rose to her feet and picked up the rabbit, walking away without waiting for him to answer. Mike followed, quickly catching up to her. Her head was down, and she was silent as they walked side by side.

"Penny for your thoughts?" It was something he always said to her when she was younger and lost in her head.

She gave him a sad smile. "Just thinking about whether I want to go back to Havenwood Falls at all."

He stopped walking, because that statement might as well have been delivered with a roundhouse kick to his stomach. Would the fates be so cruel as to make him lose his youngest daughter a second time?

That night there was a deep divide between him and Aster. She erected a wall and huddled close to her mate as they sat around the fire eating. Gage roasted the rabbit and divided it equally among the shifters. Paisley and Harlow were too grossed out and made their displeasure known while they stuck with soup. Anne kept giving him questioning looks, which meant she noticed the distance.

The distance continued until the fourth day, which is when the faint scent trail for the witch grew stronger. They were deep in the forest now. In the beginning, they crossed paths with numerous people, and at night, smoke from nearby campfires filled the air, but each day they hiked farther into the wild, there were fewer and fewer people. Orion paused in front of a pinyon pine and plucked three brown hairs off a cluster of needles.

"Jackpot!"

Gage sniffed the hairs and scowled. His eyes scanned the trees that surrounded them.

"What's wrong?" Aster asked.

"It's always the witch's scent. We haven't picked up even the slightest trace of Mina or Alice. What if this trail is intentionally leading us astray?"

"Or it's leading us to them. Remember, this witch was allegedly taken against her will," Harlow responded. "She could be leaving us breadcrumbs."

"This is taking too long!" Gage growled, and ran a hand through his hair. His eyes flashed a golden amber. That night was the full moon, and they were all feeling its pull. The urge to shift and roam the forest was driving Mike to the edge.

"Listen," he said. "Let's keep following the trail and tonight, we'll shift and follow our instincts. I think we're all going a little crazy, am I right?"

"Fuck yes!" Orion cheered, and tore off his shirt. "I'm ready now."

"Simmer down, shifter. Mr. M. said tonight," Paisley said.

"You like this, Goldie?" Orion ran his hands over his bare chest, and Paisley rolled her eyes, which only encouraged Orion, who kept his shirt off, stuffing it in a pocket of the backpack Anne was carrying. Mike couldn't help but laugh at the antics. Oh, to be young again.

That night, once the campsite was set up and the group had eaten dinner, the shifters left their clothes, plus Harlow and Paisley, behind. They slipped between the trees, the moon bathing everything in silver light, and shifted. They ran as a group, yipping with joy at the freedom of giving over to their animal halves. Aster and Anne were similar in coloring and had reddish-brown-tipped ears. Anne had a white spot on her forehead and was a little bigger than her daughter. For the first hour they ran and hunted just to get it out of their system. Ryker chuffed and started sniffing the ground, looking more like a bloodhound than a lion. His dark brown mane dragged in the dirt, picking up leaves and pine needles.

Mike inhaled deeply and noticed the witch's scent was strong. Right beneath that, not as strong, he detected his granddaughter's scent. Then he was off following the trail. He heard the thud of paws behind him and turned back to see Aster and Anne coming up on his rear. They raced up a steep incline that evened out to a plateau that turned out to be an abandoned campsite. Here the smells were concentrated, but they weren't fresh. He searched the area, leading with his nose, and found a baby's sock half buried in the loose soil underneath a shrub. Mina's scent saturated the fabric. His instinct told him they were on the right trail, and they were getting closer.

CHAPTER 8

*A*ster was tired and dirty. She dreamed of showers and indoor plumbing. If she had to sleep one more night in the tent when Orion had gas, she was going to lose it. They had been following the scent trail and knew they were getting closer, but they had been in pursuit for over two weeks. A solar-powered charger for her cell phone had been a much-needed connection to Reeve who, the last time they spoke, sounded despondent. Time was running out on the memory spell, too. She didn't have many memories to lose. It was like she had an internal countdown clock, and as each day passed, the sense of urgency grew. Aster hoped their luck was about to change. The trail they had been following was the freshest one yet, and along the river bank, where they stopped to refill water containers, new paw prints were pressed into the mud, made by more than one mountain lion.

The group approached a clearing, and Aster caught glimpses of tents through the trees. As they drew closer, she could see the tents were set up in a circle around a fire pit and in front of a small cabin. Wood smoke and voices carried on the light breeze that rustled leaves, disguising their approach. The breeze also blew their scents away from the camp. A strong whiff of her niece's scent caused Aster's nostrils to flare.

Orion, who was leading the group, stopped. His ears moved back and forth, and his mane rippled in the wind. He had been tracking in his lion form since they were so deep in the forest, the chances of running across a human slim. Being in his lion form heightened his senses, and he could provide the first line of defense if their presence was discovered.

In fact, all of the men had shifted into their animal forms as a defensive measure, and that was why Ryker was in the back of the pack. Gage and Aster's dad flanked each side, protecting the women. The sexist strategy had pissed Aster off, but she couldn't refute it was a sound strategy. The stronger members provided a well-fortified barrier. She still didn't like it and was tempted to run past Orion. Her niece was close, and if she was right, Mina was being held in the cabin.

Aster stopped, tensed, and poised to shift at the slightest indication the group's approach had been discovered. Minutes passed by, and a drop of sweat rolled down her spine, tickling, but she didn't dare move. The forest around them remained still and undisturbed. She slowly let out her breath and loosened her stance, unclenching her hands, which had automatically balled into fists. Gage had told her that would happen. She had been training with him at the Sweat Box after she expressed her desire to learn to fight and defend herself while in her human form. When she had complained about the repetitiveness of her training sessions, Gage told her she was training her body to respond on muscle memory. "When fight or flight mode kicks in, your muscles will know to fight. That's the goal, babe. You won't even have to think. Just act. It will help to control your shift, too. Less chance of public exposure."

Looking down at the half-moon impressions in the palms of her hands from her fingernails, Aster grinned. All the hard work had been worth it.

Orion took a step forward, the sound of his giant paws absorbed by the spongy moss blanketing the forest floor. His movement caught Aster's attention, and she dropped her hands to her sides. In unison, the group moved with Orion until only two stands of trees separated them from the camp, which looked like some modern gypsy encampment. Ropes were tied to tree trunks to form clotheslines, where an older woman with salt and pepper hair coiled in a bun was hanging up a shirt to dry. She was talking to a younger woman who was heavy with child. Her sundress couldn't disguise her round belly. A folding chair outside a brown tent had an acoustic guitar propped against it. Not a lot of sunlight filtered through the canopy that loomed overhead, so it seemed later than early afternoon. A shirtless man crouched in front of the fire pit, placing fresh wood in the middle of a circle of blackened stones. Large logs encircled the pit for seating. There was something vaguely familiar about his movements. His back was to them, and a long scar that started at his neck and stopped just before the waist of his jeans jogged her memory. Aster suspected, if he turned around, there'd be an even bigger scar on his chest and abdomen. Gage had caused those wounds when he went toe to toe—or paw to paw—with the guy. They had finally found Eben Brant.

Two years earlier, Eben had challenged Gage for leadership after Gage had killed Damian. After Gage won, he had ordered Eben to be exiled immediately. Eben limped away, holding his skin together and leaving a trail of blood. That was the last they had seen or heard of him.

Aster glanced over at Gage and saw he was crouched low, ears flat, nostrils flaring. A low growl rattled deep in his throat. His gaze was fixed on Eben. She reached over and placed a hand on his back, and the growling subsided. The last thing they needed was to give up their location. They were lucky to have made it that far undetected.

Suddenly, a shrill cry pierced the stillness—a cry Aster recognized—and it came from the cabin. She wanted to sprint across the clearing and barge in, but that would be reckless. There were others around, and she didn't know who was in the cabin with her niece.

Harlow whispered, and a shimmering wave radiated out from

her palm, settling over everyone before the group fanned out, threading their way through the trees to circle the clearing. The spell Harlow had cast was basically a stealth spell that muted any noise.

"I want to check the back of the cabin to see if there's another door. Going in through the back will add an element of surprise," Aster said to Harlow as they moved closer to the structure. Their movements were slow. Using trees trunks for cover, they inched forward. A shout echoed across the clearing, and chaos erupted as men shifted into mountain lions, leaving piles of tattered clothes on the ground. Aster held her breath as Gage and Eben went head to head. It was déjà vu.

"Come on," Harlow urged, gripping Aster's elbow. "Our guys will be fine. Let's take advantage of the diversion."

They sprinted to the back of the cabin and discovered a screen door. Aster wrenched it open and charged inside, Harlow right on her heels. The cabin was small and extremely rustic, a basic structure. There wasn't any plumbing, and the single room was cluttered with stained mattresses on the floor. A woman was lying on one of the mattresses. Her hair was unkempt and greasy, her white nightgown tinged a dingy gray. Aster's eyes adjusted to the dim lighting, and she noticed the woman was restrained. Rope ties around her wrists and ankles were tethered to what looked like handles, nailed to the rough floorboards, similar to how a boat was tied to a dock. The woman looked at Aster with dull eyes as if she was resigned to her fate. Remembering Reeve's story about how she was held captive in what was basically a breeding house made Aster's rage rise to the surface. She completed scanning the room and zeroed in on the older woman cowering in the corner, curled protectively over a baby. A tuft of strawberry blond hair stood up beyond the crook of the woman's arm. Relief at seeing her niece alive and in the same room flooded Aster, and she blinked tears away. She couldn't relax until she had Mina in her arms. The sound of the fighting outside grew louder. Aster saw Ryker and Orion attacking four mountain lions. They had their backs to each other and were swatting the smaller cats away like they were swatting at flies.

"Alice, give me Mina so we can end this without any more bloodshed," Aster said to the woman. She approached with her hands open and palms up, as a sign of peace even though she wanted to freak out on the woman who had baked the laced brownies and pretended to be nice, just to get close to Mina.

The older woman growled and spit in the direction of Aster's feet. Her dark eyes shone with malice, and she clutched Mina closer to her chest.

"Come any closer and the babe is dead." She moved so Aster could see that Alice's hands had shifted into paws. Long, sharp claws threatened to puncture her niece's skin.

"You wouldn't," Aster challenged. "She's a pureblood. That's why you stole her, isn't it?" Aster wasn't going to reveal that Mina's blood wasn't pure. Yes, she was the granddaughter of an alpha, but her great-grandmother was human. Revealing that information would make Mina less valuable. When Damian had Reeve on his radar, he only zeroed in on her alpha lineage. Aster looked over at Harlow, and her friend dipped her head ever so slightly. She was ready whenever Aster made her move.

"You don't deserve her. We're preserving our species, keeping the blood pure. You're a traitor to our kind if you don't agree."

"You're condoning rape and forced breeding. You're a traitor to your own gender!" The angrier Aster became, the stronger the urge to shift grew. She took a deep breath and exhaled sharply, like a bull getting ready to charge. She was done trying to talk to this woman. It was time to take action.

"Now!" she said, and a second later, Harlow began whispering while flicking the fingers of her other hand. Suddenly, Alice froze. She stared unblinking at them, mouth partly open. Aster quickly walked over and pried her niece free of the psycho's clutches. Part of the blanket she was swaddled in snagged on a claw and ripped, but her niece was unharmed.

"Oh, baby girl!" Aster cried, and hugged her niece tight,

breathing in her scent. Mina fussed briefly before yawning and letting out a contented sigh. She snuggled against Aster's chest, and her eyelids drifted closed.

"Look at you with the magic touch," Harlow said, and smiled down at Mina before gently caressing her rosy cheek. "Come on, it sounds like the fight is winding down. We have what we came for, and we should go."

"What about her?" Aster nodded in the direction of the captive woman.

Harlow walked over and knelt down by one side of the mattress and untied the knot, freeing one arm and leg. She then did the other side. Once the woman was free, Harlow gathered up the rope and crossed the room to where Alice stood, still frozen. Harlow manipulated Alice's arms so her hands were behind her back and then tied them together before securing her to an exposed wooden post that ran from floor to ceiling.

"There. That should buy us some time." Harlow spun around, her long, dark hair moving with her, and crossed back to the captive woman. "I've been training with my grandmother," she explained as she knelt down. "I froze you in place once," she said to Aster. "You don't remember, but I can freeze people or objects in place, and I can even stop time. I have more control now, and I've learned how to be selective with what I freeze. It's pretty cool, and it definitely came in handy today."

Harlow placed her hand on the woman's forehead and whispered some words under her breath. Suddenly the woman blinked and shot backwards, away from Harlow's touch.

"What just happened?" she asked, and then hissed when she lifted her arms, stopping to stare with wonder at not being anchored to the floor anymore.

"You're free," Aster said. "You can either come with us or go on your own." She turned and started moving toward the back door. She recognized Harlow's footsteps behind her and then heard a scrambling of someone hurrying after them. She glanced over her shoulder, holding her niece protectively against her chest, and saw the woman they just freed move behind Harlow. Aster tensed and opened her mouth to shout out a warning to her friend.

"Wait—please!" The woman held her hands up and took a step back. "I'm not a threat. I have no idea where I am and want to come with you. Can you help me?"

Aster looked the woman up and down. She wore cheap dollar-store flip-flops and the ragged nightgown. Aster sniffed the air to gauge the woman's scent. She didn't smell any aggression, just fear. Her posture was akin to her showing her belly and submitting. Aster didn't sense any deception either, so she agreed.

"Stick close to us and be quiet," she said, and opened the back door, preparing to fight only to discover her mom and Paisley waiting outside in the shade. Aster's mom's eyes went right to the baby in her arms, and she rushed forward.

"Is this Mina?" she asked, her voice cracking. Tears welled as she gazed upon her granddaughter for the first time.

"Do you want to hold her?" Aster shifted Mina, making sure to cradle her head, and handed her over.

"Hi, little one," Anne whispered to the sleeping baby. "I'm your grandmother. Or grandma. Maybe you'll call me Nana or Yaya. We'll see what you wind up calling me."

Aster smiled at the sight. Despite her limited memories, she was beginning to view Mike and Anne less as strangers that showed up on her doorstep and more as parents. Whatever bond was severed two years earlier was slowly knitting itself back together.

"She looks just like your sister at this age. A spitting image," Anne said. "You were both such beautiful babies."

"Aster, you didn't tell me your mom was such a badass fighter," Paisley said. "You should have seen her. We stayed behind in the woods, out of sight of the clearing, but a mountain lion snuck up on us from the opposite direction of the camp, and holy fairies! The next thing I see is your mom shifting, basically in midair. Her paws had barely hit the ground before she was charging the guy. She had him pinned, and I'm pretty sure castrated, or is it neutered?" She looked at Anne for confirmation.

"Either one works," she said with a shrug.

"It was epic! I need to learn to fight like that. Wow!"

"Are you guys okay?" Aster asked, looking for any signs of injury.

"We're fine, honey, and so is everyone else. I think the men are just toying with their prey now."

Harlow sighed and rolled her eyes.

"Cats are gonna cat, aren't they?" she asked, which caused Aster and her mom to burst out laughing.

They walked around the cabin, and Aster peered around the corner to make sure it was safe to move forward. Her mom was right—the guys had everything under control, but based on the carnage lying on the ground, they had surrendered to their animal instincts at one point. All of the purists were dead or in the process of bleeding out into the dirt, with the exception of the pregnant woman Aster had seen earlier. She was being restrained by a naked Orion, who had shifted back into his human form. Gage had also shifted back but had put on a pair of jeans. That's when Aster realized Paisley and her mom had the backpacks with their belongings. They hadn't left them behind in the trees.

"Orion didn't want pants?" Aster asked Paisley, and watched with amusement as she blushed so hard even her ears turned pink.

"I tried, but he told me he wants me to see what I've been turning down." Paisley pretended to gag, and Aster grinned when she caught the young fae checking Orion out. He was pretty spectacular to look at, she had to admit, and well equipped in all areas.

"Don't knock it till you try it, P," Harlow said. "You know what they say—once you go cat, you never go back. That's a true story." She winked, and Paisley's fair skin turned an even deeper shade of pink.

"Oh, absolutely. The things they can do with their tongues," Aster teased, and Harlow laughed as Paisley flipped them both off.

"Girls, really?" Anne admonished, which only made Harlow and Aster laugh harder. Once she started laughing, she couldn't stop. All of the stress and adrenaline from the past two weeks was over. Aster imagined she seemed a little manic, since she was losing her shit while mutilated bodies were scattered about, but that didn't matter. It felt good to release.

"What's so funny, Country Club?" Ryker asked as he sauntered toward them. He had shifted back to his human form and was completely naked, his scarred, tattooed, and extremely muscular body on full display. Aster knew not to gawk and averted her eyes. Shifters were used to nudity—it was part of the life. She had been naked countless of times in front of the den. Ryker's appearance did get her to stop laughing.

"Oh, for fuck's sake, Crusher. Put some pants on!" Harlow unzipped the bag Paisley was carrying and pulled out a pair of jeans and tossed them to her mate.

"Jealous, babe?"

"No. I know you're mine. I just don't want the whole world seeing your junk. Especially Mrs. McCabe."

A low, rumbly chuckle resonated from Ryker as he pulled on the jeans.

"Who's she?" Ryker asked, nodding in the direction of the woman they had freed. She stood off to the side, her arms wrapped tightly around her body as she surveyed the massacre. Out in the daylight, her appearance was even worse. There were burns on her skin from where the rope had been tied around her ankles and wrists. Bruises, varying in shades from black to yellow, marred her arms. The discoloration stood out against her pale skin.

"She was tied up in the cabin, and she wants to come with us," Aster explained.

"Tied up?" Ryker shook his head. "Those fucking sick bastards. Hey, girl, you got a name?" he called out to the woman, who jumped at his booming voice.

"I'll go talk to her." Aster approached the woman, who seemed to shrink into herself. "I'm Aster McCabe," she introduced herself, holding her right hand out.

"Lauren Ericson." After a moment's hesitation, she slipped her trembling hand into Aster's and shook it. "What happened here?" Lauren stared past Aster's shoulder at the carnage.

"These are former members of our den whom we exiled. They kidnapped my niece. My mate is the alpha. We fought, and they lost."

"Good," Lauren said with a sneer. "They kidnapped me, too. Six months ago, I think? They said my blood was pure and precious, and it was my duty to procreate purebloods."

At this admission, Lauren broke down, and Aster felt her own tears threaten to spill. This poor woman had endured the stuff of nightmares. Tentatively, she curled an arm around Lauren's shoulder and let the woman cry.

Aster made eye contact with Paisley and signaled for the young fae to come over. "Paisley, this is Lauren. Can you give her some of my clothes and take her to the stream we passed so she can clean up? Lauren, Paisley is a healer, and if you want, she can check you over and take care of your injuries."

Lauren nodded and wiped her nose with the back of her hand. "That would be nice, thank you."

As Paisley and Lauren walked off together, Aster watched them leave, her heart heavy with the knowledge that Paisley couldn't heal all of Lauren's wounds. It would take years to recover from the emotional damage, if she ever did. Their own kind did this; that's what bothered Aster the most. This group's twisted ideology allowed for them to mistreat their own. It was madness. The past two years had been spent rooting this evil out of their den. Though they were suspicious of everyone, Aster and Reeve had thought they could trust Alice, who was a sweet, grandmotherly type, always doting on Mina. Now they knew it was to serve dark intentions. Where was the loyalty?

A hoarse cry broke through Aster's thoughts, and she turned toward the sound to see her mom trying to soothe Mina.

"I think she's hungry," she told her mom.

"There's formula in Paisley's backpack."

The fire was still going, and there was a pot of water near the edge. It didn't take long to bring the water to a boil and warm up the formula. Once she tested it on the inside of her wrist, Aster brought the bottle to her mom who was sitting on a chair by one of the tents. Her dad was crouched next to her, gently playing with Mina's hair with a look of wonder on his weathered face. Mina greedily accepted the bottle and started sucking on the nipple, her feet kicking happily as she ate.

"Oh crap! I need to let Reeve and Patrick know we found Mina." Aster reached for her cell phone that was in the back pocket of her jeans. She didn't have a signal but tried calling anyway. "Do you have signal?" she asked her parents.

"Check. Our phones are in the bag." Aster found the phones, but they didn't have any reception either.

"Does anyone's phone have a signal?" Aster called out. The moment she asked, the woman Orion had restrained, and whom Gage was questioning, started cackling.

"Wait." Harlow closed her eyes for a few seconds. "It's a spell. We know you're working with a witch. Where is she?"

The woman threw her head back, almost headbutting Orion, and started cackling again. *She is batshit,* Aster thought.

"You know what? I have my own bag of tricks," Harlow said. She walked across the clearing, past the fire pit, to stand in front of the woman, who suddenly stopped laughing and regarded Harlow warily. "See lady, I'm a witch. A powerful witch. I can make you tell me everything we want to know."

Harlow pressed her forefinger against the woman's forehead and whispered a few words. "There. Gage, ask anything. The truth spell prevents her from lying and forces her to answer any questions she is asked."

The woman's eyes grew wide, and she started thrashing, but Orion held firm.

Gage smiled at Harlow before turning his attention to the woman. With his arms crossed over his bare chest, he was an intimidating sight. "Was this group working with anyone else?"

Clamping her mouth shut, the woman stared stonily at Gage.

Aster began to wonder if she was resistant to Harlow's spell, but a few seconds later the woman let out a gasp, like she had been holding her breath, and answered. "No. Eben paid a witch and brought her here to place the spell around the camp. It was supposed to keep technology from working, so if drones flew overhead, we'd be undetectable. We were also supposed to be shielded in a bubble of sorts that kept this camp invisible."

Harlow snorted. "Well, you didn't get your money's worth. Where is the witch?"

"Eben killed her. He was smart and didn't want to leave any trails to lead back to us."

"Were you going to stay here? You wouldn't last through winter." Gage looked around at the camp. "Why go through all the trouble?"

"Eben decided to stop here until I had the baby. Traveling so late in my pregnancy wasn't getting any easier."

"Were you with this group willingly?"

"Yes! Eben was my alpha and my mate. It's an honor to be part of creating a superior line of our species. I know who you are, Gage Barrows. My alpha told me all about you and how you're a traitor to our kind. Your niece was in better hands with us. She would have been raised the right way. The pure way."

Aster felt sick listening to this woman spew her rhetoric. She approached Gage and hooked her hand in the crook of his arm.

"Are there more of you?" she asked.

The woman faltered, and her eyes shone with tears. "No," she answered with a hoarse whisper. "Not in Colorado, at least. You succeeded in wiping us out." She went limp and started sobbing. "You ruined us!"

Aster's dad joined them, and said, "There are other purist groups throughout the country. It's a growing movement, unfortunately, but it's not new. Your grandfather experienced this ideology back in his day. At least the threat in Colorado has been eliminated . . . for now." He then exchanged a significant look with Gage.

"Something we'll have to keep an eye on," Gage replied.

"Agreed."

Seeing her dad and her mate as equals, alphas working together, made Aster swell with pride and gave her a glimpse of a future with her parents in their lives. It was moments like that when Aster wanted to return to Havenwood Falls, but then she remembered Reeve couldn't be a part of that, and the anger returned, settling in her stomach like a stone.

Just then, Harlow approached and sat down heavily on the ground, leaning back against a tree. "I removed the shielding spell. It was more complex than I thought, but it's done."

Aster grabbed her cell phone and did a happy dance when she saw she had service. She immediately called Reeve, who answered after the first ring.

"Aster, thank god! I was getting so worried! Everybody's phone was going right to voicemail. No one was responding to my texts and then you just dropped off the geo-locating app. Are you okay? Did you find Mina?"

"Yes. We have her, and she's safe. Mom is feeding her as we speak."

"Oh, thank god! Is she okay? Did those bastards hurt her?" Reeve wavered between sobs and fierce momma bear.

"She's fine, Reeve. It looks like they took care of her. Mina didn't have a scratch on her, and her clothes are clean. She hadn't been left to wallow in a dirty diaper, and her cheeks are just as full as before, so she was well fed. I'll send you a picture as soon as we hang up, okay? We have some cleaning up to do here, then we're heading home." She didn't tell her sister that cleanup meant cleaning up a crime scene. Were they going to bury the bodies, burn them, or leave them out in the open for some unsuspecting hiker to stumble across?

She ended the call, hanging up on Reeve, who was still crying tears of relief. Aster couldn't imagine what her sister was going through. Her mom held Mina up for a series of pictures, and Aster sent them to Reeve, who responded with every heart emoji.

The once-combative woman was now docile. Apparently being

compelled to tell the truth took a lot out of her. Orion released her arms, and she sank down to the ground, where she stared blankly at the dying embers of the fire.

"What are we going to do with her?" Aster asked Gage.

"We'll have to take her with us. We'll bring her back to Denver and decide what to do with her there," Gage answered.

"What about Alice? Are we bringing her back too?" Aster asked, and Gage turned to look at her.

"Alice?"

"Oh, you don't know, that's right. Alice is tied up in the cabin. She was holding Mina and threatened to kill her."

Gage's nostrils flared with this new information, and he growled, a low rumble that vibrated deep in his chest. "These are unforgivable offenses. She was disloyal, and her acts were a direct attack on den leadership."

"She's a heartless bitch. Add that to her list of offenses." Aster jumped at the voice coming from behind her. Looking over her shoulder, she relaxed when she saw it was Lauren. Paisley had healed the bruises, and the burns on her ankles and wrists were gone.

"And who are you?" Gage ran a hand through his short blond hair before crossing his arms over his chest again, his gaze narrowing on Lauren.

Aster quickly explained how she and Harlow rescued the woman.

"Did Alice mistreat you?" Gage asked.

Lauren nodded, and a visible shudder ran through her before she told them about the tortures she endured during her captivity.

When Gage asked Lauren if she wanted to be the one to kill Alice, she didn't even hesitate. She left them and entered the cabin. Moments later, a scream echoed out into the forest, the trees absorbing the sound. Then there was silence. A squeak of hinges later, Lauren emerged, wiping her hands with a white towel, staining it red with blood.

"It's done," she said, when she joined everyone where they had gathered around the fire pit. She tossed the towel on the dying fire, where it began to smoke.

Death hung in the air around them like the campground now had an aura. A shiver ran down Aster's spine as she surveyed the bodies scattered across the ground. It looked like Jason from the *Friday the 13th* movies had stopped by for a murderous rampage.

"How do you propose we clean this mess up?" she asked Gage. "We can't just leave it like this."

"Burn it," her dad suggested. "Burn it all."

"And start a wildfire? That's too dangerous. These trees will go up like kindling."

"Not necessarily," Harlow said, getting to her feet from where she had been resting against a tree. "You have a witch at your disposal, remember?" She wiggled her fingers, and embers from the fire swirled upwards like a mini tornado.

"Harlow, are you sure? It's a lot to ask you to cover up a crime scene," Aster said. She was in awe that the witch even offered. Aster's memories of Harlow were still vague. She knew they were friends, and that warm, fuzzy feeling she connected with loved ones was there, but she didn't have anything specific to draw on, so the trust was still a little thin.

If she went back to Havenwood Falls, all of her memories would return, or so she was promised. While those memories offered the chance at renewed friendship, she also knew heartache and grief waited for her. Flashes of her brother, Braden, had been surfacing more frequently. She would get glimpses, like looking at a flash of an image before it moved on to the next slide, a flash of Braden, lifeless on the ground, his body broken and bloody.

"I'm sure. It won't be the first crime scene I've covered up."

"What?" She stared at Harlow with her mouth parted, temporarily shocked speechless.

"Oh girl, we have a lot of catching up to do. I'll bring the wine. But first, let's get everyone out of the forest. It's creepy as fuck here." Harlow started to make a portal. Her arm was raised in the air, and a dark sphere began to form right before she dropped her arm and turned toward Orion. Placing her hands on her hips, she shook her head. "You have to put on pants. I'm not sending you through the portal naked."

"Oh, come on! I want to know what it feels like. I've heard it can be a rather arousing experience. If you know what I mean?" Orion wiggled his eyebrows, his gold eyes dancing with amusement as Paisley turned bright red and started giggling so hard it sounded like she forgot how to breathe.

"Knock it off, bro," Ryker said, and hit his brother upside his head with a pair of jeans. Orion continued to laugh as he pulled the pants on and buttoned them while Aster caught Paisley staring and practically drooling at the reverse strip tease. The poor girl had it bad and was in total denial.

"Now that everyone has clothes on, let's try this again. This portal will take you right to your backyard," she said to Gage, who nodded once, giving Harlow the go-ahead. She began whispering under her breath, and the wind picked up, swirling her black hair around her face. A dark hole appeared, and the area grew while the ground beneath Aster's feet started to hum with a subtle vibration. "Okay, two at a time."

Just before Aster entered, she paused and looked over her shoulder at the campground, as if she needed further confirmation the threats that had plagued her and Gage over the past two years had truly been eliminated. Nothing had changed. The dead were still dead, and there wasn't a need to linger any longer. Satisfied, she took a step, and seconds later, Aster found herself standing in her backyard on the grass at the edge of the flagstone patio and the portal was closed behind her.

Dusk was settling in, and the solar globe string lights they had suspended from the cedar pergola had begun to glow. Through the sliding glass doors that led to the patio, Aster saw the kitchen was crowded. Reeve and Patrick were already there, huddled around Mina, who was eagerly breastfeeding. Her parents stood off to the side watching, a million emotions playing on their faces: a range of joy, excitement, and sadness.

Reeve's time with her memories was running out. There was a little over a week left before their parents, Paisley, and Harlow had to return to Havenwood Falls or risk losing their memories too. Reeve wasn't able to return, so Aster had to decide if it was worth taking a trip to Havenwood Falls to reestablish a connection with a town that tossed her and Reeve out.

CHAPTER 9

The night after Mina was found and brought home, Aster pulled out the photo album and sat down in the living room with Reeve and their parents. They spent hours going through it, and Reeve and Aster slowly rediscovered their childhoods. Aster was shocked to learn that she and Reeve didn't get along and fought constantly growing up. She couldn't imagine a life without her sister. Tears fell, and there were long pauses on the pages that contained pictures of Braden. Her mom pulled out her phone and shared pictures of Braden's boy, a spitting image of his father; he'd grown considerably and was no longer the toddler Aster remembered.

Time was not on their side. With each passing day, the memory spell deadline loomed larger. Their parents had to get back to Havenwood Falls. They had a business to run, and the twins they adopted sounded like they needed some supervision. All of them were hesitant about saying goodbye when they were just getting to know each other again.

Aster rolled over and stared at Gage, who was sleeping soundly. They had the house to themselves. Her parents were staying with Patrick and Reeve. With the threat of Eben eliminated, there weren't any extra men standing guard. Everything was quiet, and still, sleep remained elusive. She sighed and rolled over again, this time to stare at the faint glimmer of stars beyond the bedroom window. The mattress shifted and then Gage was pressed up against her. His arm slid underneath hers, and his hand spanned her stomach. He kissed her bare shoulder.

"Can't sleep?" he asked.

"No." She relaxed against him.

"So do you want to talk about it?"

"About what?" she asked.

"Come on, babe. You're my mate, and we've been together for two years. I know why you're unable to sleep."

"Oh yeah, smarty pants?" She rolled over in his arms to face him, placing her palm over his tattoo. It was of his family crest, an ornamental shield with his last name, Barrows, written in fancy script at the top. "And why's that?"

"You're conflicted about going home, but you don't want to lose your parents again after just getting to know them."

Damn, he really did know her. Tears welled in her eyes, and one dripped down her face. He wiped the tear away with his thumb before cupping her cheek and placing a soft, tender kiss on her lips.

"I think you should go," he said when he ended the kiss. "Harlow and Paisley are true friends if they came all this way to help you. Your parents love you, and you need to learn more about your past. I think you'll regret it if you don't go."

"But what about Reeve? It isn't fair to her. She can never go back. I fear she'll resent me." Aster curled into his warm body. His arms wrapped around her in a comforting embrace.

"Do it for her. Be the bridge that connects you both." Her face was pressed against his chest, and his voice rumbled in her ear. "Just make me a promise . . ."

Tilting her head, she peered up at him. "What's that?"

"Come home to me. I can't live without you—you're my heart." She melted at his words and kissed his chest right above his tattoo.

"And you're mine. You couldn't keep me away. I love you, Gage Barrows."

"I love you too." Gage kissed the top of her head and held her close. It was decided, then. She was going to Havenwood Falls.

~

It was a tearful farewell. Aster's throat was thick with emotion as she watched Reeve hug their parents fiercely. When Aster told her sister that she was going to Havenwood Falls, she expected Reeve to be upset, yet she was surprisingly understanding. Reeve was mad about being banished but grateful that through Aster she'd have a connection to their parents, even if her memories of them faded. There weren't any rules in place that prevented Aster from bringing Mina for visits. At least her daughter could have a relationship with her grandparents. She didn't know how that would work with the memory spell, though. Her niece's memories would disappear every time she left Havenwood Falls. *One thing at a time*, she thought to herself as she closed the front door behind her.

Aster's suitcase was tucked in the trunk of her Sentra, next to her parents' bags. Since Harlow, Paisley, Orion, and Crusher had already left, she and her parents were driving back in Aster's car. Apparently, it was a six-hour drive. They would be arriving sometime in the afternoon.

"All set. I topped off the fluids." Gage closed the hood and stuck an oil-soaked rag in the back pocket of his jeans.

"This is in good shape," her dad said, tapping the roof. "We got it for you as a college graduation present."

"You did?" Aster tilted her head, and then a vague memory surfaced. "You had a big green bow on top, right?"

Her dad laughed and nodded, clearly pleased she had recovered another piece of her past. He stepped away from the car and looked over to where Reeve was talking to her mom, who was holding Mina. "I'm just going to say goodbye one more time."

"Okay, Dad." Aster watched him take Mina. She was so tiny next to his big build. His biceps alone were bigger than his granddaughter. Gage came to stand next to her, placing an arm around her waist, his hand resting on her hip. She leaned into him as they both watched the second round of tearful farewells.

"You'll call me when you get in?" he asked.

"Yes."

"And you'll call me if you need anything?"

"Of course." She almost laughed, because they had already been over this, but when she glanced up at him, his blue eyes were fixed on her and his expression was so serious. Turning to face him, she stuck her hands in his front pockets and tugged him forward. He placed his hands on her hips. "Babe, I'll miss you too."

"This will be the longest we've been apart." Gage lowered his forehead and pressed it against hers. "I feel like I'm letting a part of me go."

"I'll be back in a week." Standing on her tiptoes, she tilted her head and kissed him. She was so caught up in the moment, she forgot they were standing in the street with her parents just a few feet away until her dad cleared his throat.

Stifling a giggle, she started to pull away, breaking off the kiss. She knew her cheeks were flushed, and it felt like her lips were swollen. Tucking a stray hair behind her ear, she turned toward her parents, who were grinning like they just won the lottery.

"It's so good to see our girls with their mates," her mom said with a dreamy sigh.

"Thank you for taking care of our daughters," Aster's dad said, and he shook Patrick's and Gage's hands before giving Reeve a final hug.

Aster hugged Reeve and her sister held on tight.

"Call me and let me know how it is. Promise?" Reeve asked when she pulled away. Aster promised and slid into the passenger seat. Their next stop would be Havenwood Falls.

At first, her dad pointed out landmarks along the way and made small talk, but as they left the highway and starting driving through the mountains, Aster grew quiet, pensive. Traffic thinned out, and they went almost half an hour without seeing another vehicle.

Her dad picked up on her silence and glanced over at her. "Nervous?"

"A little bit," Aster admitted. "I didn't exactly leave on the greatest of terms, did I?"

"It's hard to explain. The Court is responsible for governing the supes in town and has worked tirelessly to keep Havenwood Falls a sanctuary for our kind and others. The Court's decisions are harsh, but they have to be—to protect the town and its supernatural residents."

"I still don't understand."

"Shifting in public, especially in front of humans, is a major infraction. Add in the fight and the fact that there were two deaths —that required a lot of magic to cover up. The Court had to lay down the law and send a message. It wasn't personal, baby girl. You served your sentence, and there won't be any further judgment. Hopefully once you're back in town, it will make more sense." He reached across the console and placed his hand on her knee, giving it a squeeze.

"I'm just glad you decided to come home," her mom spoke up from the backseat. "Your dad and I missed you both so much."

"It's so surreal, you know?" Aster turned in her seat, making eye contact with her mom. "I feel as if there is so much more I don't know. It's been hard to wrap my head around everything."

"That's understandable. Give yourself some time."

Just then the car went around a sharp bend, and Aster felt something ripple across her skin and a brief pressure in her head, like she needed to pop her ears, but the sensation was gone within seconds.

"What was—did you feel that?" She looked at her dad, who nodded.

"We just passed through the wards that protect Havenwood Falls, which means we have twenty-five miles to go."

Aster turned her attention back to the tree-lined road. It seemed vaguely familiar, like something out of a dream. She rolled her window down and breathed in deeply, her enhanced sense of smell processing every little scent. She detected all the organic, earthy odors like damp soil and decomposing leaves. Wildflowers blooming along the side of the road sweetened the air. Deeper in the forest, she scented urine belonging to a wolf. The farther they drove, the more she picked up hints of civilization—wood smoke, grilled meat—and soon she heard the distant chatter of voices.

Minutes later they passed a sign that said *Welcome to Havenwood Falls* in black metal lettering. The base was layered stone, which blended into the natural environment. Aster leaned forward in her seat to look out the windshield, and butterflies erupted in her stomach. After curving around yet another bend and driving even higher, they crested a ridge. Her dad slowed down to stop on the side of the road so Aster could take in the town spread out below. A reddish-brown wolf seemed to materialize out of the trees on the other side of the road. The animal watched the vehicle, and her dad rolled the window down.

"It's just me, Rusty. This is Aster's car," he called to the wolf, who raised his front right paw in the air, as if to wave, before turning away and loping off into the woods. Then Aster remembered Rusty was part of the Kasun pack and patrolled the area.

Another memory surfaced of her in her mountain lion form, crouched on a ridge and staring down at the town, only it was night and the box canyon glittered like a blanket of stars. The emotions tied to that memory hit her like a punch in the gut. She had been so angry and betrayed—by Reeve. Aster gasped and placed a hand over her heart as if in physical pain. She couldn't imagine having those feelings toward Reeve.

"You're beginning to remember more, aren't you, sweetheart?" her mom asked, placing a hand on her shoulder.

"I think I'm better off not remembering."

"Oh, honey. It's not all terrible."

Aster twisted the hem of her shirt as she processed the memory, dissecting it. Apparently, she had been dating Patrick before she met Gage, and when Reeve showed up, the mating instinct kicked in.

Reeve and Patrick were helpless against the instinct. Aster had been heartbroken and beyond angry. It didn't seem real. Aster had no romantic inclinations toward Patrick. He was like a brother to her. The next memory to surface was one of her telling Damian Stone where he could find Reeve and Patrick. *I did that? Damian Stone had been the root of all the problems with the purists, and I had willingly given up Reeve's location?*

"I was such an asshole. I did terrible things."

"We can all be assholes, baby girl," her dad said. "We all make mistakes. That's part of life. I do know that who you were before you left Havenwood Falls is not who you are now. You've grown up." He winked at her and smiled. Laugh lines fanned around his blue eyes, and a faint dimple appeared in his cheek. She noticed the stubble growing along his jaw had traces of gray. "Now come on, let's get home."

Driveways were the first sign of civilization, but the homes those driveways led to were shrouded by trees. They passed over a river, the water clear and sparkling in the afternoon sun. Then a development came into view on the left.

"Creekwood!" Aster blurted out, clapping her hands and bouncing with excitement in her seat like she was kid on the way to Disneyland. The golf course greens were perfectly manicured and busy. It was the day before the Fourth of July, and people were getting a jump on their long weekend. "Nothing has changed," she marveled as they drove through the familiar neighborhood.

Well some things had changed. They passed the Underwoods' house, and Paisley's younger brother, Dalton, was skateboarding down the driveway. He had grown since she last saw him. Two years and going from middle school to high school made a big difference.

When they approached the house she grew up in, a flood of memories washed over her. Birthdays and holidays, when she lost her first tooth and when she experienced her first shift, when Braden found his mate and when Jacob was born. It was too much all at once, and she didn't know whether she was going to throw up or cry. She just felt hot and panicky. Her dad had barely parked the car next to a pickup truck when Aster flung the door open and jumped out. She bent over, hands on her knees, gulping in fresh air. Then her mom was there, rubbing her back and telling her to breathe.

Once the feeling passed, Aster and her mom walked up the rest of the winding driveway to a walkway that led to the front door. Mountain irises were in full bloom and lined the walkway, filling the air with their sweet fragrance. Her parents' house was a large two-story made primarily of gray stone with wood trim and features. Large windows faced the street, and a wide wooden double door made up the front entrance. Her mom unlocked the door, and they stepped inside to a spacious entryway. A large ceiling fan circled overhead, suspended from the high ceiling. The living room was to the right, and it connected with the dining room by an arched entryway. To the left was her dad's office and straight ahead there was the staircase to the second floor. A hallway extended from the entryway past the staircase and straight back to the kitchen. The smell impacted Aster the most and resonated deep. A blend of her parents' scents and years of living concentrated under one roof. Home. This was home.

There were some new, unfamiliar scents mingled with the old, and she raised her nose in the air, sniffing. A move that clearly wasn't human. Just then, a man stepped into the hallway from the kitchen. He was tall and broad, with short brown hair. She recognized the sleeve tattoo on his right arm and remembered the day he stopped over for a family barbecue to show it off to her brother. Then another, more recent memory of Nicholas Jordan, whom she always called Jordan, since that's what Braden called him, surged forth, and her knees buckled. Nicholas rushed forward with his supernatural speed and caught her before she hit the slate floor.

"Easy, Aster," he said in a soothing voice as he guided her to the plush sofa in the living room.

"You were there. You tried to save Braden." Aster clung to Nicholas's shirt and when she saw the color fade from his cheeks and the sorrow in his blue eyes, she knew he still carried that pain with him. Nicholas was one of the EMTs on the scene the day Damian Stone almost destroyed her entire family. He and Braden had been best friends basically since birth, and Nicholas was just as devastated that he couldn't save his best friend. Aster recalled kneeling next to her brother's body and Nicholas delivering the news that he was gone.

"Oh, honey!" Her mom sat down next to her on the sofa. "Come here." Aster laid her head down on her mom's lap, and her mom started running her hands through her hair—a way her mom had of comforting her ever since she was little. Aster closed her eyes, and a tear spilled out.

"I'm sorry I couldn't save him," he said, and looked away, as if unable to meet her eyes. He swallowed hard and sat back, rubbing a hand along the nape of his neck.

"Nicholas, it's not your fault. We all know who killed him," Aster's mom said.

"Me," Aster thought, or at least she thought she did, but she must have said it out loud, because both her mom and Nicholas let out sharp gasps.

"What's wrong?" her dad asked. He had just come in through the front door with their bags and set them on the entryway floor before rushing into the living room.

"Aster thinks she's to blame for Braden's death," her mom explained.

"Baby girl." Her dad sat down on the other side, so Aster was sandwiched between her parents. He placed a hand on her back. "Damian Stone killed your brother. Not you."

"But I sent him after Reeve. Braden is dead because of my actions."

"No," Nicholas said. He stood up and started pacing in front of the fireplace. He exhaled sharply and turned to face them. "Your parents are right, Aster. I couldn't save your brother, but I didn't kill him. You acted out of emotion, but you didn't know what Damian Stone was going to do, and you didn't kill your brother. The guilt is still there, though, because we lost someone we love and we wish we could have done things differently to change that. I've struggled with this for two years. Now it's catching up to you. You were blissfully free of the grief. I don't know if the memory spell is a good thing or a bad thing."

"Right now, I'd say it's a bad thing," Aster replied.

"It does get better," her mom said, stroking a hand through Aster's hair. "The grief and pain will always be there, but it hurts less as time moves on. I see so much of Braden in his son, and that makes me smile. There's a part of him still here."

"I find comfort in knowing your brother went out fighting to protect his family," her dad added. "He was loyal until the end. If he had to choose how his life would end, he would want to die for a good reason and not something senseless. I can't think of a better reason. What Nicholas said is true. I carry guilt with me too. I arrived at the fight too late and it should have been me in your brother's place."

"Dad, no!" Aster cried out. She sat up and launched herself at her dad, enveloping him in a full-body hug. His strong arms wrapped around her. "It's not your fault." She sniffed and wiped tears off her cheeks. "I get it. We all wish the whole incident with Damian Stone didn't happen. He was a sick bastard, and the world is better off without him. You're right. Braden went out fighting. He wouldn't have wanted it any other way. He was always protecting me and Reeve, most often from ourselves."

She laughed through the tears, remembering how many times Braden broke up the petty fights she and her sister had over stupid things like My Little Ponies or clothes Aster borrowed without asking. He was the peacekeeper who loved his younger sisters equally and fiercely.

"That he was, baby girl."

Grief still clung to Aster, but she felt better having talked through Braden's death with her parents and Nicholas. They'd had time to process his loss, but to her it was still fresh. Hopefully as days passed, the pain and the guilt wouldn't weigh so heavy. She relaxed her hold on her dad and grabbed the glass of water. At the rate she was crying, she was going to get dehydrated.

"How were things with Roxy and Remy while we were gone?" her dad asked Nicholas. Aster eagerly waited for the response, grateful for the change in subject and curious about the two teenagers her parents had adopted. That explained the different scents she detected when she first walked in. The twins were cougar shifters like Nicholas's mate, Audrey, who was their half sister, and their scents were new to Aster.

"Everything has been fine. Roxy is her usual contained self, although she has been acting a little odd, like she's not telling Audrey and me something. Maybe she's dating someone and doesn't want us to know?" Nicholas shrugged.

"And Remy?"

"He's trying. I'll give him that. He's been going to summer classes, but I don't know how well he's doing. At least Principal Friske hasn't called. I take that as a good sign." Just the conversation alone was providing information about what hadn't changed in the two years she'd been gone. Mr. Friske was still principal at the high school. He was such a permanent fixture, he'd probably still be there in a hundred years.

"Where are they now?"

"Roxy is working at Coffee Haven, and Crusher took Remy to work out at Get Buffed!."

"Good. Crusher will keep him in line," her dad said. Aster imagined the hulking lion shifter, who filled a room with his size, was very successful at keeping people in line.

"Yeah, and the twins seem excited about the Fourth of July. Audrey is too. It will be their first one in Havenwood Falls."

"It will be a special one for sure," her dad said, looking at Aster and giving her a wink. "Thanks for taking care of them on such short notice."

"Not a problem. It gave Audrey some quality time with them and gave us a taste of what it will be like when we have our own kids."

Aster smiled at this. "You'll be a great dad, Jordan."

He grinned. "I'm warming Audrey up to the idea."

Her dad laughed and stood up, clapping Nicholas on the shoulder. "Hopefully she doesn't fight you like she tried to resist the mating call. Good luck, son."

Aster's mom stood up too. "Come on, let's get you settled in."

Aster followed her mom up the stairs, listening as she explained how the twins were staying in her old bedroom that she had shared with Reeve. Up here their scents were stronger. One was more dominant than the other, sweet and spicy in a way, like spring grass with a hint of pepper. The fact they were using her old bedroom didn't bother Aster, as she had lived on her own in the apartment above Coffee Haven and now lived in Denver, so it technically wasn't her room anymore.

"The twins don't like to be apart from each other, and Remy is very protective of his sister. They opted to share." Her mom paused in front of the door that led to Braden's old room. He had moved out long before Reeve and Aster did, but it would always be referred to as Braden's room. "If it bothers you staying in here, we can set up the guest room. I'm sure Nicholas and Audrey will go back to their place now that we're home."

"No, Mom, it's fine." Aster opened the door and stepped inside. Nothing had changed. The walls were still navy blue with white molding and trim around the windows and doors. The same navy, green, and cream plaid comforter covered the double bed, and Braden's scent lingered—faint, but it was there. It caused a lump to form in Aster's throat. In the corner there was a stack of framed pictures and posters that had been in her room. Next to the stack was a box overflowing with high school mementos, like Reeve's Miss Teen Havenwood Falls trophy. A light layer of dust covered everything. It didn't escape her notice that this had become a tomb of sorts—a place for her parents to keep all the belongings of the children they lost. She also noticed the hesitation her mom showed before following her into the bedroom.

"Perhaps I can change the sheets? Is it too much for you?"

Aster shook her head. "Leave them. It's okay. I feel closer to Braden in here."

Her mom crossed her arms over her chest and looked around the room, her green eyes misting over with tears. "I miss him so much, and I've missed you and your sister. I'm glad you're here and that we didn't lose you completely."

"Oh, Mom." Aster crossed the room and gave her mom a hug. At that moment, she despised the Court for the pain they caused her parents. How heartless, to rip their remaining children away after just losing their son. "I hate them! I hate that they tore apart our family."

"Aster, honey." Her mom stepped away and placed her hands on Aster's shoulders to look her straight in the eye. "Promise me you won't do anything. It's in the past, and the Court does things for a reason. Don't go poking that bear."

"But—"

"No!" Her mom shook Aster slightly. "Your dad swore to the Court he would never bring up Reeve's banishment. They were generous enough to shorten yours."

"Ha! By less than a week. That's not exactly generous." Aster spun out of her mom's grasp and strode across the room to the dresser. A framed picture of her family caught her attention, taken at a time when they were a complete unit—whole, happy, and alive. "How can you be okay with it?"

"I was never okay with it," her mom said with a sad sigh. "Just promise me you'll drop the matter? I can't lose you again."

The sadness in her mom's voice quieted Aster's rage. She looked over her shoulder to where her mom stood by the door. "I promise."

A few minutes later, Aster was alone in the room. She had brought her suitcase up and hung up some of her clothes. She had brought a sundress in case there was anything slightly dressy she needed to attend. For the most part she lived in jeans, leggings, or shorts and was happy to keep it that way. Once she was settled in, she stretched out on the bed and called Gage.

"I fucking miss you" was how he answered the phone, and she grinned, her heart racing at the sound of his voice.

"And I fucking miss you."

"How is it going?"

Aster sighed and rolled over onto her side, facing the window that provided a view of the street. "It's been emotional. I'm remembering everything."

She filled him in as much as she could, but kept tripping over her words, and explanations became jumbled. The spell prevented her from revealing too much. Gage offered his support, and that's really all she needed.

"I wish I could be there with you."

"You have your hands full, and I'm really okay—just internal crap I need to process or unload on a therapist," she joked.

"Me too. You haven't even been gone a day, and it feels like a month."

"Same. Will you survive without me?" she teased.

"I don't know."

"Well, I'm going to go help make dinner, and tomorrow I'm going to the Fourth of July celebration. That should be interesting."

"Call me if you need me. I hate being so far away."

"I will. Love you."

"Love you too."

She ended the call and set her phone down on the bedside table. Outside, the shadows were growing longer, but it was still hours until dark. The mouthwatering smell of steak drifted in through the open windows. When she got up and went downstairs, Aster realized her dad was grilling. He and her mom were on the back deck talking to a girl with shoulder-length sandy blond hair. She wore a long-sleeved shirt with leggings even though it was eighty degrees outside. There wasn't much to her—she was so thin she looked like a strong gust of wind would blow her over. The sound of the screen door sliding open caused all heads to turn in Aster's direction. The wind blew in her direction too, and the wild peppery scent she smelled earlier washed over her. The girl with honey-colored eyes and sandy blond hair regarded Aster cautiously as she approached.

"You must be Roxy. I'm Aster." She held her hand out to the young cougar shifter, who hesitated briefly before shaking her hand with a surprisingly firm and confident grip.

"Hi." Roxy had a soft voice and shy smile. There was a wariness about her, as if she was always on alert and ready to run.

"So, you work at Coffee Haven? I used to be the manager there. How's Willow?"

"Um, she's good." Roxy looked down at the book in her hand that had a library sticker on the spine.

"Willow is the best." There was an awkward silence. Engaging in conversation with Roxy was like pulling teeth. Either the girl was painfully shy or just didn't like talking to people. "Okay, well I'm going to see if Dad needs any help. It was nice meeting you."

Roxy looked up briefly, a flash of honey eyes, and then she was gone, disappearing inside the house. Aster stared after the slip of a girl.

"She'll warm up to you, and trust me, when she has something to say, she'll say it. Roxy just isn't talkative. She's always been aloof, except with her brother," her mom said from where she was setting out bowls of food on a side table. There were chips, a pasta salad, a potato salad, and a veggie tray in addition to a tray of rolled deli meats and cheeses. This was a spread for a party.

"Uh, what's with all the food?" Aster asked.

"We're doing family dinner tonight. You have relatives who can't wait to see you!"

Stifling a groan, Aster plastered a smile on her face. She really did want to see the rest of her family, but she was exhausted. The memory surges were taking a lot out of her, and it was still only day one of being home. "How can I help?"

"There are cases of beer and wine on the counter. If you can fill up that cooler over there, that'd be great." Her mom pointed at a large white Igloo cooler that was up against the side of the house. After several trips, the white wine and beer were packed into the ice and chilling down. She brought the red wine out and set it on the table with the food. It was from Stone Falls Winery, the local vineyard and winery in town run by the Blackstone family. Aster paused for a second when she realized she knew that without even trying and without a memory surfacing. It was just general knowledge, like it had never been wiped from her mind to begin with.

Her grandparents were the first to arrive, and the moment she saw them, all her worries about being exhausted faded. She was wrapped up in a giant bear hug from her grandpa Daniel, and her cheeks were showered with kisses from her grandma Colleen. Her dad's parents were not afraid to show affection. They hadn't changed much from her last memory of them. Her grandmother's white hair was still in her signature shoulder-length style. Her grandpa was not as muscular as her dad, but close. He kept in shape, and it showed. He didn't look eighty-seven years old, but more a spry seventy.

"Aster, dear, let us get a look at you!" her grandma said, holding Aster at arm's length for inspection. "You're just as beautiful as ever!" Her brown eyes shone with emotion. "It's so good to have you home."

Aster was pulled into another enthusiastic hug, which she willingly accepted. Her grandmother always smelled like sunshine and exuded warmth.

Her mom's twin aunts and their mates showed up next and put Aster through the same examination. By the time they had moved on to her mom, Aster's face hurt from smiling.

Great-Aunt Cordelia's husband, Great-Uncle Paul, was telling the most outrageous story from their latest trip to Las Vegas when Aster's sister-in-law showed up with Jacob walking beside her. Aster's heart just about broke when she saw her nephew and how much he had grown. He looked so much like Braden, he could have been his clone. It was remarkable and almost too much.

Jacob stopped and stared at Aster, then tilted his head and narrowed his eyes, looking at her like she was a puzzle he was trying to figure out.

"Who are you?" he blurted out.

Moving so she was kneeling in front of him, Aster held her hand out. "I'm your aunt Aster. It's so nice to meet you."

Jacob looked at her hand for a few seconds, then shrugged and shook it.

"Will you make me a s'more?" he asked.

"Jacob, not until after dinner. You know the rules," Kaitlyn, his mother, scolded.

"Yeah, but Aunt Aster might not."

His response caused Aster to laugh, and she shook her head. "I have a feeling I'd better learn them quick, before you and I both get into trouble."

From that point on, Jacob was glued to her side. He had a million and one questions about Denver and whether dinosaurs lived there. After dinner and two s'mores, he crawled up in her lap and fell asleep. She held him close and leaned down to place a kiss on top of his head, breathing in his scent when she was done.

"You're good with him," Kaitlyn said, setting a glass of white wine on the table in front of Aster before sitting down across from her with her own glass. She had put on a sweater and unclipped her hair, so it fell around her shoulders in blond waves.

"He's a good kid."

"He is, and he's a lot like his father." Kaitlyn took a sip of wine. "I really miss your brother."

"I do too."

"Are you staying?" she asked.

Aster shook her head. "I need to go back to Denver, but I'll be back to visit at least once a month. And I'm going to figure out a way to end Reeve's banishment. She needs to be here as much as me. Wait until you meet Mina."

"How are you going to do that? The Court isn't known for their flexibility."

"I don't know yet." She sipped on her wine and contemplated the problem. She had to find a way—even if it meant pleading with the assholes.

Long after dinner was over and Aster was upstairs in Braden's room, she lay awake thinking about how she could appeal to the Court. There was one detail she kept circling back to—her parents said that Michaela Petran had ruled in their favor when it came to ending Aster's sentence early. Michaela hadn't been on the Court yet when the original sentences were handed down. She and Reeve were in the same grade, and while they were competitive with one another, they got along for the most part. Aster remembered it wasn't long before she and her sister were banished that Michaela had returned to Havenwood Falls after being gone. She too had lost her memories. She'd have to feel some kind of empathy toward Reeve's situation. Would it be enough so she'd vote in the McCabes' favor?

CHAPTER 10

"I'm worried about Aster," Anne said, as she walked into their bedroom from the en suite bathroom. Stopping at the dresser, she took out her diamond stud earrings and placed them in the wooden jewelry box Mike had made for her for their first anniversary.

"Why? She's here, under the same roof and perfectly fine." Mike closed the book he was reading and set it on the bedside table next to his cell phone, giving his wife his full attention.

"She's so angry at the Court. I worry she's going to do something stupid." This last part was muffled when she stripped off her sundress. Anne crossed the bedroom to drop it in the hamper that was in the closet. Her panties and bra followed. Mike enjoyed the show and was disappointed when she put on a nightgown.

"Her anger is understandable, but I don't think she'll act on it."

Anne sighed when she slid into bed and turned on her side to face him. "This is Aster we're talking about. Our little firecracker has a history of reacting first and thinking later."

"Well, she is a redhead, like her mother," Mike teased, lifting Anne's hand to his mouth and kissing her fingertips. She narrowed her eyes at him, ever the catlike green slits. "Do you want me to talk to her?"

"No." She briefly pursed her lips. "I made her promise not to do anything. Let's just keep an eye on her, especially tomorrow, since Court members will be at the Independence Day Festival."

"Done. I have faith in our daughter. She's matured since she left Havenwood Falls, don't you think?" Mike reached over and smoothed Anne's hair away from her face. "She stayed with the group and didn't act impulsively. I was watching her and could tell she wanted to run to that cabin when she heard Mina cry, but she hesitated. She thought before acting."

"That's true. Seeing her and Reeve get along is great too. Do you remember how many fights we had to break up?"

"Oh Christ, the hairbrush incident." Mike groaned and dramatically rolled onto his back, which caused Anne to snort-laugh.

When Reeve was fifteen and Aster was thirteen, Reeve had purchased a new hairbrush that apparently only hairstylists used, and it was "very special." Reeve had told Aster that if she touched it, she was dead. Aster did more than touch it. She cut all the bristles off and dipped it in a mud puddle. Mike had arrived home to World War III. Once the chaos died down, silence ensued. The sisters didn't talk to each other for more than two weeks.

"Tomorrow is going to be a big day for Aster, and I'm sure an emotional one. She hasn't been in town yet. We just need to be there for her and rein her in if needed."

"You're right, as always, my mate." Mike cupped Anne's cheek and leaned forward, placing a kiss on her lips. "I'll make sure to keep an eye on her."

Anne reached up and placed her hand over his. "I don't want anything to get messed up." When she looked at him, he saw the fear in her eyes. "We just got her home."

Long after Anne fell asleep, Mike lay awake, staring at the ceiling and listening to his daughter's heartbeat in the other room. That was the hardest part after the kids were all gone: the silence. How many nights had he lain awake like that, listening to their heartbeats, assuring him they were safe and sleeping peacefully?

Then, one by one, they grew up and moved out, until silence filled the house. It had taken months for him to break the habit. When Roxy and Remy moved in, he became attuned to their heartbeats, a slightly faster rhythm, one of the few distinctions between mountain lion and cougar shifters. If Roxy did get accepted to the College for Supernatural Guardians, he'd have to adjust to hearing one less heartbeat again.

He didn't want anything to get messed up either. He'd talk with Aster in the morning, remind her of what was at stake and that approaching the Court in any way that was deemed inappropriate, disrespectful, or hostile could result in severe ramifications.

With that decided, he drifted off to sleep, only to be awakened by his cell phone ringing. The planning committee for the festival needed him and one of his scissor lifts to put up decorations. Anne was half awake when he told her what was going on. He slipped out of the house before the sun had even begun to rise, his plan of talking to Aster far from his thoughts.

CHAPTER 11

The next morning promised a warm, sunny day, perfect for the Independence Day Festival, where all of the events were planned for outside. Aster woke early and made a batch of blueberry scones plus one of her new recipes for raspberry sour cream scones. Her parents' kitchen was a dream. The granite countertop was perfect for setting hot trays on, and there was plenty of counter space. Sunlight spilled in through the numerous windows, so she didn't need to turn on any lights.

Remy was the first to arrive, lured by the enticing smells. He wore cargo shorts that hung on his hips and a wrinkled McCabe & Sons T-shirt. His sandy brown hair was pulled back in a man bun, and that's when Aster noticed the sides of his head were shaved. She had only met him briefly the night before. Ryker had dropped him off, and he came out to the barbecue, piled about half a cow onto his plate, and disappeared. She spotted him later, sitting on the steps of the deck with Roxy.

"Mmmm," he said with an appreciative grunt when he bit into a blueberry scone. "These are like the ones at Coffee Haven."

"I know. That's my recipe." Aster wiped her hands on her apron.

"Really? That's cool." He devoured the last bite and reached for one of the raspberry scones. He grunted in approval again and snatched up a plate with three more scones and poured a giant cup of milk before going back up to his room. Aster shook her head. Her mom used to have a coronary whenever any of the kids brought food into their rooms. She didn't want ants or any kind of bugs invading the house. Her mom must be getting soft.

Moments later, her mom shuffled into the kitchen and beamed when she saw Aster. "Oh, honey, you have no idea what it means to see you here." She pulled Aster into a fierce hug. "I don't ever want to let you go."

Aster returned the hug, squeezing just as fiercely.

"Well, it would be kind of awkward if we were stuck together like this all the time," she teased, and her mom laughed and let go.

"You always were a smartass. Glad that hasn't changed." Her mom winked and poured a cup of coffee, cradling the mug with both hands. She was already dressed for the day, wearing denim shorts and a red V-neck T-shirt. Her auburn hair was pulled back with a barrette.

"Where's Dad?"

"There was an emergency, and the festival planning committee called him early this morning. They needed one of his scissor lifts to put up decorations. Nothing like the last minute." She rolled her eyes. "We'll catch up with him in town."

"Where's Roxy? Remy was down and raided the scones."

"She's at Coffee Haven already. You remember those days, right?"

Aster sure did. Those early mornings were brutal, especially when she was out the night before roaming the woods and hunting. Some nights Patrick kept her up late. Her face scrunched up at the memory of having sex with the man who was now her brother-in-law. She immediately lost her appetite.

Later that morning, Aster and her mom walked to town together to catch the tail end of the parade. They wove their way through the crowds of people that lined the street to watch the parade. Everything was fine until they approached the corner of Main and Eighth Street. One block down on Eighth Street was

Havenwood Village, the apartment complex where Patrick used to live and where Braden died.

Aster froze and stared down Eighth Street, not seeing the pageantry for the Fourth of July, but the street blocked off by emergency vehicles, their lights flashing as she ran past, desperate to get to her sister, whom she had sent Damian Stone to find. At that moment in time, Aster didn't know her brother had already fought to his death and her dad was next as he faced off with Damian.

"Aster, honey." Her mom's gentle touch drew her back to the present. The vision faded, replaced by crowds of happy people wearing red, white, and blue and carrying small American flags. "Are you okay?"

Aster wiped her sweaty palms on her khaki shorts, took a deep breath and nodded. "Yeah, let's go."

She marched forward and crossed the street without a second glance.

Stepping into Coffee Haven was like stepping back in time and like she had never left. The bell above the door chimed, and Roxy looked over at them, her narrow face transforming when she smiled. Paintings from local artists decorated the walls. Hanging plants with colorful blossoms were suspended above tables, adding a natural, earthy vibe. There were a few customers sitting at tables inside, but most were outside in the small seating area on the sidewalk. Aster surveyed the menu, daily specials written on the chalkboard with colorful chalk.

"Unicorn Farts? What the hell is that?" Aster snorted at the name. Only Willow could get away with that.

"Well, it's about time you got your ass down here." Aster turned to see Willow coming down the short hallway from the back of the shop, where her office was located. In her arms she held a toddler, a little girl with white-blond hair like her mother and the most captivating gold eyes. She had a cherub face, and her fair skin practically glowed, a sign of her fae genes.

"Oh, my goodness!" Aster cried out, and hugged her former

boss, who was pregnant when she last saw her. "And who is this adorable creature?"

"Meet Arabella. Want to hold her?"

Aster eagerly nodded and held her hands out.

"Hi, Arabella, I'm Aster," she said as soon as the little girl was in her arms.

"Ass!" the toddler said. "Ass! Ass! Ass!" Her little fists raised in the air as she chanted. Everyone in the shop burst out laughing.

Willow tossed her long blond hair over her shoulder and grimaced. "She's approaching her terrible twos but has the vocabulary of a sailor. I blame her father. The other day she said, 'ya wee ballbag,' Scottish accent and all."

They ordered drinks, and Aster had to try the Unicorn Farts, which was more like a milkshake than coffee and had every color of the rainbow swirling on top. Willow sat with Aster and her mom so they could catch up. Their conversation was disrupted every time Willow had to chase Arabella down. The little girl wanted to meet everyone and get into everything. By the time they left, Aster's face hurt from smiling. She promised to meet Willow for lunch before she went back to Denver.

The next stop was Danzan Park, where the cookout competition was being held, hosted by Pyntz Butcher Shoppe. Aster and her mom cut down the side streets, following the smell of grilled meat. There were tables set up for arts and crafts and face painting. Vendors were selling a variety of items like pottery, artwork, jewelry, and crystals. Kids were running around with sparklers in their hands, their faces painted. Some kids were running around with turkey drumsticks that were bigger than their arms.

Aster spotted her dad talking to Nicholas's dad, standing in the shade and eating hamburgers. Ronald Jordan pulled Aster into a one-armed hug, careful to keep his plate away from her hair, and welcomed her home.

"Your folks sure missed you," he said. "Plan on sticking around?"

Aster repeated the same line she told everyone she had run

across that day because they all seemed to ask the same question. While Havenwood Falls was her hometown, her home was now in Denver, but she'd be back for visits.

Just as she was leaving to grab some food, Jacob came running up, his face painted like a tiger. Kaitlyn ran up behind him, her face flushed from the heat.

"Auntie Aster, come see!" Jacob grabbed her hand and tugged on it, urging her to follow. Who was she to ignore his request? He led her through crowds to an area set up for water gun battles. Soon they were engaged in war—Jacob and Aster versus Dalton Underwood and one his friends. Aster didn't know who won, but both teams were soaked at the end, and her belly hurt from laughing.

Her clothes were still damp when she went in search of something to drink. A beer tent called her name, and she sauntered over, bumping into a tall blond elf along the way—an elf she'd crushed on when she was a freshman in high school. He had changed a lot since then—his face was more angular and he now had sleeve tattoos on both arms.

Karson Kane smiled at her. "Hey, you're Reeve's little sis, right? I heard you were back in town. It's a bummer Reeve couldn't come back. She was always fun to hang with. How's she doing?"

"Yeah, I wish she could be here, too, and she's good. She's married and has a baby."

"That's cool. Well, tell her I said hi, not that she'll remember me." With nothing else to say, Karson continued on. He wasn't the only one of Reeve's friends Aster had run into. While Reeve may have forgotten Havenwood Falls, the people certainly had not forgotten her. The old Aster would have been jealous, but the new Aster just missed her sister. Aster shook off the melancholy thought and was pleased to run into Harlow and Crusher waiting in line at the beer tent. Crusher was in full biker mode, wearing black boots, distressed jeans, and a leather vest covered in patches over a black tank top. He wasn't the only one. There were several members of the SIN MC hanging out.

"Oh my Goddess! I'm so glad you're here!" Harlow pulled Aster into a hug. "Have your memories returned?" she whispered in her ear so as to not be overheard.

"They have. It's been . . . overwhelming. Yeah, overwhelming is the best way to describe it."

"I bet. I can't even imagine."

"I know exactly what it's like," a woman said from behind Aster, who turned around to see Michaela Petran. Of course, the moroi vampire would have heard Harlow's whisper. Michaela, like most supernaturals, had enhanced senses. "Aster, welcome home. I hope all is well?"

Aster opened her mouth, preparing to give the Court member an earful, to tell her off for their shitty rules and decisions, but then she remembered that Michaela could be an ally.

"I'm adjusting," she said instead.

"Good. I saw you over here and wanted to check in. Just take it one day at a time—that's what I did. And if you ever want to talk, stop by the inn. I'm usually there." Michaela owned Whisper Falls Inn, which had been in the Petran family since the beginning of the town.

"Okay. I'll keep that in mind." Aster watched her walk away to join Addie Beaumont, who was standing by the table for the poultry cook-off. There were stations set up for the cook-off, one for each meat variety.

"Wow," Harlow said, handing Aster a beer. "That was cool of her. Come on, let me introduce you to some of the guys."

Aster was pulled into a sea of bikers. That night, after the dance, Aster fell into bed completely exhausted. She rolled over, wanting to tell Gage about her day, then remembered he wasn't there. The next time she visited, she was bringing him. She drifted off to sleep thinking of her mate, longing to be by his side.

In the morning, it was just Aster and her parents sitting around the table on the deck drinking coffee. McCabe & Sons was closed until Monday, giving the employees and owners some time off.

E.J. FECHENDA

Since it was just the three of them, Aster decided to broach the subject of appealing Reeve's banishment.

"How do I go about doing it?"

Her dad shook his head, his mouth set in a grim line. "I don't think you'll be successful, baby girl. They seemed pretty adamant about her sentence remaining in place when we asked for yours to be shortened. In fact, I promised not to bring it up."

She scowled at his response because it wasn't what she wanted to hear. Determined, she leaned forward, placing her elbows on the table. "What if I present it as a benefit to the town? I know I tend to make decisions based on emotion, but that isn't going to work here. Asking for Reeve's banishment to end because we miss her isn't a good enough reason. It will be a waste of time."

"Agreed. So what are you thinking?" her dad asked.

"I'm thinking about proposing an alliance between the Denver den and Havenwood Falls. In the short time I've been here, I've heard other supes talking about several incidents involving outside threats. Damian's attack is just one example. Reeve was threatened, and she ran to the one place she thought would protect her. Harlow told me how the alliance between the witches and witch hunters here is unique. Then there's this Collector? If the Collector is targeting supes, isn't that a concern for supes everywhere—not just Havenwood Falls? They've expanded Sun and Moon Academy to train a supernatural army, and it's not just to protect Havenwood Falls but the world. An alliance with another den will help communicate these threats and share information. Or if the need arises, we can fight for each other. The fact that you're the alpha and your daughters are mates to the alpha and beta of the Denver den means the alliance will be built on family, trust, and loyalty."

Her dad grinned at her, laugh lines crinkling around his blue eyes. "You've really thought about this."

"I have. What do you think?" Aster raised her mug to her lips and took a sip of coffee, her eyes moving from her dad to her mom to get a read on their reactions.

"No," her mom said, at the same time her dad said, "Okay."

"Why not?" Aster challenged her mom.

"Because your father made a promise."

"Dad did, but I didn't!" Aster's ponytail swung from side to side as she stood suddenly, unable to sit still. She crossed over to the deck railing and leaned against it to stare out at the backyard.

"She has a point, Anne. It won't be us asking."

"But what if it backfires?"

Aster turned to face her parents. "I have to try. I'll regret it forever if I don't."

Her mom sighed and shook her head. "All right. I don't like it, but I understand."

Her dad drummed his hands on the table and stood up. "I'm going to go make a call." He went inside the house, and Aster looked over at her mom.

"Who is he calling?" she asked, returning to her chair.

"Most likely Elsmed Fairchild. That's who he called last time to set up a hearing with the Court."

A few minutes later, her dad returned, and he sat down heavily in his chair. He took a sip of coffee and leaned back, to survey the trees overhead, drawing out the suspense.

"Dad!" Aster kicked his leg under the table after losing her patience. He jumped and rubbed his shin, feigning injury.

"You're on, kiddo. Tuesday night you can appeal to the Court. I floated your proposal by Elsmed, and he said it has some merit."

The next five days felt like an eternity. Finally, Tuesday night arrived, and Aster sat between her parents at a table that faced a prominent wooden dais. With her memory restored, she knew exactly who everyone was, and the anxiety from her last hearing resurfaced. Elsmed still creeped her out with his glacial stare. Harlow's grandmother smiled briefly at them before returning to an all-business expression. Lawrence Mills looked like something had crawled up his butt. Michaela Petran was on the end closest to Addie Beaumont, and they were having a side conversation. Roman Bishop looked like he had better things to do and leaned back in his chair, assuming the pose of a bored teenager in class.

Mayor Barbie Stuart rapped the gavel, calling the meeting to order and ending the murmur of voices. "Aster, welcome home. I'm sure the rules were explained to you?"

"Yes."

"Good. Mike, I understand everything went well and you found your granddaughter?"

"That's correct. She's safe."

"How was it working with the Denver den?" Elsmed asked.

"It went really well. No issues. Gage, Aster's mate, is very capable."

"Good to hear. You never know when a future alliance will be needed." Elsmed winked at Aster, surprising her with his candidness. "And the threat has been eliminated?"

"Yes."

"Excellent. Now, Aster, I understand you want to appeal your sister's banishment as well as her mate's?" Elsmed didn't waste any time getting down to business.

There were rumblings among the Court, and Lawrence Mills shifted angrily in his seat, muttering something that sounded like "no respect for the rule of law."

"Michael McCabe, not even a month ago you sat in that very chair and said you had no plans of appealing Reeve's sentence," Saundra Beaumont said.

"I remember, Saundra, and I'm not. Aster is appealing. Anne and I are here for emotional support. Go ahead, baby girl." Her dad patted the top of her hands, which were tightly clenched on the table before her. It was going to take a crowbar to pry them loose.

Aster took a deep breath and stood, her chair screeching on the floor when it moved back, making her jump. Her stomach was a jumble of nerves as she approached the Court. She felt so insignificant with them looming over her. The last time she was here, they had cast her out without a second thought. She took another deep breath to settle the fear and anger she felt rising. Now wasn't the time to lose her temper.

She had dressed for the occasion. She knew her casual attire wouldn't fly with this crowd steeped in formality and tradition. Aster had chosen a black pencil skirt and an emerald green silk tank top. Instead of sneakers or flip-flops, she wore black heels that boosted her stature by three inches. All three items were purchased at Callie's Consignments earlier that day. She had taken time to style her hair, which hung in loose waves almost to the small of her back, where drops of sweat were beginning to collect. Unclenching her hands, she smoothed her skirt, drying her sweaty palms off on the fabric in the process.

"Members of the Court, thank you for your time this evening," she began, and dipped her head as a sign of respect, laying it on thick to work the odds in her favor. Then she raised her head and made eye contact, keeping her spine and shoulders straight. Speaking as a true mate of an alpha and daughter of an alpha, she proposed an alliance, pointing out it was a suggestion Elsmed had already made. When she felt her emotions rising, she stopped and took a breath, reining them in. This had to be an appeal out of logic, not emotion.

When she was done, her knees were trembling and she thought she was going to throw up.

"Thank you, Aster. You and your parents may step outside. We have a lot to discuss," Saundra said.

If the wait for the hearing was an eternity, the wait for their decision was even longer. Aster paced outside in the small reception area that looked like any other municipal office in City Hall. Her heels made a steady click-clack rhythm on the linoleum floor. She chewed on a nail that had chipped at some point, most likely when her hands were clenched into fists.

"Relax, honey," her mom said. "You did amazing in there. I'm so proud of you!"

"Your mom and I both are, baby girl."

A click of the door opening caused her to jump, and she spun around. Addie Beaumont appeared. "They're ready for you."

Her parents stood up and started moving, but Aster remained rooted to the floor. What if she'd failed to persuade them? Sure, she could be a bridge between Havenwood Falls and Denver, but it wasn't the same as having Reeve experience the comfort and joy of being home, of remembering their childhood, the good and bad. Then her parents were there, one on each side, guiding her forward. They walked into the courtroom a united front and sat down at the table. Her dad held her left hand in his, and her mom held her right hand. She grasped them tightly.

"Ms. McCabe," Lawrence Mills began. "Ordinarily I would have opposed your proposal. I'm of the belief that a sentence should never be rescinded. However, you brought up some valid points. I've lived in Havenwood Falls a long time and will die to protect this town. Recent events have made me realize that might happen sooner rather than later. An alliance with others outside of our wards has become a necessity."

Aster sat there dumbfounded. Of all the Court members, she thought for sure she'd never sway Lawrence Mills.

Next, Mathilde Augustine spoke. "Damian Stone's mindset was not unique. Each species has members who think sticking with their own kind is best. I, too, have had similar thoughts, but Harlow recently taught me I was wrong. There is strength in diversity, as there is strength in numbers. Having allies outside of town that we can call on for help in a time of need will be a benefit to Havenwood Falls. This is a matter of great importance we're working on now by creating the new academy. Your family has proven themselves loyal since your grandfather settled here in 1957. Knowing you and your sister will be outside of our wards yet still have our town's best interests in mind is a comfort."

Aster squeezed her parents' hands. This was going better than she could possibly have imagined.

Michaela Petran cleared her throat, and her unique gray-green eyes settled on Aster. "As you know, I've gone through something similar, where I had forgotten my time growing up in Havenwood Falls. Now that I'm back, I know how valuable those memories are —even if they hurt. I wasn't on the Court when Damian Stone followed Reeve and when all hell broke loose. I was dealing with my own issues back then. I've reviewed Addie's notes from this incident and the minutes from the hearing. Had I been here to cast my vote, I never would have banished either you or your sister. Reeve was coming here for help. Unfortunately, what she was running away from followed her. You and Reeve weren't villains. You were victims. We should have responded faster when he came through the wards. Everything happened too fast. He's not the only threat to have done this, and each breach allows us to strengthen our defenses."

"Are we done with the speeches?" Roman Bishop interjected, and Michaela glared at him. "I'm sure I'm not the only one with plans tonight." He ran a hand over his perfectly coiffed hair. There were a few ayes and nods. "Good. Saundra, please read the Court's decision."

Oh my God, I'm really going to throw up. Aster willed her stomach to behave.

Saundra looked straight at Aster and said the words she least expected to hear. "Effective today, Reeve McCabe and Patrick O'Shea are no longer banished. We will set terms of an alliance with Gage Barrows and Mike McCabe at a later date."

"Court dismissed," Mayor Stuart declared with a rap of the gavel. The mural behind the dais hid a secret doorway that slid open. The members stood up and filed out.

"You did it, baby girl!" Her dad picked her up and spun her around, kissing her on the cheek before setting her down, where her mom engulfed her in a hug. Aster was still stunned as they walked out together. As soon as they were in her dad's truck, she pulled her phone from her bag. It was time to call Reeve—to tell her she could come home.

~

You might also enjoy E.J.'s other stories in the Havenwood Falls universe, about the McCabe mountain lion shifters and their friends:

Fate, Love & Loyalty
Fata Morgana
Fated Beginnings
Stray With Me
Forever Loyal
Sun & Moon Academy Book One: Fall Semester

We hope you enjoyed this story in the Havenwood Falls series featuring a variety of supernatural creatures. The series is a collaborative effort by multiple authors. Have you read them all?

Find the full list and sign up for our reader group at www. HavenwoodFalls.com

ABOUT THE AUTHOR

E.J. Fechenda has lived in Philadelphia and Phoenix, and now calls Portland, Maine, home. She is the Amazon bestselling author of the New Mafia Trilogy and in addition to working on the Ghost Stories Trilogy, she's a contributing author for the Havenwood Falls series. She has a degree in Journalism from Temple University, and her short stories have been published in *Suspense Magazine* and several anthologies.

You can find her on the internet here:
Facebook: https://www.facebook.com/EJFechendaAuthor
Twitter @ebusjaneus (https://twitter.com/ebusjaneus)
Tumblr: http://ejfechenda.tumblr.com/
Bookbub: https://www.bookbub.com/authors/e-j-fechenda

ACKNOWLEDGMENTS

This was a particularly challenging story to write, since it's been two years since I wrote *Fate, Love & Loyalty*. A lot has happened in Havenwood Falls, and with the McCabe family, since then. There were some last-minute adjustments with the timeline or with shared characters, but every single author I collaborated with and called on for help at the eleventh hour made themselves available without complaint. Amy Hale, Randi Cooley Wilson, Morgan Wylie, Kristie Cook, Susan Burdorf, and C.J. Pinard, thank you for letting me use your characters. A special big shout-out goes to Victoria Escobar—thank you, dear friend, for those late night brainstorming sessions about the differences between mountain lions and cougars. Thank you for giving me some creative license with Roxy and Remy. Mike and Anne hope they're happy in their home. Liz Ferry, with Per Se Editing, I have dubbed you "Eagle Eye"—thank you for your attention to detail.

This story was written with the support of family, friends, caffeine, chocolate, wine, and during particularly manic writing sessions, lots of salty snacks. I see the need for a treadmill desk in my near future.

AN EXCERPT

~ A Havenwood Falls New Adult Novella ~

HAVENWOOD FALLS

FATE'S DEMAND

EMILY CYR

Fate's Demand (A Havenwood Falls Novella) by Emily Cyr

She's been the oracle for less than a month and she's already angered the gods. If she doesn't meet fate's demand, all of Havenwood Falls will suffer.

Lana Velis always knew she might one day inherit the powers and duties of the Oracle of Delphi, but the inheritance arriving in the middle of her last-ever college final wasn't something even she could predict.

With a power she never wanted and her testy cat, Lana must leave her best friend behind and make her way to Havenwood Falls to take over the never-ending petitioner list her ya-ya left behind. If only it were that easy. Now, not only is she saddled with a guardian she has no interest in having, but she's also forced to live with him.

And the hurdles keep coming. First, Lana must convince the Court of the Sun and the Moon to honor her title as the sacred oracle. Then she's bound by the laws of the gods to never tell someone's future if they aren't on her list—a law she struggles with, especially when she sees the unfathomable future of a little boy.

Now the gods are angry, and the Fates demand a soul in place of the one she stole—or all of Havenwood Falls will suffer the consequences. Lana must choose a soul to sacrifice, because in the end, Fate will always get its due.

FATE'S DEMAND

BY EMILY CYR

The way her short silver hair kissed that slim neck of hers sent chills throughout my whole body. That neck I'd spent two years loving, spent two years brushing my lips against. Now? Just what was I supposed to do? I was expected to just pick up the remnants of my shattered heart and move the hell on. How could anyone be expected to do that?

She knew I was there. I could tell by the way she hung all over the other woman. The one I'd caught her with. I was so stupid for still loving her, but apparently, she'd moved on long ago.

"Lana. You can't keep doing this to yourself." It was Jensen chiding me. It was always Jensen. Her kind voice had always been a balm to my soul, ever since we were kids. Now, here we were only a few finals until we graduated from college. She with a degree in education and I in graphic design. But as it was, none of that mattered, not when my heart had been so viciously ripped out.

"Earth to Lana," she prodded again. This time I glanced at her. She looked so much like the child she used to be, I couldn't help but smile at her. Her light brown skin was such a contrast to her vivid green eyes. Her spiraled ringlet curls hung around her face, making her rounded features stand out even more. She was beautiful. I was always so jealous of her. She stood at a whopping five foot seven, whereas I was five foot two on a good day. My skin seemed so pale in comparison to her richly tanned color, even though my Greek heritage gave me an olive complexion. However, she always said I never appreciated my pin-straight dark brown hair. She was right, as usual. My eyes were always my favorite feature. They were a bright blue and against my dark hair they stood out even more.

I sighed. "I know, it's just, I—" I choked on the words.

Jensen held up a slender hand in a stopping gesture. Her brow and lips tilted up slightly, causing her features to soften slightly. "I know you do. But you deserve better, girl."

Of course, she was right. "I know." There wasn't a whole lot more I could say.

"Come on, we have a final to get to. Did you even study? Greek history—shouldn't you be an expert? You being Greek and all?"

Glancing down at my phone, I realized she was correct. It was the only class the three of us shared, so it wasn't like it would be awkward or anything.

"Fuck no!" I exclaimed. I tried like hell to recall the last semester's worth of Greek history. "What were the three Fates' names again?" I blurted.

"Girl, if I have to tell you that, you're totally screwed." She laughed, shaking her head.

We walked to class as we always did, her trying to make me laugh, me brooding while trying like hell to remember the Fates' names and everything else I needed for that damn exam.

"So, what? Are you going to go back to dudes now?"

Her question caused me to choke on my own saliva.

Half coughing and half laughing, I looked at her and explained, "That's not really how it works. I'm bi. I kinda just love who I love."

"I know it's not, but I heard a laugh or two around that cock you were choking on just now, so hashtag worth it." Her crazy ass seemed to preen as her face lit up.

"You're the most inappropriate person I know." I laughed, rolling my eyes at her.

"Oh, that's so not true. You've met my mother."

"You win!" I cackled as we rounded the corner and walked into class.

This was it. My last final I'd have to take before real life would come crashing down on me.

We made our way to our seats and got settled in. My phone buzzed, and I looked down to see the text.

It was from my dad. Like I'd done for the last five years, I hit ignore. The absolute last thing I needed right then was my alcoholic father hitting me up for yet more money.

"Let me guess, your dad or ya-ya? Still letting them walk all over you?" It was her. My whole body froze at her words, not because of what she said but because of who had said it.

"Don't you have a rock to find, Cassidy?" Jensen taunted in a venom-laced tone.

Cassie looked at her in confusion.

"What?" Cassie spat. Her eyes were laser focused on Jensen.

"Oh, you know, the rock you crawled out from under and need to return to?" I heard several shocked inhalations of breath from around me at Jensen's dig.

I swear to Hades's bouncing balls my jaw hit the fucking tile floor with an audible clack.

The look of shock and hurt flashed so fast across Cassie's face, I questioned if I'd seen anything at all.

"See, this is why I found something better. You're no better than the company you keep. Remember that, Lana." She was so condescending. Come to think of it, she'd always been like that, not just to Jensen but to me as well. And her words were nothing more than a slap in the face meant to hurt me and Jensen. Then, under her breath, she said the words I thought I would never hear from someone I'd once loved: "No wonder your dad's an alcoholic."

I was so shocked I just sat there for a heartbeat. Then rage took over, and I stood to face her eye to eye. I'd had enough. Not because I actually cared about my father, but for the sheer fact that she had the gall to blame me for something I'd always blamed myself for—

something she'd known. She had the audacity to use my own insecurities against me? Yeah, fuck that.

"You know, Cassie, as I recall, I broke up with you. And, as I recall, you were trying to sext me, what, just last night? So really, who's the lucky one?"

She opened her mouth to speak, but fuck that. I wasn't having it.

"So, you want to give me advice?" I continued. "How about I give you some? You are what you eat."

The whole class was listening, including the TA and professor. I should have cared about the audience. But for once, I didn't care whom I offended or who heard my dirty laundry.

"What?" she said dumbly. Looking around for a split second, I saw the same look on nearly everyone's face.

Smiling my very best *eat shit and die* expression, I intoned, "You are what you eat. Me? I last ate a bagel. What did you eat? A rotting, stinking pus—" The world tilted and went black. But not before I saw Cassie's horrified expression. I couldn't help but laugh. Well, at least I thought I did.

Purchase *Fate's Demand* where books are sold.

www.ingramcontent.com/pod-product-compliance
Lightning Source LLC
Chambersburg PA
CBHW021131260626
47169CB00005B/1560